Captain Desmond, V.C.

BY

MAUD DIVER

AUTHOR OF

'THE GREAT AMULET,' 'CANDLES IN THE WIND,'

ETC.

"One who never turned his back, but marched breast forward,
Never doubted clouds would break ;
Never dreamed, though right were worsted, wrong would triumph ;
Held, we fall to rise, are baffled to fight better,
Sleep—to wake."

—ROBERT BROWNING.

TWELFTH IMPRESSION

WILLIAM BLACKWOOD AND SONS

EDINBURGH AND LONDON

MCMXXII

THIS BOOK IS DEDICATED TO

MY SON CYRIL,

AND TO

MRS ALAN BATTEN

IN ACKNOWLEDGMENT OF ALL THAT IT OWES TO HER GENEROUS HELP AND INTEREST.

M. D

AUTHOR'S NOTE.

In revising and partially rewriting my novel, 'Captain Desmond, V.C.,' I have been glad to make good the opportunity afforded me of bringing the Aftermath nearer to my original conception than it was in its first form. The three short chapters now substituted for the one final scene are therefore, in essence, no innovation. They represent more or less what I conceived at the time, but suppressed through fear of making my book too long; and thereby risked upsetting the balance of sympathy, which I hope the fresh chapters may tend to restore.

M. D.

CONTENTS.

BOOK I.

BOOK II.

Contents.

BOOK I.

"If we impinge, never so lightly, on the life of a fellow-mortal, the touch of our personality, like the ripple of a stone cast into a pond, widens and widens, in unending circles, through the æons, till the far-off gods themselves cannot tell where action ceases."—KIPLING.

Captain Desmond, V.C.

CHAPTER I.

JUDGE FOR YOURSELF.

"Do we move ourselves, or are moved by an Unseen Hand at a game?"—TENNYSON.

HONOR MEREDITH folded her arms upon the window-ledge of the carriage and looked out into the night: a night of strange, unearthly beauty.

The full moon hung low in the west like a lamp. A chequered mantle of light and shadow lay over the mountain-barrier of India's north-western frontier, and over the desolate levels through which the train, with its solitary English passenger, sauntered at the rate of seven miles an hour. Even this degree of speed was clearly something of an achievement, attainable only by incessant halting to take breath—for ten or fifteen minutes—at embryo stations: a platform, a shelter, and a few unhappy-looking out-buildings set down in a land of death and silence—a profitless desert, hard as the nether millstone and unfruitful as the grave.

During these pauses the fret and jar of the labouring train gave place to a babel of voices—shouting, expostulating, denunciating in every conceivable key. For the third-class passenger in the East is nothing if not vociferous, and the itch of travel has penetrated even to these outskirts of empire.

Sleep, except in broken snatches, was a blessing past

praying for, and as the moon swung downward to the hills, Honor Meredith had settled herself at the open window, to watch the lifeless wastes glide silently past, and await the coming of dawn.

She had been journeying thus, with only moon and stars, and unfamiliar scenes of earth for company, since eight o'clock; and morning was near at hand. The informal civilisation of Rawal Pindi lay fifty miles behind her; and five miles ahead lay Kushalghur, a handful of buildings on the south bank of the Indus, where the narrow line of railway came abruptly to an end. Beyond the Indus a lone wide cart-road stretched, through thirty miles of boulder-strewn desert, to the little frontier station of Kohat.

For six years it had been Honor's dream to cross the Indus and join her favourite brother, the second-in-command of a Punjab cavalry regiment; to come into touch with an India other than the light-hearted India of luxury and smooth sailing, which she had enjoyed as only daughter of General Sir John Meredith, K.C.B., and now, with the completion of her father's term of service, her dream had become an almost incredible reality.

It was not without secret qualms of heart and conscience that the General had yielded to her wish. For frontier life in those earlier times still preserved its distinctive flavour of isolation and hazard, which has been the making of its men, and the making or marring of its women; and which the northward trend of the "fire-carriage" has almost converted into a thing of the past. But sympathy with her mettlesome spirit, which was of his own bestowing, had outweighed Sir John's anxiety. On the eve of sailing he had despatched her with his blessing and, by way of practical accessory, a handsome revolver, which he had taught her to use as accurately as a man.

And now, while she sat alone in the mellow moonlight of early morning, within a few miles of the greatest river of the Punjab, not even the pain of recent parting could lessen the thrill of independence and adventure, that quickened her pulses, and stirred the deep waters of her soul.

At five-and-twenty this girl still remained heart-whole, as at nineteen: still looked confidently forward to the best that life has to give. For, despite a strong practical strain in her nature, she was an idealist at the core. She could not understand that temper of mind which sets out to buy a gold watch, and declines upon a silver one because the other is not instantly attainable. She would have the best or none: and, with the enviable assurance of youth, she never doubted but that the best would be forthcoming in good time.

For this cause, no doubt, she had failed to make the brilliant match tacitly expected of her by a large circle of friends ever since her arrival in the country. None the less, she had gone cheerfully on her way, untrammelled by criticism, quite unaware of failure, and eternally interested in the manifold drama of Indian and Anglo-Indian life. Her father and four soldier brothers had set her standard of manhood, and had set it high; and although in the past eight years many men had been passionately convinced of their ability to satisfy her needs of heart and brain, not one among them had succeeded in convincing Sir John Meredith's clear-sighted daughter.

But thought of all these things was far from her as she watched the moon dip to the jagged peaks that shouldered the stars along the western horizon. The present held her; the future beckoned with an encouraging finger; and she had no quarrel with the past.

By now the moon's last rim formed a golden sickle behind a blunt shoulder of rock; while over the eastward levels the topaz-yellow of an Indian dawn rushed at one stride to the zenith of heaven. In the clear light the girl's beauty took on a new distinctness, a new living charm. The upward-sweeping mass of her hair showed the softness of bronze, save where the sun burnished it to copper. Breadth of brow, and the strong moulding of her nose and chin, suggested powers rather befitting a man than a woman. But in the eyes and lips the woman triumphed—eyes blue-grey under very straight brows, and lips that even in repose preserved a rebellious tendency to lift at the corners. From her father, and a long line of fighting ancestors, Honor had gotten the large build of a large nature; the notable lift of her head; and the hot blood, coupled with endurance, that stamps the race current coin across the world.

A jolt of unusual violence, flinging her against the carriage door, announced conclusively her arrival at the last of the embryo stations, and straightway the stillness of dawn was affronted by a riot of life and sound. Men, women, and children, cooking-pots and bundles, overflowed on to the sunlit platform; and through their midst, with a dignified aloofness that only flowers to perfection in the East, Honor Meredith's tall *chuprassee*[1] made his way to her carriage window. Beside him, in a scarlet coat over full white skirts, cowered the distressed figure of an old ayah, who for twenty years had been a pillar of the household of Meredith.

"Hai, hai, Miss Sahib!" she broke out, lifting wrinkled hands in protest. "How was it possible to sleep in such a night of strange noises, and of many devils let loose; the rail *gharri*[2] itself being the worst devil of them all! Behold, your Honour hath brought us to an evil country, without water and without food. A country of murderers and bare-faced women. Not once, since the leaving of Pindi, have I dared close an eyelid lest some unknown evil befall me."

A statement which set her companion smiling under the shelter of his moustache and beard, at thought of the many times he had saved her slumbering form from collision against the woodwork of the train. But, with the courtesy of his kind, he forebore to discomfort her by mention of such trifling details.

"It is necessary to cross the river on foot, Miss Sahib," he said: and without more ado Honor fared forth into the untempered sunlight, closely followed by her two attendants, and a string of half-naked coolies bearing her luggage.

From the dreary little terminus a cart-track sloped to the river, which at this point sweeps southward with a strong rush of water, its steep banks forming a plateau on either hand. The narrow gorge was spanned by a rough bridge of boats lashed firmly together; and on the farther side Honor found a lone dak bungalow, its homely dovecot and wheeling

[1] Government servant. [2] Carriage.

pigeons striking a friendly note amid the callousness of the surrounding country.

An armed orderly, who had been taking his ease in the verandah, sprang smartly to his feet and saluted; and behind him, on the threshold, a red-bearded khansamah, who might have walked straight out of an Old Testament picture-book, proffered obsequious welcome to the *Major Sahib's Miss.* Honor bestowed a glance of approval upon her new protector, whose natural endowments were enhanced by the picturesque uniform of the Punjab Cavalry. A khaki tunic, reaching almost to his knees, was relieved by heavy steel shoulder-chains and a broad kummerband of red and blue. These colours were repeated in the peaked cap and voluminous turban, while over the kummerband was buckled the severe leathern sword-belt of the West.

The man held out a letter; and Honor, summarily dismissing the khansamah,—who thrust himself upon her notice with the insistent meekness of his kind,—passed on into the one sitting-room, with its bare table and half-dozen dilapidated chairs. Balancing herself on the former, she broke the seal with impatient fingers, for the sight of her brother's handwriting gladdened her like a hand-clasp across thirty miles of space.

Then she started, and all the light went out of her eyes.

"DEAREST GIRL" (she read),—

"Just a line to save you from a shock at sight of me. The old trouble—Peshawar fever. Mackay has run me to earth at last and insisted on a Board. I'm afraid it's a case of a year's sick leave at home, bad luck to it. But I see no reason to throw up our fine plan altogether. If you would like to wait out here for me, the Desmonds will gladly give you a home. He made the offer at once, and I know I couldn't leave you in better hands. Full details when we meet. It's a hard blow for us both; but you have grit enough for two, and here's a chance to prove it. Hurry up that tonga-driver.—Your loving, JOHN."

Honor read the short letter through twice; then, with

less of elasticity in her step, sought refreshment of mind and body in the hot water awaiting her in the next room.

An hour later the tonga was well on its way, speeding at a hand-gallop over the dead level of road, with never an incident of shade, or a spear-point of green, to soften the forbidding face of it; with never a sound to shatter the sunlit stillness, save the three-fold sound of their going—the clatter of hoofs, the clank and rattle of the tonga-bar rising and falling to a tune of its own making, and the brazen-throated twang of the horn, which the tonga-drivers of Upper India have elevated to a fine art.

And on either hand, to the utmost limit of vision, lay the emptiness of the desert, bounded by unfriendly hills. A pitiless country, where the line of duty smites the eye at every turn; the line of beauty being conspicuous only by its absence. A country that straightens the back, and strings up nerve and muscle; where men learn to endure hardness, and carry their lives in their hands with cheerful unconcern, expecting and receiving small credit for either from those whose safety they ensure, and who know little, and care less, about matters so scantly relevant to their immediate comfort or concern.

Honor had elected to sit in front by the strapping Pathan driver; while Parbutti, ayah, her flow of speech frozen at its source by the near neighbourhood of a sword and loaded carbine, put as much space between the orderly and her own small person as the narrow back-seat of the tonga would permit.

The English girl's eyes had in them now less of dreaminess, and more of thought. The abrupt change in her outlook brought Evelyn Desmond's pretty, effective figure to the forefront of her mind. For ten years,—the period of Honor's education in England,—the two girls had lived and learned together as sisters; and, despite natures radically opposed, a very real love had sprung up between them. They had not met, however, since Evelyn Dacre's somewhat hasty marriage to Captain Desmond, V.C., a brother officer of John Meredith; a soldier of no little promise and distinction, and a true frontiersman, both by heritage and inclination, since every Desmond who came to India went straight to the Border as a matter of course. Honor knew the man by hearsay only, but she knew every inch of her friend's character, and the knowledge gave her food for much interested speculation. There are few things more puzzling than the marriages of our friends, unless it be our own.

But after the first stoppage to change horses, Honor flung meditation to the winds, and turned her eyes and mind upon the life of the road. For, as day took completer possession of the heavens, it became evident that life, of a leisurely, intermittent sort, flourished even upon this highway to the other end of nowhere.

A line of camels, strung together like a grotesque living necklace, sauntered past, led by a loose-robed Pathan, as supercilious of aspect as the shuffling brutes who bobbed and gurgled in his wake. Or it might be a group of bullock-carts going down to Kushalghur, to meet consignments of stores and all the minor necessaries of life,—for in those days Kohat was innocent of shops. At rare intervals, colourless mud hamlets—each with its warlike watch-tower—huddled close to the road as if for company and protection. Here the monotonous round of life was already astir. Women of a remarkable height and grace, in dark-blue draperies peculiar to the Frontier, went about their work with superb movement of untrammelled limbs, and groups of shiny bronze babies shrilled to the heartsome notes of the tonga-horn. There were also whitewashed police *chokhis*,[1] where blue-coated, yellow-trousered policemen squatted, and smoked, and spat, in glorious idleness, from dawn to dusk, and exchanged full-flavoured compliments with the Pathan driver in passing. For the rest there was always the passionless serenity of the desert, with its crop of thriftless thorn-bushes, whose berries showed like blood-drops pricked from the hard heart of the land; and beyond the desert, looming steadily nearer with every mile of progress, the rugged majesty of the hills.

As the third hour of their journeying drew to an end, a sudden vision of green, like an emerald dropped on the drab face of the plain, brought a flush to Honor's cheeks, a light into her eyes.

[1] Police stations.

"It is Kohat, Miss Sahib," the driver announced with a comprehensive wave of his hand.

A breath of ice-cool air came to her from an open water-course at the roadside, and the fragrance of a hundred roses from the one beautiful garden in the station that surrounded the Deputy-Commissioner's house. They passed for a while between overarching trees, but the glimpse of Eden was short-lived. At the avenue's end they came abruptly into the cantonment itself: stony, barren, unlovely, the dead level broken here and there by rounded hummocks unworthy to be called hills. On the east, behind a protective mud-wall, lay the native city; on the north and west, the bungalows of the little garrison—flat-roofed, square-shouldered buildings, with lizard-haunted slits of windows fifteen feet above the ground, set in the midst of bare, pebble-strewn compounds; though here and there some fortunate boasted a thirsty-looking tree, or a handful of rose-bushes blooming bravely in this, the Indian month of roses.

At the foot of the highest hummock, crowned with buildings of uniform ugliness, the tonga-driver drew rein and indicated a steep pathway.

"The bungalow of the Major Sahib is above," he said, "and the Presence must needs walk."

The Presence did more than walk. In the verandah at the path's end a tall figure stood awaiting her; and before Parbutti and the orderly had collected her belongings, she was in John Meredith's arms.

The remarkable likeness between the two was very apparent as they stood together thus; though the man's face was marred by ill-health, and by the distressing prominence of his eye-bones and strongly-marked jaw. He led her into the dining-room with more of lover-like than brother-like tenderness; for despite his forty years no woman had yet dethroned this beautiful sister of his from the foremost place in his heart.

He set her down at the breakfast-table, himself poured out her tea, and dismissed the kitmutgar as soon as might be, Honor watching him the while with troubled solicitude in her eyes.

"It's crushing, John!" she said at length. "And you do look horribly ill."

"Well, my dear girl, is it likely I'd desert the regiment, and forfeit a year of your good company unless devils within were pretty imperative?"

She smiled and shook her head.

"But you ought to have told us about it sooner, . . . me, at any rate. When did you know the decision of the Board?"

"Yesterday. Desmond was with me at the time. I didn't write before that about things being uncertain, for fear the good old man should take fright and whisk you off home. And I thought that even if I couldn't square the Board, you'd find waiting out here for me the lesser evil."

"Very much the lesser evil. What a barbarian people at home would think me if they knew it! And you must go, . . . when?"

"In four or five days; as soon as my leave is sanctioned."

"And, naturally, I stay here with you till then."

"Well, . . . partially. But when your heavy luggage came yesterday, it seemed simpler to send it straight to the Desmonds, and that you should settle in and sleep over there. We're all sitting in one another's pockets here, and you and I can be together all day, never fear. Will that arrangement suit your Royal Highness?"

"My Royal Highness is as wax in your hands," she answered, with a swift softening of face and voice. "I won't start being autocratic till I get you back again. Only—sit down at once, please. You don't look fit to stand."

He obeyed with unconcealed willingness, at the same time handing her a note.

"It is from Mrs Desmond. She is expecting you over there this afternoon."

Honor looked mutinous.

"But I want to stay with you. I shall see plenty of Evelyn later."

"Still, I think we must spare her an hour to-day. The little woman's keen to see you, and I'd like Desmond to feel that we appreciate his prompt kindness. He'll be down at the Lines all the afternoon. It's our day for tent-pegging. You might ride down with Mrs Desmond, and bring me news of what my men are doing. I'm mad at not being able to be there myself."

She deserted her breakfast, and knelt down beside him.

"Dear man! Of course I'll go and find out all about it from Captain Desmond. I needn't stay long to do that."

"No. You can say you want to get back to me. Desmond will understand."

"He's rather a fine fellow, isn't he?"

"One of the best I know. The last man who ought to be hampered by a woman."

"I might take that as a dismissal! How about yourself!"

"Ah, that's quite another matter." And he laid a hand upon the soft abundance of her hair. "Mine is only a two years' contract. And, in any case, *I* would never allow myself to be handicapped by a woman—not even by you. But I don't feel so certain about Desmond."

"Poor little Evelyn! Do you mean, . . . is there any question of her really hampering him, . . . seriously?"

Meredith hesitated. A half-smile hovered in his tired eyes.

"As I'm strongly against the whole affair, and have hardly forgiven him yet for marrying at all, it is fairer for me to say nothing about her one way or the other. You must judge for yourself."

CHAPTER II.

I WANT TO BE FIRST.

> "A breath of light, a pulse of tender fire,
> Too dear for doubt, too driftless for desire."
>
> —SWINBURNE.

SIXTEEN months earlier, Evelyn Dacre—having come out to India with a party of tourist friends—had chanced to spend Christmas week at Lahore: a week which brings half the Punjab together for purposes of festivity and sport. Here, by some mysterious process, which no science will ever be able to fathom or explain, she had cast an instantaneous and unaccountable spell over a man of rare singleness of purpose, whose heart was set to court action, danger, hardship in every conceivable form: a man for whom a girl-wife fresh out from "Home" seemed as hazardous an investment as could well be imagined.

But with all his fine qualities of head and heart, Theo Desmond was little given to cool deliberation in the critical moments of life. This chance-met girl, fragile as a flower and delicately tinted as a piece of porcelain, full of enthusiasm for her new surroundings and of a delight half shy, half spontaneous in the companionship of a man so unlike the *blasé*, self-centred youths of her limited experience, had, for the time being, swept him off his feet. And men are apt to do unaccountable things during those hot-headed moments when the feet are actually off the ground.

A moonlight picnic; an hour of isolated wandering in a garden of tombs; the witchery of the moment; the word too much; the glance that lingered to a look;—and the irrevocable was upon them. Desmond had returned to the Frontier, to a circle of silently amazed brother officers; and in less than three months from their time of meeting the two had become man and wife.

Honor, having been away in England at the time, had had but a second-hand hearing of the whole affair; and for all the keenness of her present disappointment, a natural spark of interest was aroused in her at the prospect of spending a year with this unequally yoked husband and wife.

She found her friend awaiting her in the verandah: a mere slip of womanhood, in a grey habit.

"Oh, *there* you are at last, Honor!" she cried eagerly. "It's grand to see you again! I'm dreadfully sorry about Major Meredith—I am, truly. But it's just lovely getting you on a long visit like this. Come in and have tea before we start."

And taking possession of the girl with both hands, she led her into the house, talking ceaselessly as she went.

"It's really very charming of you two to be so pleased to have me," Honor said quietly, as she settled herself, nothing loth, in the spaciousness of Captain Desmond's favourite chair. Then, because her head still hummed with the clatter of travel, she fell silent; following with her eyes the movements of this graceful girl-wife, whose engaging air of frankness and simplicity was discounted, at times, by an odd lack of both dimly shadowed in the blue-green eyes.

Evelyn Desmond's eyes were, not without reason, her dearest bit of vanity. The tint of the clear iris suggested sea shallows on a day of light cloud—more green than blue; yet with just enough of the sky's own colour to lend the charm of a constant variability, that harmonised admirably with her iridescent changes of mood.

Honor Meredith, who understood her curious mingling of charm and unsatisfactoriness better than any one else in the world, noted her afresh, inwardly and outwardly, with the result that she desired more than ever to know the man who had been hardy enough to place his life's happiness in the hollow of Evelyn's clinging, incompetent hands.

At this juncture Mrs Desmond sank on to a low stool

beside her, set her own cup and plate unceremoniously on the carpet, and laid a caressing hand upon her knee.

"It *does* feel like old times," she said. "And I so badly want to show you to Theo."

The young simplicity of the words brought a very soft light into Honor's eyes.

"I promised John I would go down just in order to be 'shown to Theo,'" she answered smiling. "But you must put off showing me to the rest till another day. I'm a little tired: and I can't keep my mind off John for very long just now."

"You still love him better than any one in the world, then?"

"Isn't the fact of my coming here to stay two years sufficient proof of that?"

"The very greatest proof imaginable!" Mrs Desmond flung out her hands with a pretty, characteristic gesture. "I'm only wondering if you know what you've let yourself in for? I thought India was a lovely place *till* I came here. Theo warned me it wouldn't be a bit like Pindi or Lahore. But that didn't seem to matter, so long as I had him. Only I am so seldom *able* to have him! The regiment swamps *every*thing. The men are always in uniform, and always at it; and the aggravating part is that they actually like that better than anything."

Honor laid her hand over the one that rested on her knee. She saw both sides of the picture with equal vividness.

"What a dire calamity!" she said gently. "I am afraid that on the Frontier, if a man is keen, his wife is bound to stand second; and if only she will accept the fact, it must surely be happier for both in the long-run."

Mrs Desmond looked up at her with pathetic eyes.

"But I don't *want* to accept the fact. I want to be first always: and I ought to be. It's easy enough for *you* to talk, because you haven't a notion how nice Theo is! When you've married a man like that, and buried yourself in a howling wilderness because of him, he ought to belong more to you than to his sacred Frontier Force! But Theo seems to be the private property of half the regiment! There's his chief friend Major Wyndham, and the Boy, his subaltern, he thinks the world of them; and they seem to live in the house. Then there's a tiresome old Ressaldar always coming over to do Persian with him for his Higher Proficiency exam.; and I don't find it half amusing to be one of a mixed crowd like that!"

Her whimsical air of woe disarmed all save the mildest disapproval. It was one of Evelyn Desmond's unfair advantages that she always did manage to disarm disapproval, even in her least admirable moments; and the smile deepened in Honor's eyes.

"It seems to me, Evelyn," she said quietly, "that your husband must be a very large-hearted man."

"Why, of course! That's just the trouble, . . . don't you see?"

"Yes, I do see; and I am woman enough to sympathise. But it will do you no harm, dear, to be one of a crowd, and to get out of the glass case you have been kept under ever since you were born. Show me this wonderful Theo now. People's faces tell me a great deal, you know; and you have roused my curiosity."

"Look round and see if you can recognise him," was the laughing answer.

There were some half-dozen photographs of men, in uniform and out of it, set about the incongruous room; but the girl's eyes were speedily caught and riveted by a full-length presentment of a Punjab cavalryman, which stood, solitary and conspicuous, on the upright piano. She rose and went quickly towards it.

"I choose here," she said decisively. "Am I right?" And seeing that Evelyn nodded, she went on: "What a very remarkable picture. So extraordinarily alive! One can see how he hates standing still inside that frame!"

Then she fell into a long silence: for she was a practised observer of men and things, and the face before her compelled attention. The keynote of the whole was vigour: not mere impetuosity, though that was present also, but a sustained, indwelling vigour, that keeps endeavour bright.

Evelyn stood watching her in no little wonderment, awaiting further comment.

"Don't you like him?" she asked at length.

"Decidedly; if that picture does him justice."

"Well, come on down to the tent-pegging, and find out for yourself."

From the bungalows crowning the mound a bare road sloped northward to the cavalry lines. Along it the two women rode at a foot's pace; for Evelyn still had much to say, and the girl was a notable listener. But even so the parade-ground below them came rapidly into view—a level expanse of brown earth, hard as a usurer's heart, varied only by lines of featureless mud huts, and backed by the dragon's teeth of the hills, brown also, save where sharply defined shadows broke the prevailing monotony of hue.

But the foreground of this toneless setting vibrated with life, movement, colour.

Groups of native troopers, in blue belted tunics and turbans of blue and gold, occupied the central space. English officers, in undress uniform, rode to and fro among them, criticising, encouraging, and generally directing the course of events. In an open *shamianah*,[1] eight or ten men divided their attention between a table at the back of the tent and the four ladies of the station, who perforce converted military events into those friendly gatherings which are the mainstay of Anglo-Indian life. Native onlookers, of all races and ranks, formed a mosaic border to the central theme; and a jumble of rollicking Irish airs from the Sikh band set Honor's foot tapping the air with brisk precision.

"Wait, Evelyn," she said. "I would like to see those four Pathans take the pegs from here. One gets the effect better from rising ground."

And Evelyn, whose knowledge of effects was limited to hats and hairdressing, drew rein obediently, her eyes probing the crowd for the one figure, to whom the rest were mere accessories, and rather troublesome accessories at that.

But Honor's eyes and mind were set upon the four Pathans drawn up in line at the starting-point, the sunlight flashing from their lance-heads, and from every link of eight steel shoulder-chains; their faces inscrutable; their

[1] Marquee.

eyes points of living fire. A pathway of straw softened the ground for galloping, and in the midst of it four pegs awaited the furious onset.

The horses, all eagerness to be off, tossed impatient heads, straining impotently at the tightened rein. On a given word they sprang forward with a thundering rush of hoofs, swooping down upon the pegs at lightning speed, the men's faces level with the flying manes, their lance-heads skimming the ground. Followed the stirring moment of impact, the long-drawn shout, steadily rising to a yell of triumph, as four lances whirled aloft, each bearing the coveted morsel of wood spiked through the centre.

The girl drew a deep breath, and her face glowed with that pagan exultation in bodily strength and prowess, which all the refining fires of civilisation will never burn out of the human heart. But as she turned with praise on her lips, Evelyn leaned eagerly towards her.

"Theo has seen us. He is coming up here. Look!"

And Honor looked accordingly.

A man on a superb bay "waler" had detached himself from the crowd, and was coming towards them at a swinging trot, sitting the horse as though he were part of the animal. Honor realised at a glance that here was that stimulating thing, a positive personality alive to the finger-tips, realised also with what success the photographer had caught and rendered the living essence of the man. Desmond was dark as his wife was fair, though a hint of chestnut in his moustache, and a peculiar light in the hazel-grey eyes, suggested fire not far below the surface. The whole face was stamped with that sovereign quality of sympathy which, even in a world of failure, never fails of its reward.

His wife effected an introduction in her own ingenuous fashion. "There, Theo, . . . this is Honor, that you have heard so much about."

Desmond saluted.

"I'm uncommonly glad to meet you, Miss Meredith," he said; but before Honor could reply Evelyn made haste to interpose.

"Theo, . . . I can't have you calling her Miss Meredith! She's just like my sister, and you must simply be Honor and Theo, . . . d'you see?"

Desmond's eyes showed a flicker of amusement.

"Perhaps you'll allow us to shake hands first," he suggested, and the friendliness of his grasp dispelled the sense of isolation that weighed upon the girl at thought of her brother's departure.

"How did that last performance strike you? Pretty good, wasn't it?"

"Splendid. They went by like a wall. Such magnificent riding."

"They were your brother's men. Wish he could have seen them. He's so tremendously keen. They've tied with my Sikhs, so there'll be an exciting finish. Won't you come down and see it out?"

"I think not, thanks, if it doesn't seem unfriendly. I really only came because John and Evelyn wished it, just to make your acquaintance and see how things were going, and I would honestly like to go straight back to him now, . . . if I may. He said you would understand."

"He was right. I'll see you to the gate myself. Go on down to the *shamianah*, Ladybird, the Boy is looking out for you. I'll not be gone long."

And with a rebellious crumpling of her forehead Evelyn obeyed.

"I am afraid the Major's news must have been rather a shock to you, Miss Meredith," Desmond went on, as their horses mounted the slope. "But we've all been expecting it this long while. He takes too little leave and steadily overworks himself, . . . that's the truth. But then, . . . you should see what he's done for the regiment in the last ten years!"

The spark of enthusiasm in the man's tone struck an answering spark from his companion.

"That's the true way to look at it," she declared warmly. "So many people simply call him a fool. It's the fashion to sneer at enthusiasm in these days."

"We don't sneer at it in this part of the world," Desmond replied with quiet emphasis. "I see now why the Major said I should find you the right sort for the Frontier and a help to . . . my Evelyn. I have transplanted her to a very rough soil, I only hope she's fit to stand it."

"*I* think so. She has been too carefully sheltered till now; and it's just a matter of adapting herself to fresh conditions. You may count on me to do all I can for her while I am here."

"Your name is sufficient guarantee for that!" he answered simply; and the implied compliment to her brother quickened every pulse in her body.

They parted at Major Meredith's gate, Desmond promising to report the result of the final contest on his way home; and the girl sat watching him thoughtfully till a dip in the road hid him from view.

CHAPTER III.

THE BIG CHAPS.

"Love that is loud or light in all men's ears,
. . . .
That binds on all men's feet, or chains, or wings."
—SWINBURNE.

HONOR woke early, springing from dreamless sleep to alert wakefulness, as is the way of vivid natures, and the first sight that greeted her was the huddled form of Parbutti, her chin between her knees, her dark eyes bright and watchful.

Honor's smile was answered by a flash of light across the old woman's face as she arose and salaamed to the ground.

"Behold, while the Miss Sahib slept like a little child, I have laid out the riding-gear as of custom, and now I go to prepare the *terail*[1] for *chota hazri*.[2] They are not ill folk in this compound, Hazúr; and there goes but one word among them, that our Sahib is a diamond fit for a king's turban, understanding the heart of black men, giving no shame words, neither smiting with his foot as do many officer-sahibs. It is well for us, who come strangers to a country of murderers, to be of the household of such a Sahib. Nay, then, child of my heart, I will cease from idle talk, . . . it is an order. Doth not my pearl and the light of my life await her chota hazri?"

And the old woman, whose garrulity was as dust in the balance when weighed against twenty years of faithful service, shuffled out of the room.

[1] Tray. [2] Small breakfast.

Half an hour later Honor was in the saddle—a gallant figure in well-cut brown habit and white helmet, the sunlight finding out gleams of bronze in her abundant hair, while all about her shone the uncompromising blue and gold of a mid-March morning—fresh without sharpness, and fragrant with the ethereal fragrance of dawn.

She followed the downward road, noting a landmark here and there for guidance. Her delight was in the rhythm of movement; in the waiting stillness of earth and sky; the momentous pause between all that has been, and all that shall be, which gives a dramatic sense of responsibility to the day's first hours.

Her eyes rejoiced in the least detail of form and light and colour; in the signs of reviving life; the alert ubiquitous sentries, the sharp alternations of sun and shadow on hills naked and unpromising as the harsh face of poverty; hills that for all time have had but one gift for the giving—"not peace, but a sword." From the cavalry Lines behind her the trumpet call to "stables" set the blood stirring in her veins, with that peculiar thrill which no other instrument can produce. The very spirit of battle breathes in the sound.

An expectant interest glowed within her like a star. It was her great good-fortune to be blessed with that poetic understanding which is neither deceived by custom nor dulled by repetition, which sees all things—even the most familiar—virginally fresh, as on the morning of creation.

Her random wanderings brought her to a stretch of unmetalled road, and at the road's edge, some few hundred yards away a man on a white horse had drawn rein at sight of her. Instantly her thought alighted on Evelyn's husband, but nearer view revealed a different type of man—taller, and equally erect, yet lacking in the suggestion of force and virility that emanated from Captain Desmond, even in repose. With a rapidity born of much practice Honor took stock of him, from his helmet to his boots, as he sat awaiting her, with a coolness which at once amused her and piqued her interest. A slim square chin, indeterminate colouring, and eyes of a remarkable thoughtfulness under very level brows, went to make up a satisfying, if not very striking whole.

"A modest, understanding sort of man," was Honor's mental verdict. "A student every inch of him. I wonder how in the world he comes to be a soldier."

By this time Dilkusha had been drawn up, and the man who ought not to have been a soldier was saluting her with a singularly charming smile, that began in the eyes, and broke up the gravity of the face as sunshine breaks up a cloud.

"You must be Miss Meredith," he said. "One doesn't meet a new face haphazard in Kohat, and . . . you are wonderfully like your brother. I am Major Wyndham. You may have heard the name?"

"Why, . . . yes. You are Captain Desmond's friend."

"You couldn't give a completer description of me! I hear you are to put up with them till Meredith comes back."

"Yes. They have been quite charming about it, and I am so glad not to be driven away from the Frontier at once. I have been longing to get to it for years."

He watched her while she spoke, his quietly observant eyes missing no detail of her face.

"And now you have got here, I wonder how it will strike you after the imposing official circles of Simla and Lahore. You'll find none of the 'beer and skittles' of the country up here. But the Frontier has its own fascination all the same; especially when a man has the spirit of it in his blood. Desmond, for instance, wouldn't give a brass farthing for life out of sight of those hard-featured hills. Do you know him and his wife at all?"

"I never saw him till yesterday, except in the distance at polo matches. But I have known her since she was quite a child."

"And I have known Desmond since he was thirteen. Rather odd! You can't fail to be good friends with *him* Miss Meredith."

"Are you as rabid as my brother and the Colonel because the poor man has dared to marry?" she asked, with an incurable directness which to some natures was a stumbling-block, and to others her chiefest charm. "It seems to be a part of the regimental creed."

"It is. And I subscribe to it . . . *as* a creed. But my

belief has not yet been tried in the fire. Desmond is the keenest soldier I know; yet he has seen fit to marry. I have an immense faith in him, and, whatever others may think, I prefer to reserve my judgment."

"If only a few more of us had the wisdom to do that," the girl said softly. "How much easier life would be for every one!"

Wyndham smiled.

"I have a notion that life isn't meant to be easy," he said. "And the fact remains that Meredith and the Colonel are right in principle. Few men are strong enough to stand the strain of being pulled two ways at once, and marriage is bound to be a grave risk for a man whose heart is set on soldiering—Frontier soldiering above all. But then Desmond loves a risk better than anything else in life."

And with an abrupt laugh he dismissed the subject.

"I must be going on now," he added. "But no doubt we shall meet again soon. I am constantly over at the bungalow."

And, saluting her again, he trotted leisurely northward to the cavalry Lines.

His thoughts as he went hovered about the girl. The mere picture she left upon his brain was not one to be lightly set aside by a man with an ardent eye for the beautiful, and a spirit swift to discern those hidden elements which gave to Honor Meredith's beauty its distinctive quality and charm.

Some men are born with a genius for looking on at life, a form of genius not to be despised. They are of the type from which great naturalists, great philosophers are made; men quick to perceive, slow to assert; men whose large patience rests upon freedom from the fret of personal desire. Of such was Paul Wyndham, and in his accepted rôle of onlooker he fell to pondering upon the new element in his own immediate drama.

If only Desmond had chosen for his helpmate such a girl as Miss Meredith, how different might have been the regiment's feelings in regard to the unwelcome fact of his marriage. Yet Wyndham was aware of an instant recoil from the idea, aware that he personally preferred matters as they stood. With which conclusion he spurred his horse to a canter, as though he could thus outrun the quickened current of thought and feeling which this unlooked-for meeting had set stirring in his brain.

Meantime Honor Meredith had fallen in with another member of her newly-adopted family:—a big, raw-boned Irishwoman, who wore her curling reddish hair cropped short, answered to the name of "Frank," and dressed chronically in a serviceable skirt and covert coat, and a man's shikarri helmet. When riding, the skirt was replaced by that of a country-made habit; and in the simplest evening gown this large-featured, large-hearted woman stood a martyr confessed. For ten years she had been the only woman in a regiment of sworn bachelors; had nursed her "brother officers" whenever need arose; had shared their interests, their hardships, their amusements; till,—in the symbolism of the India she loved,—they and the regiment had become "her father and her mother, her people and her God."

At sight of Honor she hurried her grey country-bred across the road, and held out a square, loosely-gloved hand.

"It's bound to be Miss Meredith!" she exclaimed, in a pronounced brogue, with a flash of white even teeth—her sole claim to beauty. "It's very welcome you are to Kohat and to the regiment. I'm Frank Olliver, . . . Captain Olliver's wife. I'll turn now and ride back a bit of the way with you. Then we can talk as we go. 'Tis the worst of bad luck about your brother. When'll he be leaving?"

"In four or five days. He moves across into our bungalow this morning. It was splendid of Captain Desmond to think of it."

"Ah, Theo's just made that way!" Then, noting a glimmer of surprise in Honor's face, her wide smile shone out once more. "Is it shocked you are because I speak of him so? Well, . . . truth is, I'm a privileged person since I pulled him through typhoid seven years ago, when by rights he should have died. I'm a rare hand, anyway, at dropping the formalities with them that suit me taste. Though, by the same token, I've taken uo liberties with little Mrs Desmond yet. It's queer. We don't seem to get much further with her; though we'd be glad enough to do it for Theo's sake. You mustn't mind straight speech from me, Miss Meredith. Sure I must have been born with the whole truth in me mouth, for as fast as I open me lips a bit of it slips out. I'll be finding she's your half-sister, or first cousin, or some such thing!"

Honor laughed outright. It would clearly be impossible to take amiss anything that this woman might choose to say. The kindliness of her soul shone through her plain face, like sunlight through a window-pane.

"Her mother is a distant connection of ours," the girl admitted frankly. "And we were brought up for a time like sisters. It must have been rather a startling change for her from a country town at home to a Border station; and she is very young still, and very devoted to her husband."

"She is that, . . . after a queer fashion of her own. But Theo's bound to make his mark on the Frontier, like his father before him; and you know the proverb, 'He travels the fastest who travels alone.' 'Tis hardly meself, though, that should be upholding such a saying as that!"

"No, indeed! No woman ought to uphold it. And, after all," Honor added, with a very becoming touch of seriousness, "there may be better things for a man than to travel fast. He may learn more by travelling slowly, don't you think? And I should imagine that fast or slow, Captain Desmond is bound to arrive in the end—Now I must turn in here, and see if John is awake. I'll come and see you when he is gone. I can spare no time for any one else till then!"

Frank Olliver beamed in unqualified approbation.

"You're just a brick, Miss Meredith," she declared with ready Irish warmth. "An' 'twas a fine wind indeed that carried you up to Kohat."

Honor found her hand enclosed in a grasp as strong as a man's; and three minutes later Mrs Olliver—whose seat on a horse was as ungainly as her hand on its mouth was perfect — had become a mere speck on the wide sunlit road.

Honor entered the hall of her new home pondering

many things. She laid aside her sun helmet, and in obedience to the promptings of her interested soul turned her steps toward the drawing-room.

The door was ajar, and passing between the looped gold and white *phulkaris*, she came to a stand-still; for the room was not empty.

Captain Desmond, in undress uniform, sat at the piano with his back towards her. His white helmet lay, spike downward, on the carpet; and an Aberdeen terrier—ears rigidly erect, head tilted at a critical angle—sat close beside it, watching his master with intent eyes, in which all the wisdom and sorrow of the ages seemed writ.

While the girl hesitated on the threshold, Desmond struck a succession of soft chords in a minor key; and she stood spell-bound, determined to hear more. Music was no mere accomplishment to her, but a simple necessity of life; and this man possessed that rare gift of touch, which no master in the world can impart, because it is a produce neither of hand nor brain, but of the player's individual soul. Desmond's fingers were unpractised, but he gave every note its true value; and he played slowly, as though composing each chord as it came, or building it up from memory. It was almost as if he were thinking aloud; and Honor had just decided that she really had no business to be overhearing his thoughts, when an apprehensive "woof" from the Aberdeen brought them suddenly to an end.

Desmond swung round upon the music-stool, and at sight of her sprang up hastily, a dull flush showing through his tan.

"Amar Singh told me you were out," he said, as they shook hands.

"So I was. I only came in this minute. Won't you let me hear a little more, please?"

He shook his head with good-humoured decision.

"I never play to any one . . . except Rob, who, being a Scots Covenanter, disapproves on principle."

"I call that selfish. It's such a rare treat to hear a man play well. I was delighted when you began. I thought pianos were unheard of up here."

"Well, . . . they are hardly a legitimate item in a Frontier officer's equipment! This one was . . . my mother's," he laid a hand on the instrument, as though it had been the shoulder of a friend. "The fellows sat upon me, I assure you, when I brought it out. Told me it was worse than a wife. But I've carried my point, . . . wife and all. And now, perhaps you will reward me,—if I haven't been too ungracious to deserve it?"

He whisked away his solitary photo, and opened the piano.

"How do you know I play?" she asked, smiling. She liked his impetuosity of movement and speech.

"I don't know. I guessed it last night. You carry it in your head?"

"Yes; most of it."

"Real music? The big chaps?"

"Very little else, I'm afraid."

"No need to put it that way here, Miss Meredith. A sonata, please. The Pathetic."

She sat down to the piano with a little quickening of the breath and let her fingers rest a moment on the keyboard. Then—sudden, crisp, and vigorous came the crash of the opening chord.

Honor Meredith's playing was of a piece with her own nature—vivid, wholesome, impassioned. Her supple fingers drew the heart out of each wire. Yet she did not find it necessary to sway her body to and fro; but sat square and upright, her head a little lifted, as though evolving the music from her soul.

Desmond listened motionless to the opening bars; then, with a long breath of satisfaction, moved away, and fell to pacing the room.

The Scots Covenanter, scenting the joyful possibility of escape, trotted hopefully to heel: but, being a dog of discernment, speedily detected the fraud, and retired to the hearth-rug in disgust. Thence he scrutinised his master's irrational method of taking exercise, unfeigned contempt in every line of him, from nose-tip to tail.

The sonata ended, Honor let her hands fall into her lap, and sat very still. She had lost all thought of her companion in the joy of interpretation; but Desmond's voice at her side recalled her to reality.

"Thank you," he said. "I haven't heard it played like *that* . . . for five years. If you can do much of this sort of thing you'll find me insatiable. We're bound to be good friends at this rate, and I see no reason why we should not comply with Ladybird's request to us. Do you, . . . Honor?"

She started and flushed at the sound of her name; then turned her clear eyes full upon him, the shadow of a smile lifting the rebellious corners of her mouth.

"No reason at all, . . . in good time, Captain Desmond."

He returned her look with an equal deliberation.

"Is that a hint to me to keep my distance?"

"No. Only to . . . 'go slow,' if you'll forgive the expressive slang. It's so much wiser in the long-run."

"Is it? Bad luck for me. I've never managed it yet, and I doubt if I ever shall. The men of my squadron call me *Bijli-wallah Sahib*,[1] and I didn't earn the name by going slow, . . . Miss Meredith. If I have been overbold, your music was to blame. But Ladybird seemed to wish it; and, believe me, I did *not* mean it to seem like impertinence. Why, there she is herself, bless her; and we're neither of us ready for breakfast!"

[1] *Bijli*—lightning.

CHAPTER IV.

ESPECIALLY WOMEN.

"We are fearfully and wonderfully made—especially women."
—THACKERAY.

THE afternoon sunlight flung lengthening shadows across the cavalry Lines, where men and native officers alike were housed in mud-plastered huts, innocent of windows; and where life was beginning to stir anew after the noontide tranquillity of the East.

The eighty horses of each troop stood, picketed with ample lengths of head and heel rope, between the lines of huts occupied by their sowars; while at the permanently open doorways squatted the men themselves,—Sikhs, Punjabi-Mahomedans, Pathans, each troop composed entirely of one or the other,—smoking, gambling, or putting final touches to their toilet in the broad light of day. The native officers alone aspired to a certain degree of privacy. Their huts were detached a little space from those that guarded the horses; and flimsy walls of grass matting, set around them, imparted a suggestion of dignity and aloofness from the common herd.

The hut of Jemadar Alla Dad Khan, of the Pathan troop of Desmond's squadron, boasted just such a matting wall, with a gateless gateway, even as in the bungalows of Sahibs; and withinsides all was very particularly set in order. There was an air of festivity in the open courtyard, on either side of which lay two smoke-grimed rooms, that made up the entire house.

For this was a red-letter day in the eyes of the Jemadar,

and of Fatma Bibi, his wife, who had spent a full hour in adorning her plump person, and emphasising its charms according to the peculiar methods of the East. That done, she came forth into the sunlight, attired as becomes a Mahomedan woman who is expecting a visit of ceremony. Above her mysteriously draped trousers she wore a sleeveless coat, adorned with crescent-shaped pockets and a narrow gold braid. A *sari*[1] of gold-flecked muslin was draped over her head and shoulders, and beneath it her heavily oiled hair made a wide triangle of her forehead. The scarlet of betel-nut was upon her lips; the duskiness of kol shadowed her lashes. Ornaments of glass and silver encircled her neck and arms, and were lavishly festooned around her delicate ears.

Her entire bearing exhaled satisfied vanity like a perfume, as she sat at ease upon a bare *charpoy*[2] watching her husband's preparations for the expected guests.

He was arrayed in full-dress uniform, even to the two cherished medals on his chest; and his appearance sorted strangely with the peaceful nature of his occupation.

In the midst of the courtyard he had set forth—not without a secret glow of pride—as exact an imitation of the Sahibs' "afternoon tea" as his limited knowledge and resources would permit. From the mess khansamah he had borrowed a japanned tea-tray that had seen much service, a Rockingham teapot, chipped at the spout, two blue-rimmed cups and saucers, and half a dozen plates, which last he had set round the table at precisely equal distances from each other. Two of them were left empty for the use of his guests, and the other four were piled with dainties suitable for so high an occasion—sugar-topped biscuits (beloved of natives throughout the land), raw pistachio nuts, Cabul grapes and oranges. Then, because the central space had a barren aspect, the sugar-bowl was promoted to the place of honour for lack of a more suitable adornment.

The only two chairs the courtyard contained were set opposite to one another, and it was uplifting to reflect that in a short time they would be occupied by his captain's own

[1] Veil. [2] String-bed.

Memsahib and the Generailly Sahib's Miss, they having, of their great condescension accepted his hospitality by the gracious favour of the Captain Sahib himself.

"According to this fashion, are all things made ready, O Fatma Bibi, when there is a tea-drinking in the bungalows of Sahibs," he announced, for the enlightenment of his wife, who had seen little of the world beyond the four mud walls roofed by her private patch of sky, and therefore could not be expected to have accurate acquaintance with the mysterious ways of Sahibs.

Fatma Bibi acknowledged the information with just such a nod as a mother might bestow on a contented child. Despite her limited experience of the outer world, she knew herself many degrees wiser than her husband in matters of far greater moment than the setting out of a few plates and cups after the manner of the Sahib-log, who, in respect of food and feeding are completely and comprehensively "without sense," as all India knows.

"Bear in mind also," the man went on, sublimely unconscious of his wife's indulgent attitude, "that the Memsahib knoweth the simplest words of Hindostani only; but Meredith Miss Sahib will render our speech unto her, making all things clear. Behold—they come."

The sound of hoofs, and the thud of a "dandy" set down outside confirmed his words; and not many minutes later the Jemadar ushered two Englishwomen into the presence of his wife,—Evelyn, looking more flower-like than usual, in a many-frilled gown of creamy muslin and a big simple hat to match.

"By the goodness of the Captain Sahib's heart my house is honoured beyond deserving," the man gave them greeting as they crossed the threshold, while Fatma Bibi's eyes rested in frank curiosity upon the exceeding whiteness and simplicity of the English "Mem," whose appearance was so direct a contrast to her own.

"Without doubt these women of *Belait*[1] possess no true beauty," she assured herself, with a nod of satisfaction, as she resumed her seat and the new-comers accepted their appointed chairs.

[1] England.

It was a strange meal, and Evelyn Desmond was, in all respects, the least happy of the oddly assorted quartette. She made a conscientious, if not very successful, effort to drink the pale block tea, and eat the strange mixture of foods pressed upon her by the Jemadar, who would obviously feel disheartened if his guests did not empty all four plates at a sitting. Nor was this the least of her troubles. Fatma Bibi's valiant attempts at conversation filled her with a bewilderment and discomfort, bordering on irritation. In an impulse of childish wickedness, she caught herself wishing heartily that Theo had never seen fit to distinguish himself by saving the Jemadar's life.

She looked enviously across the table at Honor, who, by a few spontaneous questions, set both at their ease. She spoke of her father, and the man's face glowed.

"How should men forget the Generailly Sahib, who have beheld him, as did we of the *Rissalar*,[1] in war time, leading men and horses and guns through the terrible mountain country beyond Peshawur? We that serve the British Raj, Miss Sahib, are not men of ready tongue; but our hearts are slow to forget."

In proof thereof, the good Jemadar—his tongue effectually unloosed for the moment—regaled his guests with tale upon tale of bygone raids and murders and of swift retribution meted out by those watch-dogs of the Border, the Punjab Frontier Force; tales set forth with the Oriental touch of exaggeration which lent colour to a narrative already sufficiently inspiring.

"These things have I seen, Miss Sahib," he concluded, with a sudden deepening of his voice, "and these things have I done, through the godlike courage of my Captain Sahib Bahadur"—the man saluted on the words—"who, in the beginning of my service, when I lay wounded almost to the death, amid bullets that fell like hail, bore me to safety on his own shoulders, earning thereby the Victoria Cross that he weareth even now. True talk, Hazúr. Among all the officer Sahibs of Hind, and I have seen more than a few, there be none like unto my Captain Sahib for courage and greatness of heart."

[1] Regiment.

At this point Evelyn's voice broke in on a note of querulous weariness.

"Do come away, Honor. I've eaten queer things enough to give me indigestion for a week; and I can't understand a word any one is saying. What was he getting so excited about just now?"

"Something that must make you feel a very proud woman, Evelyn," the girl answered; and with a thrill in her low voice she translated the man's last words.

Mrs Desmond flushed softly; praise of her husband being only a few degrees less acceptable than praise of herself.

"It sounds very magnificent," she agreed, without enthusiasm, "but I daresay he doesn't really mean half of it. These natives never do. Anyway, please say the polite and proper things and let's get home as soon as possible. I'm sure we've done enough to satisfy even Theo by this time."

And Honor, who would fain have listened to their host for another half-hour, had no choice but to obey.

"Why, Evelyn," she said, as they left the striped sun and shadow of the lines, "you never told me that Captain Desmond won his V.C. by saving the Jemadar's life. I want to hear all about it, please."

Evelyn smiled, and shrugged her shoulders.

"You probably know as much as I do. Theo never *will* tell about himself. Besides, in my own heart, I think he was rather foolish to risk getting killed several times over just for the sake of a *native*." The scorn that some few Anglo-Indians never lose lurked in her tone. "Of course it's very nice for him to have the V.C., and I suppose he thought it was worth while just for that. But I hope he won't go in for any *more* things of that sort. There's *me* to be considered now."

Such peculiar views on the subject of heroism smote Honor to silence, and with a hurried murmur that Dilkusha seemed impatient to get home she set the mare into a trot.

Arrived in the cool dimness of her own drawing-room, Evelyn Desmond sank gratefully into a chair, her skirts billowing softly about her.

"How refreshing it is here, after that glaring courtyard! This place is getting too hot already. I *do* wish Theo would let me go to Simla again this year. Last season the Walters asked him to let me join them; and it was simply lovely. Though I didn't half like leaving him behind; and I suppose I shan't like it much this year either."

"Then why go at all?" suggested practical Honor. "You're not obliged to. Surely Mrs Olliver stays?"

"Mrs Olliver! She's not a woman! She's a Regimental Institution. I can't think *what* the men see in her to make such a fuss about! A plain, badly-made Irishwoman, who dresses abominably. And she's much too casual with all of them—especially with Theo, even if she *did* save his life from typhoid fever."

Honor made no immediate reply. It was only charitable to suppose that an overdose of sunshine and block tea was responsible for the note of irritation in Evelyn's tone.

"I suppose you think I ought to imitate her," Mrs Desmond went on, after an expectant pause. "Kohat is hateful enough in the cold weather, and with heat and cholera, and flies added, it would kill me outright! Besides, I don't believe a man loves one any better for that sort of thing in the end. He probably gets horribly bored, and doesn't like to say so. Besides—Theo *prefers* me to go, he *said* so; and that settles everything quite comfortably for us both. By the way, I've been planning a sort of introduction picnic for you, only that stupid tea-party put it out of my head. I'll make out a list of people at once and send the invitations out this evening."

She crossed over to her bureau, which, apart from the piano, was the only piece of furniture the room contained that in England would be considered worthy of the name.

While she sat absorbed in her congenial task, Desmond entered equipped for polo, and after a few words with Honor went over to his wife.

"What are you so taken up with, Ladybird?" he asked.

"Something lovely! A picnic—for Honor."

Desmond laughed.

"Six for her and half a dozen for yourself! Let's see who we're inviting."

He ran his eye down the list of guests—twelve in all. At sight of the last two names—Mr Kresney, Miss Kresney—

he frowned sharply, and taking up his wife's discarded pencil ran a broad black line through both.

She pushed his hand aside with an unusual display of irritation.

"What did you do *that* for?" she demanded, a ring of defiance in her voice. "I want to ask the Kresneys; and I will—all the same."

"Indeed, little woman, you'll do nothing of the sort."

"Why? What's wrong with them, Theo? They're quite decent people, as far as I can see."

"Which doesn't prove that you can see very far! You must just take my word for it, that whatever else they may be, the Kresneys are not our sort at all."

"I suppose you really mean they're not up to *Frontier Cavalry form!*" she retorted, not without a thrill of fear at her own daring; for the pride of the Frontier Force is a deeply-rooted pride; and, considering its records, not unjustifiable after all.

Desmond's eyes flashed fire, and a sharp retort rose to his lips. But, after a brief silence, he answered his wife with a restraint that spoke volumes to the girl at the tea-table behind him.

"Your taunt is unjust and untrue. In a general way we accept most people for what they are, out here. But one has to draw the line somewhere, even in India. If I were Deputy-Commissioner, the Kresneys would be asked along with the rest. But, in my position, I am free to make distinctions. And I have very good reasons for not asking Kresney to an informal picnic of my particular friends. On neutral ground, such as the club, or the tennis-courts, I have nothing to say; though I should naturally feel pleased if you considered my wishes a little in this matter."

"Well, then, why can't you consider *mine* a little too? I told Miss Kresney about it, and she's expecting to come."

"I'm sorry for that; I don't want to hurt the girl's feelings. But you can't take people up just for once and ignore them afterwards. The truth is, they both see plainly enough that you haven't quite got the hang of things out here yet, and they are naturally taking full advantage of the fact."

Evelyn's passing gentleness evaporated on the instant.

"They're *not!*" she protested wrathfully. "And it's horrid of you to say such things! They like me, I don't see why I shouldn't be nice to them. Besides, this is *my* picnic—I planned it—and if *I'm* the hostess I can ask who I please." The touch of young importance that sounded through the petulance of her tone dispelled the last shadow of Desmond's annoyance and set him smiling.

"Why, of course, Ladybird—within reasonable limits. But after all, the hospitality offered is mine; and what's more, the hostess is mine into the bargain!"

He laid his hand lightly against the rose-flush of her cheek, but she jerked it impatiently aside.

"Oh, well, if you will take it that way," he said, in a tone of resigned weariness, and turning abruptly on his heel came across to Honor, whose cheeks were almost as hot as Evelyn's own.

"I'm glad Alla Dad Khan made himself interesting this afternoon," he remarked conversationally. "Ressaldar Rajinder Singh, who commands my Sikh troop, is very anxious to come and pay his respects some day soon. You see, as your father's daughter and the Major's sister you are a rather special person for us all. But I must be off now. The fellows will be waiting. I'll arrange about the Sirdar to-morrow."

On the threshold he paused and looked towards his wife, who still sat with her back to the room, her head supported on her hand.

"Good-bye, Ladybird," he said, and there was marked kindliness in his tone.

She acknowledged the words with a scarcely perceptible movement, and a few minutes later the rattle of hoofs on the road came sharply to their ears.

Honor's anger flamed up and overflowed.

"Oh, Evelyn, how *can* you behave like that to him!"

Still no answer; only, after a short silence, Evelyn rose and faced her friend. Then Honor saw that her cheeks were wet and her eyes brimming with tears.

It is to be feared that her first sensation was one of pure annoyance. Evelyn thoroughly deserved a scolding: and here she was, as usual, disarming rebuke by her genuine distress.

"*Now*, I suppose he'll go—and get *killed!*" she said, in a choked voice.

"My dear child, what nonsense! He'll come back safe enough. You don't deserve that he should be so patient with you—you don't indeed!"

Evelyn looked up at her with piteous drowned eyes, whose expression had the effect of making Honor feel altogether in the wrong.

"He shouldn't have made such disagreeable remarks about me and the Kresneys, then," she said brokenly. "All the same, I wanted to speak to him. But—I was crying, and I couldn't make a scene—with *you* there. And now—if anything happens to him, and—I never see him again,—it'll be all *your* fault!"

With that finely illogical conclusion she swept out of the room, leaving Honor serenely unimpressed by her own share in the impending tragedy, yet not a little troubled at thought of the man who, for the rest of his natural life, lay at the mercy of such bewildering methods of reasoning.

CHAPTER V.

AN EXPURGATED EDITION.

"A little lurking secret of the blood;
A little serpent secret, rankling keen."

THE Kresneys looked in vain for the coveted invitation, and the trifling circumstance loomed largely on their narrow horizon.

Owen Kresney possessed in a high degree that talent for discovering or inventing slights which is pride of race run crooked, and reveals the taint of mixed blood in a man's veins. As District Superintendent of Police he had relieved his predecessor in the middle of the hot weather. His sister being at Mussoorie, he had arrived alone; and, in accordance with the friendly spirit of the Frontier, had been made an honorary member of the station Mess, where he had found himself very much a stranger in a strange land.

The man's self-conceit was unlimited; his sense of humour *nil;* and in less than a month he had been unanimously voted a "*pukka*[1] bounder" by that isolated community of Englishmen, who played as hard as they worked, and invariably "played the game"; a code of morals which had apparently been left out of Kresney's desultory education. The fact revealed itself in a hundred infinitesimal ways, and each revelation added a fresh stone to the wall that sprang up apace between himself and his companions.

Among them all Desmond and Wyndham represented, in the highest degree, those unattainable attributes which Kresney was secretly disposed to envy; and his narrow soul solaced itself by heartily detesting their possessors. This

[1] Thorough.

ability to recognise the highest without the least desire to reach it, breeds more than half the pangs of envy, hatred, and malice that corrode the lesser natures of earth. But there were also, in Kresney's case, personal and particular reasons which served to nourish these microbes of the soul.

Toward the close of the hot weather the man's growing unpopularity had been established by an incident at Mess, which brought him into such sharp contact with Desmond as he was not likely to forget.

There had been a very small party at dinner. Several of the older men were absent on leave, and three were on the sick list, no uncommon occurrence in Frontier stations. Thus it had chanced that Desmond was the senior officer present.

The wine had already been round twice when the sound of a lady's name, spoken in passing, had diverted Kresney's attention from his own dissatisfied thoughts.

It chanced that he had met this same lady at Murree a year ago, and that she had roundly snubbed his advances towards intimacy. The unexpected mention of her name revived that sense of injury which smoulders in such natures like a live coal; and on the same instant awoke the desire to hit back with the readiest weapon available.

Forgetful of the restriction imposed by the rigid code of the mess-table, he launched the first disparaging comment that sprang to his mind.

Directly the sentence was out, he could have bitten his own tongue for pure vexation.

It fell crisp and clear into a chasm of silence, as a dropped pebble plashes into a well.

The stillness lasted nearly a minute, and while it lasted Kresney felt the fire of Desmond's glance through his lowered lids. Then some one hazarded a remark, and the incident was submerged in a renewed tide of talk.

When dinner broke up, with a general movement towards the ante-room, Kresney became aware that Desmond was at his side.

"You will be good enough to come into the verandah with me," he had said in a tone of command; and Kresney, feeling ignominiously like a chidden schoolboy, had had no choice but to obey.

Before that brief interview was ended, the man had heard the truth about himself for the first time in his life, with the sole result that he registered in his heart an unquenchable hatred of the speaker.

But Desmond had been in no mood just then to reckon with after-results. All the inborn chivalry of the man was up in arms, less against the spoken words than against the petty spite underlying them—the cowardly hit at a woman powerless to defend herself. In an unguarded moment he gave full vent to the scorn and disgust that consumed him, and lashed the man without mercy.

Then—realising the utter inability to alter the other's peculiar point of view—natural magnanimity checked his impetuous outburst:

"I don't know whether you are aware," he said, "that after to-night I should be justified in asking the Mess President to remove your name from the list of Honorary Members. But that is rather a strong measure, and I decided instead to speak a few straight words to you myself. If they've been a trifle too straight, I am sorry. But remarks of the kind you made this evening are inadmissible at a mess-table; or, for that matter, at any other table where—gentlemen are present. Now, if you give me your word to keep the rules of the Mess strictly in future, I will give you mine that this incident shall never be mentioned to any one by me, or by any one of the fellows here to-night."

Kresney had given the required promise none too graciously. But his effort at perfunctory thanks stuck in his throat; nor did Desmond appear to expect them. With a brief reassurance in respect of his own silence he turned back into the Mess; and there, so far as externals went, the incident had ended.

Yet, on this still March evening, as Kresney strolled back and forth on his narrow verandah, enjoying an after-dinner cigar, every detail of that detested interview darted across his memory for the hundredth time, like a lightning-streak across a cloud. Wounded, in the most susceptible part of his nature, Kresney saw no reason to deny himself the satisfaction of hitting back. Whatever may have been his principles in regard to debts in general, he was scrupulously punctilious in settling debts of malice,—indirectly, if possible; and in this instance personal antipathy added zest to the mere duty of repayment.

Very early in the cold weather Kresney had become aware that an effective weapon lay ready to his hand, and had taken it up without scruple or reluctance. Evelyn Desmond's natural lack of discernment, her blindness to the subtle impertinence of flattery, and her zeal for tennis—a game seldom patronised by cavalrymen,—had worked all together for good; and Kresney had gone forward accordingly, nothing loth.

He had looked to the riding picnic to mark a definite step in advance, and Mrs Desmond's intention of inviting them was beyond doubt. Remained the inference that Desmond had used either authority or persuasion to prevent it.

The idea stirred up all the dregs of the man's soul. A sudden bitterness overwhelmed him—a sense of the futility of attempting to strike at a man so obviously favoured by the gods; a man who held his head so resolutely above the minor trivialities of life.

But the will to strike would soon or late evolve a way. There were other means of achieving intimacy with a woman as inexperienced as little Mrs Desmond, and he would get Linda to help him. Linda was a good girl, if a trifle stupid. At least she had the merit of believing in him and obeying his wishes with unquestioning fidelity—a very creditable merit in the eyes of the average man.

These reflections brought him to a standstill by one of the doors that opened into the drawing-room. It was a long narrow room of an aggressively Anglo-Indian type—overcrowded with aimless tables, painted stools and chairs in crumpled bazaar muslins, or glossy with Aspinall's enamel. The dingy walls were peppered with Japanese fans, China plates, liliputian brackets, and photographs in plush frames. Had Miss Kresney taken her stand on each door-sill in turn and flung her possessions, without aim or design, at the whitewashed spaces around her, she could not have produced a more admired disorder. This she recognised with a thrill of pride; for she aspired to be artistic, and some misguided friend had assured her that the one thing needful was to avoid symmetry or regularity in any form.

Her own appearance harmonised admirably with her surroundings. She wore the shapeless tea-gown beloved of her kind—made in the verandah, and finished with dingy lace at the neck and wrists, and even at this hour a suggestion of straw slippers showed beneath the limp silk of her gown. Yet, as Evelyn Desmond saw her on the tennis-courts, she was a neatly clad, angular girl of eight-and-twenty, with a suppressed, furtive air that was an unconscious reflection upon her brother's character. In her heart she cherished a lurking admiration for Desmond, and aspired to become the wife of a cavalry officer—Harry Denvil being the temporary hero of her dreams.

When her brother entered the room she was fitfully engaged in perpetrating a crewel-work atrocity for one of her many chairs.

He did not speak his thought at once, but stood looking down at her critically through the smoke-wreaths of his cigar. The major share of good looks certainly rested with himself; but for eyes set too near together, and the relentless lines that envy and ill-humour pencil about a man's mouth, the face was attractive enough, in its limited fashion. He had the same air of being "off duty" which pervaded his sister, and his Japanese smoking-suit showed signs of being a very old friend indeed.

"Look here, Linda," he began at last, "when are we playing tennis again with little Mrs Desmond?"

"I think it was Tuesday," she said.

"Well, then, ask her to tea here first, d'you see?"

Linda's brown eyes—it pleased her to call them hazel—widened with surprise.

"Oh, my! D'you think she would reallee come? It was nastee of her to leave us out of her picnic like that, after she told me all about it, too."

Miss Kresney's insistence on the consonants and the final vowels was more marked than her brother's; for although three-fourths of the blood in her veins was English, very few of her intimate associates could make so proud a boast without perjuring their souls: and there are few things more infectious than tricks of speech.

"Yes, of course," he acquiesced readily. "But I'm jolly well certain that was not her doing. She'll come, right enough, if you ask her nicely. At all events it is worth trying, if only on the chance of annoying her insufferable husband."

"If you wish it, certainlee. I would like to be better friends with Mrs Desmond. Only, I do not quite see why you dislike *him* so much more than the others."

Kresney hesitated before replying. It was not often that Linda aspired to question either his motives or decisions; and he had begun to suspect that her loyalty wavered, by a hair's-breadth, where Desmond was concerned. After all, why not tell her an expurgated edition of the truth. The idea commended itself to him for many reasons, and even as she was beginning to wonder at his silence he sat down beside her and spoke; the sting of humiliation stimulating his inventive faculty as he went on.

Desmond himself would scarce have recognised the incident, but Miss Kresney was clearly impressed.

"You see, Linda," her brother concluded, "a fellow can't be expected to stand that sort of thing without hitting back, and I am trying to hit back a bit now. It is only fair. These Frontier Force chaps need a lot of setting down, I can tell you. They fancy they hold all India in their hands. And what is it they do after all, except play polo like maniacs, and play all manner of foolish pranks at Mess? They make a god out of this Desmond, here; and the fellow is as proud as the devil. He will be jolly well mad if his wife gets really friendly with me. As he will not ask us there, we will ask her here—you see? And you must be as nice as you can. Say pretty things to her—that pleases her more than anything: and make yourself useful, if you get the chance. She's not half a bad little woman; and if you help me, Linda, I shall get in with her yet in spite of her conceited prig of a husband."

The smile that accompanied the words was not a pleasant

one, but the girl returned it with an uncritical fervour of affection.

"You know I am always glad to please you, Owen. I am onlee sorree you did not tell me all about it sooner."

Her ready championship put him in high good-humour with himself and the world at large.

"You really *are* no end of a good girl, Linda," he said, as he rose to his feet. "I shall ask Denvil to tea for you on Tuesday; and you shall have a new frock as soon as ever I get next month's pay. Not a thing made in the verandah; but a good style of frock from Mussoorie or Lahore, whichever you please; and you can ask Mrs Desmond to help you choose it. Her dresses are always first class, and she is interested in such things."

CHAPTER VI.

GENIUS OF CHARACTER.

"For still the Lord is Lord of Might,
In deeds, in deeds, He takes delight."
—R. L. S.

EVELYN DESMOND'S picnic was an accomplished fact. At four o'clock, in the full glare of a late March sun, a business-like detachment of twenty horses, and one disdainful camel, proceeded at a brisk trot along the lifeless desolation of the Bunnoo Road. The party kept in close formation, straggling of any sort being inadmissible when the bounds of the station have been left behind. Ten of the riders were English, and an armed escort guarded them in front and rear; the camel, in gala trappings of red and blue, being responsible for provisions, enamelled iron tea-things, and the men's guns.

Notwithstanding the absence of the Kresneys, Evelyn Desmond was in a mood of unusual effervescence. Harry Denvil rode at her side, and the two kept up a perpetual flow of such aimless, happy nonsense as is apt to engender vague regret in the hearts of those who have arrived at greater wisdom.

Three miles of riding brought them to the welcome refreshment of a river running crystal clear over a bed of pebbles. Beside the river rose an isolated plateau—abrupt, inconsequent, and, like all things else in the tawny landscape, unsoftened by a blade of living green.

The face of the rock was riddled with rough, irregular holes, as though Titans had been using it for a target. Around and above it a bevy of blue rock-pigeons—circling, dipping, and darting with a strong rush of wings—shone like iridescent jewels, green and blue and grey, against the unstained turquoise of the sky, whose intensity of colour made generous atonement for the lack of it on earth. At the foot of the cliff a deep pool mirrored the calm wonder of the sky.

Here the camel was brought to his knees, and the escort, dismounting, formed a wide circle of sentries round the little party, the under-note of danger suggested by their presence giving a distinct flavour to the childishly simple affair. The white man's craze for carrying his food many miles from home, in order to eat it on the ground, remains a perpetual bewilderment to the natives, who express their opinion on the matter in all frankness and simplicity by christening it the "dinner of fools."

Pigeon-shooting was the established amusement of afternoons spent under the cliff; and, the meal being over, sport was soon in full progress, Frank Olliver and Mrs Jim Conolly handling their guns as skilfully as any man present.

While Honor stood watching them, Wyndham drew near and remained by her for a few seconds without a word. Then: "Shall we go and sit over by the river, Miss Meredith, and leave them to their sport?" he asked suddenly, his eyes and voice more urgent than he knew.

"Yes; I'd far rather watch the birds than shoot them. They are too beautiful to be killed for the sake of passing the time. But you probably don't see it that way—men seldom do."

"I must be the eternal exception, then!" he answered, as they turned away. "It's not a creditable confession for a right-minded man: but I shrink from taking life, even in the exigencies of my profession."

At that she turned upon him with a spontaneous frankness of interest, which had lured many men to their undoing.

"Will you think me very ill-mannered if I ask how you ever came to choose such a profession at all? I wondered about it the first time I saw you."

"Do I look as hopelessly unsoldier-like as all *that?*"

"No—a thousand times, no!" And the quick colour flamed in her cheeks.

"Well, then?"

"I only meant—I see a good deal in faces, and—yours gave me a strong impression that you would prefer reading and thinking to acting and striving."

His smile had in it both surprise and satisfaction.

"You were not far out there. Let us sit down on this rock for a bit. I would like to answer your question. May I light a cigarette?"

"Do."

He took his time over the simple operation. His impulse towards unreserve puzzled him, and several seconds of silence passed before he spoke again; silence, emphasised by broken snatches of talk and laughter; by the sharp crack of guns; and the whirring of a hundred wings, like the restless murmuring in the heart of a shell.

"It may sound strange to you," he began, not without an effort, "but the truth is that my choice of a profession was simply the result of my friendship with Desmond. I think I told you we were at school together. *His* future was a foregone conclusion, and when it came to the point —I chose just to throw in my lot with his. I am quite aware that many people thought me a fool. But we have had twelve years of it together here, he and I; and it has certainly been good enough for me."

He spoke in a tone of great quietness, his eyes set upon the shining reaches of the river which, by now, ran molten gold in the westering sunlight.

"Thank you for telling me," she said; and the simple words set his pulses travelling at an unreasonable rate of speed. "I had no idea friendship could ever mean quite so much."

"It doesn't in nine cases out of ten. But I think that's enough about myself. It isn't my habit to entertain ladies with egotistical monologues!"

"But then, properly behaved ladies don't ask you direct personal questions, do they?"

"Well—no—not often."

And they exchanged one of those smiles that ripen intimacy more speedily than a month of talk.

"I'm quite unrepentant, all the same!" she said. "And I'm rather wanting to ask you another. It's about Captain Desmond this time. May I?"

"Ask away!"

"Well, I want to know more of how he won his V.C. Evelyn could give me no details when I asked her; and it struck me just now that you were probably there at the time."

"Yes, indeed, I *was*," he said, with a new ring in his voice. "There were a few bad minutes when we in the valley felt morally certain we had seen the last of him."

She turned on him with kindling eyes.

"Oh, tell me—please! Tell me everything. I am soldier enough to understand."

"I verily believe you are! And, since you wish it, you shall have it in full. It happened during a rising of the Ghilzais six years ago. They had given us rather a stiff time of it for some weeks, and on this occasion a strong body of them had to be dislodged from a height where they were safely entrenched behind one of their stone sangars, ready to pick off any of us who should attempt the ascent. But the thing had to be done, like many other hopeless-looking things, and a party of infantry and cavalry were detailed for the duty,—a company of Sikhs, and twenty-five dismounted men of Desmond's squadron, led by himself. Our main force was stationed in the valley, you understand, and the advance was covered by three mountain guns. The men were deployed in an extended line at the foot of the hill, and began a careful ascent, taking advantage of every scrap of cover available, the Ghilzais picking them off with deadly certainty whenever they got the smallest chance. About two-thirds of the way up Alla Dad Khan was bowled over and lay out in the open dangerously wounded, under the full brunt of the enemy's fire. In a flash Desmond was out from under the rock he had just reached. He crossed that open space under a rain of bullets it made one sick to see, and got the poor fellow up in his arms. It seemed a sheer impossibility for him to get back under cover alive, hampered as he was by the wounded man, who—as you know—is a much bigger fellow than himself. I gave up every shred of hope as I watched, and one or two of the sowars near me broke down and cried like children. But if ever I beheld a miracle it was during those few astounding minutes—the worst I've ever known. His clothes were riddled with bullets; two of them passed clean through his helmet; yet except for a flesh wound in the left arm, he was untouched."

Wyndham paused, and the girl drew in a long breath.

"Oh, I can see it all!" she said softly. "But isn't there more?"

"A little more, if you want it."

"Please."

"Well, the hill was successfully cleared, and you may imagine the welcome we gave Theo, when at last he got back to camp, with his uniform in ribbons and his helmet gone. I don't know when I've heard such cheering from natives. Besides saving the Jemadar, the success of the whole affair had been due to his leadership and example. He wouldn't hear of it, of course; but when the account came out in the 'Gazette,' he found himself belauded from start to finish, with a V.C. conferred on him to crown all. One couldn't say much to him even then. He's not the sort."

Honor's cheeks were on fire, her eyes like stars; and it is characteristic of Paul Wyndham that he noted these facts without a shadow of envy.

"The genuine modesty of genius," she said; and Paul bent his head in acquiescence.

"Theo's genius is of the best kind," he added; "it is genius of character, of a wide sympathetic understanding of men and things. And on the Frontier, Miss Meredith, that sort of understanding counts for more than anywhere else in the country. We control our fellows here as much by love and respect as by mere discipline. Get a native to love you, and believe in you, and you are sure of him for good. That is why officers like Theo and your brother, who hold their men's hearts in their hands, are, without exaggeration, the pillars on which the safety of India rests. It is when the cry of 'Jehad' runs like fire along the Border, and the fidelity of our troops is being tampered with, that we get the clearest proof of this. At such times pay, pension, and Orders of Merit have no more power to restrain a Pathan than a thread of cotton round his ankle. But there's just one thing he will *not* do—he will not desert, in his hour of need, an officer whom he has found to be just, upright, and fearless, and whom he has praised as a hero to his own people."

Wyndham's unwonted eloquence, and the glow of feeling underlying it, lifted the girl to fresh heights of enthusiasm.

"Oh, how glad I am to have come here!" she said with sudden fervour. "Captain Desmond was talking in much the same strain just before we started; and one cannot listen to him without catching the fire of his enthusiasm, which is surely the best kind of fire that ever came down from heaven!"

Just as she finished speaking, Desmond himself strode up to them.

"I say, Paul, old man," he remonstrated, "isn't it some one else's turn for an innings by this time? Mrs Conolly is keen to have a talk with Miss Meredith before we start. You both looked so absorbed that she begged me not to interrupt! I ought to have introduced her to you before starting, Miss Meredith. She's the wife of our acting Civil Surgeon and quite an old friend of yours, it seems. Will you come?"

The girl rose and turned to Wyndham with a friendly smile. "You and I can have our talk out another time, can't we?"

"By all means."

He sat watching her as she left him, with a tender concentration of gaze, his brain stunned by a glimpse into undreamed-of possibilities; into a region of life whereof he knew nothing, and had believed himself content to know nothing all his days.

Mrs Jim Conolly was a large woman, nearer forty than thirty. Twenty years of India, of hot weathers resolutely endured, of stretching small means to the utmost limit and beyond it, had left their mark, in sallowness of skin, in broken lines of thought between her brows, and of restrained endurance about her firmly-closed lips. She had the air of a woman who has never allowed herself to be worsted by the minor miseries of life; and in India the minor miseries multiply exceedingly. Unthinking observers stigmatised her face as harsh and unprepossessing; but it was softened and illumined by a glow of genuine welcome as she greeted Honor Meredith.

"I wonder if you have the smallest recollection of me?" she said. "My last glimpse of you was in a dak gharri at Pindi, when you were first starting for home nineteen years ago, and the sight of what you have grown into makes me feel a very old woman indeed! Do you remember those Pindi days at all?"

"Bits, here and there, quite vividly. I had been wondering already why I seemed to know your face. It was you who had the two nice babies I loved so dearly. Haven't you any for me to play with now?"

"Yes, my two youngest are still with me. But they are rather big babies by this time. You must come over and see them soon, and we will pick up the threads of our dropped friendship, Honor. Your father and mother were very good to me in the old days, but you were my chief friend from the start. You have grown into a very beautiful woman, dear," she added, in a lower tone; "and if you ever want help or advice while you are here alone, I hope you will turn to me for it as readily as you would to your own mother. I haven't seen Lady Meredith for years. Sit down under the cliff with me, and give me some news of them all."

By the time dusk had set in the little party was back again in Desmond's compound, the escort deserting them at the gate; and as Honor Meredith prepared to dismount, Paul Wyndham came forward, a certain restrained eagerness in his eyes.

"May I?" he asked, with the diffidence of a man unused to making such requests.

"I generally manage all right, thanks."

"You might make an exception, though—just this once."

For an instant of time his hands supported her—an instant of such keen sensation that, when it was passed, he pulled himself up sharply—called himself a fool, and in the same breath wished that she had been a few degrees less skilful in springing lightly to the ground.

Ready-made talk was, for the moment, beyond him; and he departed something hastily, leaving Honor and his friend alone together in the darkening verandah.

Voices and laughter came out to them from the drawing-room, where Evelyn and Denvil were carrying on their young foolishness with undiminished zeal; and Desmond turned upon the girl the irresistible friendliness of his eyes.

"You enjoyed yourself, I hope,—Miss Meredith?"

"Immensely, thank you,—Captain Desmond."

Her tone was a deliberate echo of his; and their eyes met in mutual laughter.

"Aren't we good friends enough now to drop the formality?" he asked. And at the question a lightning vision came to her of the scene on the hillside, so vividly described by his friend.

"Yes—I think—we are," she said slowly.

"That's right. I think so too."

"I seem to have made quite an advance in that direction this afternoon," she added, in no little surprise at her own boldness.

"How's that? Paul?"

"Yes."

"Oh! so that was the engrossing subject. I might have known Paul wasn't likely to be expatiating on himself."

"He gave me a stirring account of a certain day in October, six years ago," she went on, with an unconscious softening of her voice.

Desmond's short laugh had in it a genuine touch of embarrassment.

"Did he? That was superfluous of him. The good fellow would have done no less himself in the circumstances. Listen to those two children in there! How finely they're enjoying themselves! I say, Harry!" he shouted to the invisible Denvil, who came forth straightway;—a squarely built, chestnut-haired boy, his sea-blue eyes still full of laughter; "have you quite decided to invite yourself to dinner?"

"*Rather*—if you'll have me?"

"Of course I'll have you. Cut away and make yourself respectable."

And as the boy vanished in the darkness Desmond turned to find his wife's figure in the open doorway, its purity of outline thrown into strong relief by the light within.

She stood on the threshold balancing herself on the tips of her toes in a light-hearted ecstasy of unrest, and flung out both hands towards her husband.

"Oh, Theo, it was delicious! I had lovely fun!"

She came and nestled close to him with the confiding simplicity of a child; and Honor, under cover of the dusk, slipped round by the back of the house to her own room.

CHAPTER VII.

BRIGHT EYES OF DANGER.

"My mistress still, the open road;
And the bright eyes of danger."
—R. L. S.

BY mid-April, life in the blue bungalow had undergone an unmistakable change for the better; and Theo Desmond, sitting alone in the congenial quietness of his study, an after-dinner pipe between his teeth, a volume of Persian open before him, and Rob's slumbering body pressed close against his ankles, told himself that he and his wife, in befriending Honor Meredith at a moment of difficulty, had without question entertained an angel unawares. Evelyn had blossomed visibly in the pleasure of her companionship; while he himself found her good to talk with, and undeniably good to look at.

There was also a third point in her favour, and that by no means the least. Her sympathetic rendering of the great masters of music had renewed a pleasure linked with memories sacred beyond all others. Althea Desmond bid fair to retain undivided supremacy over the strong son, who had been the crown and glory of her life. Death itself seemed powerless to affect their essential unity. Her spirit —vivid and vigorous as his own—still shared and dominated his every thought; and her photograph, set in a silver frame of massive simplicity, stood close at his elbow, while he reviewed the changes wrought in the past few weeks by the unobtrusive influence of John Meredith's sister.

The mere lessening of strain and friction in regard to the countless details of an Indian household was, in itself, an unspeakable relief. During the first few months of his marriage he had persevered steadily in the thankless task of instructing his cheerfully incompetent bride in the language and household mysteries of her adopted country. But the more patiently he helped her the more she leaned upon his help; till the futility of his task had threatened to wear his temper threadbare, and to put a severe strain on a relationship more complex than he had imagined possible.

Now, however, the tyranny of trifles was overpast. The man's elastic nature righted itself, with the spring of a finely-tempered blade released from pressure, and as the passing weeks revealed his wife's progress under Honor's tuition, he readily attributed her earlier failures to his own lack of skill.

As a matter of fact, her power to cope with Amar Singh—Desmond's devoted Hindu bearer—and the eternal enigmas of charcoal, *jharrons*,[1] and the *dhobie*,[2] had not increased one whit: and she knew it. But the welcome sound of praise from her husband's lips convinced her that she must have done something to deserve it. She accepted it, therefore, in all complacency, without any acknowledgment of the guiding hand upon the reins.

Great peace dwelt also in the compound, where a colony of servants and their families lived their unknown lives apart; and great pride in the heart of Parbutti, since Amar Singh had so far unbent as to prophesy that the Miss Sahib would without doubt become a Burra Mem before the end of her days.

While Desmond sat alone in this warm April evening, studying the fantastic Persian characters with something less than his wonted concentration, the sound of the piano came to him through the half-open door.

For a few moments he listened, motionless, to the first weird whispering bars of Grieg's Folkscene, "Auf den Bergen," then the book was pushed hastily aside and the lamp blown out. Rob—rudely awakened from a delectable dream of cats and the naked calves of unsuspecting coolies—found himself plunged in darkness, and his master vanishing through the curtains into the detested drawing-room.

[1] Dusters. [2] Washerman.

Evelyn was installed on the fender-stool of dull red velvet, her hands clasped about her knees, her head raised in expectation. A dress of softly flowing white silk, and a single row of pearls at her throat, intensified her fragile freshness, as of a lily of the field, a creature out of touch with the sterner elements of life. It was at such moments that her husband was apt to suffer a contraction of heart, lest, in an impulse of infatuation, he had undertaken more than he would be able to perform.

She patted his favourite chair; then, impulsively deserting her seat, crouched on the hearth-rug beside him and nestled her head against his knee.

"I told her to play it! I knew it would bring you at once," she whispered, caressing him lightly with a long slim hand.

"You shall sing to me afterwards yourself," he said, "a song in keeping with your appearance to-night. You look like some sort of elf-maiden in that simple gown and my pearls. Only one touch wanted to complete the effect!"

With smiling deliberation he drew out four tortoise-shell pins that upheld the silken lightness of her hair, so that it fell in a fair soft cloud about her neck and shoulders.

"Theo! How dare you!"

And as she turned her face up to him, in laughing remonstrance, he was struck anew by the childishness of its contour, in spite of the pallor, which had become almost habitual of late. Taking it between his hands he looked steadfastly into the limpid shallows of her eyes, as though searching for a hidden something which he had little hope to find.

"Ladybird, what a baby you are still!" he murmured, "I wonder *when* you mean to grow into a woman?"

Then with a start he became aware that Amar Singh, having entered noiselessly through the door behind him, stood at his side in a pose of imperturbable reverence and dignity.

"Olliver Memsahib *ghora per argya*,"[1] he announced with discreetly lowered lids; while Evelyn, springing up with rose-petal cheeks and a small sound of dismay, must

[1] Has come on a horse.

needs try and look as if ladies in evening dress habitually wore their hair hanging loose about their shoulders.

Honor swung round upon the music-stool as Frank Olliver, in evening skirt and light drill jacket strode into the room.

Before she could bring out her news, a blare of trumpets, sounding the alarm, startled the quiet of the night, and Desmond leapt to his feet.

"There you are, Theo, man," she said. "You can hear for yourself. It's a fire in the Lines. Geoff and I caught sight of the flare just now from our back verandah. He's gone on ahead; but I said I'd look in here for you."

"Thanks. Tell 'em to saddle the Demon, will you? I'll be ready in two minutes."

And Mrs Olliver vanished from the room.

As Desmond prepared to follow her, his wife's fingers closed firmly on the edge of his dinner-jacket.

She was sitting now in the chair he had left; and turned up to him a face half beseeching, half resentful in its frame of soft hair.

"Why must *you* go, Theo? There are heaps of others who—aren't married."

"Don't be a little fool, child!" he broke out in spite of himself. Then gently, decisively, he disengaged her fingers from his coat; but their clinging grasp checked his impatience to be gone.

He bent down, and spoke in a softened tone. "I've no time for arguments, Evelyn. I am simply doing my duty."

He was gone—and she remained as he had left her, with hands lying listlessly in her lap, and a frown between her finely pencilled brows,—mollified, but by no means convinced.

Honor had hurried into the hall, where Frank Olliver greeted her with impulsive invitation.

"Why don't you 'boot and saddle' too, Honor, an' ride along with us?"

"I only wish I could! I'd love to go! But I *must* stay with Evelyn. She is upset and nervous about Theo as it is."

"Saints alive! How *can* you put up with her at all—at

all!" muttered irrepressible Frank. "But hush, now, here's the blessed fellow himself!"

Theo Desmond strode rapidly down the square hall, hung with trophies of the chase and implements of war—an incongruous figure enough, in forage cap and long brown boots with gleaming spurs, his sword buckled on over his evening clothes. He snatched a long clasp-knife from the wall in passing, and the Irishwoman, with an nod of approval, hurried out into the verandah, where the impatient horses could be heard champing their bits.

Desmond had a friendly smile for Honor in passing.

"Pity you can't come too. Be good to Ladybird. Don't let her work herself into a fever about nothing."

For eight breathless minutes the grey and the dun sped through the warm night air, under a rising moon, their shadows fleeing before them, long and black,—two perspiring saïses following zealously in their wake;—till their riders drew rein before a pandemonium of scurrying men and horses, silhouetted against a background of fire.

The great pile of sun-dried bedding burnt merrily: sending up fierce tongues of flame, that shamed the moonlight, as dawn shames the lamp. A brisk wind from the hills caught up shreds and flakes from the burning mass, driving them hither and thither, to the sore distraction of man and beast.

Lithe forms of grass-cutters and water-carriers, in the scantiest remnants of clothing, leaped and pranced on the outskirts of the fire, like demons in a realistic hell.

In valiant spurts and jerks, alternating with ignominious flight, they were combating that column of flame and smoke with thimblefuls of water, flung out of stable buckets, or squirted from mussacks. They were beating it also with stript branches, making night radiant with a thousand sparks.

But the soaring flames jeered at their pigmy efforts; twinkled derisively on their glistening bodies; and assailed the vast composure of the skies with leaping blades of light.

To the bewildering confusion of movement was added a

no less bewildering tumult of sound, whose most heart-piercing note was the maddened scream of horses; and whose lesser elements included shouts of officers and sowars; high-pitched lamentations from the audience of natives; the barking of dogs; and the drumming of a hundred hoofs upon the iron-hard ground.

During the first alarm of the fire, which had broken out perilously close to the quarters occupied by Desmond's squadron, the terrified animals, in their frenzied efforts to break away from the ropes, had reduced the Lines to a state of chaos. Those of them, and they were many, who succeeded in wrenching out their pegs, had instinctively headed for the parade-ground beyond the huts; their flight complicated by wandering lengths of rope that trailed behind them, whirled in mid-air, or imprisoned their legs in treacherous coils; while sowars and officers risked life and limb in attempting to free them from their dilemma.

The restless brilliance gave to all things a strange nightmare grotesqueness: and a blinding, stifling shroud of smoke whirled and billowed over all.

As the riders drew up, there was a momentary lull, and before dismounting Desmond flung a ringing shout across the stillness.

"*Shahbash*,[1] men, *shahbash!* Have no fear! Give more water—water without ceasing!"

He was answered by an acclamation of welcome from all ranks.

"*Wah! Wah!* Desmin Sahib *argya*!"[2] the sowars of his squadron called to one another through the curling smoke; and the new arrivals were speedily surrounded by a little crowd of officers and men: Wyndham, Denvil, Alla Dad Khan, and Ressaldar Rajinder Singh, in the spotless tunic and vast silken turban of private life.

The Jemadar took possession of the Demon's bridle, and Desmond, leaping lightly to the ground, hurried straightway to the relief of a distressed grass-cut. The man had been rash enough to attempt the capture of two horses at once, and now stood in imminent danger of being kicked to death by his ungrateful charges.

[1] Well done. [2] Has come.

Desmond took both horses in hand, holding them at arm's length, and soothing them with his voice alone.

"Here you are, Harry!" he said, as Denvil came to his assistance. "This poor fellow will go with you now, quietly enough."

Handing over his second horse to the grass-cut, he vanished into the darkness; where, betwixt stampeding horses and the incredible swiftness of fire, he found more than sufficient scope for action.

He came to a stand-still, at length, for a second's breathing space;—and lo, Rajinder Singh emerging suddenly from the heart of pandemonium, breathless with haste, a great distress in his eyes.

"Hullo, Ressaldar!" Desmond exclaimed. "What's up now?"

The tall Sikh saluted.

"The knife, Sahib! Give me your knife! It is *Sher Dil*,[1] fallen amongst his ropes. He is like to strangle——"

"Great Scott! I'll see to it myself."

And he set out, full speed, Rajinder Singh after him, protesting at every step.

The great black charger, the glory of the squadron and of his owner's heart, was in a perilous case. So securely had he entangled himself in the head-rope that, despite the freedom of his heels, and spasmodic efforts to regain his feet, he remained pinned to earth, not many yards from where the fire was raging,—his fear and misery increased by wind-blown fragments of lighted straw, by the roar and crackle of the burning pile.

Desmond saw at a glance that his rescue might prove a dangerous business, but Rajinder Singh was beside him now, still hopeful of turning him from his purpose.

"Hazúr—consider—the horse is mine——"

"No more words!" Desmond broke in sharply. "Stay where you are!"

He plunged forthwith into the stinging, blinding smoke; dexterously avoiding the hoofs of Sher Dil, subduing his terror with hand and voice, though himself half choked, and constantly forced to close his eyes at the most critical

[1] Lion Heart.

moments; while the task of avoiding the burning fragments that fell about him seemed in itself to demand undivided attention.

Rajinder Singh, stationed at the nearest possible point, anxiously watched his Captain's progress; and here Paul Wyndham joined him hurriedly.

"Who is that?" he asked. "The Captain Sahib?"

"To my shame, your honour speaks truth," the old man made answer humbly. "His heart was set to do this thing himself——"

"Have no fear," Wyndham reassured him kindly; and, with a sharp contraction of heart, ran to his friend's assistance.

Desmond had already stooped to slit the rope that pressed so cruelly against the charger's throat; and, as Wyndham reached him, the animal gave a last convulsive plunge; threw out his forelegs in an ecstasy of freedom; and struck his deliverer full on the shoulder.

"Damnation!" Desmond muttered, as he fell to the ground, and Sher Dil staggered, panting, to his feet.

Rajinder Singh sprang forward with a smothered cry. But, quick as lightning, Desmond was up again, and had secured the morsel of rope dangling by the horse's head. Only his left arm hung limp and helpless, the droop of the shoulder telling its own tale.

"Collar-bone," he said laconically, in reply to the mute anxiety of Paul's face. "Same old spot again!"

"It might just as well have been—your head," Paul answered, with a twist of his sensitive mouth. He had not quite got over his few moments of acute suspense.

Desmond laughed.

"So it might, you old pessimist! But it wasn't! Here you are, Ressaldar Sahib! Never have I seen a horse so set on killing himself. But it was needful to disappoint him on your account."

Rajinder Singh, who had come forward, plucking the muslin scarf from his shoulders for a bandage, saluted in acknowledgment of the words.

"How is it possible to make thanks, Hazúr. . . . ?"

Desmond laid a hand on the man's shoulder.

"No need of thanks," said he. "This fine fellow hath already thanked me in his own rough fashion, clapping me on the shoulder,—forgetful of his great strength,—because he had no power to say 'Shahbash!'"

The old Sikh shook his head slowly, a great tenderness in his eyes.

"Such is the gracious heart of the Captain Sahib, putting a good face even upon that which is evil. Permit, at least, that we make some manner of bandage till it be possible to find the Doctor Sahib."

It was permitted; and the useless arm having been strapped into place, Wyndham insisted upon his friend's departure; a fiat against which Desmond's impetuous protests were launched in vain. For, like many men of habitually gentle bearing, Paul Wyndham's firmness was apt to be singularly effective on the rare occasions when he thought it worth while to give proof of its existence.

"I'll ride back with you myself," he announced, in a tone of finality, "and go on to the Mess for Mackay afterwards. The worst is over now, and you'll only let yourself in for a demonstration if your men find out that any harm has come to you." The diplomatic suggestion had the desired effect; and they rode leisurely back to the bungalow, under a moon no longer robbed of its radiance.

Few words passed between them as they went; but on arriving at the squat, blue gate-posts Wyndham drew rein and spoke.

"Good-night, dear old chap. Take a stiff 'peg' the minute you get in. I'm in need of one myself."

"Sorry if I gave you a bit of a shock, old man," Desmond answered smiling, and rode at a foot's pace toward the house.

"Here I am, Ladybird!" he announced, on entering the drawing-room; and Evelyn, springing from the depths of his chair, made an eager movement towards him.

But at sight of his bandaged arm and damp dishevelled appearance she halted with lips apart. A curious coldness crept into her eyes and entirely banished the young look from her face.

"Theo—you're hurt—you've broken something."

"Well, and if I have?" he answered laughing. "It's a mere nothing. Only a collar-bone."

"Your collar-bone isn't nothing. And I can't *bear* to see you all hideous and bandaged up like that. I knew something would happen! I was sure it would!"

The light of good-humour faded from his eyes.

"Well, well, if you knew it all beforehand, no need to make so many words about it now. Let me sit down. It's been stifling work and—I'm tired."

He sank into the chair and closed his eyes, his face grown suddenly weary. His wife drew near to him slowly, with more of pained curiosity than of solicitude in her face, and laid a half-reluctant hand on the arm of his chair.

"Does it hurt, Theo?" she asked softly.

"Nothing to bother about. Mackay will be here soon."

"Won't you tell us how it happened?"

"There's not much to tell, Ladybird. Rajinder Singh's charger kicked me while I was cutting his head-rope—that's all. The good old chap was quite upset because I would'nt let him do it himself."

"Well, I think you *ought* to have let him. It wouldn't have mattered half so much if *he*——"

"That's enough, Evelyn!" the man broke out in a flash of genuine anger. "If you're only going to say things of that sort, you may as well hold your tongue."

And once again he closed his eyes, as if in self-defence against further argument or upbraiding.

His wife stood watching him with a puzzled frown, while Honor, a keenly interested observer, wondered what would happen next.

Her sympathy, as always, inclined to the man's point of view. But a passionate justness, very rare in women, forced her to acknowledge that Evelyn's remonstrance, if injudicious, was not unjustifiable. The girl saw clearly that the sheer love of danger for its own sake, which Frontier life breeds in men of daring spirit, had impelled Desmond to needless and inconsiderate risk; saw also that his own perception of the fact added fire to his sharp retort.

He stirred at length, with an uneasy shifting of the damaged shoulder.

"This bandage is hideously uncomfortable," he said in a

changed tone. "Could you manage to untie it and fix it up more firmly till Mackay comes?"

Thus directly appealed to, Evelyn cast a nervous glance at Honor. The girl made neither sign nor movement, though her hands ached to relieve the discomfort of the wounded man; and after a perceptible moment of hesitation, Evelyn went to Desmond's side, her heart fluttering like the heart of a prisoned bird.

With tremulous fingers she unfastened the knot behind his shoulder, and, having done so, rested her hand inadvertently on the broken bone. It yielded beneath her touch, and she dropped the end of the bandage with a little cry.

"Oh, Theo, it *moved!* I can't touch it again! It's . . . it's horrible!"

Her husband stifled an exclamation of pain and annoyance.

"Could *you* do it for me, Honor?" he asked. "It can hardly be left like this?"

She came to him at once, and righted the bandage with deft, unshrinking fingers, rolling part of the long scarf into a pad under his arm to ease the aching shoulder.

"Thank you," he said. "That's first-rate."

And as he shouted for a much-needed "peg," Honor passed quietly out of the room.

Evelyn remained standing a little apart, watching her husband with speculative eyes. Then she came and stood near him, on the side farthest from the alarming bone that moved at a touch.

"I'm sorry, Theo. Are you very cross with me?"

Her lips quivered a little, and the pallor of her face caught at his heart.

"No, no. We won't make mountains out of molehills, eh, Ladybird? Kiss and be friends! like a good child, and get to bed as fast as possible. Mackay will be here soon, and you'll be best out of the way."

He drew her down and kissed her forehead. Then, as she slipped silently away through his study, and on into the bedroom beyond, he lay back with a sigh in which relief and weariness were oddly mingled. He was devoutly thankful when the arrival of James Mackay dispelled his disturbing train of thought.

CHAPTER VIII.

STICK TO THE FRONTIER.

"We know our motives least in their confused beginning."
—BROWNING.

HONOR sat alone in the drawing-room, a basket of socks and stockings at her elbow, her thoughts working as busily as her needle. This girl had reduced the prosaic necessity of darning to a fine art; and since Evelyn's efforts in that direction bore an odd resemblance to ill-constructed lattice windows, Honor had taken pity on the maltreated garments very early in the day.

Evelyn herself was at the tennis-courts, with the Kresneys and Harry Denvil, a state of things that had become increasingly frequent of late; and a ceaseless murmur of two deep voices came to Honor's ears through the open door of the study, where Desmond was talking and reading Persian with his friend Rajinder Singh.

Honor enjoyed working to the accompaniment of that sound. It had grown pleasantly familiar during the past week, in which Desmond had been cut off from outdoor activities. When the Persian lesson was over, he would come in to her for a talk. Then there would be music, and possibly a game of chess; for Desmond was an enthusiastic player. They had spent one or two afternoons in this fashion already, since the night of the fire; and their intimacy bid fair to ripen into a very satisfying friendship.

To the end of time, writers and thinkers will continue to insist upon the impossibility of such friendships; and to the end of time, men and women will persist in playing with this form of fire. For it is precisely the possibility of fire under the surface which lends its peculiar fascination to an experiment old as the Pyramids, yet eternally fresh as the first leaf-bud of spring.

In the past five years Honor had established two genuine friendships with men of widely different temperaments; and she saw herself now—not without a certain quickening of heart and pulse—in a fair way to establishing a third.

The hum of voices ceased; there were footsteps in the hall; a few hearty words of leave-taking from the Englishman, and two minutes later he stood before her, his left sleeve hanging limp and empty; the arm and shoulder strapped tightly into place beneath the flap of his coat.

"Not gone out yet?" he said, a ring of satisfaction in his tone. "Going to join Ladybird at the club later on?"

"No. As she had this engagement I stayed at home in case you might be glad to have some one to 'play with' after your long lesson was over."

"Just like you!" he declared, with a touch of brotherly frankness, which was peculiarly pleasing to this brother-loving girl. "I've been rather overdoing the Persian this week. You must give me some Beethoven presently. And if you really mean to 'play with' me you must also leave off looking so aggressively industrious."

His eyes rested, in speaking, on the rapid movement of her needle, and he became suddenly aware of the nature of her work.

"Look here, Honor," he exclaimed. "I draw the line at that! Ladybird ought not to allow it. We've no right to turn you into a domestic drudge."

"Ladybird—as you so delightfully call her—knows me far too well to try and stop me when she sees I mean to have my own way! Shall you mind if I go shares in your special name for her? It suits her even better than her own."

"Yes, it seems to express her, somehow—doesn't it?"

An unconscious tenderness invaded his tone, and his glance turned upon a panel photograph of his wife in her wedding-dress that stood near him on the mantelpiece. Watching it thus, he fell into a thoughtful silence, which Honor made no attempt to break. Speaking or silent his companionship was equally acceptable to her: and while she awaited his pleasure a great hole, made by the removal of one of Evelyn's "lattice windows," filled up apace.

Of a sudden he turned from the picture, and, drawing up a low chair, sat down before her, leaning a little forward, his elbow resting on his knee. The urgency and gravity of his bearing made her at once lay down her work.

"Honor," he began, "I'm bothered . . . about Ladybird, . . . that's the truth. I wonder if I can speak without fear of your misunderstanding me?"

"Try me! I am only too glad to help her in any way."

His intense look softened to a smile.

"You've made that clear enough already. I begin to wonder what she will do when John comes back to claim you again. You so thoroughly understand her, and thoroughly—love her."

"She is a creature born to be loved."

"*And* to be kept happy," he added very quietly. "But the vital question is whether that is at all possible in Kohat, or in any other of our stations; for Kohat is by no means the worst. She hates the place, doesn't she? She's counting the days to get away to the Hills. You know you can't look me straight in the face and say she is happy here."

The unexpected attack struck Honor into momentary silence. Desmond was fatally quick to perceive the shadow of hesitation, transient as a breath upon glass; and when she would have spoken he silenced her with a peremptory hand.

"Don't perjure yourself, Honor. Your eyes have told me all I wanted to know."

Distress gave her a courage that surprised herself.

"Indeed they have done nothing of the kind! You ask a direct question, and you are bound in fairness to hear my answer. The life here is still very new to Evelyn, and she has not quite found her footing yet;—that is all. I have had it from her own lips that the place matters very little to her so long as she is—with you; and you go too far in saying that she is not happy here."

But her words did not carry conviction. He was still under the influence of his wife's curious aloofness since the night of the fire.

"You're trying to let me down gently, Honor," he said, with a rather cheerless smile. "And you may as well save yourself the trouble. Only—this is where you must *not* misunderstand me, please,—no shadow of blame attaches to Ladybird if she isn't happy. I had no right to bring her up to this part of the world, knowing it as I did; and I've no right to keep her here. That's the position, in a nutshell."

"Do you mean you ought to—send her away?"

"No—*take* her away."

Honor started visibly.

"But—surely—that's impossible?"

"I think not," he said, in a matter-of-fact tone that distressed her more keenly than any display of emotion. "It's merely a question of facing facts. If I had money enough, I could throw up the Army and take her home. But, as matters stand, I can only do the next best thing, and give up—the Frontier, by exchanging into a down-country regiment."

"*The Frontier* . . . ! Theo! Do you realise what you are saying?"

"Perfectly."

"Oh, but it's folly—worse than folly! To give up what you have worked for all these years—the men who worship you—your friends, the regiment——"

"They would survive the loss. I don't flatter myself I'm indispensable. Besides, this isn't a question of me or my friends. I am thinking of Ladybird."

The coolness of his tone, and the set determination of his mouth, chilled her fervour like a draught of cold air.

"Oh, if only Major Wyndham were here!" she murmured desperately.

"Thank God he is not! And if he were, it would make no difference. I shouldn't dream of discussing such a matter with him or—any of them. When my mind is made up, I shall tell him; that is all."

He rose as though the matter were ended; but Honor had no mind to let him shut the door upon it—yet.

"It is strange that you can speak so," she said, "when

you must know, better than any one, what your leaving the regiment would mean—to Major Wyndham."

"Yes—I know," he answered quietly, and the pain in his eyes made her half regret her own daring. "The only two big difficulties in the way are my father—and Paul."

"*I* see a whole army of others almost as big."

"That is only because you are always in sympathy with the man's point of view."

"A matter like this *ought* to be looked at first and foremost from the man's point of view. The truth is, Theo, that you have simply appealed to me in the hope of having your own Quixotic notion confirmed. You want me to say, 'Yes, go; you will be doing quite right.' And—think what you will of me—I flatly refuse to say it!"

He regarded her for a few seconds in an admiring silence, the smile deepening in his eyes. Then:

"Don't you think you are a little hard on me?" he said at length. "It is not altogether easy to do—this sort of thing."

Honor made no immediate reply, though the strongest chords of her being vibrated in response to his words. Then she rose also, and stood before him; her head tilted a little upwards; her candid eyes resting deliberately upon his own. Standing thus, at her full height, she appeared commandingly beautiful, but in the stress of the moment the fact counted for nothing with either of them. All the hidden forces of her nature were set to remove the dogged line from his mouth; and he himself, looking on the fair outward show of her, saw only a mind clear as crystal, lit up by the white light of truth.

For an instant they fronted one another—spirits of equal strength. Then Honor spoke.

"If I *do* seem hard on you, it is only because I want, above all things, to convince you that your idea is wrong from every point of view. You have paid me a very high compliment to-day. I want you to pay me a still higher one: to believe that I am speaking the simple truth, as I see it, from a woman's standpoint, not merely trying to save you from unhappiness. May I speak out straight?"

"As plainly as you please, Honor. Your opinion will not be despised, I promise you."

"Well, then—is it fair on Evelyn to make her upbringing responsible for such a serious turn of the wheel? Would you give her no voice in the matter—treat her as if she were a mere child?"

"She is very little more than a child."

"Indeed, Theo, she is a great deal more. She is a woman, . . . and a wife. The woman's soul isn't fully awake in her yet; but it may come awake any day. And then—how would she feel if she ever found out——"

"She never would——"

"How can you tell? Women find out most things about the men they—care for. It's a risk not worth running. Would she even acquiesce if you put the matter before her now, child as she is?"

"Frankly, I don't know. Possibly not. She isn't able to see ahead much, or look all round a subject."

"Shall you be very angry if I say that you haven't yet looked thoroughly round this one? The idea probably came to you as an impulse—a very fine impulse, I admit; and, instead of fairly weighing pros and cons, you have simply been hunting up excuses that will justify you in carrying it out; because, for the moment, Evelyn seems a little discontented with things in general."

The hard lines about his mouth relaxed.

"You *are* speaking straight with a vengeance, Honor!"

"I know I am. It's necessary sometimes, when people are—obstinate!" And she smiled frankly into his troubled face. "Oh, believe me, it's fatal for the man to throw all his life out of gear on account of the woman. It's putting things the wrong way about altogether. In accepting her husband, a woman must be prepared to accept his life and work also."

"But, suppose she can't realise either till—too late?"

"That's a drawback. But if she really cares, it can still be done. I am jealous for Evelyn. I want her to have the chance of showing that she has good stuff in her. Give her the chance, Theo; and if she doesn't quite rise to it, don't feel that you are in any way to blame."

"I'd be bound to feel that."

"Then I can only say it would be very wrong-headed of

you." Her eyes softened to a passing tenderness nevertheless. "Let the blame, if there is any, rest on my shoulders; and we'll hope that the need may never arise. Now, have I said enough? Will you—*will* you leave things as they are, and put aside your impossible notion for good?"

The urgency of her request so touched him that he answered with a readiness which surprised himself.

"No question but you're a friend worth having! I promise you this much, Honor. I will think very thoroughly over it all, since you accuse me of not having done so yet! And we'll let the matter rest for the present, anyway. I'd like to get you both to the Hills as soon as possible. These Kresneys are becoming something of a nuisance. It's past my comprehension how she can find any pleasure in their company. But she has little enough amusement here, and I'm loth to spoil any of it. She'll enjoy going up to Murree, though, sooner than she expected; and as Mackay insists on my taking fifteen days before getting back to work, I can go with you, and settle you up there in about a week's time. You'll see after her, for me, won't you, Honor? She's a little heedless and inexperienced still; and you'll keep an eye on household matters more or less?"

"Of course I will, and make her see to them herself, too; though it seems rather like expecting a flower to learn the multiplication table! She is so obviously just made to be loved and protected."

"*And* kept happy," he insisted, with an abrupt reversion to his original argument.

"Yes—within reasonable limits. Now, sit down, please, and light up. You've been all this time without a cigar!"

But the cigar was hardly lighted before they were startled by a confused sound of shouting from the compound;—a blur of shrill and deep voices, punctuated by the strained discordant bark of a dog;—a bark unmistakable to ears that have heard it once. Desmond sprang out of his chair.

"By Jove! A mad pariah!"

Lifting Rob by the scruff of his neck, he flung that amazed and dignified person with scant ceremony into the study, and shut the door; then, judging by the direction of the sound, hurried out to the front verandah, snatching up a heavy stick as he passed through the hall. Honor, following not far behind, went quickly into her own room.

Desmond found his sun-diffused compound abandoned to a tumult of terror. Fourteen servants and their belongings had all turned out in force, with sticks, and staves, and valiant shakings of partially unwound turbans, against the unwelcome intruder—a mangy-coated pariah, with lolling tongue and foam-flecked lips, whose bones showed through hairless patches of skin; and whose bared fangs snapped incessantly at everything and nothing, in a manner gruesome to behold. A second crowd of outsiders, huddled close to the gates, was also very zealous in the matter of shouting, and of winnowing the empty air.

As Desmond set foot on the verandah, a four-year-old boy, bent on closer investigation of the enemy, escaped from the "home" battalion. His small mother pursued him, shrieking; but at the first snap the dog's teeth met in the child's fluttering shirt, and his shrieks soared, high and thin, above the deeper torrent of sound.

In an instant Desmond was beside him, the stick swung high over his head. But a low sun smote him straight in the eyes, and there was scant time for accurate aim. The stick merely grazed the dog's shoulder in passing; and Desmond almost lost his balance from the unresisted force of the blow.

The girl-mother caught wildly at her son; and prostrating herself at a safe distance, babbled incoherent and unheeded gratitude. The dog, mad with rage and pain, made a purposeful spring at his one definite assailant; and once again Desmond, half-blinded with sunlight, swung the heavy stick aloft. But before it fell a revolver shot rang out close behind him; and the dog dropped like a stone, with a bullet through his brain.

A shout of quite another new quality went up from the crowd; and Desmond, turning sharply on his heel, confronted Honor Meredith, white to the lips, the strong light making an aureole of her hair.

The hand that held the revolver quivered a little, and he caught it in so strong a grip that she winced under the pressure.

"It would be mere impertinence to say 'thank you,'" he murmured with low-toned vehemence. But his eyes, that sought her own, shamed the futility of speech. "The sun was blinding me; and if I'd missed the second time——"

"Oh, hush, hush!" she pleaded with a quick catch of her breath. "Look, there's Rajinder Singh coming back."

"He must have seen what happened; and by the look of him, I imagine *he* will have no great difficulty in expressing his feelings."

Indeed, the tall Sikh, whose finely-cut face and cavernous eye-bones suggested a carving in old ivory, bowed himself almost to the ground before the girl who had saved his admired Captain Sahib from the possibility of a hideous death.

But in the midst of an impassioned flow of words, his deep voice faltered; and squaring his shoulders, he saluted Desmond with a gleam of fire in his eyes.

"There be more things in the heart of a man, Hazúr, than the tongue can be brought to utter. But, of a truth, the Miss Sahib hath done good service for the Border this day."

Desmond flung a smiling glance at Honor.

"*There's* fame for you!" he said, with a lightness that was mere foam and spray from great deeps. "The whole Border-side is at your feet!—But what brought you back again, Rajinder Singh?"

"Merely a few words I omitted to say to your Honour at parting."

The words were soon spoken; and the crowd, breaking up into desultory groups, was beginning to disperse, when, to his surprise, Desmond saw his wife's jhampan appear between the gate-posts, and pause for a moment while she took leave of some one on the farther side. Instinctively he moved forward to greet her; but, on perceiving her companion, changed his mind, and stood awaiting her by the verandah steps.

The dead dog lay full in the middle of the path; and Honor, still holding her revolver, stood only a few yards away. At sight of these things the faint shadow of irritation upon Evelyn's face deepened to disgust, not unmixed with fear, and her voice had a touch of sharpness in it as she turned upon her husband.

"Who on earth put that horrible dog there, Theo? And why is Honor wandering about with a pistol? I met a whole lot of natives coming away. Has anything been happening?"

"The dog was mad, and Honor shot him," Desmond answered, with cool abruptness. Her manner of parting from Kresney had set the blood throbbing in his temples. "I only had a stick to tackle him with; and she very pluckily came to my rescue."

While he spoke, Honor turned and went into the house. She was convinced that Evelyn would strike a jarring note, and in her present mood felt ill able to endure it.

Evelyn frowned.

"Oh, Theo, how troublesome you are! If the dog had bitten a few natives, who'd have cared?"

"Their relations, I suppose. And there was a child in danger, Evelyn."

"Poor little thing! But you really can't go about trying to get killed for the benefit of any stray sort of people. I am thankful I wasn't here!"

"Yes—it was just as well," her husband answered drily, as he handed her out of the jhampan. "What brought you back so early?"

"The sun was too hot. I had a headache; and we were all playing abominably. I'm going in now, to lie down."

She paused beside him, and her eyes lingered upon his empty coat-sleeve. Lifting it distastefully between finger and thumb, she glanced up at him with a droop of her delicate lips.

"When is it going to be better? I hate to see you looking all one-sided like that."

"I'm sorry," he answered humbly. "But Nature won't be persuaded to hurry herself—even to please you." He scrutinised her face with a shade of anxiety.

"You do look white, Ladybird. How would it be if I took you to Murree in a week's time?"

"It would be simply lovely! *Can* you do it—really? Would you *let* me go so soon?"

"*Let* you go? Do you think I want to keep you here a moment later than you care to stay?"

"Theo!" Instant reproach clouded the April brightness of her face. "How horrid you are! I thought you liked to have me here as long as possible."

He laughed outright at that. He was apt to find her unreasonableness more charming than irritating.

"Surely, little woman, that goes without saying. But if the heat is troubling you, and headaches, I like better to have you where you can be rid of both; and as the notion seems to please you, we'll consider the matter settled."

Between nine and ten that evening, when the three were sitting together in the drawing-room, the outer stillness was broken by a sound of many footsteps and voices rapidly nearing the house. No native crowd this time. The steps and voices were unmistakably English; and Desmond rose hastily.

"This must be Rajinder Singh's doing! It looks as if they meant to overwhelm us in force."

Evelyn had risen also, with a slight frown between her brows.

"Can't I go to bed before they come, Theo? I'm very tired, and they're sure to make a dreadful noise."

"I'm afraid that won't do at all," he said decisively, a rare note of reproof in his tone. "They probably won't stop long, and you must please stay up till they go."

As he spoke, Harry Denvil in white Mess uniform, scarlet kummerband, and jingling spurs, plunged into the room.

"I'm only the advance guard! The whole regiment's coming on behind—even the Colonel—to drink Miss Meredith's health!" He turned upon the girl and shook hands with her at great length. "All the same, you know," he protested laughing, "it's not fair play for *you* to go doing that sort of thing. Wish I'd had the chance of it myself!"

Such speeches are impossible to answer; and Honor was thankful that the main body of troops arrived in time to save her from the futile attempt.

But she was only at the beginning of her ordeal.

By the time that Mrs Olliver and six men had wrung her

hand with varying degrees of vigour, each adding a characteristic tribute of thanks and praise, her cheeks were on fire; and a mist, which she tried vainly to dispel, blurred her vision.

Through that mist, she was aware of Frank vigorously shaking hands with Desmond, scolding and blessing him in one breath. "Ah, Theo, man, you're a shocking bad lot!" was her sisterly greeting. "Never clear out o' one frying-pan till you're into the next! Thank the Powers Miss Meredith was handy." And swinging round on her heel she accosted the girl herself. "No mistaking the stock *you* come of, Honor, me dear!"

Submerged in blushes, Honor could scarce command her voice. "But really—I only——"

"You only hit the bull's eye like a man, Miss Meredith," Captain Olliver took her up promptly. "The Major never told us he was adding a crack shot to the regiment!" And he swept her a bow that reduced her to silence.

More overwhelming than all were the few direct words from Colonel Buchanan himself; a tall, hard-featured Scot, so entirely absorbed in his profession that he never, save of dire necessity, set foot in a lady's drawing-room.

Paul Wyndham introduced him, and moved aside, leaving them together. For an instant he treated the girl to the quiet scrutiny of clear blue eyes, unpleasantly penetrating. He had scarcely looked at her till now. Still unreconciled to Desmond's marriage, he had resented the introduction of a third woman into the regiment; and he found himself momentarily bewildered by her beauty.

"I ought to be better acquainted with you, Miss Meredith," he said a little stiffly, sincerity struggling through natural reticence, like a light through a fog. "I'm no lady's man, as you probably know, but I had to come and thank you to-night. Desmond's quite my finest officer—no disrespect to your brother; he knows it as well as I do——"

"Here you are, Colonel!" Geoff Olliver thrust a long tumbler into his senior's hand. "We're going to let off steam by drinking Miss Meredith's health before we go back."

Honor looked round hastily, in hopes of effecting an escape, and was confronted by Desmond's eyes looking straight into her own. He lifted his glass with a smile of the frankest friendliness; and the rest followed his example.

"Miss Meredith, your very good health."

The words went round the room in a deep disjointed murmur; and Frank Olliver, stepping impulsively forward, held out her glass to the girl.

"Here's to your health and good luck, with all my heart, Honor, . . . the Honor o' the regiment!" she added, with a flash of her white teeth.

Uproarious shouts greeted the spontaneous sally.

"Hear, hear! Well played, indeed, Mrs Olliver! Pity Meredith couldn't have heard that."

Olliver laid a heavy hand on Desmond's shoulder.

"Tell you what, old chap," he said. "You must come back with us; and, by Jove, we'll make a night of it. Finest possible thing for you after a week's moping on the sick list; and we'll just keep Mackay hanging round in case you get knocked out of shape. I'll slip into uniform myself and follow on. That suit you, Colonel?"

"Down to the ground; if Mackay has no objection."

But Mackay knew his men too well to have anything of the sort; and Desmond's eyes gleamed.

"How about uniform for me, sir?" he asked. "I could manage it after a fashion."

Colonel Buchanan smiled.

"No doubt you could! But I'll overlook it to-night. The fellows want you. Won't do to keep them waiting!"

Followed a babel of talk and laughter, in the midst of which Honor, who had moved a little apart, became aware that Desmond was at her side.

"Never mind them, Honor," he said in a low voice. "They mean it very well, and they don't realise that it's a little overwhelming for us both. I won't pile it on by saying any more on my own account. *Wait* till I get a chance to repay you in kind—that's all!"

His words spurred her to a sudden resolve.

"You have the chance now, if it doesn't seem like taking a mean advantage of—things."

"Mean advantages are not in your line. You've only to say the word."

"Then *stick to the Frontier!*" she answered, an imperative ring in her low voice. "Doesn't to-night convince you that you've no right to leave them all?"

His face grew suddenly grave.

"The only right is to stand by Ladybird—at all costs."

"Yes, yes—I know. But remember what I said about her side of it. Give her the chance to find herself, Theo; and give *me* your word now to think no more about leaving the Border. Will you?"

He did not answer at once, nor did he remove his eyes from her face.

"Do you care so much what I do with the rest of my life?" he said at last very quietly.

"Yes—I do; for Ladybird's sake."

"I see. Well, there's no denying your privilege—now to have some voice in the matter. I give you my word, and if it turns out a mistake, the blame be on my own head. The fellows are making a move now. I must go. Good-night."

The men departed accordingly with much clatter of footsteps and jingling of spurs; and only Mrs Olliver remained behind.

Evelyn Desmond had succeeded in slipping away unnoticed a few minutes earlier. She alone, among them all, had spoken no word of gratitude to her friend.

CHAPTER IX.

WE'LL JUST FORGET.

"Les petites choses ont leur importance; c'est par elles toujours qu'on se perde."—DOSTOIEVSKY.

"So the picnic was a success?"

"Yes, quite. Mrs Rivers was so clever. She paired us off beautifully. My pair was Captain Winthrop of the Ghurkas; an awfully nice man. He talked to me the whole time. He knows Theo. Says he's the finest fellow in Asia! Rather nice to be married to the 'finest fellow in Asia,' isn't it?"

"Decidedly. But I don't think we needed *him* to tell us that sort of thing." A touch of the girl's incurable pride flashed in her eyes.

"Well, I was pleased all the same. He said he was never so surprised in his life as when he heard Theo had married; but now he had seen me, he didn't feel surprised any more."

"That was impertinence."

"Not a bit! I thought it was rather nice."

A trifling difference of opinion; but, in point of character, it served to set the two women miles apart.

Evelyn's remark scarcely needed a reply; and Honor fell into a thoughtful silence.

She had allowed herself the rare indulgence of a day "off duty." Instead of accompanying Evelyn to the picnic, she had enjoyed a scrambling excursion with Mrs Conolly —whose friendship was fast becoming a real possession— and her two big babies; exploring hillsides and ravines; hunting up the rarer wild flowers and ferns; and lunching off sandwiches on a granite boulder overhanging infinity. This was her idea of enjoying life in the Himalayas; but the June sun proved a little exhausting; and she was aware of an unusual weariness as she lay back in her canvas chair in the verandah of "The Deodars,"—a woodland cottage, owing its pretentious name to the magnificent cedars that stood sentinel on either side of it.

Her eyes turned for comfort and refreshment to the stainless wonder of the snows, that were already beginning to don their evening jewels—coral and amethyst, opal and pearl. The railed verandah, and its sweeping sprays of honeysuckle, were delicately etched upon a sky of warm amber, shading through gradations of nameless colour into blue, where cloud-films lay like fairy islands in an enchanted sea. Faint whiffs of rose and honeysuckle hovered in the still air, like spirits of the coming twilight, entangling sense and soul in a sweetness that entices rather than uplifts.

Evelyn Desmond, perched lightly on the railings, showed ethereal as a large white butterfly, in the daintiness of her summer finery against a background of glowing sky. She swung a lace parasol aimlessly to and fro, and her gaze was concentrated on the buckle of an irreproachable shoe.

Honor, withdrawing her eyes reluctantly from the brooding peace of mountain and sky, wondered a little at her pensiveness; wondered also where her thoughts—if mere flittings of the mind are entitled to be so called—had carried her.

As a matter of fact, she was thinking of unpaid bills; since human lilies of the field, though they neither toil nor spin, must pay for irreproachable shoes and unlimited summer raiment.

The girl's own thoughts, as they were apt to do in leisure moments, had wandered to Kohat: to the men who were working with cheerful, matter-of-fact courage in the glare of the little desert-station; and to the one brave woman, who remained in their midst to hearten them by her own indomitable gladness of soul.

The beauty of the evening bred a longing—natural in one so sympathetic—that they also could be up on this green hill-top, under the shade of the deodars, enjoying the exquisite repose of it all.

"Have you heard from Theo this week, Ladybird?" she asked suddenly. It was the first time she had used the name, for habit is strong; and Evelyn looked up quickly, the colour deepening in her cheeks.

"Don't call me Ladybird!" she commanded, with unusual decision. "It belongs to Theo."

Honor noted her rising colour with a smile of approval.

"I'm sorry, dear," she said gently. "I quite understand. But—have you heard lately?"

Evelyn's face cleared as readily as a child's.

"Oh, yes; I forgot to tell you. I had quite a long letter this morning. Perhaps you would like to read it."

And drawing an envelope from her pocket she tossed it into Honor's lap.

The girl glanced down at it quickly; but allowed it to lie there untouched. She knew that Desmond wrote good letters, and she would have dearly liked to read this one. But a certain manly strain in her forbade her to trespass on the privacy of a letter written to his wife.

"Thank you," she said; "I think I won't read it, though. I don't suppose Theo would care about his letters being passed on to me. I only want to know if things are going on all right."

"Oh, yes; in the usual sort of way. They've had trouble with those wretched Waziris. Two sentries murdered last week; and some horses stolen. Oh! and Mrs Olliver has had a bad touch of fever; and there's cholera in the city, but they don't think it'll spread. What a gruesome place it is! And what a mercy we're not there now. By the way," she added, working her parasol into a crack between two boards, "I met the Kresneys as I was coming home."

"The Kresneys! Here?"

Honor sat suddenly upright, all trace of weariness gone from her face.

"Yes. They're up for six weeks, and they seemed so pleased to see me that—I asked them in to dinner to-night."

"Evelyn!"

"Well—why not?" A spark of defiance glinted through the dark curves of her lashes.

"You know Theo would hate it."

"I daresay. But he isn't here; so it can't matter to him. And he need not know anything about it."

"My dear! That would be worse than all!"

Evelyn frowned.

"Really, Honor, for a clever person, you're rather stupid. It would be simply idiotic to tell him what is sure to annoy him, when the thing's done and he can't prevent it."

The girl leaned back with an impatient sigh.

"If you feel so sure it will annoy him, why on earth do you do it? He is so good to you in every possible way."

A great longing came upon her to disclose all that he had been ready to relinquish five weeks ago.

"*I* know that without your telling me," Evelyn retorted sharply. "But I think I might do as I like just while I'm up here. And I mean to—whatever you say. The Kresneys came here, instead of going to Mussoorie, chiefly to see me. I can't ignore them; and I won't."

"Well, for goodness' sake, don't ask them to the house again, that's all." Then, because she could scarcely trust herself to say more on the subject, and because she had no wish to risk a quarrel, she added quickly: "A parcel came while we were out. Perhaps you'd like to open it before dinner."

Evelyn was on her feet at once—the Kresneys forgotten as though they were not.

"It must be my new dress for the General's garden-party. How lovely!"

"Another dress? Your almirah's choked with them already."

"Those are only what I got at Simla last year."

"You seem to have gone in rather extensively for dresses last year," Honor remarked, a trifle critically. Since their arrival in Murree she had become better acquainted with the details of Evelyn's wardrobe; and the knowledge had troubled her not a little. "How about your trousseau?"

"Mother gave me hardly *any* dresses. She said I wouldn't need them on the Frontier. But I *must* have decent clothes, even in the wilderness."

"Yes, I suppose so. Still you will find continual dresses from Simla a terrible drain on a limited allowance."

A delicate flush crept into Evelyn's cheeks, and her eyes had an odd glitter that came to them when she felt herself hard-pressed, yet did not intend to give in.

"What do *you* know about my allowance?"

"I happen to know the amount of it," Honor answered quietly. "I also know the cost of clothes such as you have been getting in Simla, and—I am puzzled to see how the two can be made to fit. You do *pay* for your things, I suppose?" she added, with a flash of apprehension. She herself had never been allowed to indulge in bills.

Evelyn's colour ebbed at the direct question; and she took instant refuge in anger and matrimonial dignity, as being safer than truth.

"Really, Honor, you're getting rather a nuisance just lately. Scolding and preaching never does me a scrap of good—and you know it. What I do with my allowance isn't anybody's business but my own, and I won't be treated as if I were a child. After all"—with a fine mingling of dignity and scorn—"*I'm* the married woman. You're only a girl—staying with me; and I think I might be allowed to manage my own affairs, without *you* always criticising and interfering."

By this time Honor had risen also; a line of sternness hardening her beautiful mouth. Beneath her sustained cheerfulness lay a passionate temper; and Evelyn's unexpected attack stung it fiercely into life. Several seconds passed before she could trust herself to speak.

"Very well, Evelyn," she said, at length, "from to-day there shall be an end of my criticism and interference. You seem to forget that you asked for my help. But as you don't need it any longer I will hand over the account books to you to-morrow morning; and you had better give Nazar Khan some orders about dinner. There isn't very much in the house."

Only once before had Evelyn seen her friend roused to

real indignation; and she was fairly frightened at the effect of her own hasty words.

"Oh, Honor, don't be so angry as that!" she pleaded brokenly. "You know I simply can't——"

But with a decisive gesture Honor set her aside, and walking straight past her, mounted the steep staircase to her own room.

Arrived there, she stood still as one dazed, her hands pressed against her temples. There were times when this girl felt a little afraid of her own vehemence; which, but for the heritage of a strong will, and her unfailing reliance on a Higher Judgment, might indeed have proved disastrous for herself and others.

With controlled deliberation of movement, she drew a chair to the hired dressing-table, which served as davenport, and began to write.

She set down date and address and the words, "My dear Theo,"—no more. What was it she meant to say to him? That from to-day Evelyn must be left to manage her affairs alone; that she could no longer be responsible for her friend's doings, social or domestic; but that she was willing to remain with her for the season, if he wished it? How were such things to be worded? Was it even possible to say them at all?

Her eye fell upon the envelope containing his last letter. Mechanically she drew it out and read it through again very slowly. It was a long letter, full of their mutual interests; of the music and the Persian,—which she was now studying under his tuition;—of Wyndham, Denvil, Mrs Olliver, and his men; very little about himself. But it was written as simply and directly as he spoke,—the only form of letter that annihilates space; and it was signed, "Always your friend, Theo Desmond."

Before she reached the signature the fire had faded from her eyes. She returned it to the envelope, took up the sheet on which three lines were written, and tearing it across and across, dropped it into the cane basket at her side.

"I can't do it," she murmured. "What right have I to let him call himself my friend, if I fail him the first time things take an unpleasant turn?"

She decided, nevertheless, that Evelyn might well be allowed to realise her own helplessness a little before the reins were again taken out of her hands. Then she went downstairs and out into the golden evening, to cool her cheeks and quiet her pulses by half an hour of communing with the imperturbable peace of the hills.

Evelyn, standing alone in the drawing-room, bewildered and helpless as a starfish stranded by the tide, heard Honor's footsteps pass the door and die away in the distance. An unreasoning fear seized her that she might be going over to Mrs Conolly to stay there for good; and at the thought a sob rose in her throat. Flinging aside her parasol, which fell rattling to the floor, she sank into the nearest chair and buried her face in the cushion.

She knew right well that her words had been ungrateful and unjust; yet in her heart she was more vexed with Honor for having pushed her into a corner than with herself for her defensive flash of resentment. More than all was she overwhelmed by a sense of utter helplessness, of not knowing where to turn or what to do next.

"Oh, if only Theo were here!" she lamented. "He would never be unkind to me, I know." Yet the ground of her woe reminded her sharply that if her husband had knowledge of the bills lying at that moment in her davenport, he might possibly be so unkind to her—as she phrased it—that she did not dare tell him the truth. He had spoken to her once on the subject of debt in no uncertain terms; and she had resolved thenceforth to deal with her inevitable muddles in her own way,—the simple fatal way of letting things slide, and hoping that they would somehow come right in the end. But there seemed no present prospect of such a consummation; and for a while she gave herself up to a luxury of self-pity. Tides in her mind ebbed and flowed aimlessly as seaweed. Everything was hopeless and miserable. It was useless trying to be good; and she supposed Honor would never help her again.

Then her thoughts stumbled on the Kresneys. It must be nearly half-past six, and dinner was at a quarter past eight. But, as things now stood, their coming was impossible. She must send them a note to say Honor was not well; for who could tell how this new, angry Honor might choose to behave if they arrived in spite of all?

The need for action roused her, and she went over to her davenport. But on lifting the lid her eyes fell upon the little sheaf of bills—and again the Kresneys faded into insignificance. She took up the detested slips of paper; laid them out one by one on the table; and, sitting down before them, contemplated them with knitted brows and a hopeless droop of her lips.

No need to look into them in detail. She knew their contents, and the sum of them by heart. She knew that they amounted in all to more than six hundred rupees; and that another four hundred, possibly more, was still owing in different directions.

Where in all the world was such a sum to be found without Theo's help? An appeal to Honor would be worse than useless. Honor was so stupid about such things. Her one idea would be immediate confession. A hazy notion haunted Evelyn that people who were in straits borrowed money from somewhere, or some one. But her knowledge of this mysterious transaction went no further; and even she was able to perceive that from so nebulous a starting-point no definite advance could be made. She had also heard of women selling their jewels, and wondered vaguely who were the convenient people who bought them; though this alternative did not commend itself to her in any case.

Yet by some means the money must be found. Her earliest creditors were beginning to assert themselves; to thank her in advance for sums which she saw no hope of sending them; and, worse than all, she lived in daily dread lest any of them should be inspired to apply to Theo himself. Look where she would a blank wall confronted her; and in the midst of the blankness she sat, a dainty, dejected figure, with her pitiless pile of bills.

"Krizney, Miss Sahib, *argya*."[1]

The kitmutgar's voice jerked her back to the necessities of the moment.

Well, mercifully, Honor was out. It would be a comfort

[1] Has come.

to see any one, and get away from her own thoughts. Also she could explain about the dinner; and, hastily gathering up her papers, she sent out the customary "salaam."

"Oh, Mrs Desmond, I *do* hope I am not disturbing you." Miss Kresney came forward with a rather too effusive warmth of manner. "But you forgot to mention if you dine at a quarter to eight or a quarter past; and I was not certain if you meant us to dress or not."

Miss Kresney would probably have been amazed could she have seen these two Englishwomen dining together.

"Why, yes," Evelyn answered simply, "we always dress in the evening, Honor and I. But—please don't think me very rude—I'm afraid I must ask you and your brother to put off coming till—some other night. I was just going to send you a note; because Honor is—not at all well. She has been out in the sun all day, and her head is bad. She must keep quiet to-night. You see, don't you, that I can't help it? It isn't my fault."

Linda Kresney's face had fallen verv blank; but she pulled herself together, and called up a cold little smile.

"Of course not, Mrs Desmond. How could I think it is *your* fault, when you have always been so veree kind to us? We often say it is a pity every one is not so kind as you are. I am sorry Miss Meredith is not well." An acid note invaded her voice. She had her own suspicions of Honor, as being too obviously Captain Desmond's friend. "My brother will be terribly disappointed. No doubt we can come some day veree soon instead."

But Evelyn was too self-absorbed to detect the obvious hint.

"Yes—I hope so," she agreed, without enthusiasm; then, seeing puzzled dissatisfaction in Linda Kresney's eyes, made haste to add: "Perhaps you'll stay a little now, as you are not coming to-night. It's quite early still, and I'm all alone."

Miss Kresney sat down with unconcealed alacrity, and Evelyn followed her example, laying her hand on the telltale papers. The trouble of her mind showed so clearly in her eyes and lips, that the girl, who had begun to grow really fond of her, was emboldened to risk a vague proffer of sympathy. She had never as yet found the opportunity her brother so desired of making herself useful; and she was quick-witted enough to perceive that Fate might be favouring her at last.

"I am afraid you have been worried about something, Mrs Desmond," she began warily. "Perhaps after all I had better not stay here, bothering you to make talk. Unless perhaps—I can help you in any way. I should be very glad to, if you will not think me officious to say so. I cannot bear to see you look so unhappee. It is not bad news from Kohat, I hope?"

Evelyn's smile was a very misty affair.

"Oh, no—it's not that," she said, and broke off short.

Miss Kresney waited for more—her face and figure one fervent note of interrogation. She had tact enough to realise that she could not press verbal inquiry further.

But her air of interested expectation was not lost on Evelyn Desmond. A pressing need was urging her to unburden her mind through the comforting channels of speech. Cut off, by her own act, from the two strong natures on whom she leaned for sympathy and help, there remained only this girl, who would certainly give her the one, and might possibly give her the other, in the form of practical information. It was this last thought that turned the scale in Miss Kresney's favour; and Evelyn spoke.

"I think it's very nice of you to mind that I am unhappy, and to want to help me. But I don't know whether you can; because it's—it's about money."

The merest shadow of astonishment flittered across Miss Kresney's face. But she said no word, and Evelyn went on—her nervousness giving way rapidly before the relief of speech.

"I have a whole heap of bills here, for dresses and things, that I simply can't pay for out of my allowance. It's not because my husband doesn't give me enough," she added, with a pathetic flash of loyalty. "He gives me all he can possibly spare. But I'm stupid and unpractical. I just order clothes when I want them, and never think about the price till the bill comes in, and then it's soo late! My mother did it all before I married.

I wish to goodness she had taught me to manage for myself; but it's no use thinking of that now. The question is—where can I get money to pay these bills without troubling my husband about them. I must find some way to do it, only—I don't the least know how. Aren't there natives out here who buy people's jewels, or—or lend them money when they want it in a hurry? I thought—perhaps—you might know whether I could manage to do it—up here?"

The surprise in Miss Kresney's face deepened to alarm.

"Oh, but indeed, Mrs Desmond, you cannot do anything like that. The native money-lenders are veree bad people to deal with; and they ask such big interest, that if you once start with them it is almost impossible to get free again. You say you are inexperienced about money, and that would make it far worse. You cannot do anything of that kind—reallee."

Evelyn rose in an access of helpless impatience.

"But if I can't do that, what *can* I do?" she cried. "I've got to do *some*thing—somehow, don't you see? Some of them are beginning to bother me already, and—it frightens me."

A long silence followed upon her simple, impassioned statement of the case. Miss Kresney was meditating a startling possibility.

"There is only one thing that I can suggest," she ventured at length, "and that is I could lend you some money myself. I haven't a great deal. But if three hundred rupees would help you to settle some of the bills, I would feel only too proud if you would take it. There will be no interest to pay; and you could let me have it back in small sums just whenever you could manage it."

With a gasp of incredulity Evelyn sank back into her chair.

"D'you *mean* that?"

"Of course I do."

"Oh, Miss Kresney, I don't know why you should be so kind to me! How can I take such a lot of money—from you?"

"Why not, if I am glad to give it?"

Indeed the sum seemed to her an inconsiderable trifle beside the certainty of Owen's praise, of Owen's entire satisfaction.

For a clear three minutes Evelyn Desmond sat silent, irresolute; her mind a formless whirl of eagerness and uncertainty, hope and fear. The novelty of the transaction rather than any glimmering of the complications it might engender held her trembling on the brink; and Miss Kresney awaited her decision with downcast eyes, her fingers mechanically plaiting and unplaiting the silken fringe of the tablecloth.

Sounds crept in from without and peopled the waiting stillness. Evelyn Desmond had no faintest forewarning of the grave issues that hung upon her answer, yet she was unaccountably afraid. Her driven heart cried out for the support of her husband's presence; and her voice, when words came at last, was pitifully unsteady.

"It is so difficult not to say Yes."

"Why will you not say it, then? And it would all be comfortably settled."

"Would it? I don't seem able to believe that. Only if I *do* say Yes, you must promise not to tell—your brother."

"I am afraid that would not be possible. How could I arrange such a thing without letting my brother know about it?"

"Then I can't take the money."

Evelyn's voice was desperate but determined. Some spark of intuition enabled her to see that any intrusion of Kresney set the matter beyond the pale of possible things; and nothing remained for Linda but compromise or retreat.

She unhesitatingly chose the former. A few reassuring words would cost little to utter; and if circumstances should demand a convenient forgetfulness, none but herself need ever be aware of the fact. She leaned across the table, and her tone was a triumph of open-hearted sympathy.

"Mrs Desmond, you know quite well that I cannot leave you unhappy like this. If you are so determined that my brother must not know, I think I could manage without his help. Come to the Hotel to-morrow at half-past ten, and we will send off three hundred rupees to those who are troubling you most for payment."

Miss Kresney was as good as her word. She drew three hundred rupees in notes from her own small bank account, and herself went with Evelyn to the post-office whence they were safely despatched to Simla.

Some three evenings later, Owen Kresney bade his sister good-night with a quite phenomenal display of affection.

"You're a regular little trump, Linda!" he declared. "I never gave you credit for so much good sense. By Jove! I'd give a month's pay for a sight of Desmond's face if he ever finds *this* out! I expect he stints that poor little woman and splashes all the money on polo ponies. Glad you were able to help her; and whatever you do, don't let her pay you back too soon. If you're short of cash, you've only to ask me."

For the space of a week Honor held inflexibly aloof; and the effort it cost her seemed out of all proportion to the mildness of the punishment inflicted. It is an old story—the inevitable price paid by love that is strong enough to chastise. But this great paradox, the corner-stone of man's salvation, is a stumbling-block to lesser natures. In Evelyn's eyes Honor was merely cruel, and her own week of independence a nightmare of helpless irritation. She made one effort at remonstrance; and its futility crushed her to earth.

During the evening of their talk the matter had been tacitly avoided between them; but when, on the following morning, Honor laid books and bills upon the davenport where Evelyn sat writing, she caught desperately at the girl's hand.

"Honor, it isn't fair. How *can* you be so unkind?"

Honor drew her hand decisively away.

"Please let the subject alone," she said coolly. "If you persist in talking of it, you will drive me to go and sit in my own room—that's all."

A week later, however, when she returned from a ride to find Evelyn again at the detested davenport, her head bowed upon her arms, like a flower broken with the wind, all the inherent motherhood in her rose up and overflowed. Hastily crossing the room she knelt down beside the small tragic figure and kissed a pearl-white fragment of forehead; the only spot available at the moment. "Poor darling!" she whispered. "Is it really as bad as all that?"

Caresses from Honor were so rare that for an instant Evelyn was taken aback; then she laid her head on the girl's shoulder with a sigh of pure content.

"Oh, Honor! the world seems all broken to pieces when *you* are unkind to me!"

Honor kissed her again.

"I won't be unkind to you any more; and we'll just forget from this minute that it ever happened at all."

But to forget is not to undo; and during their brief estrangement Evelyn Desmond had added a link to the chain of Fate, whose strongest coils are most often wrought by our own unskilful fingers.

CHAPTER X.

A SQUARE BARGAIN.

"The faith of men that ha' brothered men,
By more than easy breath;
And the eyes o' men that ha' read wi' men,
In the open books of death."

—KIPLING.

"BEHOLD! Captain Sahib,—there where the sky touches earth. In the space of half an hour we arrive."

Desmond lifted sun-weary eyes to the horizon, and nodded.

When a man is consumed with thirst, and scorched to the bone, by five hours of riding through a furnace seven times heated in the teeth of a blistering wind, he is chary of speech; and the two rode forward in silence—mere specks upon the emptiness of earth and sky—keeping their horses to the long-distance canter that kills neither man nor beast. A detachment of forty sabres followed in their wake; and the rhythmical clatter rang monotonously in their ears.

The speck on the horizon was an outpost—a boundary mark of empire,—where a little party of men watched, night and day, for the least sign of danger from the illusive quiet of the hills.

It is these handfuls of men, natives of India all, stationed in stone watch-towers twenty miles apart along the Border, who keep the gateway of India barred; and who will keep it barred against all intruders for all time. The unobtrusive strength of India's Frontier amazes the new-comer. But only those who have spent their best years in its service know the full price paid for the upkeep of that same strength in hardship, unremitting toil, and the lives of picked men.

As the riders neared the post its outline showed, stern and clear-cut, against the blue of the sky. A single circular room, loop-holed and battlemented, set upon an outward sloping base of immense solidity, and surrounded by a massive stone wall:—a tower in which ten men could hold their own against five hundred. The look-out sentry, sighting the detachment afar off, gave the word to his companions, who lowered the ladder that served them for staircase; and when Desmond's party drew rein the door in the wall stood open to receive them.

During the halt that followed, the men, having fed and watered their horses, took what rest they might in patches of burning shadow within the wall. Though the sun-saturated masonry breathed fire, it served to shelter them from the withering wind that scours the Border at this fiery time of year.

Desmond, who had breakfasted five hours earlier on stale bread and a few sardines, lunched, with small appetite, on biscuits and a slab of chocolate, and moistened his parched throat with tepid whisky-and-water. Quenching his thirst was an achievement past hoping for till Kohat itself should be reached.

He had left the station with his detachment early on the previous day; had relieved four outposts between dawn and dusk, covering eighty miles of desert road, with four brief halts for rest; and had spent a night of suffocating wakefulness in a sun-baked windowless room, built out from the base of the last post relieved. It was all in the day's work —as Frontier men understand work. The exposure and long hours in the saddle had little effect upon his whipcord and iron frame: but a sharp attack of fever—unrecorded in his letter to his wife—had slackened his alertness of body and spirit; and it was with an unusual sense of relief that he faced the last twenty-mile stretch of road, leaving behind him six fresh men to take up the task of watching the blank, unchanging face of the hills.

Three hours later, the little party turned their horses' heads towards Kohat. The sun still smote the uncomplaining earth, and many miles of riding lay before them. But at least it was the beginning of the end; a fact which the two stout-hearted chargers seemed to recognise as clearly as their riders. The Ressaldar, who had not failed to note his Captain's slight change of bearing, proposed a short cut across country well known to himself.

"Hazúr," he urged, "there runs a long deep nullah, straight as a lance, across the plain; and as the sun falls lower, it would give some measure of shade."

"Well spoken, Ressaldar Sahib! I have had my fill of the road. I'm for the nullah. Come on, men."

And, striking out across country, they vanished from the earth's surface, entering one of those giant clefts in the clay soil formed by the early downrush of torrents from the hills.

Suddenly, in the midst of a swinging canter, the Ressaldar reined in his horse, and the rest followed suit. The old Sikh threw up his head, as a stag will do at the first whisper of danger. In the strong light his chiselled face, with its grey beard scrupulously parted and drawn up under his turban, showed lifeless as a statue; and his eyes had the far-off intentness of one who listens with every fibre of his being.

Desmond watched him in a growing bewilderment that verged on impatience.

"What's up now?" he demanded sharply.

But no flicker disturbed the rigid face: the keen eyes gave no sign. The old man raised a hand as if enjoining silence, dismounted hastily, and, kneeling down, pressed his ear close against the ground.

Desmond's suspense was short-lived but keen.

In less than ten seconds the Ressaldar was beside him, one hand on his bridle, a consuming anxiety in his eyes.

"Hazúr, it is a spate from the hills," he said between quick breaths. "It is coming with the speed of ten thousand devils and there are five miles to go before we can leave the nullah."

"Mount, then," the Englishman replied with cool decision. "We can but ride."

And swiftly, as tired horses could lay legs to ground, they rode.

Desmond could catch no sound as yet of the oncoming danger; but the practised ears of the native detected its increase, even through the rattle of hoofs that beat upon the brain like panic terror made audible.

"Faster,—faster!" he panted. His Captain's danger was the one coherent thought in his mind. Desmond merely nodded reassurance; and shifting a little in his saddle, eased matters as far as possible for *Badshah Pasand*.[1]

The ground raced beneath their horses' hoofs. The serene strip of sky raced above their heads. The imprisoning walls fell apart before their eyes, seeming to divide like a cleft stick as they drew near, and reeling away on either hand as they passed on. All things in earth and heaven seemed fleeing in mortal haste save only themselves.

Theo Desmond heard the voice of the enemy at last:—an ominous roar, growing inexorably louder every minute. At the sound his head took a more assured lift; his mouth a firmer line; and the fire of determination deepened in his eyes.

By a movement of the rein he urged Badshah Pasand to renewed effort. But the devoted animal was nearing the end of his tether, and his rider knew it. Thick spume flakes blew backward from his lips, and the sawing motion of his head told its own tale.

Sher Dil, who was still going lustily, gained upon him by a neck, and the Ressaldar turned in his saddle.

"The spurs, Hazúr—the *spurs!*" he entreated, knowing well his Captain's abstemiousness in this regard.

But Desmond shook his head. Badshah Pasand was doing his utmost; and neither man nor beast can do more. He merely rose in the stirrups, pressed his heels lightly against the quivering flanks and, leaning forward, spoke a few words of encouragement almost in the charger's ear.

The sensitive animal sprang forward with a last desperate output of strength; and in the same instant a hoarse shout broke from Rajinder Singh.

"An opening—an opening, Captain Sahib By the mercy of God we are saved!"

Five minutes later the whole party drew rein on the upper

[1] Beloved of kings.

levels of earth, and their sometime pursuer swept tumultuously onward fifteen feet below.

Desmond's eyes had an odd light in them as he turned from the swirling waters to the impassive face of the man who had saved their lives.

"I do—not—forget," he said with quiet emphasis.

The old Sikh shook his head with a rather uncertain smile.

"True talk, Hazúr. I had known it without assurance. Yet was mine own help no great matter. It was written that my Captain Sahib should not die thus!"

"That may be," Desmond answered gravely, for he had been strangely upheld by the same conviction. "Yet there be also—these others. In my thinking it is no small *matter* that, except for your quickness of mind and hearing, forty-four good men and horses would now be at the mercy of that torrent. But this is no time for words. It still remains to reach Kohat before sundown."

The sun was slipping behind the hills, with the broad smile of a tyrant who fully enjoys the joke, when Desmond drew up before his own verandah and slid to the ground.

"Thank God that's over!" he muttered audibly. But he did not at once enter the house. His first care, as always, was for the horse he rode; and with him it was no mere case of the "merciful man," but of sheer love for that unfailing servant of the human race.

He accompanied Badshah Pasand to the stable, superintended the removal of his saddle, and looked him carefully all over. That done, he issued explicit orders for his treatment and feeding: the great charger—as though fully aware of his master's solicitude,—nuzzling a mouse-coloured nose against his shoulder the while.

Arrived in the comparative coolness of the hall, he shouted for a drink, and a bath. Then, turning towards the drawing-room, promised himself a few minutes blessed relaxation in the depths of his favourite chair.

But passing between the gold-coloured curtains he saw that which checked his advance, and banished all thought of relaxation from his brain.

Harry Denvil—whose buoyancy and simplicity of heart

had led Desmond to christen him the Boy—sat alone at Evelyn's bureau, his head between his hands, despair in every line of his figure.

Desmond regarded him thoughtfully, marvelling that the sounds of his own arrival should have passed unheard. Then he went forward, and laid his hand on the Boy's shoulder.

"Harry! I don't seem to recognise *you* in that attitude. Anything seriously wrong?"

Denvil started, and revealed a face of dogged dejection.

"You here?" he said listlessly. "Never heard you come in."

"That's obvious. But—about yourself?"

The Boy choked down a sigh.

"Why the deuce should I bore you with myself, when you're hot and tired? I've been a confounded fool; if not worse, and the devil's in the luck wherever I turn."

But Desmond waited in expectant silence for the Boy's trouble to overflow. While he waited, the coveted "drink" arrived, and he empted the long tumbler almost at a gulp. The station had run out of ice—a cheerful habit of Frontier stations; but at least the liquid was cool and stinging.

"Well?" he said at length, Denvil having returned to his former attitude. "I want something more explicit. How am I to help you, if you slam the door in my face?"

"Don't see how you can help me. I've only been . . . a great many kinds of a fool: and *you*——"

"Well, what of me? I've been plenty of kinds of fool in my time, I assure you. Money's the backbone of your trouble, no doubt. Nothing worse, I hope?"

Denvil's honest eyes met his own without flinching.

"No, on my honour—nothing worse. The money's bad enough." And the trouble came out in a quick rush of words—explanatory, contrite, despairing—all in one breath. For the Boy had Irish blood in his veins; and the initial difficulty over, he found it an unspeakable relief to disburden his soul to the man who had "brothered" him ever since he joined the Force.

Desmond, perceiving that the overflow, once started, was likely to be exhaustive and complete, took out pipe and tobacco, balanced himself on the arm of a chair, and listened gravely to the Boy's disjointed story.

It was a long story, and a commonplace one, if even the most trivial record of human effort and failure can be so styled. It was the story of half the subalterns in our Imperial Army—of small pay, engulfed by heavy expenses, avoidable and unavoidable; the upkeep of much needless uniform; too big a wine bill at Mess; polo ponies, and other luxurious necessities of Indian life, bought on credit; the inevitable appeal to the "*shroff*,"[1] involving interest upon interest; the final desperate attempt to mend matters by high stakes at cards, and fitful, injudicious backing of horses, most often with disastrous results.

"Have you the smallest idea what the total damage amounts to?" asked Desmond, when all was said. "I'm bound to know everything now."

Denvil nodded.

"Close on fifteen hundred, I think," he answered truthfully.

"Why, in Heaven's name, didn't you tell me all this sooner?"

"Oh, I kept hoping to get square somehow—without that. I wanted to stay in your good books; and I saw you were rather down on chaps who are casual about money. But I seem to be made that way, and——"

"So are most of us, my dear chap. But it's up to you to make yourself some other way, if you don't want to come a cropper and leave the Service. I hope I am no Pharisee, but I've been reared to believe that living in debt is an aristocratic, and rather mean form of theft. My notion of you doesn't square with that; and I know a good man when I see one. You'll never mend matters, I assure you, by playing the fool over horses and cards. How about your mother?"

Denvil looked down at the blank sheet of foreign note-paper before him, and answered nothing. He was the only son of his mother, and she was a widow.

"Can't you see that the fact of your having no father to pull you up sharp puts you on your honour to keep straight in every way, on her account? Does she know anything about all this?"

[1] Native money-lender.

"How *could* I tell her?" the Boy murmured, without looking up. "She thinks me no end of a fine chap; and—and—I'm hanged if I know how to answer her letters since—things have got so bad——"

"When did you write last?"

"About six weeks ago."

Desmond flung out an oath.

"Confound you!" he cried hotly. "What do you think she's imagining by now? All manner of hideous impossibilities. I suppose you never gave *that* a thought——"

The Boy looked up quickly, pain and pleading in his blue eyes. "I say, Desmond, don't hit so straight. I know I've been a brute to her; and I feel bad enough about it, without being slanged—by *you*."

Theo Desmond's face softened, and he took the Boy's shoulders between his hands.

"My dear lad," he said gently. "I'm sorry if I hit too hard. But I feel rather strongly on that subject. I've no wish to slang you. I only want to set you on your feet and *keep you* there. So we may as well get to business at once."

"Set me on my feet! How the devil's *that* to be done?"

Desmond smiled.

"It's simply a question of making up one's mind to things. In the first place we must sell Roland. He's the best pony you have."

Harry straightened himself sharply, but Desmond's gesture commanded silence.

"It's a cruel wrench, I know," he said gently. "Few men understand that better than myself. But it's all you can do. And you're bound to do it. You can advertise him as trained by me. He's safe to fetch seven hundred that way."

Denvil bent his head in desperate resignation.

"You are down on a fellow, Desmond. How about the other eight?"

"That will be—my affair."

Again the Boy was startled into protest.

"Look here! That's impossible. I couldn't pay you back within the next three years."

"Did I say anything about paying me back?"

"*Desmond*—you don't mean——?"

Their eyes met, and Denvil was answered. He brought his fist down on the bureau with such force that Evelyn's knick-knacks danced again.

"By God, I won't have it!" he protested passionately. "I'll not take such a sum of money from you."

Desmond's smile showed both approval and amusement.

"No call for violence, Boy! I told you my mind was made up; and it's folly wasting powder and shot against a stone wall."

"Look here, though—can you manage it—easily?"

"Yes, I can manage it." And in the rush of relief Harry failed to note the significant omission of the adverb. "But it's to be a square bargain between us. No more *shroffs;* no more betting, or I come down on you like a ton of coals for my eight hundred. Stick to whist and polo in playtime. Polish up your Pushtoo, and get into closer touch with your Pathans. Start Persian with me, if you like, and replace Roland with the money you get for passing. But first of all write to your mother, and tell her the chief part of the truth. Not my share in it, please. That remains between ourselves and—my wife. She'll understand, never fear. Now—shake hands on that, and stick to it, will you?"

"Desmond, you *are* a trump!"

"No need for compliments between you and me, Harry. Shut up and get on with your letter."

Then, because his mind was freed from anxiety, he realised that the Boy's hand felt like hot parchment, and that his eyes were unusually bright.

"You've got fever on you," he said brusquely. "Feel bad?"

"Pretty average. My head's been going like an engine these two days. Couldn't eat anything yesterday or get a wink of sleep last night. That's what set my conscience stirring perhaps."

Desmond laughed.

"Likely as not! I'm off for Mackay all the same. Get into my chair and stay there till further orders. Don't bother your head about that letter. It shan't miss the mail. I'll write it myself to-night."

An invisible reminder from the doorway that the Heaven-born's bath had long been waiting, elicited a peremptory order for the Demon; and Amar Singh departed, mystified but obedient. The Sahib he worshipped, with the implicit worship of his race, was a very perplexing person at times.

James Mackay's verdict—given well out of the patient's hearing—was immediate and to the point.

"Typhoid, of course—104°. Fool of a boy not to have sent for me sooner. Ought to have been in bed two days ago. Get him there sharp, and do what you can with wet sheets and compresses. I'll wire for a nurse, but we shan't get one. Never do. Not a ounce of ice in the place, and won't be for three days. That's always the way. He'll keep you on the go all night by the looks of him. May as well let the Major do most of it. You'd be none the worse for a few hours in bed yourself."

A certain lift of Desmond's head signified tacit denial, and the astute Scotsman knew better than to insist. Meeting Wyndham at the gate, he counselled a policy of non-resistance.

"The fellow's overdone without knowing it," he said. "Take my advice, man, and let him gang his ain gait. Fever or no, he's hard as nails, and he'll be glad enough to knock under in twenty-four hours' time."

Throughout that night of anxious battling with the fire of fever the two Englishmen seemed translated into mechanical contrivances for the administering of milk, brandy, and chicken-broth; for the incessant changing of soaked sheets, that were none too cool at best; and for allaying, as far as might be, a thirst that no water on earth can quench.

Nothing draws men into closer union than a common danger, or a common anxiety; and in the past twelve years these two had stood shoulder to shoulder through both many times over. But their zeal produced no manifest results. Denvil's temperature rose steadily, and his stress of mind broke out in a semi-coherent babble of remorse and self-justification, of argument and appeal, of desperate reckonings in regard to ways and means. Desmond left his station by the bed and crossed over to his friend, who was noiselessly washing a cup and saucer.

"Don't hear any more of that than you can help. Fact, you might as well take your chance of a short rest till he's quieter. I'll come and tell you, no fear."

Paul glanced up with his slow smile from the saucer he was polishing with elaborate care.

"On your word, Theo?"

"On my word."

And he retired obediently to his own room—the room that in the cold weather had belonged to Honor Meredith; that, even now, empty casket though it was, awoke in him a subtle sense of her presence; of the strength and cheerfulness that crowned her beauty like a diadem, and transformed his outlook on life.

The letter to Mrs Denvil was written in the small hours. Harry never discovered its contents; but his mother, after reading it half a dozen times, locked it up with a hoard of sacred treasures pertaining to her boy. And soon after six, in the pitiless gold of dawn, the two men cantered leisurely down to early parade.

Here Desmond's attention was arrested by the absence of Rajinder Singh. Hailing a lesser native officer, he learnt that the Ressaldar had been ill with sun-fever all night, and was still quite unfit for work. Hindus are creatures of little or no stamina, and they go down like mown grass before the unhealthy heat of the Frontier.

Desmond despatched a message to the stricken man, adding that he himself would come to make inquiry before eleven o'clock. On his return he found Harry temporarily quieter, and fallen into a light sleep.

"I must see Frank about him," he reflected, "on my way back from the Lines." For Frank was the regimental standby in every emergency, and would claim the lion's share of the nursing as a matter of course.

True to his word, Desmond was back on the deserted parade-ground by half-past ten, his syce pursuing him closely, a flat paper parcel under his arm. It contained a full-length photo of himself in the silver frame that had held his mother's picture, because frames were not to be procured at an hour's notice in Kohat, and he had a great wish that his gift should be complete: a lasting memento—such as the old Sikh would keenly appreciate—of their stirring ride, and of the fact that he owed his life to the man's remarkable quickness of ear and brain.

Rajinder Singh lived alone; for the Sikh, when he enters Imperial service, leaves his wife behind in her own village. His one-roomed hut was saturated with heat, and almost devoid of light. It contained a chair, a strip of matting, and a low string-bed, with red cotton quilt and legs of scarlet lacquer. Mud walls and floor alike were scrupulously clean. Sacred vessels, for cooking and washing, were stowed away out of reach of defilement. Above his bed the simple-hearted soldier had nailed a crude coloured print of the *Kaiser-i-Hind* in robes and crown; and on the opposing wall hung a tawdry looking-glass, almost as dear to his heart.

The Sirdar was nominally in bed; that is to say, he lay on the bare strings, beneath his cotton quilt, fully dressed in loose white tunic and close-fitting trousers. His turban alone had been discarded, and stood ready-folded beside him, a miracle of elaborate precision.

At the sound of hoofs he sat up instantly, his uncut hair and beard flowing down to his waist. In less than twenty seconds both had been twisted to a deft knot high on the head, his turban adjusted at an irreproachable angle; and, as Desmond's figure darkened the doorway, he staggered to his feet and saluted with a trembling hand.

"Sit down, sit down!" his Captain commanded him; and he obeyed, rather suddenly, with a rueful smile.

"The years steal away my strength, Hazúr. A little fever, and my bones become as water—yea, though I had once the might of ten in this dried-up arm."

Desmond smiled and shook his head.

"No reason to speak evil of the years, after yesterday, and the fever hath the power of seven devils over any man. I have been all night beside Denvil Sahib, who lieth without sense and strength this morning, young as he is."

"Denvil Sahib! I had not known. Is it fever also?"

"Yes,—the great fever. A matter of many weeks, and sore trouble of mind; for disease takes strong hold upon the strong. And what will come to the squadron, with both my troop commanders laid in their beds?"

"*Na*,—na, Hazúr. I will arise, even as I am——"

"That you will not, Sirdar Sahib," Desmond interposed with kindly decision; "we will rather give Bishan Singh a chance to prove that he is fit for promotion. I have had the assurance from him many times in words. Now I will have it in deeds—the fittest language for a soldier."

The deep-set eyes gleamed approval.

"Great is the wisdom of the Captain Sahib, understanding the deceitfulness of man's heart. Bishan Singh's tongue is as a horse without bit or bridle. If head and hand carry him as far, he will do well."

"True talk," Desmond answered, smiling. Then with the incurable diffidence of the Englishman when he is moved to do a gracious action, he held out his parcel. "See here, Rajinder Singh. This is a small matter enough for your acceptance. A token merely that—I do not forget."

"*Hazúr!*"

The eagerness of a child transfigured the man's weather-beaten face, and his fingers plucked unsteadily at the string.

Desmond took out a knife and slit it without a word.

For a long moment Rajinder Singh gazed upon the miracle before him in silent wonder. To the unsophisticated native—and there are happily many left in India—a photograph remains an abiding miracle; a fact to be accepted and reverenced without explanation, like the inconsistencies of the gods.

"In very truth, it is the Captain Sahib himself!" he muttered with the air of one who makes an amazing discovery. Then, grasping his possession in both hands, he held it out at arm's length, examining every detail with loving care; glancing from the counterfeit to the original as if to satisfy himself that the artist had omitted nothing; for Desmond was wearing the undress uniform of the picture.

"*Bahut, bahut salaam*,[1] Sahib!" he broke out in a tremulous fervour of gratitude. "It is your Honour's self, as I said, lacking only speech. Feature for feature—cord for cord. All things are faithfully set down. Behold, even these marks upon the scabbard,—the very scar upon your Honour's hand! Now, indeed, hath God favoured me

[1] Many, many thanks.

beyond deserving; for my Captain Sahib abideth under this my roof until I die."

Rising unsteadily, in defiance of Desmond's mute protest, he removed the cherished looking-glass, hung the photo in its place, and, drawing himself up to his full six-feet-two of height, gravely saluted it.

"*Salaam, hamara,*[1] Captain Sahib Bahadur!"

Then he turned to find Desmond, who had risen also, watching him intently, his full heart in his eyes.

"I thought it would give you pleasure," he said, in a tone of restrained feeling, "but I had no knowledge that it would please you as much as that. I am very glad I thought of it. But now," he added more briskly, "enough of talk. There waiteth more work to be done than a man can accomplish before dark. Get you back to bed, Ressaldar Sahib, and stay there until I order otherwise."

Once outside, he sprang to the saddle, and set off at a canter through the withering, stupefying sunlight towards Captain Olliver's bungalow.

[1] Salaam, my Captain Sahib.

CHAPTER XI.

YOU DON'T KNOW DESMOND.

uffer with men, and like a man be strong."—MYERS.

FRANK OLLIVER, looking remarkably fresh and cool in a holland gown of severe simplicity, greeted him from the verandah with a flour-covered hand. At the sound of hoofs, her ready brain had sprung to the right conclusion, and she hurried out to save him the necessity of dismounting. She had learned to know the value of minutes to a hard-worked man.

"Geoff told me," she said, a rare seriousness veiling the laughter of her eyes. "It's cruel bad news, but you mustn't dream of being anxious yet awhile, Theo, man. I'll be round by half-past eleven sharp; stay till you two are through with your work; rest this afternoon and come on again at seven, till morning. You'll just take one clear night in bed before I let you go shares in *that* part o' the work. You can trust him to me, can't you, though I *am* a mad Irishwoman? I'll promise not to be waking up the patient to take his sleeping draught, or any such cleverness!"

Her nonsense dispelled Desmond's gravity. "I can trust you as far as that, I think!" he answered with a laugh; "but I won't have you knocking yourself up again over this. The lad's my subaltern, and it's my business. You shall take to-night, though, if you've a mind to, and my best thanks into the bargain. God alone knows where we should ll be without you."

"Just precisely where you are at present, no doubt!" the softened tone betrayed her appreciation of his honest praise. "It's just a bad habit you've got into, that's the truth, and I've not the heart to break you of it either. But 'tis no time now for playing ball with compliments. I'm busy over a cake. My cook has a pain, an' swears 'tis cholera. An' what with dosing him, an' trying to convince him he's a fool, and seeing after Geoff's tiffin, I'll be melted to one tear-drop presently; but the good man'll have to dine at Mess to-night."

Desmond gathered up his reins, and she waved to him as he rode away.

Punctually at the half-hour she entered the sick-room—cool, practised, business-like, and took over her case as composedly as any trained nurse. For in those early days nursing was as persistent a feature of the hot weather as the punkah itself, and her skill had been acquired in a hard school.

The Boy had been installed, for greater comfort, in Desmond's own bed; and he greeted her with a faint smile of recognition.

"Poor, dear old fellow," she murmured tenderly, pushing the damp hair from his brow; "wait only till the ice comes, an' we'll pull you round finely, never fear."

His lids fell under her soothing touch, and sprinkling her fingers with lavender water she passed them across and across his forehead; a look in her eyes the while that none save her "brother officers" had ever seen there; a look such as her children might have seen, had she been so blest.

Among acquaintances Mrs Olliver passed for a masculine woman, boisterous and good-humoured, though somewhat lacking in the lesser proprieties and affectations which passed for delicacy of feeling. But with all her angularity and mannish ways, she was a fine mother wasted: and in her heart she knew it. There are too many such among us. A mystery of pain and unfulfilled hope which there seems no justifying, save that at times the world is the gainer by their individual loss; and Frank Olliver, being denied the blessedness of children, mothered all the men of her regiment, the formidable Colonel not excepted.

Having charmed her patient into a light sleep, she made

a noiseless tour of the room, smiling at the revelation of Paul Wyndham's hand in the exquisite neatness wherewith all things had been set in order. A towel pinned to the punkah frill brought the faint relief of moving air nearer to Denvil's face. In the hasty manner of its pinning Theo's workmanship stood revealed, and the smile deepened in her eyes. She knew each least characteristic of these her grown children; knew, and loved them, with a strong unspoken love.

Her next move brought her to the thermometer. It registered 95° A long while after sundown the mercury might drop three degrees, certainly not more. She cast an anxious glance at the sleeper, and her quick eye caught the lagging of the punkah, broken by fitful jerks, which denotes that the coolie—squatting on his heels in the verandah—is pulling the inexorable rope in his dreams.

Opening the outer door and letting in a blast as from the mouth of hell, she reasoned with that much-enduring human machine in a forcible Irish whisper, that set the towel flapping and billowing like a flag in a wind. The room was none the cooler for his exertions, but in such intensity of heat mere movement of the air serves to prevent suffocation.

Mrs Olliver sat down beside her patient and her mind reverted to her own domestic calamity. She wondered with a simple practical wonderment, devoid of fear, whether or no she had a case of cholera in her compound. To-morrow it would be well to ascertain the truth; and in the meantime she dismissed the matter from her mind.

Before tiffin was over at the station Mess, Wyndham made his appearance, and with a friendly nod of welcome took the reins out of her hands. But by seven o'clock she was back at her post; and one look at Harry's flushed face and unseeing eyes convinced her that the next twelve hours would make a high demand upon her energies, and her resolute hopefulness of heart.

Desmond came in before Mess. His eyes were grave and anxious, and for many minutes he stood looking down upon the boy in silence; the slim uprightness of his figure emphasised by the close-fitting white uniform, with its wide splash of scarlet at the waist Then he crossed to the table and studied the chart, that strange hieroglyph, like a negative print of forked lightning, so full of dread meaning to those who can read it aright. The latest entry was 106°.

"You saw Mackay?" he asked, under his breath.

"I did."

"You're in for a hard night of it. I'd better stay up and help."

"I'll not have you at any price," she answered bluntly.

He frowned. But the fact that he did not insist spoke volumes to her understanding heart.

"Swear you'll send Amar Singh to wake me if it seems necessary."

"I will—no fear."

"He'll sit handy, just outside, all night and help you in any possible way. He's a jewel at times like this. I'll look in again when I get home."

"Come back early," she commanded with a sudden smile, "and have a solid night of sleep. It's plain your needing it badly."

"Thanks. I believe I am. I'll make a fresh start afterwards and take my fair share of the work. Jove! It's a furnace of a night. There goes the trumpet; I'll be back before long."

His words were truer than he knew.

Shortly after nine o'clock, while Mrs Olliver was persuading her semi-delirious patient to swallow two tablespoonfuls of chicken-broth, quick footsteps and the clink of spurs made her sit suddenly upright, with a listening look in her eyes. She knew the country of her service well enough to be prepared for anything at any hour of the day or night—and she was barely surprised when, two minutes later, Desmond stood before her in his forage cap, his sword buckled on over his mess-jacket and held high to prevent it from clanking

"What is it?" she asked in a hurried whisper. "A beacon fire alight?"

He nodded, and passed a handkerchief across his forehead, for he had come at lightning speed.

"A raid of sorts—out Hangu way. Can't tell if it'll be a big thing or not. The whole garrison's ordered out."

It was a matter of seconds, and he spoke in a breathless rush.

"I dashed on ahead to give you a few instructions. Olliver is ordering Griselda to be saddled and brought across at once. If the affair looks serious we'll send an orderly back to fetch a doolie from the hospital, come on here for you and the Boy, and see you safely to the Fort, where you must stay till further orders. Get all possible necessaries together, and be ready to leave at a moment's notice."

"If we move him to-night, Theo, 'twill be—the end of it all."

A spasm of pain crossed his face.

"I hope to God it mayn't be necessary. But we must take our chance of that. It won't be safe for you to have a light in the house, with every door open, and the city full of *budmashes*.[1] Can you manage with just a night-light carefully screened?"

"Sure I can. I'll manage to see with me fingers well enough!"

"Right! Amar Singh'll sit outside the door. He'll not sleep a wink, I promise you."

The suspicion of a tremor in her brave smile caught at his heart. He pressed her shoulder with a reassuring hand.

"Sorry Olliver couldn't see you before leaving," he said gently. "Hullo, there's Paul; I must be off. God bless you for a plucky woman, Frank. We'll all get back—sometime, never fear." And in an instant she was alone.

Nothing remained but to blow out the lamp and set the screened night-light on a table farthest from the outer doors. Its uncertain flicker served to make darkness visible and through the darkness she crept back to her station by the bed.

Denvil, who had fallen into an unrefreshing sleep, stirred and tossed with broken mutterings that threatened every moment to break out into the babble of delirium; and for a while she sat beside him in a stunned quietness, her ears

[1] Bad characters.

strained to catch the sounds that came up from below—the hasty gathering of men and horses and mules; the jingle of harness; brisk words of command; the tramping of many feet. Comforting sounds, since they spoke of the protective presence of Englishmen.

But those that followed were less reassuring, for they were sounds of massed movement, of an organised body under way: the muffled tread of infantry, the cheerful clatter of cavalry at the trot. She knew the order of their going, to the minutest detail. A vision of it all was photographed upon her brain as she had witnessed it these many times within the past ten years; and perhaps owing to the mental vividness of her race, custom had not yet ground the edge off the poignant moment of departure.

Rapidly, inexorably, the sounds retreated toward the hills; and as they drew farther away she listened the more intently. It was as if her spirit, freed from her body, followed the men she loved, till the unheeding night absorbed them—till hearing, stretched to its utmost limit, could catch no lightest echo of sound.

Then silence, intensified by stifling darkness, enveloped her, pressing in upon heart and brain like an invisible force that held her prisoner against her will.

The practical side of her fought squarely against this obsession of the intangible; but it persisted and prevailed. The mocking shadows crowded about her, compelled her to a discomfortable realisation of her solitude in a station needing the perpetual alertness of armed men to ensure peace and safety. For Kohat city boasted a creditable average of bad characters and murder cases—a corpse more or less on the Border being of no more consequence than the fall of a sparrow; and the Waziris had of late been unusually daring in regard to Government horses and carbines. Nor was it an unknown thing for them to creep past the sentries on very black nights into the station itself; and for all her courage, Frank Olliver was by no means fearless. The two are a contradiction in terms. Only the unimaginative are fearless, and only the keenly imaginative, capable of feeling fear in every fibre, ever scale the heights of true courage.

Save for the wakeful vigilance of sentries, the huddled

bungalows of the cantonment lay below her empty as a handful of shells on a lone shore; and in the overpowering stillness each least sound stood out crisp and clear-cut as twigs against a winter sunset; the fitful rustle of bedclothes; Rob breathing peacefully in a distant corner; the whisper of the punkah; the querulous creaking of the rope answered by a whine from the back verandah, where a resigned coolie swayed a basket of damp straw, packed with bottles of milk and soda-water for Denvil's consumption during the night.

The reiteration of these still small voices grew distracting as the whisper of an unseen clock. They dominated the silence, paralysing thought, and compelling her to note every change in their pitiless regularity.

Resolved to break the spell by the only definite action available, she decided to prepare for the emergency which her brain refused to face. But on rising she was arrested by a voice from the bed—a voice not of speech but of song, a snatch from a burlesque the Boy had played in during the winter:

"My name it is Abanazar
If you want me you needn't go far;
I'm sure to be found, if you'll only look round,
Number Seventy, Suddar Bazaar."

Denvil's deep baritone, distorted to a guttural travesty of itself, rose to a shout on the ascending notes of the last line. Then, without pause for breath, came the voice of speech—hurried, expressionless, heartrending to hear.

"Safe for an encore, that—what? Should ha' been Desmond, though. See him in tights you'd think he could slip through a wedding-ring. Done it too, by Jove! Better than horses that, in the long-run.—How about Grey Dawn?—Confound your luck! Always a dead cert till I lay anything on. Hold hard, though. . . . I'm done with all that now. . . . Wouldn't go back on Desmond—not for a mine of gold. *You* don't know Desmond;—wait till you're in a hole! Eight hundred rupees, I tell you—more than his month's pay! Said I was to keep quiet about it too. Not mail-day to-morrow, is it? Where's the use of writing to her? She'd never understand. Look out—some one's coming,—there by the door. Great Scott! It's—it's mother!"

The voice broke into an unnatural sound between a laugh and a sob, and Frank, who was already praying for the lesser evil of silence, bent over the Boy, soothing him with tender words and tone, as though she were his mother in very deed.

The delusion was strong upon him. He clung to her fiercely when she would have risen to fetch milk, overwhelming her with a rush of disjointed questions varied by snatches of enthusiasm for Desmond, till exhaustion reduced him to incoherent mutterings; and she was free at last to grope for milk and brandy and a fresh packing of wet sheets.

He grew quieter after a space, and sank into a more restful sleep, leaving Frank Olliver to face another spell of whispering silence; her ears strained now to catch the dread sound of a single horseman returning from the hills.

The first white streak of dawn found her still at her post, with hands quietly folded and unclosed eyes; found Amar Singh wide-eyed also, his lean face and figure rigid as a stone image, a bared sword lying like a flash of light across his knees.

And with the dawn came also the far-off mutter of the footsteps that night had stolen from her; an inverted repetition of the same sounds in a steady crescendo that rang like music in her ears—a sound to lift the heart.

The massed tramping of men and horses broke up at length, scattered in all directions, and within five minutes she looked up to find her husband in the doorway—a thick-set man, with more of force than perception in his blunt features and heavily-browed eyes.

She rose and went to him straightway, her face alight with satisfaction, and he took a friendly hold of her arm by way of greeting. They had always been more like good comrades than man and wife, these two.

"Well, old girl," he said, "there was no show after all, you see. It seems that the raid didn't quite come off; and we had our scamper for nothing, worse luck! The Boy going on all right?"

"'Tis hard to tell. He's in a quiet sleep just now, anyway."

"You may as well come out of this, then, and give us some breakfast. I'm going to the Major's room to tidy up."

As his wife stepped back into the sick-room, Theo Desmond came quickly towards her.

"Well done," he said heartily; "you didn't expect us quite so soon, did you? Not a shot fired, and I should have been swearing all the way home—but for the Boy. Looks peaceful enough now, doesn't he? Temperature any lower?"

"Just a little, these last few hours. But he's been talking a deal of madness, poor fellow."

"What about?" he asked sharply. "Money?"

She smiled, with an odd mixture of pride and tenderness in her eyes.

"Faith, I can see what's been happening, Theo, clear as daylight. But I'll say no word to a soul, not even Geoff; you know that sure enough."

"Yes, I know it. But I'll feel grateful when he stops airing the subject."

Her low laugh had a break in it, and he scanned her face keenly.

"You're played out, Frank. I was afraid you were hardly fit for this sort of thing yet. You don't do a stroke more till to-morrow morning. Come along now and have five grains of quinine and some food. Amar Singh can mount guard in case the Boy wakes up."

Paul Wyndham greeted her with his nod and smile, which were apt to convey more friendliness than other people's words. Desmond set her ceremoniously in the place of honour; and the 6.30 breakfast, prepared at ten minutes' notice, and eaten in Mess uniform, proved a remarkably cheerful affair; one of those simple, commonplace events which, for all their simplicity, go far to cement friendship and form refreshing oases along the dusty path of life.

The morning post-bag contained an envelope in Evelyn's handwriting; and, the Ollivers being gone, Theo retired to the study to enjoy it at his leisure. It proved to be short, and contained little beyond querulous upbraiding. Her husband could almost catch the tone of her voice as he read; and the light of satisfaction left his face. Evelyn had an insatiable appetite for long and detailed letters, though she by no means returned them in kind; and it appeared that Theo had not written for a week. In the fulness of his days he had not realised the fact which was now brought forcibly to his notice.

"It's just laziness and selfishness," she wrote in her sweeping fashion, "when you *know* how I look out for your letters, to leave me a whole week without a line. If it was *me*, there might be some excuse, because there's always something or another going on, and I never seem to get a minute to sit down and write. But you must have hours and hours of spare time in the long days down there. I expect you play chess with Major Wyndham all the while, and quite forget about writing to me. I suppose if you were ill *some one* would have the decency to write and tell me. But if you don't write yourself *directly* you get this, I shall think something dreadful has happened; and it's such a nuisance not to know if you are all right. I can't enjoy things properly a bit."

And so on, *ad lib.*, *da capo*, until the end.

Having read it through twice, with a flicker of amusement in his tired eyes, he sat down straightway, wrote for a quarter of an hour at the top of his speed, and left the letter ready for the afternoon post. It contained a polite apology for remissness, followed by an account in bare outline of his doings during the past five days; a few details in regard to Harry's illness; and an intimation that if letters were short, she must remember that, for the present, every hour of spare time would be taken up with nursing the Boy or writing detailed accounts to his mother. And, in truth, before that wearisome illness was over Mrs Denvil and her boy's Captain had struck up a lasting friendship across six thousand miles of sea.

On her return from a tennis party the following afternoon Evelyn Desmond found the letter awaiting her; and her face took such rueful lines as she read it, that Honor's anxiety was roused.

"*Evelyn*—what is it?" she asked, a slight catch in her breath.

Evelyn shrugged her shoulders in meek resignation.

"Oh, it's only rather more Kohatish than usual! Mr

Denvil seems to be quite bad with typhoid, and Theo has been galloping over half the Frontier after out-posts—such rubbishy work for a man like that! And—oh, you'd better read it all for yourself. You needn't bother about it having been written for *me*. It might just as well be a paragraph out of a newspaper!"

With a childish grimace she tossed the letter across the table. But hid in her heart lay the rankling knowledge that she had been both hasty and unjust to her husband, who had emphasised the fact by ignoring it,—a method peculiarly his own.

Honor read every line of the closely-written pages with eager interest, read also the much that had not been written, that Evelyn had failed to discern; and a great thankfulness overwhelmed her that she had refrained from adding her own passing vexation to the burden of work and anxiety already resting on her friend's shoulders.

Her spoken comment was brief and characteristic.

"Oh, how I envy Mrs Olliver! We're just playing at life up here, you and I, like two dolls, while she is living the real thing down there."

Evelyn Desmond, in utter astonishment, flung annoyance to the winds.

"Really and truly, Honor," she declared, with conviction, "you are the most amazing person I've ever known!"

CHAPTER XII.

NOW IT'S DIFFERENT.

"A word! how it severeth!
O Power of Life and Death,
In the tongue, as the preacher saith."
—BROWNING.

THE great monsoon—a majestic onrush of cloud hurtling across the heavens, with dazzle of lightning and clangour of thunder—had long since rolled up from India's coast-line to her utmost hills; bringing new forms of torment to the patient plains; filling mountain and valley and water-courses innumerable with the voice of melody.

On the cedar-crowned heights of Murree, dank boughs dripped and drooped above ill-made houses, that gave free admittance to the moist outer world; tree ferns, springing to sudden life on moss-clad trunks and boughs, showed brilliant as emeralds on velvet. The whole earth was quick with hidden stirrings and strivings, the whole air quick with living sound—plash of rain-drops; evensong of birds; glad shouting of cicadas among the branches, and the laughter of a hundred fairy falls.

Theo Desmond drank in the cool green wonder of it all with a keenly perceptive enjoyment; drew into his lungs deep draughts of the strong, clean mountain air; watched the frail curtain of mist swaying, lifting, spreading to a pearl-white film, till, through a sudden rent, the red gold of sunset burned, deepening to a mass of velvet shadow the inexpressible blue of rain-washed hills.

His post of observation on this August evening was the saturated verandah of "The Deodars," where he had flung himself full length in Honor's canvas chair, a pipe between his teeth; hands locked behind his head; lavishly muddied boots and gaiters outstretched; the whole supple length of him eloquent of well-earned relaxation and repose.

Three days earlier he had ridden up through a world of driving mist and rain in the wake of Harry Denvil's doolie; having secured a blessed month of respite for himself and two months for the Boy, who, by the efforts of three tireless nurses and a redoubtable Scotch doctor, had been dragged back from death; and was but just beginning to take hold on life and health again.

From outset to close he had clung to the support of Desmond's presence with the tenacity of an exhausted body and a fevered brain;—a tenacity which could not fail to touch the older man's heart, and which had made it difficult for others to take their due share in the nursing. Thus the slow weeks of dependence on one side, and unwearied service on the other, together with the underlying bond between them, had wrought a closeness of friendship to which the Boy had long aspired; and which promised to add depth and stability to the warmth and uprightness of heart that were already his. Harry Denvil's present need was for a tacit wiping out of the past, an unquestioning trust in regard to the future; and his Captain, after the wordless manner of men, gave him full assurance of both. It is just this power to draw out the best and strongest by the simple habit of taking it for granted that marks the true leader; the man who compels because he never insists; whose influence is less a force than a subtle radiation.

And now, as Theo Desmond sat alone fronting a world compact of mist and fire, and the fragrance of moist earth, his mind was mainly concerned with the Boy's future, and with certain retrenchments of his own expenditure, whereby alone he could hope to cancel the debts that remained after the disposal of Roland. His sole trouble in respect of these retrenchments lay in the fact that they must, to some extent, affect his wife. If only she could be persuaded to see the necessity as clearly as he did himself, all would be well. She and Harry had been good friends from the outset. He hoped—he believed—she would understand

Light footsteps on the boards behind him brought a smile to his lips; but he neither turned nor stirred. An instant later, hands cool and imponderable as snowflakes rested on his forehead, and silken strands of hair brushed it softly as his wife leaned over him, nestling her head against his own.

"Are you very happy sitting there?" she whispered.

"Supremely happy."

"Why? Because you're so nice and wet, and messy?"

"Yes; and a few other reasons as well."

"What other reasons? Me?"

"Naturally, you dear little goose! Come round and let me get a sight of you, instead of perching behind me like a bird."

She came round obediently, standing a little away from him,—a slim strip of colour that reflected the uncertain sea-tint of her eyes,—and looked down upon his disordered appearance with a small grimace.

"I'm not *sure* that I love you properly, Theo, when you're *quite* as muddy as that."

"Oh yes, you do; come on!"

And putting out an arm, he drew her down till she knelt beside him, her hands resting on his knee. He covered them quietly with one of his own.

"Ladybird, it's turning out a glorious evening! Come for a walk."

"Oh, Theo, *don't* be so uncomfortably energetic! I hate going out in the wet. You only came in half an hour ago, and you've been walking all day."

He laughed—the glad laugh of a truant schoolboy—and knocked the ashes out of his pipe.

"I'm capable of walking all night too! Only then you might imagine the hot weather had turned my brain. But indeed, little woman, if you had been sickened with sunlight and scorched earth as I have been for the last three months, you'd understand how a man may feel a bit light-headed in the first few days that he's quit of it all."

"And was I very horrid to be playing up here in the cool all the time?" she asked, pricked by the memory of Honor's words to one of her rare touches of compunction.

"My dear, what nonsense! It would have been double as bad if you had been there too."

Sincerity rang in his tone, and she noted the fact with a sigh of relief. She was not altogether heartless, this fragile slip of womanhood. She merely desired, like many of us, the comfort of being selfish without the unbecomingness of appearing so.

"We'll sit out here together and talk till it gets dark," she announced with a pretty air of decision, lest the invitation to walk should be renewed. "Stay where you are, and I'll fetch a stool. It's quite a treat to see you looking lazy for once in a way."

She brought a stool and established herself close to him. He acknowledged her presence without removing his eyes from the storm-tossed glory of the sky.

"Look, Ladybird—look!" he urged in a low tone. "We can talk afterwards."

But her attention was caught and riveted by the reflection of the glory in her husband's face.

"Does it please you so tremendously?" she asked in honest bewilderment. "Just a sunset! You've seen hundreds of them before."

He smiled and answered nothing. Speech and emotion inhabit different hemispheres of a man's brain; woman alone is rash enough to force them into unwilling union.

The clinging garment of mist, driven and dispersed by day's last flash of self-assertion, lay heaped and tumbled in the valleys, and the mountains stood knee-deep in an opalescent sea of foam. It was as though Nature, in a mood of capricious kindliness, had rent the veil, that mortals might share in the triumphal passing of the sun, whose supremacy had been in eclipse these many days.

Above the deep-toned quiet of earth, blurred and ragged clouds showed every conceivable tone of umber and grey, from purest pearl-white to darkest depths of indigo. Only low down, where a blue-black mass ended with level abruptness, a flaming strip of day was splashed along the west—one broad brush-stroke, as it were, by some Titanic artist whose palette held liquid fire. Snows and mist alike caught and flung back the radiance in a maze of rainbow hues;

while beyond the bank of cloud a vast pale fan of light shot outward and upward to the very zenith of heaven. Each passing minute wrought some imperceptible change of grouping, form, or colour; blurred masses melted to flakes and strata on a groundwork of frail blue; orange deepened to crimson; and anon earth and sky were on fire with tints of garnet and rose. Each several snow-peak blushed like an angel surprised in a good deed. Splashes of colour sprang from cloud-tip to cloud-tip with invisible speed, till even the chill east glowed with a faint hue of life.

And in the midst of the transient splendour, enveloped by the isolation of the falling day, husband and wife sat silent, absorbed in strangely opposite reflections. Verily they dwelt in different planets, these two who had willed to be one, but whom forces more potent held inexorably apart.

Desmond had long since passed beyond the border-line of definite thought; while Evelyn's mind rapidly reverted to the more congenial atmosphere of things terrestrial. An unknown force was urging her to speak openly to her husband, to rid herself of the shadow that had begun to tarnish the bright surface of life. It would be easier to speak in dusk than in bald daylight—easier also before the bloom of reunion had been rubbed off by the prosaic trivialities of life. In her present position, too, it would be possible to avoid his gaze; and she found a singular difficulty in tampering with facts when Theo's eyes were on her face.

She watched him speculatively for a few moments, and wondered what change would come over him when her tale was told. Anger frightened and repelled her; and for all his hastiness she had seldom seen more than a mere spark of his inner fire.

He seemed to have forgotten her existence; and by way of gentle reminder she shifted her position.

"Theo," she said under her breath.

He felt the movement without catching the sound of his name, and turned to her quickly, impulsive speech upon his lips.

"By the way, Ladybird, there's something I want to tell you, and this is a good opportunity."

The coincidence so startled her that her own half-fledged

impulse scurried back to its nest. Nor was she certain whether the sigh that escaped her expressed disappointment or relief.

"What is it?" she asked—"something nice?"

The characteristic question set him smiling.

"You must judge for yourself. It chiefly concerns the Boy. You're fond of him, aren't you?"

"Yes; he's nice enough. But why?"

"You wouldn't mind if we put ourselves out a little to get him out of a difficulty?"

"Well, that would rather depend on what we had to do." Her tone, though still pleasant, was guarded. "What kind of difficulty?"

"Money."

She turned her face away something suddenly, and felt very thankful that day was fading from the sky.

"Do you mean—lending him money?" she asked blankly.

"No—giving it. I prefer it that way. There's no need to tell you his troubles in detail; it would hardly be fair to him. They are of a kind you can't know anything about; and I hope you never will."

In the fewest possible words he gave her an outline of Harry's story; of the parting with Roland, and the promise he had exacted in return for his help. He spoke throughout with such unfailing kindness that vexation pricked and stung her, like thorns under the skin. She might have told him after all. He would not have been angry. Now she had been forestalled. She failed to perceive that the backslidings of his wife must of necessity touch him more nearly than those of his subaltern, and that to her own extravagance was added a host of petty evasions and deceits such as a man of his type would be little able to condone or understand.

"You see," he was saying when her mind harked back from the excursion into her own point of view, "the poor fellow has done all he can towards putting matters straight, and I am thankful I can manage the rest myself, so as to give him a fair start for the future."

"But how much is—*your* share?" she asked, almost in a whisper.

"Rather more than eight hundred rupees."

"And you have actually—*done* it, Theo?"

"Yes. You surely couldn't have wished otherwise?"

For a moment she hesitated, then her repressed bitterness brimmed over.

"Oh, I don't know. Only I think you might have considered *me* a little first. I've more right to your money than he has; and if you can afford to throw away eight hundred rupees on a careless, extravagant subaltern, you could quite well let me go to Simla; or at least add something to my dress allowance. It's not so very easy to manage on the little you give me."

She spoke with averted face in a tone of clear hardness, and each word smote her husband like a small sharp stone.

"I am sorry you see it that way," he said, a new restraint in his voice, "and that you don't find your allowance sufficient. I give you all I can, and you seem to have pretty frocks enough, anyhow. If I had eight hundred rupees to throw away,—as you choose to express it,—I should hardly have spoken of putting ourselves out; in fact, I shouldn't have spoken at all. But you have been such good friends with the Boy all along that I hoped you would be ready to help give him a hand up. I can only manage such a sum by knocking two hundred off my pay for the next four months. This means cutting down expenses a little; but we can easily do it, Ladybird—*if* we pull together."

At any other time such an appeal from Theo would have proved irresistible, would have drawn them into a closer union of thought and purpose than they had ever attained as yet. But the appeal came at the wrong moment, and Evelyn Desmond sat silent, her hands so fast interlocked that her rings bruised their delicate surface.

"I am thinking of the Boy's mother as well as himself, you see," her husband urged with increasing gentleness; "he is her only son, and she is wrapped up in him; and I know from experience what that means."

She lifted her head and faced him.

"You think a great deal too much about—those sort of stray people, Theo, and it's rather hard on me. Why am *I* to be made uncomfortable on account of Mrs Denvil, when I've never even met her in my life?"

"If you can't see that for yourself, Ladybird, I'm afraid I can't tell you. I've no taste for preaching sermons."

"It would be rather a mercy if you had no taste for acting them either," she retorted, with a little laugh that failed to take the edge off her words. "*I* don't much like them in any form. How are you going to cut down expenses?"

"Chiefly in ways that need not concern you. But to start with, I'm afraid I must take you and Honor down with me on the third of next month. I can do nothing while I am crippled by a double establishment. You'll barely miss four weeks up here, and the heat is over earlier in Kohat than in the Punjab. Paul gets his leave when mine is up, and he will spend it here with the Boy, so as to take the last month of rent off my hands."

"So you've *settled* it all without saying a word to *me?*"

"Yes. I had to fix things up before I left. It's a pity the difficulty includes Honor, but I don't think she'll mind when I tell her why."

"Oh dear, no; *Honor* won't mind. I believe she's happier in Kohat,—but——"

"But *you* are *not?*" he broke out abruptly, leaning forward and searching her face with anxious eyes.

The vehement question startled her.

"I never said *that,* Theo—and it isn't true. Only—I do hate the ugliness and the heat, and September's the loveliest month of all up here."

"Doesn't it make things any easier to feel you are helping the Boy by giving up these few weeks of enjoyment?"

"No—it doesn't. Not a bit."

Desmond frowned.

"Try and fancy yourself in a strait like that, Evelyn, and the thundering relief it would be to get out of it."

His words stabbed her unwittingly.

"I'm not good at fancying things, and I'm not good at cutting down expenses either—I was never taught. I hope you don't do these uncomfortable sort of things often, Theo. It seems to me you're too much inclined to rush in and help people without stopping to think of—of other people at all! It would have been much better for the Boy if you'd left him to get clear of his muddle, instead of upsetting every one by spending money on him that you can't really spare."

Her husband leaned farther back into the shadow, his mouth hardened to a rigid line. All that he chose to say on the subject had been said.

Emboldened by his silence, and the fact that his face was hidden from her, she continued her small flow of remonstrance, undermining herself more completely with each fresh word.

"It was all very well while you were a bachelor for you to go throwing your life and your money about so foolishly. But now it's different; and I don't think you have a right to do it any more. Where's the good of us trying so hard to live on our pay, if it's only to be flung about to help subalterns who don't try at all? You can't cure Mr Denvil of being casual; and for all your generosity, you'll probably find him in just as bad a hole again by this time next year."

The words stung him to sharp retort.

"I never asked for *your* opinion of the Boy, Evelyn; and you seem to forget that he has given me his word."

"Oh, no doubt he has! It's easy enough to make promises when one's unhappy; but it isn't so easy to keep them when things get smooth again." And she nodded her head wisely, for her conviction sprang from the depths of personal experience.

Her husband rose and walked to the verandah's edge. Here he remained standing, his hands thrust deep into the pockets of his Norfolk coat, his eyes fixed absently on the last gleam of light in the west, where all that now remained of the sunset's stormy splendour was a handful of filmy fragments, like rose petals dropped from some Olympian rose-bush, and the sickle of a young moon, outrivalled by the mellow radiance of the evening star. The snows lay dead and cold, awaiting the resurrection of dawn. Their chill pallor struck at his heart in a manner new to him.

Evelyn studied his eloquent outline with a mild surprise. She was not a little proud of her valiant protest against his mistaken ideas; and he was surely not foolish enough to be annoyed because she had talked practical common-sense.

She went to him at last, and lightly touched his arm.

"You look as solemn as a funeral, Theo! Why don't you speak?"

"Because I have no more to say. Too much has been said already. I am sorry I mentioned the matter at all."

With that he turned from her and entered the house.

Honor met him on the threshold, and her eyes were quick to catch the lurking shadow in his. But she merely said what she had come to say.

"Mr Denvil is longing for you. I have done my small best to amuse him; only there comes a stage when nothing will satisfy him but you. Where's Evelyn?"

"Outside there. It's time she came in."

Honor found her by the verandah rails, standing like a pensive ghost in the dying light.

"Studying the sunset, Evelyn?" she remarked cheerfully. "That's a new departure for you!"

Whereat Evelyn flung out both hands—a pretty appealing gesture all her own.

"Oh, Honor, Theo's been *so* troublesome! And he wants to take us down on the third of next month. He will explain to you the why of it all; perhaps you'll understand better than I could. Such high-flown notions don't appeal to me a bit. *I* think Theo is rather like that silly man in the Middle Ages who was always trying to fight windmills, or sheep, or something; and there really ought to be a law to prevent people who want to go about being unselfish to everybody from ever having wives at all!"

CHAPTER XIII.

IT ISN'T FAIR.

> "Though thou repent, yet have I still the loss;
> The offender's sorrow yields but weak relief
> To him who bears the strong offence's cross."
>
> —SHAKESPEARE.

THE measure of a man's worth is not to be found in a heroic impulse or a fine idea, but in the steadfast working out of either through weeks and months—when the glow has faded from the heights, when the inspiration of an illumined moment has passed into the unrecognised chivalry of daily life; and the three months following upon that crucial August evening put no light tax upon Desmond's staying power,—the power that is the corner-stone of all achievement.

Border life is, in every respect, more costly than life in "down country" cantonments. To keep within the narrow bounds of his pay was already a difficult matter; and such minor retrenchments as could be achieved were inadequate to meet his present need. He saw that he would be called upon to part with one or two cherished possessions, acquired in days of young extravagance; and possibly to break into the few hundred rupees laid aside for emergencies shortly after his marriage.

Wine, cigars, and cigarettes must be banished outright; and he limited himself to one pipe and one "peg" a-day. Stores of all kinds were ruthlessly cut down; and only the Anglo-Indian housewife knows what it means to be flung almost entirely upon the tender mercies of the Bazaar. Informal dinner-parties, for which the Desmonds were famous, became rare events; and nights at Mess—a favourite and justifiable luxury—were reduced in number as far as might be without eliciting remonstrance from his brother officers. For in India, and more especially in the Army of India, it is profoundly true that "no man liveth unto himself." In the Land of the Open Door the second of the two great commandments is apt to be set before the first; and nowhere, perhaps, is the bond of union stronger, more compelling, than in the isolated regiments of the Frontier Force. But, with due regard for this unwritten law, Desmond accomplished much in those few months of unremitting self-denial; and if his friends noted certain changes in his way of life, they accepted these in the true spirit of comradeship, without question or comment.

Even Wyndham kept silence, though he had fuller knowledge of his friend's abstemiousness, and was disturbed by a great longing to remove the hidden cause. But intimate speech played a minor part in the friendship of these two men. The very depth and strength of their feeling for each other constrained them to a particular reticence in the matter of self-expression.

On the first occasion of Paul's dining at the blue bungalow, after his return from Murree, Desmond spoke a few words of apology for the absence of wine and cigars.

"Sorry to treat you shabbily, old man," he said, when they were alone. "Just a little necessary economy. It won't last long."

Paul nodded, smiling, and quietly proffered his own cigar-case.

"At least you'll not refuse one of mine, Theo," he said; and their talk drifted into the fertile channel of "shop," and the prospect of serious collision with Russia, which at that time loomed on the political horizon.

Paul was thus left to draw his own conclusions, which were not complimentary to his friend's wife. For reserve has its drawbacks, like every other virtue; and those who practise it often, forget that if there is a time for silence, there is also a time for speech.

Evelyn clung tenaciously to her disapproval of the whole proceeding. The scarcity of stores, and of pleasant little dinners, were the only retrenchments that directly disturbed her comfort, and she made the most of them, though the problems of housekeeping fell mainly upon Honor's shoulders. The girl's readiness to accept Evelyn's burden, as a matter of course, could not fail to rouse Desmond's admiration: and these three months of friction and stress, of working bravely together for one end, went far to strengthen the bond of their friendship.

Evelyn contented herself with a thinly veiled air of martyrdom, and with raising objections whenever opportunity offered. Only after Denvil's first dinner did she venture a direct attack. For on this occasion economy was not. Wine and cigars appeared with the dessert; and the two men sat an inordinately long while over both. But the inner significance of her husband's acts being a sealed book to Evelyn Desmond, she spent the evening in a state of suppressed irritation, which, on the Boy's departure, overflowed in petulant reproof.

"Why did you have everything different to-night just because of Mr Denvil?" she demanded in a note of challenge.

"Because I preferred it so."

Desmond's tone was polite, but final. He sat down and opened a book in self-defence. But Evelyn was not to be baulked by a policy of masterly inactivity. She remained standing before him.

"Is it going to be like that every time he comes?"

"Yes."

"Theo—it's perfectly ridiculous the way you put yourself out for that boy!" she protested with unusual heat, kindled by a hidden spark of jealousy. "It's bad enough to have you giving up everything, and making Honor and me thoroughly uncomfortable, without this sort of nonsense on the top of it all."

Honor glanced up in quick remonstrance; but Desmond caught the look in her eyes, and it was enough. "Haven't you the sense to see that just because he is so fond of you he *ought* to be allowed to know how much trouble he has given you. It's the only way to make him more careful, now he's back again; and if you *will* go on in this way, I shall end in speaking to him myself."

She had overshot the mark.

Desmond shut the book with a snap; flung it on the table, and sprang up with such anger in his eyes that his wife shrank back instinctively. Her movement, slight as it was, checked the impetuous speech upon his lips.

"You will do nothing of the sort," he said in a restrained voice. "It is a matter entirely between him and me; and that's an end of the subject, once for all."

Evelyn, startled into silence, stood motionless till the study door closed behind her husband; then, with a sigh of exasperation, hurried out of the room, leaving Honor to her own disturbing thoughts.

Each month was forcing upon the girl a clearer revelation of the clash of temperament, which threatened to bring about serious disunion between these two, whose happiness had become a vital part of her life; and her spirit was troubled beyond measure. The strongest passion of Honor Meredith's heart was the true woman's passion—to protect and help. But worldly wisdom warned her that her hands were tied; that man and wife must work out their own salvation, or the reverse, without help or hindrance from her.

Since their return from Murree such flashes of dissension had become increasingly frequent between them. It is astonishing how quickly two people can fall into a habit of discord. Abstinence from tobacco was not without its effect upon Desmond's nerves and temper, tried as they were by Evelyn's pin-prick methods of warfare; while she herself was often strung into irritability by her own unacknowledged troubles.

The passing relief wrought by Miss Kresney's loan had evaporated with the realisation that she had only contracted a debt in another direction—a debt more embarrassing than all the rest put together; for she knew that she would never have the courage to speak of it to her husband. Miss Kresney had told her to take her time in the matter of repayment, and she had taken it in generous measure. Not a fraction of the three hundred rupees had been repaid as yet; and, by way of atonement, Evelyn felt constrained to a more decisive friendliness with both brother and sister—a fact which Owen Kresney noted with satisfaction; and which did not improve matters between herself and Theo.

As the weeks wore on he devoted his spare time more exclusively to polo and Persian; continuing his lessons to Honor; and rarely spending his evenings in the drawing-room, unless the girl's music held him spell-bound, and ensured the avoidance of dangerous topics. Evelyn retorted by a renewed zest for tennis and tea-parties; an increasing tendency to follow the line of least resistance, regardless of results. Thus Honor found herself thrown more and more upon the companionship of Mrs Olliver, Mrs Conolly, and Paul Wyndham, whose anxiety for Theo she guessed at, even as they guessed her own, though never a word on the subject passed between them.

Evelyn's anxiety was reserved exclusively for herself. She had sense enough to perceive that nothing could defer the day of reckoning much longer; and on a certain afternoon in early December she exhumed her detested sheaf of bills and sat down at her bureau to a reconsideration of the hopelessness of things in general.

A panel of winter sunshine, flung across the room from the verandah door, enveloped her in a glow of light and warmth. The drowsiness of an Indian noon brooded over the compound. Honor was out riding with Paul Wyndham; Theo busy in the next room, and very unlikely to interrupt her, she reflected with a pang of regret. In an hour's time she was going over to tea and tennis with the Kresneys; and had decided that, after six months of silence, some mention must be made of a fixed scale of repayment, to begin with the New Year. But in that event, what hope of meeting any of those other demands, that were again being urgently brought to her notice? What possibility of ordering the two new gowns—bare necessities, in her esteem—to grace the coming Christmas week at Lahore?

This same "week" is the central social event of the Punjab cold weather, when most officers on the Border are certain of their fifteen days' leave; when from all corners of the Province men and women gravitate towards its dusty capital—women with dress baskets of formidable size; men armed with polo-sticks, and with ponies, beloved cricket-bats and saddles.

Through all the dismal coil of things, this one hour of festivity gleamed on Evelyn Desmond's horizon like a light in a dark room. For one brief blessed week she would be in her element, would escape from the galling restraint of economy; and, more than all, in the background of her mind there lurked a hope that by some means she might recapture that vigorous, self-poised husband of hers, whose love was, after all, the one real necessity of her life; and whom she now saw slipping slowly, surely out of reach. But to recapture she must recaptivate; and to that end faultless frocks were indispensable.

She leaned her head upon her hands, and fell to building extravagant air-castles that eclipsed all practical considerations whatsoever.

So complete was her abstraction, that she failed to hear the study door open, and was rudely startled back to reality by her husband's voice at her elbow, sharp and stern, as she had never heard it till now.

"What *is* the meaning of this, Evelyn?" he demanded, bringing his hand down on the desk beside her; and one glance at the half sheet lying beneath it was enough. That particular bill had grown painfully familiar during the last few months. It was from Lahore, and its total was no less than three hundred rupees. Her husband's waiting silence was more disconcerting than speech.

"It's mine," she murmured breathlessly; and snatched at the offending scrap of paper, tearing it in two.

"The bill is mine now," Desmond rebuked her with studied equanimity. "You can't cancel it by destroying it. No doubt you've got another copy. Will you let me have it and any others you happen to have by you?"

"Where's the use of that? . . . You can't pay off anything now."

"I can and will pay off every penny. But I must know exactly how you stand."

For all his coldness, the assurance fell on her heart like rain on thirsty soil. Where the money was to come from she could not guess. But she knew enough of the man to feel sure that his words would be fulfilled to the letter.

One consideration only withheld her from reply. How much did she dare confess to him even now? Not Miss Kresney's transaction; nor the need of new dresses for Lahore. But the rest! . . . What an unspeakable comfort it would be to fling all the rest on to his shoulders, that seemed broad and strong enough to carry her burdens and his own.

Her hesitancy pricked him to impatience.

"Well, Evelyn, I am waiting for your answer. Are there other bills besides that one?—Yes or No. I want the truth. Don't stop to embroider it."

At that the blood flew to her cheeks. She sprang up and faced him, tremulous, but defiant.

"If you say things like *that* to me, I won't tell you anything at all . . . ever." And turning sharply away, to hide her tears, she went over to the mantelpiece and leaned upon it, keeping her back towards him.

Desmond followed her.

"I am sorry if I hurt you," he said, a touch of bitterness in his tone. "But the fact that I can speak so without doing you a gross injustice hurts me more than you are ever likely to understand."

"You make it all seem much worse—than it really is," she answered without looking round. "I haven't done anything dreadful, after all. Heaps of people get into debt. You weren't so angry with Mr Denvil; and—and—if you hadn't been in such a hurry to help him, you'd have found it easier to help me now."

"No need to fling that in my teeth, or drag the Boy into the discussion. The cases are not parallel, and you have only yourself to thank that my money went to him instead of you. In my anxiety to avoid anything of this sort, I have questioned you several times, and each time you have told me a lie. The whole pile of bills are nothing to me in comparison with that. I suppose I ought to have known that you could hardly dress as you do on the little I can spare. But I was fool enough to trust you implicitly." He paused, and added with greater gentleness: "What's more,

I shall trust you again, unless you make that quite impossible. But I warn you—Ladybird, that if ever you do kill my trust in you, you will kill—everything else along with it."

"*Theo!*"

There was sharp pain in the cry, and she swung round, flinging out her hands with a pathetic gesture of entreaty. He did not take them as she half hoped he would; but stood looking at her in a thoughtful silence. Then, "If you care as much as that," he said slowly, "it lies with you not to fling away the thing you care for. Will you please let me see those bills."

"They are on the bureau. You can take them."

She turned again to the mantelpiece, for her lips were not quite steady.

"You were going to tell me about them, perhaps?"

"N—no. I wasn't."

He sighed; and taking up the papers, looked through them absently, too deeply troubled to grasp their contents.

"Are these all?" he asked quietly.

"Nearly all."

"Have you any idea of the total?"

"About six hundred rupees."

A short silence followed, during which she again heard the rustle of paper behind her, and longed for a sight of his face.

"I am afraid this knocks the Lahore week on the head," he said at length. "I am bound to run down for the Polo Tournament, of course; but I can come straight back, and we must do without the rest of it this year."

The incredible words roused Evelyn to open mutiny. Once more she faced him, her head flung backward, a ring of resolve in her voice.

"No, Theo, . . . I *won't* do without the rest of it. *You* don't care, I daresay! So long as you can win the Punjab Cup, nothing else matters. But Christmas week is my only bit of real pleasure in all the cold weather, and I *will* go down for it, . . . what*ever* you say."

Theo Desmond was completely taken aback; and when surprise gave place to speech, his tone suggested the iron hand under the velvet glove.

"My dear little woman, you are talking nonsense. If I find it impossible to manage Lahore, you will remain here. There can be no question about that."

But Evelyn persisted with the courage of despair.

"Then you mustn't find it impossible, . . . that's all! There has been nothing but giving up ever since we came from Murree. I'm sick of it; and I won't give up Christmas week, too. It's quite hard enough for me as it is, being stranded in the most hopeless part of India because of you, without your grudging my few little pleasures as well." And sinking into a chair, she hid her face in her hands.

The victory is more often to the unscrupulous than to the strong. His wife's injustice cut Desmond to the quick. Impulsive renunciation sprang to his lips; and was only checked by the remembrance that he had given Honor his word.

"Evelyn—Evelyn," he pleaded with sudden vehemence, "for Heaven's sake have a little consideration for facts—if you have none for me. I grudge you nothing—I have never done so—and you know it. But—if you really find Frontier life intolerable, I can only give you free leave to go home, directly I scrape together the money for your passage."

"Go home——?" she echoed in blank bewilderment. "What do you mean?"

"What I say."

"But—wouldn't you come too?"

"No. I have no leave due now; and if I had, I couldn't afford to take it."

"You want me to go?" she flashed out in a tremor of apprehension. "I'm only a hindrance to you here. That's the real truth, I suppose?"

"I never said that, and I have given you no grounds for thinking it."

"But do you, Theo—*do* you?"

Her eyes searched his face for confirmation of her suspicion, and found none.

"What I want or don't want is beside the mark," he said. "I naturally wish to see you happy; and as that evidently can't be managed here, I am willing to let you go and be happy elsewhere."

Her eyes fell and her answer came almost in a whisper.

"But I couldn't be happy anywhere else—without you."

"Is that the truth?"

"Yes."

"You'd prefer to stay here—with me?"

"Yes."

He laid his hand for an instant on her bent head.

"Stay then, Ladybird, by all means. Only, for pity's sake, spare me any more of the sort of things you said just now."

"And you won't stop me from going to Lahore, Theo?—Promise."

A swift change of expression crossed his face.

"I can't promise that. I'll do my best not to disappoint you, but I must get all these cleared off before I think of anything else."

"How *can* you manage to clear them off—now?"

"Why trouble your head about side issues? They will all be paid before Christmas; that ought to be enough for you."

"But it's not enough. Tell me what you are going to do—tell me. I won't be pushed on one side like a child."

Desmond frowned.

"Well—if you insist on having it, I am going to sell Diamond."

She started and caught at his arm. For all his matter-of-fact coolness, she knew what those half-dozen words meant to her husband.

"No,—no Theo. Not Diamond! He's the best of them all."

"Exactly. He'll sell quicker and fetch a longer price than any of the others; that's why—he must go."

"But the tournament? Captain Olliver's mad about winning the Cup this year."

"I know that. So am I. I shall manage about a third pony, no fear. Time enough to think of that later. I must go and make out those advertisements."

He set his teeth upon the word and turned to leave her, but her voice arrested him half-way to the door.

"Theo!"

"Well?"

"Are you *sure* there's nothing else that can be done? It—it isn't fair for you to lose the pony you love best, just because of a few dressmakers' bills."

At that his pent-up bitterness slipped from leash.

"Upon my soul, Evelyn, you're right. But there's no other way out of the difficulty, so let's have no more words about it: they don't make things easier to bear."

CHAPTER XIV.

I SIMPLY INSIST.

"The fountains of my hidden life,
Are, through thy friendship, fair."
—EMERSON.

NOT many days later Desmond's advertisements appeared simultaneously in the only two newspapers of Upper India; and he set his face like a flint in anticipation of the universal remonstrance in store for him, when the desperate step he had taken became known to the regiment.

He was captain of the finest polo team on the frontier; the one great tournament of the year—open to every Punjab regiment, horse and foot—would begin in less than a fortnight; and he, who had never parted with a polo pony in his life, was advertising the pick of his stable for sale. A proceeding so unprecedented, so perplexing to all who knew him, could not, in the nature of things, be passed over in silence. Desmond knew—none better—that victory or defeat may hang on the turn of a hair; that, skilled player though he was, the introduction of a borrowed pony, almost at the last moment, into a team trained for months to play in perfect accord was unwise, to say the least of it; knew also that he would be called upon to justify his own unwisdom at so critical a juncture, when all hearts were set on winning the coveted Punjab Cup.

And justification was out of the question,—there lay the sting.

Loyalty to Evelyn sealed his lips; and even the loss of his best-loved pony was less hard to bear than the possibility of being misjudged by his brother officers, whose faith in him had come to be an integral part of his life.

In his present cooler frame of mind he saw that his action had been over-hasty; but with men of vehement temperament, to think is to feel, to feel is to act,—reflection comes last, if it ever comes at all. The first heat of vexation, the discovery of his wife's untrustworthiness and the sacrifice it entailed, had blinded him to all minor considerations.

But these were details that could not be put into words. The thing was done. To put a brave face on it, and to shield Evelyn from the result of her own misdoing—there lay his simple duty in a nutshell. The risk must be accepted, and the Punjab Cup carried off in its despite. This man owed more than he knew to the "beholden face of victory"; to his life-long determination that, no matter what happened, he must conquer.

In the meanwhile immediate issues demanded his full attention.

Harry Denvil, as might be expected, sounded the first note of protest.

He invaded the sacred precincts of his senior's study with audacious lack of ceremony.

"Forgive me, Desmond: but there was no one in the verandah, and I couldn't wait. Of course you know what's in the wind. The Colonel came on that advertisement of yours in 'The Pioneer' just before tiffin, and you should have heard him swear! He showed it to Major Wyndham, and asked: 'Was it a practical joke?' But the Major seemed quite cut up; said he knew nothing about it, and you would probably have good reasons to give. The rest didn't take it so quietly; but of course *I* understood at once. For God's sake, old chap, cancel that confounded advertisement, and take back your eight hundred. I can borrow it again from the *shroff*, just for the present. Anything's better than letting you in for the loss of Diamond at a time like this."

He broke off more from lack of breath than lack of matter; and Desmond, who had risen to cope with the intruder, put both hands upon the Boy's shoulders, a great kindliness softening his eyes.

"My dear Harry, don't distress yourself," he said. "I

appreciate your generosity a good deal more than I care to say. But you are not in any way to blame for the loss of Diamond."

"But, Desmond—I don't understand——"

"There are more things in heaven and earth . . .!" Desmond quoted, smiling. "It's like your impertinence to understand everything at four-and-twenty."

"Oh, shut up!" the other retorted, laughing in spite of himself. "Can't you see I'm in earnest? You don't mean to tell me——?"

"No, Harry, I don't mean to tell you anything about it. I'm not responsible to you for my actions. Stay and have a pipe with me to cool you down a bit. Not another word about my affairs, or I take you by the shoulders and put you outside the door."

Thus much for Denvil. But the rest could not be treated in this summary fashion.

Wyndham put in an appearance at polo that afternoon. He played fitfully; and at other times rode out to the ground, which lay a mile or so beyond the station. To-day it chanced—or possibly Paul so contrived it—that he and Desmond rode home together, a little behind the others.

A low sun stretched out all the hills; distorted the shadows of the riders; and flung a golden pollen of radiance over the barren land.

The habit of silence was strong between these two men; and for a while it lasted unbroken. Desmond was riding his favourite pony, a spirited chestnut Arab, swift as a swallow, sensitive as a child, bearing on his forehead the white star to which he owed his name. The snaffle hung loose upon his neck, and Desmond's hand rested upon the silken shoulder as if in a mute caress. He knew what was coming, and awaited Paul's pleasure with stoical resignation.

Wyndham considered the strong, straight lines of his friend's profile thoughtfully; then he spoke:

"You gave us all rather a shock this morning, Theo."

"I'm sorry for that. I was afraid there'd be some bother about it. But needs must—when the devil drives."

"The devil that drives you is your own incurable pride," Paul answered with unusual warmth. "You know, without forcing me to put it in words, that every rupee I possess is at your service. You might have given me a chance before going such lengths as this."

Desmond shook his head. The man's fastidious soul revolted from the idea of using Paul's money to pay his wife's bills.

"Not in these circumstances," he said. "It wasn't pride that held me back; but a natural sense of the justice and —fitness of things. You must take that on trust, Paul."

"Why, of course, my dear chap. But how about the fitness of parting with that pony just before the tournament? As captain of the team, do you think you are acting quite fairly by the Regiment?"

The shot told. Among soldiers of the best sort the Regiment is apt to be a fetish, and to Desmond the lightest imputation of disregard for its welfare was intolerable.

"Is that how the other fellows look at it?" he asked, a troubled note in his voice.

"Well, if they do, one can hardly blame them. They naturally want to know what you mean to do about the tournament after you have let your best pony go? I take it for granted that you have some sort of plan in your head."

"Yes. I am counting on you to lend me Esmeralda. It's only the 6th now; and if I train her for all I'm worth between this and the 20th, I can get her up to the scratch."

Paul's answering smile was oddly compact of tenderness and humour.

"So that's your notion? You'll deign to make use of me so far? Upon my soul, Theo, you deserve that I should refuse, since you won't give me the satisfaction of doing what would be far more to the purpose."

Desmond looked his friend steadily in the eyes.

"You'll not refuse, though," he said quietly, and Paul shook his head. By way of thanks, Theo laid his hand impulsively upon Wyndham's arm.

"I'm sure you understand, dear old man, that it's not easy or pleasant for me to part with Diamond, or to shut you out and refuse your help; but I can't endure that the rest of them should think me slack or careless of their interests."

"They know you far too well to think anything of the sort. By the way, what arrangements are you making for Lahore?"

"None at all. Honor will go, I daresay; and I shall run down for the polo. But fifteen days' leave is out of the question."

Paul turned sharply in his saddle.

"Now, look here, Theo—you're going too far. I make no offer this time. I simply insist!"

Desmond hesitated. The thought of Evelyn was knocking at his heart.

"You know I hate accepting that sort of thing," he objected, "even from you."

Wyndham laughed.

"That's your peculiar form of selfishness, my dear chap. You want to keep the monopoly of giving in your own hands. Very wholesome for you to have the tables turned. Besides," urged the diplomatist, boldly laying down his trump card, "it would be a great disappointment to your wife not to go down with us all and see the matches."

"Yes. That's just the difficulty."

"I'm delighted to hear it! The Lahore week shall be my Christmas present to her and you; and there's an end of *that* dilemma."

"Thank you, Paul," Desmond said simply. "I'll tell her to-night. Come over to dinner," he added as they parted. "The Ollivers will be there; and I may stand in need of protection."

The sound of music greeted him from the hall, and he found Honor playing alone in the dusk.

"Please go on," he said, as she rose to greet him. "It's what I want more than anything at this moment."

The girl flushed softly, and turned back to the instrument. Any one who had heard her playing before Desmond came in, could scarcely have failed to note the subtle change in its quality. She made of her music a voice of sympathy, evolved from the heart of the great German masters; whose satisfying strength and simplicity—so far removed from the restless questioning of our later day—were surely the outcome of a large faith in God; of the certainty that effort, aspiration, and endurance, despite their seeming futility, can never fail to be very much worth while.

In this fashion Honor reassured her friend to his complete comprehension; and while he sat listening and watching her in the half light, he fell to wondering how it came about that this girl, with her generous warmth of heart, her twofold beauty of the spirit and the flesh, should still be finding her central interest in the lives of others rather than in her own. Was the inevitable awakening over and done with? Or was it yet to come? He inclined to the latter view, and the thought of Paul sprang to his mind. Here, surely, was the one woman worthy of his friend. But then, Paul held strong views about marriage, and it was almost impossible to picture the good fellow in love.

Nevertheless, the good fellow was, at that time, more profoundly, more irrevocably in love than Desmond himself had ever been, notwithstanding the fact of his marriage. His theories had proved mere dust in the balance when weighed against his strong, simple-hearted love for Honor Meredith. Yet the passing of nine months found him no nearer to open recantation. If a man has learnt nothing else by the time he is thirty-eight, he has usually gained possession of his soul, and at no stage of his life had Paul shown the least talent for taking a situation by storm. In the attainment of Honor's friendship, this most modest of men felt himself blest beyond desert; and watch as he might for the least indication of a deeper feeling, he had hitherto watched in vain. It never occurred to him that his peculiarly reticent form of wooing—if wooing it could be called—was hardly calculated to enlighten her as to the state of his heart. He merely reined in his great longing and awaited possible developments; accepting, in all thankfulness, the certain good that was his, and determined not to risk the loss of it without some hope of greater gain.

But of all these things Desmond guessed nothing as he sat, in the dusk of that December evening, speculating on the fate of the girl whose friendship he frankly regarded as one of the goodliest gifts of life.

When at last she rose from the piano, he rose also.

"*Thank* you," he said with quiet emphasis. "How well you understand!"

"Don't let yourself be troubled by anything the Ollivers may say or think," she answered softly. "You are doing your simple duty, Theo, and I am sure Major Wyndham, even without knowing all the facts, will understand quite as well—as I do."

With that she left him, because the fulness of her understanding put a check upon further speech.

That night, when the little party had broken up without open warfare, and Desmond stood alone with his wife before the drawing-room fire, he told her of Wyndham's generosity.

"You'll get your week at Lahore, Ladybird," he said. "And you owe it to Paul. He wishes us to accept the trip as his Christmas present."

"Oh, Theo . . .!" A quick flush revealed her delight at the news, and she made a small movement towards him; but nothing came of it. Six months ago she would have nestled close to him, certain of the tender endearments which had grown strangely infrequent of late. Now an indefinable shyness checked the spontaneous caress, the eager words upon her lips. But her husband, who was looking thoughtfully into the fire, seemed serenely unaware of the fact.

"You're happy about it, aren't you?" he asked at length.

"Yes—of course—very happy."

"That's all right; and I'm glad I wasn't driven to disappoint you. Now get to bed; and sleep soundly on your rare bit of good luck. I have still a lot of work to get through."

She accepted his kindly dismissal with an altogether new docility; and on arriving in her own room gave conclusive proof of her happiness by flinging herself on the bed in a paroxysm of stifled sobbing.

"Oh, if only I had told him sooner!" she lamented through her tears. "Now I don't believe he'll ever really forgive me, or love me properly again."

And, in a measure, she was right. Trust her he might, as in duty bound; but to be as he had been before eating the bitter fruit of knowledge was, for the present at all events, out of his power.

Since their momentous talk nearly a week ago, Evelyn had felt herself imperceptibly held at arms' length, and the vagueness of the sensation increased her discomfort tenfold. No word of reproach had passed his lips, nor any further mention of Diamond or the bills; nothing so quickly breeds constraint between two people as conscious avoidance of a subject that is seldom absent from the minds of both. Yet Theo was scrupulously kind, forbearing, good-tempered—everything, in short, save the tender, lover-like husband he had been to her during the first eighteen months of marriage. And she had only herself to blame,—there lay the sharpest pang of all. Life holds no anodyne for the sorrows we bring upon ourselves.

As the days wore on she watched Theo's face anxiously, at post time, for any sign of an answer to that hateful advertisement; and before the week's end she knew that the punishment that should have been hers had fallen on her husband's shoulders.

Coming into breakfast one morning, she found him studying an open letter with a deep furrow between his brows. At sight of her he started and slipped it into his pocket.

The meal was a silent one. Evelyn found the pattern of her plate curiously engrossing. Desmond, after a few hurried mouthfuls, excused himself and went out. Then Evelyn looked up; and the tears that hung on her lashes overflowed.

"He—he's gone to the stables, Honor," she said brokenly. "He got an answer this morning;—I'm sure he did. But he—he won't tell me anything now. Where's the *use* of being married to him if he's always going on like this? I wish—I wish he could sell—*me* to that man, instead of Diamond. He wouldn't mind it *half* as much——"

And with this tragic announcement—which, for at least five minutes, she implicitly believed—her head went down upon her hands.

Honor soothed her very tenderly, realising that she sorrowed with the despair of a child who sees the world's end in every broken toy.

"Hush—hush!" she remonstrated. "You mustn't think anything so foolish, so unjust. Theo is very magnanimous.

Evelyn. He will see you are sorry, and then it will all go smoothly again."

"But there's the—the other thing," murmured the pretty sinner with a doleful shake of her head. "He won't forgive me that; and he *doesn't* seem to see that I'm sorry. I wanted to tell him this morning, when I saw that letter. But he somehow makes me afraid to say a word about it."

"Better not try yet awhile, dear. When a man is in trouble, there is nothing he thanks one for so heartily as for letting him alone till it is well over."

Evelyn looked up again with a misty smile.

"I can't think why you know so much about men, Honor. How do you find out those sort of things?"

"I suppose it's because I've always cared very much for men,"—she made the statement quite unblushingly. "Loving people is the only sure way of understanding them in the long-run."

"*Is* it? . . . You are clever, Honor. But it doesn't seem to help me much with Theo."

Such prompt, personal application of her philosophy of the heart was a little disconcerting. The girl could not well reply that in love there are a thousand shades, and very few are worthy of the name.

"It *will* help you in time," she said reassuringly. "It is one of the few things that cannot fail. And to-day, at least, you have learnt that when things are going hardly with Theo, it is kindest and wisest to leave him alone."

Evelyn understood this last, and registered a valiant resolve to that effect.

But the day's events gave her small chance of acting on her new-found knowledge. Desmond himself took the initiative: and save for a bare half-hour at tiffin, she saw him no more until the evening.

Perhaps only the man who has trained and loved a polo pony can estimate the pain and rebellion of spirit that he was combating, doggedly and in silence; or condone the passing bitterness he felt towards his uncomprehending wife.

He spent more time than usual in the stables, where Diamond nuzzled into his breast-pocket for slices of apple and sugar; and Diamond's *sais* lifted up his voice and wept, on receipt of an order to start for Pindi with his charge on the following day.

"There is no Sahib like my Sahib in all Hind," he protested, his turban within an inch of Desmond's riding-boot. "The Sahib is my father and my mother! How should we serve a stranger, Hazúr,—the pony and I?"

"Nevertheless, it is an order," Desmond answered not unkindly, "that thou shouldst remain with the pony, sending word from time to time that all goeth well with him. Rise up. It is enough."

Returning to the house, he hardened his heart, and accepted the unwelcome offer from Pindi.

"What a confounded fool I am!" he muttered, as he stamped and sealed the envelope. "I'd sooner shoot the little chap than part with him in this way."

But the letter was posted, nevertheless.

He excused himself from polo, and rode over to Wyndham's bungalow, where he found Paul established in the verandah with his invariable companions—a pipe, and a volume of poetry or philosophy.

"Come along, and beat me at rackets, old man." he said without dismounting. "I'm 'off' polo to-day. We can go for a canter afterwards."

Wyndham needed no further explanation. A glance at Theo's face was enough. They spent four hours together; talked of all things in heaven and earth, except the one sore subject; and parted with a smile of amused understanding.

"Quite like old times!" Paul remarked, and Desmond nodded. For it was a habit, dating from early days, that whenever the pin-pricks of life chafed Theo's impatient spirit, he would seek out his friend, spend an hour or two in his company, and tell him precisely nothing.

Thanks to Paul's good offices, dinner was a pleasanter meal than the earlier ones had been. But Evelyn looked white and woe-begone; and Honor wisely carried her off to bed, leaving Desmond to his pipe and his own discouraging thoughts.

These proved so engrossing that he failed to hear a step in the verandah, and started when two hands came quietly down upon his shoulders.

No need to ask whose they were. Desmond put up his own and caught them in a strong grip.

"Old times again, is it?" he asked, with a short satisfied laugh. "Brought your pipe along?"

"Yes."

"Good business. There's your chair,—it always seems yours to me still. Have a 'peg'?"

Paul shook his head, and drew his chair up to the fire with deliberate satisfaction.

"Light up, then; and we'll make a night of it as we used to do in the days before we learned wisdom, and paid for it in hard cash."

"Talking of hard cash—what price d'you get?" the other asked abruptly."

"Seven-fifty."

"Will that cover everything?"

"Yes."

"Theo,—why, in Heaven's name, won't you cancel this wretched business, and take the money from me instead?"

"Too late now. And, in any case, it's out of the question, for reasons that you would be the first to appreciate—if you knew them."

"But look here—suppose I do know——"

Desmond lifted a peremptory hand.

"Whatever you think you know, for God's sake don't put it into words. I'm bound to go through with this, Paul, in the only way that seems right to me. Don't make it harder than it is already. Besides," he added, with a brisk change of tone, "this is modern history! We're pledged to old times to-night."

Evelyn's fantastic French clock struck three, in silver tones, before the two men parted.

"It's an ill wind that blows no good, after all!" Desmond remarked, as he stood in a wide splash of moonlight on the verandah steps. "I feel ten years younger since the morning. Come again soon, dear old man; it's always good to see you."

And Paul Wyndham, riding homeward under the myriad lamps of heaven, thanked God, in his simple devout fashion, for the courage and constancy of his friend's heart.

CHAPTER XV.

GOOD ENOUGH, ISN'T IT?

"One crowded hour of glorious life."
—SCOTT.

THE dusty parade-ground of Mian Mir, Lahore's military cantonment, vibrated from end to end with a rising tide of excitement.

On all sides of the huge square eight thousand spectators, of every rank and race and colour, were wedged into a compact mass forty or fifty deep: while in the central space, eight ponies scampered, scuffled, and skidded in the wake of a bamboo-root polo-ball; their hoofs rattling like hailstones on the hard ground.

And close about them—as close as boundary flags and distracted native policemen would permit—pressed that solid wall of onlookers—soldiers, British and native, from thirty regiments at least; officers, in uniform and out of it; ponies and players of defeated teams, manfully resigned to the "fortune o' war," and not forgetful of the obvious fluke by which their late opponents had scored the game; official dignitaries, laying aside dignity for the occasion; drags, phaetons, landaus, and dog-carts, gay as a summer parterre in a wind, with the restless parasols and bonnets of half the women in the Punjab; scores and scores of *saises*, betting freely on the match, arguing, shouting, or shampooing the legs of ponies, whose turn was yet to come; and through all the confused hubbub of laughter, cheering, and mercifully incoherent profanity, a British infantry band hammering out with insular assurance, "We'll fight and we'll conquer again and again."

It was the last day of the old year—a brilliant Punjab December day—and the last "chukker" of the final match for the Cup was in full progress. It lay between the Punjab Cavalry from Kohat and a crack Hussar team, fresh from Home and Hurlingham, mounted on priceless ponies, six to each man, and upheld by an overweening confidence that they were bound to "sweep the board." They had swept it accordingly; and although anticipating "a tough tussle with those game 'Piffer'[1] chaps," were disposed to look upon the Punjab Cup as their own property for at least a year to come.

Desmond and his men—Olliver and two native officers—knew all this well enough; knew also that money means pace, and weight, and a liberal supply of fresh mounts, and frankly recognised that the odds were heavily against them. But there remained two points worth considering they had been trained to play in perfect unison, horse and man · and they were all in deadly earnest.

They had fought their way, inch by inch, through the tournament to this final tie; and it had been a glorious fight so far. The Hussars, whose self-assurance had led them to underrate the strength of the enemy, were playing now like men possessed. The score stood at two goals all, and electric shocks of excitement tingled through the crowd.

Theo Desmond was playing "back," as a wise captain should, to guard the goal and ensure the completest control over his team; and his mount was a chestnut Arab with three white stockings and a star upon his forehead.

This unlooked-for circumstance requires explanation.

A week earlier, on returning from his morning ride to the bungalow where Paul and his own party were staying, Desmond had been confronted by Diamond in a brand-new saddle-cloth marked with his initials; while Diamond's *sais*, with a smile that displayed every tooth in his head, salaamed to the ground.

"Well, I'm shot!" he exclaimed. "Dunni,—what's the meaning of this?

The man held out a note in Colonel Buchanan's hand-

[1] Abbreviation of Punjab Irregular Frontier Force.

writing. Desmond dismounted, flung an arm over the Arab's neck, and opened the note with a strange quickening of his breath.

The Colonel stated, in a few friendly words, that as Diamond was too good a pony to be allowed to go out of the Regiment, he and his brother officers had decided to buy him back for the Polo Club. Major Wilkinson of the Loyal Monmouth had been uncommonly decent over the whole thing; and, as captain of the team, Desmond would naturally have the use of Diamond during the tournament, and afterwards, except when he happened to be away on leave.

It took him several minutes to grasp those half dozen lines of writing; and if the letters grew indistinct as he read, he had small cause to be ashamed of the fact.

On looking up, he found Paul watching him from the verandah; and dismissing the *sais* he sprang up the steps at a bound.

"Paul,—was it your notion?"

But the other smiled and shook his head.

"Brilliant inspirations are not in my line, old chap. It was Mrs Olliver. She and the Colonel did most of it between them, though we're all implicated, of course; and I don't know when I've seen the Colonel so keen about anything in his life."

"God bless you all!" Desmond muttered under his breath. "I'm bound to win the Cup for you after this."

And now, as the final "chukker" of the tournament drew to a close, it did indeed seem that the ambition of many years was on the eve of fulfilment. Excitement rose higher every minute. Cheers rang out on the smallest provocation. General sympathy was obviously with the Frontier team, and the suspense of the little contingent from Kohat had risen to a pitch beyond speech.

All the native officers and men who could get leave for the great occasion formed a picturesque group in the forefront of the crowd; Rajinder Singh towering in their midst, his face set like a mask; his eyes fierce with the lust of victory. Evelyn Desmond, installed beside Honor in a friend's dog-cart, sat with her small hands clenched, her face flushed to the temples, disjointed murmurs breaking from her at intervals. Honor sat very still and silent, gripping the iron bar of the box-seat, her whole soul centred on the game. Paul Wyndham, who had mounted the step on her side of the cart, and whose hand clasped the bar within half an inch of hers, had not spoken since the ponies last went out; and to all appearance his concentration equalled her own. But her nearness affected him as the proximity of iron affects the needle of a compass, deflecting his thoughts and eyes continually from the central point of interest.

And what of Frank Olliver?

Her effervescent spirit can only be likened to champagne just before the cork flies off. Perched upon the front seat of a drag, with Colonel Buchanan, she noted every stroke and counter-stroke, every point gained and lost, with the practised knowledge of a man, and the one-sided ardour of a woman. She had already cheered herself hoarse; but still kept up a running fire of comment, emphasised by an occasional pressure of the Colonel's coat-sleeve, to the acute discomfiture of that self-contained Scot.

"We'll not be far off the winning post now," she assured him at this juncture. "Our ponies are playing with their heads entirely, and the others are losing theirs because of the natives and the cheering. There goes the ball straight for the boundary again!—Well done, Geoff! But the long fellow's caught it—Saints alive! 'Twould have been a goal but for Theo. How's *that* for a fine stroke, now?"

For Desmond, with a clean, splitting smack, had sent the ball flying across three-fourths of the ground.

"Mind the goal!" he shouted to his half-back, Alla Dad Khan, as Diamond headed after the ball like a lightning streak, with three racers—maddened by whip and spur and their own delirious excitement—clattering upon his tail; and a fusilade of clapping, cheers, and yells broke out on all sides.

The ball, checked in mid career, came spinning back to them with the force of a rifle-bullet. The speed had been terrific, and the wrench of pulling up wrought dire confusion. Followed a sharp scrimmage, a bewildering jumble of horses and men, rattling of sticks and unlimited breaking of the third commandment; till the ball shot out again into the open, skimming, like a live thing, through a haze of fine white dust, Desmond close upon it, as before; the Hussar "forwards" in hot pursuit.

But their "back" was ready to receive the ball, and Desmond along with it. Both players struck simultaneously. Their cane-handled sticks met with a crack that was heard all over the ground. Then the ball leapt clean through the goal-posts, the head of Desmond's stick leapt after it, and the crowd scattered right and left before a thundering onrush of ponies. Cheer upon cheer, yell upon yell, went up from eight thousand throats at once. British soldiers flung their helmets in the air; the band lost its head and broke into a triumphant clash of discord; while Colonel Buchanan, forgetful of his Scottish decorum, stood up in the drag and shouted like any subaltern.

He was down in the thick of the *melée*, ready to greet Desmond as he rode off the battlefield, a breathless unsightly victor, covered with dust and glory.

"Stunningly played—the whole lot of you!"

"Thank you, sir. Good enough, isn't it?"

A vigorous handshake supplied the rest; and Desmond trotted forward to the dog-cart, where Evelyn greeted him with a rush of congratulation. Honor had no word, but Desmond found her eyes and smile sufficiently eloquent.

"Best fight, bar none, I ever had in my life!" he declared by way of acknowledgment. "We're all off to the B.C. Mess as soon as the L.G. has presented the Cup, and we've got some of the dust out of our throats. Come along, Paul, old man."

And he went his way in such elation of spirits as a captain may justly feel whose team has carried off the Punjab Cup in the face of overwhelming odds.

CHAPTER XVI.

SIGNED AND SEALED.

" Leave the dead moments to bury their dead;
Let us kiss, and break the spell."
—OWEN MEREDITH.

THE Fancy Ball, given on Old Year's night by the Punjab Commission, was, in Evelyn's eyes, the supreme event of the week; and when Desmond, after a mad gallop from the Bengal Cavalry Mess, threw open his bedroom door, he was arrested by a vision altogether unexpected, and altogether satisfying to his fastidious taste.

A transformed Evelyn stood before the long glass, wrapt in happy contemplation of her own image. From the fillet across her forehead, with its tremulous wire antennæ, to the sandalled slipper that showed beneath her silken draperies, all was gold. Two shimmering wings of gauze sprang from her shoulders; her hair, glittering with gold dust, waved to her waist; and a single row of topaz gleamed on the pearl tint of her throat like drops of wine.

"By Jove, Ladybird,—how lovely you look!"

She started, and turned upon him a face of radiance.

"I'm the Golden Butterfly. Do you like me, Theo, really?"

"I do;—no question. Where on earth did you get it all?"

"At Simla, last year. Muriel Walter invented it for me." Her colour deepened, and she lowered her eyes. "I didn't show it to you before,—because——"

"Yes, yes,—I know what you mean. Don't distress

yourself over that. You'll have *your* triumph to-night, Ladybird! Remember my dances, please, when you're besieged by the other fellows! Upon my word, you look such a perfect butterfly that I shall hardly dare lay a hand on you!"

"You may dare, though," she said softly. "I won't break in pieces if you do."

Shy invitation lurked in her look and tone; but apparently her husband failed to perceive it.

"I'll put you to the test later on," he said, with an amused laugh. "I must go now, and translate myself into Charles Surface, or I'll be late."

Left alone again, she turned back to her looking-glass and sighed; but a single glance at it comforted her surprisingly.

"He was in a hurry," she reflected, by way of further consolation, "and I've got four dances with him after all."

Theo Desmond inscribed few names on his programme beyond those of his wife, Mrs Olliver, and Honor Meredith.

"You must let me have a good few dances, Honor," he said to her, "and hang Mrs Grundy! We are outsiders here, and you and I understand one another."

She surrendered her programme with smiling submission. "Do you always order people to give you dances in that imperative fashion?"

"Only when I'm set on having them, and daren't risk refusal! I'll go one better than Paul, if I may. I didn't know he had it in him to be so grasping."

And he returned the card on which the initials P. W. appeared four times in Wyndham's neat handwriting.

Never, in all his days had Paul asked a woman to give him four dances; and as he claimed Honor for the first of them, he wondered whether his new-found boldness would carry him farther still. Her beauty and graciousness, her enthusiasm over the afternoon's triumph, exalted him from the sober levels of patience and modesty to unscaled heights of aspiration. But not until their second valse together did an opening for speech present itself.

They had deserted the packed moving mass, in whose midst dancing was little more than a promenade under difficulties, and stood aside in an alcove that opened off the ballroom.

"Look at Evelyn. Isn't she charming in that dress?" Honor exclaimed, as the Golden Butterfly whirled past, like an incarnate sunbeam, in her husband's arms. "I feel a Methuselah when I see how freshly and rapturously she is enjoying it all. This is my seventh Commission Ball, Major Wyndham! No doubt most people think it high time I hid my diminished head in England. But my head refuses to feel diminished,"—she lifted it a little in speaking,—"and I prefer to remain where I am."

"On the Border?"

"Yes. On the Border for choice."

"You were keen to get there, I remember," he said, restraining his eagerness. "And you are not disappointed, after nine months of it?"

"Disappointed?—I think they have been almost the best months of my life."

She spoke with sudden fervour, looking straight before her into the brilliant, shifting crowd.

Paul's pulses quickened. He saw possibilities ahead.

"Do you mean——? Would you be content to live there—for good?"

His tone caught her attention, and she turned to him with disconcerting directness of gaze.

"Yes," she said quietly, "I would be quite content to live on the Frontier—with John, if only he would have me. Now we might surely go on dancing, Major Wyndham."

Paul put his arm about her in silence. His time had not yet come; and he took up his burden of waiting again, if with less hope, yet with undiminished resolve.

Honor, meanwhile, had leisure to wonder whether she had imagined that new note in his voice. If not,—and if he were to repeat the question in a more definite form—how should she answer him?

In truth she could not tell. Sincere admiration is not always easy to distinguish from love of a certain order. But Paul's bearing through the remainder of the dance convinced her that she must have been mistaken, and she dismissed the subject from her mind.

Leaving her in charge of Desmond, Wyndham slipped on his greatcoat, and spent half an hour pacing to and fro, in the frosty darkness, spangled with keen stars. Here, forgetful of expectant partners, he took counsel with his cigar and his own sadly sobered heart. More than once he asked himself why those months on the Frontier had been among the best in Honor Meredith's life. The fervour of her tone haunted him with uncomfortable persistence; yet, had he put the question to her, it is doubtful whether she could have given him a definite answer, even if she would.

But although the lights and music and laughter had lost their meaning for him, the great ball of the year went forward merrily in regular alternations of sound and silence, of motion and quiescence, to its appointed end.

It was during one of the intervals, when eye and ear enjoyed a passing respite from the whirling wheel of things, that Desmond, coming out of the cardroom—where he had been enjoying a rubber and a cigarette—caught sight of a gleaming figure standing alone in the pillared entrance to the Hall, and hurried across the deserted ballroom. His wife looked pathetically small and unprotected in the wide emptiness of the archway, and the corners of her mouth quivered as though tears were not far off.

"Oh, Theo,—I *am* glad!" she said as he reached her side. "I wanted you—long ago, but I couldn't find you anywhere in the crowd."

"What's the trouble, little woman?" he asked. "Quite surprising to see you unappropriated. Any one been bothering you?"

"Yes — a man. One of the stewards introduced him——"

The ready fire flashed in his eyes.

"Confound him! Where is he? What did he do?"

"Nothing—very much. Only—I didn't like it. Come and sit down somewhere and I'll tell you."

She slipped her hand under his arm, and pressed close to him as they sought out a seat between the rows of glass-fronted book-shelves in which the Lawrence Hall library is housed.

"Here you are," he said. "Sit down and tell me exactly what happened."

She glanced nervously at his face, which had in it a touch of sternness that recalled their painful interview three weeks ago.

"I—I don't think he really knew what he was talking about," she began, her eyes on the butterfly fan, which she opened and shut mechanically while speaking. "He began by saying that fancy balls were quite different to other ones; that the real fun of them was that every one could say and do just what they pleased, and nothing mattered at all. He said his own dress was specially convenient, because no one could expect a Pierrot to be responsible for his actions. Then he—he said that by coming as a butterfly I had given every man in the room the right to—to catch me if he could. Wasn't that hateful?"

"Curse him!" muttered Desmond under his breath. "Well—was that all?"

She shook her head with a rueful smile.

"I don't half like telling you, Theo; you look so stern. I'm afraid you'll be very angry."

"*Not* with you, dear. Go on."

"Well, I told him I didn't see it that way at all, and he said of course not; butterflies never *did* see that people had any right to catch them; yet they got caught all the same. Then he took tight hold of my hands, and came so close to me that—I was frightened, and asked him to take me back to the ballroom at once. He said it wasn't fair, that the whole twelve minutes belonged to him, and he wouldn't be cheated out of any of it. Then when I was getting up to go away, he—he laughed, and put his arm round me, so that I couldn't move, though I tried to—I did, truly."

At that her husband's arm went round her, and she yielded with a sigh of satisfaction to its protective pressure.

"The brute didn't dare to—kiss you, did he, Ladybird?"

"Oh, no—no. The music began, and some people came by, and he had to let me go. Do men often behave like that at balls, Theo?"

"Well—no; not the right sort!" Desmond answered, a gleam of amusement in his eyes. "But there's always a good sprinkling of the wrong sort in a crowd of this kind, and the stewards ought to be more careful."

"The trouble is that—I gave him two dances. The next one is his, and I *can't* dance with him again. That's why I so badly wanted to find you. Listen, they're tuning up now. Must I go and sit in the ladies' room till it's over?"

"Certainly not. Come out and dance it with me."

"Can I? How lovely! I was afraid you were sure to be engaged."

"Of course I am. But as you happen to need me, that doesn't count."

She leaned forward suddenly, and gave him one of her quick, half-shy kisses, that were still so much more like the kisses of a child than of a woman grown. "It is nice to belong to a man like you," she murmured caressingly. "You really are a dear, Theo! And after I've been so bad to you, too!"

"What's forgiven should be forgotten, Ladybird," he answered, tightening the arm that held her. "So that's a closed subject between us,—you understand? Only remember, there must be *no more* of that sort of thing. Do you want the compact signed and sealed?" he added, smiling.

"Yes—I do." And he sealed it accordingly.

Two bright tears glistened on her lashes, for she had the grace to realise that she was being blessed and trusted beyond her deserts. A sudden impulse assailed her to tell him everything—now, while his forgiveness enfolded her and gave her a transitory courage. But habit, and dread of losing the surpassing sweetness of reconciliation sealed her lips; and her poor little impulse went to swell the sum of unaccomplished things.

He frowned at sight of her mute signals of distress.

"No, no, little woman. That's forbidden also! Come along out; and if that cad attempts to interfere with us, I'll send him to the right about effectually, I promise you."

"But who *is* your real partner?" she asked, as they rose to go.

"You are,—who else? My permanent partner!" he answered, smiling down upon her. "I haven't a notion who the other is. Let's stop under this lamp and see."

He consulted his card, and his face clouded for a moment.

"It's Honor! That's rough luck. But at least one can tell her the truth, and feel sure she'll understand. There she is by that pillar, wondering what has come to me. Jove! How splendid she looks to-night! I wish the Major could set eyes on her."

The girl's tall figure, in its ivory and gold draperies, showed strikingly against a mass of evergreens, and the simple dignity of the dress she had herself designed emphasised the queenly element in her beauty.

"Did you think I had deserted you altogether?" Desmond asked, as they drew near.

"I knew you would come the first moment you could."

"You have a large faith in your friends, Honor."

"I have a very large faith—in you!" she answered simply.

"That's good hearing. But I hardly deserve it at this minute. I have come to ask if I may throw you over for Ladybird?" And in a few words he explained the reason of his strange request.

One glance at Evelyn's face told Honor that the untoward incident had dispelled the last shadow of restraint between husband and wife; and the loss of a dance with Theo seemed a small price to pay for so happy a consummation.

The valse was in full swing now,—a kaleidoscopic confusion of colour, shifting into fresh harmonies with every bar; four hundred people circling ceaselessly over a surface as of polished steel.

Desmond guided his wife along the edge of the crowd till they came again to the pillared entrance. Here, where it was possible to stand back a little from the dancers, they were confronted by a thick-set, heavy-faced man wearing the singularly inept-looking costume of a Pierrot. Face and carriage proclaimed that he had enjoyed his dinner very thoroughly before setting out for the ball; and Evelyn's small shudder fired the fighting blood in Desmond's veins. It needed an effort of will not to greet his unsuspecting opponent with a blow between the eyes. But instead, he stood his ground and awaited developments.

The man bestowed upon Evelyn a bow of exaggerated politeness, which italicised his scant courtesy towards her partner.

"There's some mistake here," he said bluntly. "This is *my* dance with Mrs Desmond, and I've missed too much of it already."

"Mrs Desmond happens to be my wife," Theo made answer with ominous quietness. "I don't choose that she should be insulted by her partners; and I am dancing this with her myself."

The incisive tone, low as it was, penetrated the man's muddled brain. His blustering assurance collapsed visibly, increasing fourfold his ludicrous aspect. He staggered backward, muttering incoherent words that might charitably be construed as apology, and passed on into the library, making an ineffectual effort to combine an air of dignified indifference with the uncertain gait of a landsman in a heavy sea.

Desmond stood looking after him as he went in mingled pity and contempt; but Evelyn's eyes never left her husband's face.

His smouldering anger, and the completeness of his power to protect her by a few decisive words, thrilled her with a new, inexplicable intensity,—an emotion that startled her a little, and in the same breath lifted her to an unreasoning height of happiness.

Unconsciously she pressed close against him as he put his arm round her.

"You're all safe now, my Ladybird," he said with a low laugh. "And honour is satisfied, I suppose! The creature wasn't worth knocking down, though I could hardly keep my fists off him at the start."

And he swept her forthwith into the heart of the many-coloured crowd.

The valse was more than half over now, and as the music slackened to its close some two hundred couples vanished into the surrounding dimness, each intent on their own few minutes of enjoyment. Evelyn Desmond, flushed, silent, palpitating, remained standing at her husband's side, till they were left practically alone under one of the many arches that surround the great hall.

"That was much too short, wasn't it?" he said. "Now we must go and look up Honor, and see that she is not left in the lurch."

At that she raised her eyes, and the soft shining in them lent a quite unusual beauty to her face.

"Must we, Theo,—really? Honor's sure to be all right, and I'm so badly wanting to sit out—with you."

"Are you, really? That's a charming confession to hear from one's wife. You look different to-night, Ladybird. What's come to you?"

"I don't know," she murmured truthfully; adding so low that he could barely catch the words, "Only—I don't seem ever to have understood—till just now how much—I really care——"

"Why,—*Evelyn!*"

Sheer surprise checked further speech, and with a man's instinctive sense of reserve he looked hastily round to make sure that they were alone.

She misread his silence, and slipped a hand under his arm.

"You're not angry, are you—that I—didn't understand sooner?"

"Good heavens, no!"

"Then come—please come. Honor gave me the whole dance. Besides—look!—there she goes with Major Wyndham. She's always happy with him!"

Desmond smiled. "That's true enough. No need for us if Paul is in the field. Come this way, Ladybird. I know the Lawrence Hall of old."

They sought and found a sofa in a retired, shadowy corner.

"That's ever so nice," she said simply. "Sit down there."

He obeyed, and there was a momentary silence between them. Then the emotion astir within her swept all before it. Turning suddenly, she flung both arms round his neck and hid her face upon his shoulder, her breath coming in short, dry sobs, like the breath of an overwrought child.

Very tenderly, as one who touches that which he fears to bruise or break, he drew her close to him, his own pulses quickened by a remembrance of the words that gave the clue to her strange behaviour, and during those few minutes between dance and dance, Evelyn Desmond arrived at a truer knowledge of the man she had married, in the girlish ignorance of mere fascination, than two years of life with him had brought to her half-awakened heart.

CHAPTER XVII.

YOU WANT TO GO!

"White hands cling to the tightened rein,
  Slipping the spur from the booted heel,
Tenderest voices cry 'Turn again!'
  Red lips tarnish the scabbarded steel.
High hopes faint on a warm hearth-stone;
He travels the fastest who travels alone."

—KIPLING.

FOR the first six weeks of the new year life flowed serenely enough in the bungalow on the mound.

Relieved of the greater part of her burden, and re-established in her husband's heart, Evelyn Desmond blossomed like a flower under the quickening influences of spring. Light natures develop best in sunshine: and so long as life asked no hard things of her, Evelyn could be admirably sweet-tempered and self-forgetful—even to the extent of curbing her weakness for superfluous hats and gloves and shoes. A genuine sacrifice, this last, if not on a very high plane. But the limits of such natures are set, and their feats of virtue or vice must be judged accordingly.

To Honor, whose very real sympathy was infallibly tinged with humour, the bearing of this regenerate Evelyn suggested a spoilt child who, having been scolded and forgiven, is disposed to be heroically, ostentatiously good till next time; and her goodness at least was whole-hearted while it lasted. She made a genuine effort to handle the reins of the household: waxed zealous over Theo's socks and shirts; and sang to his accompaniment in the evenings. Her zest for the tennis-courts waned. She joined Frank and Honor in their frequent rides to the polo-ground, and Kresney found himself unceremoniously discarded like a programme after a dance.

Wounded vanity did not improve his temper, and the ever-present Linda suffered accordingly. For Kresney, though little given to the weakness of generosity, never failed to share his grievances liberally with those about him.

"What is this that has come to little Mrs Desmond?" he demanded one evening on a querulous note of injury. "Whenever I ask her to play tennis now she always manages to be engaged. I suppose, because they have won that confounded Punjab Cup, she thinks she must give herself airs like the rest of them. But I tell you what, Linda, we have got to make her understand that she is not going to get money out of us, and then chuck us in the dirt like a pair of old gloves,—you see? You must tell her you are in a hole now, because of that three hundred rupees; that you have been forced to get cash from me to go on with, and to let me know about your little business with her; and you are afraid I may refer the matter to her husband. It would bring his cursed pride down with a run if he knew that his wife had practically borrowed money from me, and he could say nothing against *us* for helping her. It is she who would suffer; and I am not keen to push her into a hot corner if she can be made to behave decently enough to suit me. So just let her know that I will make no trouble about it so long as she is friendly, like she used to be. Then you can ask her to tea; and I bet you five rupees she accepts on the spot!"

Meantime Evelyn Desmond went on her way, in ignorance of the forces that were converging to break up her newly-gotten peace of mind. For the time being her world was filled and bounded by her husband's personality. The renewal of his tenderness and his trust in her eclipsed all the minor troubles of life: and with the unthinking optimism of her type she decided that these would all come right somehow, some time, sooner or later.

What Desmond himself thought did not transpire.

Evelyn's happiness gave him real satisfaction; and if he were already beginning to be aware that his feeling for her left the innermost depths of his nature unstirred, he never acknowledged the fact. A certain refinement of loyalty forbade him to discuss his wife, even with himself. Her ineffectualness and the clinging quality of her love made an irresistible appeal to the vein of chivalry which ran, like a thread of gold, through the man's nature; and if he could not forget, he could at least try not to remember, that her standard of uprightness differed widely and radically from his own.

When Kresney's tactics resulted in a partial revival of her friendliness towards him, Desmond accepted the fact with the best grace he could muster. Since his promise to the man made definite objection impossible, he decided that the matter must be left to the disintegration of time; and if Kresney could have known how the necessity chafed Desmond's pride and fastidiousness of spirit, the knowledge would have added relish to his enjoyment of Evelyn's society.

Thus the passing of uneventful days brought them to the middle of February—to the end of the short, sharp Northern winter, and the first far-off whisper of the wrath to come; brought also to Honor Meredith a sudden perception that her year with the Desmonds was very nearly at an end. John's latest letter announced that he hoped to get back to the life and work he loved by the middle of April; and the girl read that letter with such strangely mixed feelings that she was at once puzzled and angered by her own seeming inconsistency. John had always stood unquestionably first in her life. It would be altogether good to have him with her again—to be able to devote herself to him entirely as she had dreamed of doing for so many years. And yet. . . . There was no completing the broken sentence, which, for some unaccountable reason, ended in a sigh.

Honor was sitting at the time in her favourite corner of the drawing-room, on a low settee constructed out of an empty case, cunningly hid, and massed with cushions of dull red and gold. As her lips parted in that unjustifiable sigh she looked round at the familiar pictures and hangings;

at Desmond's well-worn chair, and the table beside it with his pipe-rack, a photo of his father, and half a dozen favourite books; at the graceful outline of Evelyn's figure where she stood by the wide mantelshelf arranging roses in a silver bowl, her head tilted to one side, a shaft of sunlight from one of the slits of windows, fifteen feet up the wall. turning her soft fair hair to gold.

From Evelyn's figure, Honor's glance travelled to the photograph of Desmond on the piano, and lingered there with a softened thoughtfulness of gaze. What deep roots she had struck down into the lives of these two since her first sight of that picture! A year ago the man had been a mere name to her; and now——

The clatter of hoofs, followed by Desmond's voice in the verandah, snapped the thread of her thought, and roused Evelyn from the contemplation of her roses.

"Theo *is* back early!" she exclaimed: and on the words he entered the room, elation in every line of him, an unusual light in his eyes.

"What *has* happened to make you look like that?" she asked. "Somebody left you a fortune?"

Desmond laughed, with a peculiar ring of enjoyment.

"No fear! Fortunes don't grow hereabouts! But we've had stirring news this morning. A big party of Afridis has crossed the Border and fired a village, murdering and looting cattle and women on a very daring scale. The whole garrison is under orders for a punitive expedition. We shall be off in ten days, if not sooner."

Evelyn's colour ebbed while he was speaking, and she made a quick movement towards him. But Desmond taking her shoulders between his hands, held her at arm's length, and confronted her with steadfastly smiling eyes.

"No, no, Ladybird—you're going to be plucky and stand up to this like a soldier's wife, for my sake. The Frontier's been abnormally quiet these many months. It will do us all good to have a taste of real work for a change."

"Do you mean . . . will there be much . . . fighting?"

"Well—the Afridis don't take a blow sitting down. We have to burn their crops, you see; blow up their towers; enforce heavy fines, and generally knock it into their heads that they can't defy the Indian Government with impunity. Yes; it means fighting—severe or otherwise, according to their pleasure."

"Pleasure!—It sounds simply horrible; and you—I believe you're *glad* to go!"

"Well, my dear, what else would you have? Not because I'm murderously inclined," he added smiling. "Every soldier worth his salt is glad of a chance to do the work he's paid for. But that's one of the things I shall never teach you to understand!"

Evelyn turned hurriedly back to her roses. Her throat felt uncomfortably dry, and two tears had escaped in spite of herself.

"How long will you be gone?" she asked, addressing her question to the flowers.

"A month or six weeks. Not longer."

"But won't any one be left to guard the station? In this horrible place we women don't seem to count a bit. You all rush off after a lot of stupid Afridis."

"Not quite all. An infantry regiment will come up from Pindi: and we leave Paul's squadron behind. Just like his luck to be out of it, poor old man. But six weeks will be gone in no time. This sort of thing is part and parcel of our life up here. You're not going to fret about it, Ladybird—are you?"

He turned her face gently towards him. To his astonishment eager entreaty shone through her tears, and she caught his hand between her own.

"No, Theo, I needn't fret, because—if somebody has to stay—it can just as easily be you. You're married and Major Wyndham isn't."

Desmond stepped back a pace, incredulous anger in his eyes. "Evelyn! Are you crazy? It's not the habit of British officers to sneak behind their wives when they're wanted at the front. It comes hard on you: but it's the price a woman pays for marrying a soldier and there's no shirking it——"

For answer she clung to his hand, pressing it close against her heart. Instinctively she understood the power of her weakness, and exercised it to the full. Perhaps, also, an undefined fear of Kresney gave her courage to persist; and the least mention of the man's name at that instant might have averted many things.

"Only this time, please," she murmured, bringing the beseeching softness of her eyes and lips very close to his set face. "You'll be sorry afterwards if you leave me alone —just now."

"Why just now? Besides, you won't be alone. You will have Honor."

"Yes. But I want you. It has all been so lovely since Christmas. Theo—darling,—I *can't* let you go, and—and perhaps be killed by those horrid Afridis. Every one knows how brave you are. They would never think you shirked the fighting. And Major Wyndham would do anything you asked him. Will you—*will* you?"

Desmond's mouth hardened to a dogged line, and he drew a little away from her; because her entreaty and the disturbing nearness of her face made resistance harder than he dared allow her to guess.

"My dear little woman, you haven't the smallest notion what you are asking of me. I never bargained for throwing up active service on your account; and I'll not give the fellows a chance to insult you by flinging marriage in my teeth."

"That means—you insist on going?"

"My dear—I can do nothing else."

She threw his hand from her with a choking sob.

"Very well, then, go—go! I know, now, that you don't really—care, in your heart—whatever you may say."

And turning again to the mantelpiece, she laid her head upon her arms.

For a few moments Desmond stood regarding her, a great pain and tenderness in his eyes.

"It is rather cruel of you to put it that way, Ladybird," he said gently. "Can't you see that this isn't a question—of caring, but simply of doing my duty? Won't you try and help me, instead of making things harder for us both?"

He passed his hand caressingly over her hair, and a little shiver of misery went through her at this touch.

"It's all very well to talk grandly about duty," she answered in a smothered voice. "And it's no use pretending to love me—when you won't do anything I ask. But—you *want* to go."

Desmond sighed, and instinctively glanced across at Honor for a confirmation of his resolve not to let tenderness undermine his sense of right. But that which he saw banished all thought of his own heartache.

She sat leaning a little forward, her hands clasped tightly over Meredith's letter, her face white and strained, her eyes luminous as he had never yet seen them.

For the shock of his unexpected news had awakened her roughly, abruptly to a very terrible truth. Since his entrance into the room she had seen her phantom palace of friendship fall about her like a house of cards; had seen, rising from its ruins, that which her brain and will refused to recognise, but which every pulse in her body confirmed beyond possibility of doubt.

Desmond's eyes looking anxiously into hers, roused her to a realisation of her urgent need to be alone with her incredible discovery. Her lips lost their firmness; the hot colour surged into her cheeks; and smoothing out John's letter with uncertain fingers, she rose to her feet.

But in rising she swayed unsteadily; and in an instant Desmond was beside her. He had never before seen this girl's composure shaken, and it startled him.

"Honor, what has upset you so?" he asked in a low tone. "Not bad news of John?" For he had recognised the writing.

She shook her head, fearing the sound of her own voice, and his unfailing keenness of perception.

"You must be ill, then. I was afraid you were going to faint just now. Come into the dining-room and have a glass of wine."

She acquiesced in silence. It would be simplest to let him attribute her passing weakness to physical causes. And she went forward blindly, resolutely, with a proud lift of her chin, never looking at him once.

He walked beside her, bewildered and distressed, refraining from speech till she should be more nearly mistress of herself, and lightly holding her arm, because she was so evidently in need of support. She tightened her lips and mastered an imperious impulse to free herself from his touch. His unspoken solicitude unnerved her; and a sigh of pure relief escaped her when he set her down upon a chair, and went over to the sideboard for some wine.

She sipped it slowly, supporting her head, and at the same time shielding her eyes from his troubled scrutiny. He sat beside her, on the table's edge, and waited till the wine-glass was half empty before he spoke.

"Did you feel at all ill this morning? I'll go for Mackay at once to make sure there's nothing wrong."

"No—no." There was a touch of impatience in her tone. "Please don't bother. It is nothing. It will pass."

"I didn't mean to vex you," he answered humbly. "But you are not the sort of woman who goes white to the lips for nothing. Either you are ill, or you are badly upset. You promised John to let me take his place while he was away, and if you are in any trouble or difficulty,—don't shut me out. You have done immensely much for both of us. Give me the chance to do a little for you. Remember, Honor," his voice took a deeper note of feeling, "you are more to me than the Major's sister or Ladybird's friend. You are mine, too. Won't you tell me what's wrong?"

At that she pulled herself together and faced him with a brave semblance of a smile.

"I am very proud to be your friend, Theo. But there are times when the truest friendship is just to stand on one side and ask no questions. That is what I want you to do now. Please believe that if you could help me, even a little, I would not shut you out."

"I believe you—and I'll not say another word. You will go and lie down, perhaps, till tiffin time?"

"No. I think I will go to Ladybird. She badly needs comforting. You broke your news to us rather abruptly, you know. We are not hardened yet, like Frank, to the boot-and-saddle life here."

"I'm sorry. It was thoughtless of me. We are all so used to it. One's apt to forget——"

He rose and took a few steps away from her; then, returning, stood squarely before her. She had risen also, partly to prove her own strength, and partly to put an end to the strain of being alone with him.

'Honor," he asked, "was I hard with Ladybird? And am I an unpardonable brute if I insist on holding out against her?"

"Indeed, no! You mustn't dream of doing anything else."

She looked full at him now, forgetful of herself in concern for him.

"I was half afraid—once, that you were going to give way."

"Poor Ladybird! She little guessed how near I came to it. And maybe that's as well, after all."

"Yes, Theo. It would be fatal to begin that way. I quite see how hard it is for her. But she must learn to understand. When it comes to active service, we women must be put altogether on one side. If we can't help, we are at least bound not to hinder."

Desmond watched her while she spoke with undisguised admiration.

"Would you say that with the same assurance, I wonder, if it were John? Or if it happened to be—your own husband?"

A rush of colour flooded her face, but she had strength enough not to turn it aside.

"Of course I would."

"Then I sincerely hope you will marry one of us, Honor. Wives of that quality are too rare to be wasted on civilians!"

This time she bent her head.

"I should never dream of marrying any one—but a soldier," she answered very low. "Now I must go back to my poor Evelyn and help her to see things more from your point of view."

"How endlessly good to us you are," he said with sudden fervour. "I know I can count on you to keep her up to the mark, and not let her make herself too miserable while we are away."

"Yes—yes. I am only so thankful to be here with her—this first time."

He stood aside to let her pass; and she went out quickly, holding her head higher than usual.

He followed at a little distance, still perplexed and thoughtful, but refraining from the least attempt to account for her very unusual behaviour. What she did not choose to tell him he would not seek to know.

On the threshold of the drawing-room he paused.

His wife still stood where he had left her, disconsolately fingering her roses, her delicate face marred with weeping. Honor went to her straightway; and putting both arms round her kissed her with a passionate tenderness, intensified by a no less passionate self-reproach.

At the unnerving touch of sympathy Evelyn's grief broke out afresh.

"Oh, Honor—Honor, comfort me!" she sobbed, unaware of her husband's presence in the doorway. "You're the only one who really cares. And he is so—so pleased about it. That makes it worse than all!"

A spasm of pain crossed Desmond's face, and he turned sharply away.

"Poor little soul!" he reflected as he went; "shall I ever be able to make her understand?"

CHAPTER XVIII.

LOVE THAT IS LIFE!

"Love that is Life;
Love that is Death,
Love that is mine!"
—GIPSY SONG.

NOT until night condemned her to solitude and thought did Honor frankly confront the calamity that had come upon her with the force of a blow, cutting her life in two, shattering her pride, her joy, her inherent hopefulness of heart.

The insignificant fact that her life was broken did not set the world a hair's breadth out of gear; and through the day she held her head high, looking and speaking as usual, because she still had faith and strength and courage; and, having these, the saddest soul alive will not be utterly cast down.

She spent most of her time with Evelyn; and succeeded in so far reconciling her to Theo's decision that Evelyn slipped quietly into the study, where he sat reading, and flinging her arms round him whispered broken words of penitence into the lapel of his coat; a proceeding even more disintegrating to his resolution than her attitude of the morning.

Honor rode out to the polo-ground with them later on in the day, returning with Paul Wyndham, who stayed to dinner, a habit that had grown upon him since the week at Lahore. She wondered a little afterwards what he had talked of during the ride, and what she had said in reply; but since he seemed satisfied, she could only hope that she had not betrayed herself by any incongruity of speech or manner.

During the evening she talked and played with a vigour and cheerfulness which quite failed to deceive Desmond. But of this she was unaware. The shock of the morning had stunned her brain. She herself and those about her were as dream-folk moving in a dream while her soul sat apart, in some vague region of space, noting and applauding her body's irreproachable behaviour. Only now and then, when she caught Theo's eyes resting on her face, the whole dream-fabric fell to pieces, and stabbed her spirit broad awake.

Desmond himself could not altogether shut out anxious conjecture. By an instinct he could hardly have explained, he spoke very little to the girl, except to demand certain favourite pieces of music, most of which, to his surprise, she laughingly refused to play. Only, in bidding her good-night, he held her hand a moment longer than usual, smiling straight into her eyes; and the strong enfolding pressure, far from unsteadying her, seemed rather to revive her flagging fortitude. For who shall estimate the virtue that goes out from the hand-clasp of a brave man, to whose courage is added the strength of a stainless mind?

At last it was over.

She had left the husband and wife together, happy in a reconciliation of her own making; had dismissed Parbutti, bolted the door behind her, and now stood like one dazed, alone with God and her grief, which already seemed old as the stars,—a thing preordained before the beginning of time.

She never thought of turning up the lamp; but remained standing very straight and still, her hands clenched, all the pride of her maidenhood up in arms against that which dominated her, by no will of her own.

She knew now, past question,—and the certainty crimsoned her face and neck,—that she had loved him unwittingly from the moment of meeting; possibly even from that earlier moment when she had unerringly picked out his face from among many others. Herein lay the key to her instinctive recoil from too rapid intimacy; the key to the peculiar quality of her intercourse with him, which had been from the first a thing apart; as far removed from her friendship with Wyndham as is the serenity of the foothills from the life-giving breath of the heights.

And now—now that she had been startled into knowledge, the whole truth must be confronted, the better to be combated;—the truth that she loved him—with everything in her—with every thought, every instinct of soul and body. Nay, more, in the very teeth of her shame and self-abasement, she knew that she was glad and proud to have loved him, and no lesser man, even though the fair promise of her womanhood were doomed to go down unfulfilled into the grave.

Not for a moment did she entertain the cheap consolatory thought that she would get over it; or would, in time, give some good man the husk of her heart in exchange for the first-fruits of his own. She held the obsolete opinion that marriage unconsecrated by love was a deadlier sin than the one into which she had fallen unawares; and which, at least, need not tarnish or sadden any life save her own. This last brought her sharply into collision with practical issues. In the face of her discovery, dared she—ought she to remain even a week longer under Theo's roof?

Her heart cried out that she must go; that every hour of intercourse with him was fraught with peril. The fact that his lips were sealed availed her nothing; for these two had long since passed that danger point in platonic friendship when words are discarded for more direct communing of soul with soul. Theo could read every look in her eyes, every tone of her voice, like an open book, and she knew it; though she had never acknowledged it till now. All unconsciously he would wrest her secret from her by force of sympathetic insight; and she, who implicitly believed in God, who held suicide to be the most dastardly sin a human being can commit, knew that she would take her own life without hesitation rather than stand proven disloyal to Evelyn, disgraced in the eyes of the man she loved. She did not think this thing in detail. She merely knew it, with the instinctive certainty of a vehement temperament that feels and knows apart from all need of words.

Her character had been moulded by men—simple, upright men; and she had imbibed their hard-and-fast notions of honour, of right and wrong. She had power to turn her back upon her love, to live out her life as though it were not, on two conditions only. No one must ever suspect the truth. No one but herself must suffer because of it. Conditions hard to be fulfilled.

"Oh, *Theo!*"

The cry broke from her unawares—a throb of the heart made vocal. It roused her to reality, to the fact that she had been standing rigidly in the middle of the room,—how long she knew not,—seeing nothing, hearing nothing, but the voice of her tormented soul.

She went forward mechanically to the dressing-table, and leaning her hands upon it, looked long and searchingly into her own face. Her pallor, the ivory sheen of her dress, and the unnatural lustre of her eyes, gave her reflection a ghostly aspect in the dim light; and she shuddered. Was this to be the end of her high hopes and ideals,—of her resolute waiting and longing and praying for the very best that life and love could give? Was it actually she,—John's sister—her father's daughter—who had succumbed to this undreamed-of wrong?

At thought of them, and of their great pride in her, all her strained composure went to pieces. She sank into a chair and pressed both hands against her face. But no tears forced their way between her fingers. A girl reared by four brothers is not apt to fall a-weeping upon every provocation; and Honor suffered the more keenly in consequence.

Suddenly the darkness was irradiated by a vision of Theo, as he had appeared on entering the drawing-room that morning, in the familiar undress uniform that seemed a part of himself; bringing with him, as always, his own magnetic atmosphere of alertness and vigour, of unquestioning certainty that life was very much worth living. Every detail of his face sprang clearly into view, and for a moment Honor let herself go.

She deliberately held the vision, concentrating all her soul upon it, as on a face that one sees for the last time, and wills never to forget. It was an actual parting, and she felt it as such—a parting with the man who could never be her friend again.

Then, chafing against her momentary weakness, she pulled herself together, let her hands fall into her lap with a slow sigh that was almost a sob, and wondered, dully, whether sleep would come to her before morning. Certainly not until she had considered her position dispassionately,—neither ignoring its terrible possibilities, nor exaggerating her own sense of shame and disgrace,—and had settled, once for all, what honour and duty demanded of her in the circumstances.

One fact at least was clear. Her love for Theo Desmond was, in itself, no sin. It was a force outside the region of will,—imperious, irresistible. But it set her on the brink of a precipice, where only God and the high compulsion of her soul could withhold her from a plunge into the abyss.

"Mine own soul forbiddeth me: there, for each of us, is the eternal right and wrong." For Honor there could be no thought, no question of the false step, or of the abyss; and sinking on her knees she poured out her heart in a passionate prayer for forgiveness, for light and wisdom to choose the right path, and power to walk in it without faltering to the end.

When at last she rose, her lips and eyes had regained something of their wonted serenity. She knew now that her impulse to leave the house at once had been selfish and cowardly; that Evelyn must not be deserted in a moment of bitter need; that these ten days must be endured for her sake—and for his. On his return, she could find a reasonable excuse for spending a month elsewhere till John should come to claim her. Never in all her life had she been called upon to make so supreme an effort of self-mastery; and never had she felt so certain of the ultimate result.

She turned up the lamp now, and looked her new life bravely in the face, strong in her reliance on a Strength beyond her own,—a Strength on which she could make unlimited demands; which had never failed her yet, nor ever would to the end of time.

CHAPTER XIX.

IT'S NOT MAJOR WYNDHAM.

"I will endure; I will not strive to peep
Behind the barrier of the days to come."
—OWEN MEREDITH.

FOR a few hours Honor slept soundly. But so soon as her bodily exhaustion was repaired, grief and stress of mind dragged her back to consciousness. She woke long before dawn; woke reluctantly, for the first time in her life, with a dead weight upon heart and brain; a longing to turn her face to the wall and shut out the unconcerned serenity of the new day.

But though hearts be at breaking-point, there is no shutting out the impertinent details of life. And on this particular morning Honor found herself plunged neck-deep in prose. Domestic trifles thrust themselves aggressively to the fore. Parbutti assailed her after breakfast with a voluble diatribe against the dhobi's wife, whose eldest son was going to and fro in the compound unashamed, wearing a shirt made from the Memsahib's newest jharrons. She did not feel called upon to add that her own under-jacket had begun life upon Evelyn Desmond's godown shelves. It was not a question of morals. It was the lack of a decent reserve in appropriating her due share of the Sahib's possessions which incensed the good lady against the dhobi's wife. Such unreserve in respect of matters which should be hid might rouse suspicion in other quarters; therefore it behoved Parbutti to be zealous in casting the first stone.

Honor listened with weary inattention, promised investigation of the matter, and passed on to the godown—a closet of broad shelves stocked with an incongruous assortment of household goods, and smelling strongly of kerosine oil and bar soap.

Here it was discovered that the oil had been disappearing with miraculous celerity, and Amar Singh cast aspersions on the *kitmutgar* and his wife. A jealous feud subsisted between him and them; and as ruler-in-chief of the Sahib's establishment, the bearer made it a point of honour to let no one cheat Desmond save himself. He had a grievous complaint to lodge against a *sais*, who had been flagrantly tampering with the Desmonds' grain, adding a request that the Miss Sahib would of her merciful condescension impart the matter to the Sahib. "For he sitteth much occupied, and his countenance is not favourable this morning."

Honor complied, with a half-smile at the irony of her own position, which, until to-day, she had accepted without after-thought, and which of a sudden seemed unendurable.

Desmond, much engrossed in regimental concerns, and anxious to get off to the Lines, was inclined to irritability and abruptness; and the delinquent, who, with his charger ready saddled, awaited the Sahib's displeasure in the front verandah suffered accordingly. He bowed, trembling, to the ground, and let the storm sweep over his head; making no defence beyond a disarming reiteration of his own worthlessness, and of his everlasting devotion to the Protector of the Poor.

Turning back to the hall for his helmet, Desmond encountered Honor in the doorway, and his wrath gave place to a smile of good fellowship that brought the blood into her cheeks.

"Hope my volcanics didn't horrify you," he said apologetically. "It seems almost as cowardly to fly out at those poor chaps as to strike a child; but they have a genius for tripping one up at critical moments."

He paused, and scanned her face with kindly anxiety. "You're all right again now? Not troubled any more—eh?"

"No. I'm perfectly well. Don't bother your head about me, please. You have so much more important things to think about."

Her colour deepened; and she turned so hastily away that, in spite of his impatience to be gone, Desmond stood looking after her with a troubled crease between his brows. Then he swung round on his heel, vaulted into the saddle, and straightway forgot everything except the engrossing prospect of the campaign.

But for all his preoccupation, he had not failed to note the wistfulness in Evelyn's dutifully smiling eyes. He was more than usually tender with her on his return, and successfully banished the wistfulness by giving up his polo to take her for a ride. Honor stood watching them go, through tears which rose unbidden from the depth of her lonely grief, her haunting sense of disloyalty to the two she loved. She dashed them impatiently aside the instant they moistened her lashes; and betook herself for an hour's rest and refreshment to Mrs Jim Conolly,—"Mrs Jim" was her station name,—whose open-hearted love and admiration would give her a much-needed sense of support.

She entered her friend's drawing-room without formal announcement, to find her seated on a low sofa, barricaded with piles of cotton frocks and pinafores, which had suffered maltreatment at the hands of that arch-destroyer of clothes and temper—the Indian dhobi.

"Don't get up, please," the girl said quickly, as Mrs Conolly gathered her work together with an exclamation of pleasure. "I've just come for a spell of peace and quietness, to sit at the feet of Gamaliel and learn wisdom!"

She settled herself on the carpet,—a favourite attitude when they were alone together,—and with a sigh of satisfaction leaned against her friend's knee. The older woman put an arm round her shoulders, and pressed her close. Her mother's heart went out in very real devotion to this beautiful girl, who, strong and self-reliant as she was, turned to her so spontaneously for sympathy, counsel, and love.

"Arrogant child!" she rebuked her, smiling. "Remember who it was that sat at the feet of Gamaliel! But what particular kind of wisdom are you wanting from me to-day?"

"No particular kind. I'm only liking to have you near me. One is so sure of your faith in the ultimate best, that there is encouragement in the touch of your hand."

She took it between both her own, and rested her cheek against the other's arm, hiding her face from view.

Mrs Jim smiled, not ill pleased. She was one of those rare optimists who, having frankly confronted the evil and sorrow, the ironies and inconsistencies of life, can still affirm and believe that "God's in his Heaven; all's right with the world." But an unusual note in the girl's voice perplexed her.

"Are you in special need of encouragement just now, dear?" she asked. "Is that big baby of yours making you anxious on account of this expedition?"

"No—oh no! She is going to behave beautifully. The shock upset her at first, and she wanted Theo to stay behind. It was hard for him; but he held out; and I think I have helped her to see that he was right. He has taken her for a ride this afternoon and she is very happy."

"She has a great deal to thank you for, Honor," the elder woman said gravely. "I felt from the first that you were in rather a difficult position between those two, and you have filled it admirably. I have said very little to you about it, so far; but I have watched you and thought of you unceasingly; and I believe Major Meredith would be prouder of you than ever if he could realise that you have turned your time of waiting to such good account."

Honor's cheek still rested against Mrs Conolly's arm, and the warmth that fired it penetrated the thin muslin of her blouse. She wondered a little, but said nothing; and after a short pause Honor spoke in a low voice and with an attempt at lightness which was not a conspicuous success.

"You think too well of me, so does John. I have done little enough. Only, I care very much for—them both, and I want them to be happy—that's all."

"There are always two ways of stating a fact," the other answered, smiling. "And—do you know, Honor, *I* care very much for you—if you were my own child, I could hardly care more—and, frankly, I want to see *you* happy in the same way." She laid her free hand over the two that held her own. "It would be a sin for a woman like you not to marry. I take it for granted you have had chances enough, and I have sometimes wondered——"

The girl lifted her head and sat upright. She had come here to escape her trouble, and it confronted her at every turn.

"Please—please don't begin wondering about that," she said decisively, "or I shall have to get up and go away; and I don't want to do that."

"No, no! my child, of course not. We will talk of other things."

But the shrewd woman said within herself: "There *is* some one after all," adding a heartfelt hope that it might be Major Wyndham. Thus her next remark was more relevant to the forbidden subject than Honor was likely to guess.

"I hear Major Wyndham's squadron remains behind. You are glad, I suppose? You seem to be good friends."

"Yes; it will be a great comfort to have him when one will be missing—all the rest. There are very few men in the world like Major Wyndham; don't you think so? He has the rare secret of being in it, yet not of it. I sometimes wonder whether anything could really upset that self-contained tranquillity of his, which makes him such a restful companion."

Here was high praise, and Mrs Jim echoed it heartily; yet in spite of it, perhaps because of it, she was far from content. "It is not Major Wyndham," she decided, regretfully. "But then,—who else is it likely to be?"

At this moment children's voices sounded in the garden and Honor sprang impulsively to her feet. "Oh, there are Jimmy and Violet!" she cried. "Let me go and be foolish with them for a little and give them their tea. We can play at wisdom again afterwards—you and I."

With that she hurried out into the garden; and in surrendering herself to the superbly unconscious egotism of childhood, found passing respite from the torment of her own thoughts. But it was some time before Mrs Conolly returned to her interrupted work.

Paul Wyndham dined again at the blue bungalow that night; and it soon became evident to Honor that something had succeeded in upsetting the schooled serenity which was the keynote of the man's character. Desmond kept the conversation going with unflagging spirit, obviously for his friend's benefit; but he never once mentioned the campaign; and Honor began to understand that Paul rebelled, with quite unusual vehemence, against an order which sent his friend on active service without him. Then it occurred to her that he must have been unlike himself the night before, and that she, in her blind self-absorption, had noticed nothing. Remorse pricked her heart and gave additional warmth to her manner,—a fact which he was quick to perceive, and to misinterpret.

The men sat a long while over their cigars, and thereafter went into the study at Paul's request.

Honor had been right in her guess. The fiat of separation, coming at a time of active service, had roused him as he was rarely roused; had proved to him, if proof were needed, that in spite of the strong love, which had opened new vistas of thought and emotion for him during the past year, his feeling for Desmond was, and always would be, the master-force of his life. That he should be condemned to play the woman's part and sit with idle hands while his friend risked life and limb in the wild mountain country across the Border, seemed for the moment more than he could accept in silence.

He was obliged to own grudgingly that the Colonel was justified in his decision,—that as Second in Command he was the right man to remain in charge of the station. But the acknowledgment did not make the necessity one whit less detestable in his eyes; and to-night the two men's positions were reversed. It was Paul who moved to and fro with long restless strides; while Theo, enveloped in a cloud of blue smoke, sat watching him in profound sympathy and understanding, making occasional attempts at consolation, with small result.

During the next ten days Honor Meredith discovered how much may be achieved and endured with the help of use and wont; discovered also that habit is the rock on which man's soul shall be wrecked or anchored in his evil day.

She forced herself to speak of Theo more often than she had done hitherto; for she now understood the reason of her instinctive reserve where he was concerned; and the mere effort of breaking through it was a help. She succeeded in talking to him also, if with less frankness, still with something of her old simplicity and ease; and in playing his favourite preludes and sonatas, even though they stirred unsounded depths of emotion, and made the burden laid upon her shoulders seem too heavy to be borne.

One habit alone seriously hindered her. Her spirit of candour—which was less a habit than an elemental essence—chafed against the barrier between her and those she loved. For she now found herself constrained to avoid the too discerning eyes of Paul and Mrs Conolly, and, above all, of Theo himself. Men and women whose spirit hibernates more or less permanently in its temple of flesh have small knowledge of the joy of such wordless intercourse; such flashes of direct speech between soul and soul; but Honor felt the lack of it keenly. She experienced, for the first time in her life, that loneliness of heart which is an integral part of all great sorrow.

But when things are at their worst we must needs eat and sleep, and find some degree of satisfaction in both. Honor was young, practical, healthy, and her days were too well filled to allow of time for brooding; nor had she the smallest leaning toward that unprofitable occupation. She sought and found refuge from her clamorous Ego,—never more clamorous than at the first awakening of love,—in concentrating thought and purpose upon Evelyn; in bracing her to meet this first real demand upon her courage in a manner befitting Theo Desmond's wife.

And she reaped her measure of reward. Evelyn bore herself bravely on the whole. Theo's manifest approbation acted as a subconscious pillar of strength. But on the last day of all, when the strain of standing morally on tiptoe was already producing its inevitable effect, an unlooked-for shock brought her back to earth with the rush of a wounded bird.

The troops were to march at dawn; and in the evening it transpired that Theo intended to dine at Mess, returning, in all probability, just in time to change and ride down to the Lines. The programme was so entirely a matter of course on the eve of an expedition, and his squadron had absorbed so much of his attention, that he had forgotten to speak of the matter earlier; and the discovery was the last touch needed to upset Evelyn's unstable equilibrium. Her collapse was the more complete by reason of the strain that had gone before.

At the first she entreated him to give up the dinner and to spend his last evening with her; and upon his gentle but definite answer that such a departure from precedent was hardly possible, she fell to sobbing with the passionate unrestraint of a child. In vain Desmond tried to reason with her, to assure her that these big nights on the eve of active service were a time-honoured custom; and that all married officers attended them as a matter of course.

"I would willingly stay at home to please you, Ladybird," he added, "but the fellows would probably come round and carry me off by main force. It would all be done in the way of a joke, of course; but can't you see that any lack of regimental spirit on my part is a reflection on you, which I won't have at any price?"

No, she could see nothing, poor distracted child, except that he was rewarding her cruelly ill for the genuine effort at control she had made for his sake; and having once lost hold upon herself, all the pent-up fears and rebellion, at loss of him, found vent in a semi-coherent outbreak of reproaches and tears, till Desmond finally lost his patience, and went off to change for Mess in a mood of mind ill-tuned to the boisterous night ahead of him.

"Big nights," an immemorial feature of army life, are a specially marked feature of the Frontier, where the constant recurrence of Border warfare, and the hardness of existence generally, produce more frequent outbursts of the schoolboy spirit that characterises the British soldier of all ranks; that carries him unafraid and undismayed through heartbreaking campaigns; keeps him cheerful and uncomplaining in the face of flagrant mismanagement, fell-climates, disaster, and defeat. Big nights, sixty years ago, left a goodly number of men, either under the table or in a condition only a few degrees less undignified. But, in spite of the outcry against modern degeneration, these things are not so to-day; and the big nights of the Frontier Force, on the eve of active service, are singularly free from this, the least admirable part of the programme.

The week before departure was necessarily a week of hard work, culminating in the task of getting all details into perfect marching order, and setting every item in readiness for the start at dawn. This done, the British predilection for "letting off steam" resulted in a night of uproarious hilarity, incomprehensible to those ignorant of the conditions which gave it birth, and unable to realise its tonic effect on men who are setting out to face danger, hardship, and possibly a violent death.

Wild games and contests were the order of the evening,—the wilder the more acceptable. Cock-fighting, mock-polo matches, or gymkhanas,—on such occasions nothing comes amiss in the way of riotous foolishness pure and simple. The senior officer forgets his seniority; the most dignified lets fall the cloak of dignity for a few exhilarating hours.

Colonel Buchanan himself entered with zest into the maddest innovations which Desmond or Olliver could devise; and those who knew Paul Wyndham, in his normal habit as he lived, would scarce have recognised him masquerading as Desmond's polo pony, in a inter-regimental match played with billiard balls, brother officers doing duty for mounts and cues for polo-sticks. It was all excellent fooling; and the bar of grey in the east came far too soon.

Close on five o'clock Desmond re-entered the bungalow; his scarlet kummerbund disordered; his white mess-jacket in a hundred creases; yet alert and ready in every fibre for the day's march that lay before him.

The grey twilight of dawn was already creeping in through the skylights and long glass doors, as he passed through the drawing-room into his study.

Here he came to a standstill with a low exclamation of surprise.

On his cane deck-lounge Evelyn lay fast asleep, her face so turned upon the cushion that its delicate profile showed clear as a cameo against a background of dull blue. Her white dinner dress gleamed ghostly in the dusk of morning.

One bronze slipper had fallen off; and one bare arm hung limply over the chair's edge, the fingers curled softly upwards. A slender chain bangle, with a turquoise pendant, had almost slipped over her hand.

Desmond drew nearer with softened tread, and stood looking down upon her, a world of tenderness in his eyes;—tenderness touched with the reverence a finely tempered man is apt to feel in the presence of a child or woman asleep. For by some mysterious process sleep sanctifies a face; perhaps because it is half brother to death.

Evelyn's face was white as her dress, save for the coral tint of her lips. Their downward droop, the red line along her eyelids, and the moist handkerchief clutched in her right hand, were more heart-stirring than tears.

He knelt down beside her and lightly caressed her hair.

"Ladybird," he said softly, "time to wake up."

His touch brought her back to life with an indrawn breath like a sob; and at sight of him her arms went round his neck.

"Theo, darling," she whispered, drawing his head down close to hers. "I—was dreaming—that you were gone. I suppose you are going very soon now?"

"Yes; in about an hour."

She held him closer.

"I was bad and selfish to you last night, Theo. I didn't mean to be; but—I was. Honor made me understand."

"Bless her brave heart!" he said fervently. "She comes of the best stock I know. By the way, I am sure she never told you to spend the night here."

"No. She thought I had gone to bed. But I was too unhappy to trouble about that—and——"

"You thought I might turn up before morning,—wasn't that it?"

"Y—yes." She flushed softly on the confession.

"Poor dear little soul!"

He drew her to her feet, slipped on the fallen shoe, and put his arm round her. "Come along to the dressing-room and help me to get into my khaki."

She walked beside him in so strange a confusion of happiness and misery that it was impossible to say where one ended and the other began. In the semi-darkness she tripped and stumbled on the threshold, and he caught her close to him, holding her thus for a long moment. Then he began to dress.

At this point the long lean form of Amar Singh appeared in the doorway. But at sight of the Memsahib, arrayed for dinner, he departed as noiselessly as he had come; not without a lurking sense of injury, since it was clearly his privilege to do those last offices for his Sahib of twelve years' standing.

Evelyn, anxious to show that she could be useful on occasion, followed Theo to and fro like a shadow; handed him the wrong thing at the wrong moment with pathetic insistence; and hindered his progress by a host of irrelevant questions. But some women can hinder more engagingly than others can help; and in any case Theo Desmond was in no humour to lose patience with his wife that morning.

Once her attention was caught and held by Desmond's sword and revolver, laid ready on a small table. She regarded them with a kind of fearful fascination. They were no longer mere ornaments of his uniform, but actual death-dealers, going forth to do murderous work. The short blue muzzle of the revolver had a sinister look, and a point of light at the tip winked like a mocking eye.

"Theo," she said suddenly in an awestruck undertone, "do you know what I was dreaming when you woke me? I dreamt that you were fighting with Afridis,—ever so many of them,—and you were all alone. I thought they were going to—kill you every minute. They were running after you——"

Here Desmond dispelled the tragic vision with a shout of laughter.

"They'll never get the chance to do *that*, Ladybird, so long as I have the use of my bare hands, let alone my sword!"

"But, Theo, just think, if you were all alone, and you were bound to get killed if you stayed, and there was me at home praying to get you back safe; wouldn't you be allowed to run away—even then?"

Desmond smiled; but he did not answer at once. The

ludicrous suggestion, with its unconscious touch of pathos, hurt him more than he cared to acknowledge.

"It isn't a case of being allowed," he said. "I should never be left quite alone like that; and anyway, they don't lav down a code of morals for us in the Queen's Regulations. It is understood that a British officer will play the man, even in desperate straits."

She knitted her brows wistfully. "Yes, of course. Only—it seems rather hard on—the wives and mothers."

"You never said a truer word, little woman. That's why they need to have such good grit in them,—don't you see?"

"Yes—I see. But mayn't you just get out of the way of a bullet if you happen to see it coming?"

Desmond shook his head.

"One generally happens to feel it before one gets a chance of seeing it," he said. "But now, let's have done with nonsense. Buckle on my sword and we'll go to breakfast. The whole house is astir."

She set the leathern belt round his waist, and tried to fasten it; but her fingers trembled in spite of herself, and a mist blinded her eyes. He took the heavy strap from her very gently, and fastened it himself.

"You won't change and ride out a little way with us as the others mean to?" he asked.

"N—no; I couldn't. I don't want to make you ashamed of me, Theo."

For answer he held out his arms; and there was a long silence in the dimly lighted room.

Then he led her to the door of their room, and himself went out to the breakfast-table with a brisk elasticity of tread. He would not have been the man he was, if even the pang of parting could altogether quench his ardour to be gone.

In the dining-room he found Honor ready equipped for the start. She looked paler than usual, and there were blue shadows under her eyes; but she answered his greeting cheerfully enough, and busied herself with pouring out his tea.

"Ladybird is changing into a morning gown," he explained. "She never went to bed last night poor child!"

"Oh, I wish I had known that! I did my best to comfort her."

"So she told me: and you succeeded. You generally do."

He glanced at her thoughtfully, a shade of anxiety in his eyes. "You're not looking as fit yourself as you did a fortnight ago," he said.

"Don't talk nonsense," she answered with a touch of impatience.

"Well, I hope it may be nonsense. But I feel responsible for you. Take good care of yourself, please, while I am away; and—take care of my Ladybird as well. . . . Hullo, there's Paul!"

Wyndham entered as he spoke, wearing the undress uniform of station life: and Honor had seldom been so glad to see him as at that moment.

The two men stood facing one another for quite a long time. Then they smiled, and sat down to breakfast. Both knew that in that long look they had said all that need ever be said between them and it sufficed.

Evelyn came in a few minutes later, pale and subdued, but not uncheerful. Her real sorrow, and no less real determination to control it, gave a rare touch of dignity to the grace and simplicity that were hers by nature;—a fact which her husband was quick to perceive and admire. Both men, by a natural instinct, were a trifle more attentive to her than usual, without the least hint of intrusion upon the privacy of her grief; and it is in just such acts of unobtrusive chivalry that Englishmen, of the best type, stand unrivalled throughout the world.

The meal over, Evelyn accompanied them into the verandah, and stood smiling and waving her hand to them as they rode away, with a composure born of a stunned sense of the unreality of it all. Theo was just going down to the Lines, and he would be back to tiffin as a matter of course. Nevertheless, half an hour later the rims of her eyes were again reddened with weeping: and donning a sun-hat, she hurried out to a point where she could watch the little force move across the space of open country between the cantonment and the bastioned fort that stands at the entrance to the hills.

By the time Evelyn reached her coign of vantage, the cavalcade was already nearing the prescribed mile where the final parting would take place, to the strains of "Auld Lang Syne"; a piece of gratuitous torment, honoured by custom, which many would have willingly foregone.

The slowly retreating mass, half enveloped in dust, showed a few shades darker than the desert itself. A patch of vermilion indicated the Pioneer band, now blaring forth, with placid unconcern, "The Girl I Left Behind Me!" Lesser specks denoted officers, riding out, like the rest of the station, to speed the parting troops.

The cavalry riding in the van were a mere moving dust-cloud, followed by artillery, infantry, ambulance doolies, borne by half-naked Kahars; while a jumble of men and animals, camp-followers and transport, formed, as it were, a disorderly tail to the more compact body. Camels, groaning under tent-poles and heavy baggage, shuffled and swayed on the outskirts, with leisurely contempt; grass-cutters bobbed cheerfully along on ponies of no birth or breeding, that appeared oddly misshappen under vast loads of grass: and at the last came miniature transport carts, closely followed by the rear-guard, a mixed body of all arms.

While Evelyn still watched, the halt was called, and the disturbing strains of parting reached her where she stood. Hill, plain, and nearer objects lost their crispness of outline; and she went back to the silent house awaiting her,—the lively strains of the return march already sounding in her ears.

As she stood still for a moment, fighting against her emotion, Owen Kresney rode past. She barely acknowledged his greeting; and he had the tact to pass on without speech. For the man saw plainly that the coveted opportunity for striking a blow at Desmond, behind his back, was very near at hand; and he could afford to bide his time.

CHAPTER XX.

THE DEVIL'S PECULIARITY?

"This is the devil's peculiarity, he attacks us through our softest places."
—SUDERMANN.

AFTER the departure of the troops, life settled down gradually into its normal groove.

Frank Olliver had moved into the blue bungalow, at Desmond's request, an arrangement more satisfying to Honor than to his wife; and the Pioneer Regiment from Pindi had added a couple of ladies to the station. These were made welcome with the prompt friendliness which is India's distinctive charm; and the bachelors, in due course, made the circuit of Kohat's handful of bungalows. The station was a few degrees less cheerful, owing to the absence of its own particular men; but in India spirits must be kept up at all costs, if only as an antidote to the moral microbes of the land; and the usual small sociabilities flourished accordingly.

Evelyn took part in these at first with a chastened air. Not that she assumed what she did not feel; but that her grief, when it reached a less acute stage, gave her a soothing sense of importance; a kind of dismal distinction, such as a child feels in the possession of a badly cut finger or a loose tooth. The wind bloweth where it listeth; and such thistledown natures are entirely at its mercy. They cannot take deep root, even where they would. For them the near triumphs over the far. Like Esau, they will sell their birthright cheerfully for a mess of pottage; and they are the raw material of half the tragedies in the world.

Thus, with the passing of uneventful days, Evelyn began

to find it rather uninteresting to be quietly and comfortably unhappy; and the aspect of subdued plaintiveness which she half consciously adopted was, in truth, singularly becoming. She was one of those favoured women who have the good fortune to do most things becomingly. Her very tears became her, as dewdrops do a rose.

Frank commented on the fact to Honor, in characteristic fashion.

"Sure, 'tis a thousand pities we can't all of us look so pretty when we put on a melancholy face! It makes me look such a scarecrow meself, that I'm bound to keep on smiling, out o' sheer vanity, even if me heart's in two!"

"That's one way of putting it," Honor answered, with a very soft light in her eyes. She had begun to understand lately that this brave woman was by no means so inured to the hardship and danger of the men she loved as she would fain have them and the world believe: and the two drew very near to one another in these weeks of eager looking for news from the hills.

It is not to be supposed that Kresney failed to observe the gradual change in Evelyn's bearing. The man displayed remarkable tact and skill in detecting the psychological moment for advance. He contented himself at first with conversations in the Club Gardens and an air of deferential sympathy, which was in itself a subtle form of flattery. But on a certain afternoon of regimental sports, when Evelyn appeared, radiant and smiling, in one of her most irresistible Simla frocks, with an obviously appreciative Pioneer subaltern in attendance, Kresney perceived that the time to assert himself had arrived.

After a short but decisive engagement, he routed that indignant subaltern; and with a quiet assurance which by no means displeased her, took and kept possession of Mrs Desmond for the remainder of the afternoon.

That evening he enjoyed his after-dinner cigar as he had not enjoyed it for many weeks. Mrs Desmond was obviously tired of her pretty pathetic pose; and he intended to avail himself to the utmost of her rebound towards light-heartedness. He flattered himself that he read her like an open book; that she would be as wax in his hands if he chose to push his advantage. But for all his acuteness, he failed to detect the one good grain hid in a bushel of chaff; or to perceive that it was not indifference, but the very burden of her anxiety, that drove Evelyn to seek distraction in the form of any amusement lying near to her hand.

Letters from the Samana were few and brief. The last ones had brought news that the expedition seemed likely to prove a more serious affair than had been anticipated. Unknown to Honor, Evelyn cried herself to sleep that night, and awoke to the decision that she would not be so foolishly unhappy any more. She would shut her eyes to the haunting horrors, and forget. Theo had forbidden her to make herself too miserable. Why should she not obey him? And she proceeded to do so in her own equivocal fashion.

After the first effort it was fatally easy to slip back into the old habit of accepting Kresney's companionship, and his frequent invitations to the house;—fatally easy to slip even a few degrees farther without the smallest suspicion of his hand on the reins. She took to riding with him—sometimes in the early mornings, sometimes in the evenings; and these leisurely rides—for Evelyn was no horsewoman—suited Kresney's taste infinitely better than tennis. By cautious degrees they increased in frequency and duration; till it became evident to the least observant that little Mrs Desmond was consoling herself to good purpose.

Honor watched the new trend of events with suppressed wrath and disgust. That a woman who had won the love of Theo Desmond should descend, even for passing amusement, upon such a travesty of manhood, roused in her a bitterness of rebellion which she had no right to feel; but which, being only human, she could not altogether banish from her heart. Nor were matters made easier by Frank Olliver's periodical outbursts on the subject. The hot-headed Irishwoman had a large share of the unreasoning prejudice of her race. She hated as she loved, wholesale, and without reason. She could make no shadow of excuse for Evelyn Desmond; and was only restrained from speaking out her mind by a wholesome fear of her own temper, and a desire to avoid a serious breach with Theo Desmond's wife. But with Honor it was otherwise. Honor, she maintained, had a right to speak, and no right to be silent; and goaded thus, the girl did at length make a tentative effort at remonstrance.

But upon her first words Evelyn flushed hotly.

"For goodness' sake, Honor, don't start interfering again!" she said, in a tone which effectually quenched further discussion.

Thus, without definite intention, they drifted a little apart. Honor, haunted by a sense of having failed Theo at a time of need, found what consolation she might in her growing intimacy with Paul Wyndham; while Evelyn went on her way unchallenged, blind to every consideration but the need of escape from the haunting dread that she would never see her husband again. The dissonance between her feelings and her actions troubled her no whit. Her notions of loyalty were peculiar and inconsistent, like herself; and it is probable that she never gave a thought to Kresney's interpretation of her conduct, or to the dangerous nature of the game she was playing.

The man himself was well content, and increasingly self-satisfied. He could be an intelligent and mildly amusing companion, when it served his turn; and he was beginning to lose sight of Desmond in keen enjoyment of the oldest pastime in the world. They fell into occasional spells of silence now as they rode—silence such as familiarity breeds, and which is not without a degree of danger at a certain stage of intimacy between a man and a woman.

They had been riding thus, for some time, on an afternoon of early March. Their horses' heads had been turned homeward; for the sun was near to setting, and on the Frontier it is unsafe to be out after dusk. Evelyn's reins lay loose upon the grey mare's neck and her long lashes shadowed her cheek. She seemed to have forgotten her companion's presence. Kresney's eyes rested speculatively on her finely chiselled profile. He found her, on close acquaintance, more charming than he had expected. She possessed an elusiveness that captivates more surely than beauty. A man could never feel quite certain of her. She had not been in a very "coming-on disposition" that afternoon. His interest was piqued in consequence, and he was in the mood to dare a good deal.

He would have given much to know what she was thinking of; and the knowledge would have administered a wholesome shock to his vanity. He decided to surprise her with the question, and read the answer in her too expressive face.

"What *is* the absorbing subject?" he demanded suddenly. His tone was a sufficient index of his progress during the past fortnight.

She flushed and laughed softly, without looking up; and he drew his own conclusions.

"I don't tell my thoughts! But I'm sorry if I was rude. I was thinking, for one thing," she added lightly and mendaciously, "that I wish it was nearer time to go up to the Hills."

"I don't wonder at that. You're wasted in a place like Kohat."

"That's rubbish!" she rebuked him. But her pleasure in the words was self-evident.

"And that's modesty!" he capped her promptly, enjoying the deepening carnation of the cheek turned towards him. "Will it be Murree again this year?"

"Yes; I suppose so." She spoke without enthusiasm.

"Wouldn't you prefer Simla?"

"Well, naturally—a thousand times."

"Then why not go there? I would come up too, like a shot. I can get a couple of months this year, and we'd have a ripping time of it. Shall we call it settled—eh?"

She sighed and shook her head.

"It's too expensive. Besides, there seems to be something wrong with Simla. My husband doesn't like it much; nor does Honor."

The implication in Kresney's laugh was lost upon Evelyn Desmond.

"Oh, well, of course Simla isn't much of a place for husbands," he explained loftily, "or for girls. It's the bachelors who have a good time there,—*and* the married women."

"Is it? How odd! I should think anybody who cared

about dancing and acting, and all that sort of thing, would be bound to have a lovely time in Simla."

She looked him so simply and straightly in the face that he felt unaccountably ashamed of his questionable remark, and the laugh that had preceded it—a sensation to which he was little accustomed.

"Yes, yes; daresay you're right," he agreed airily. "But if you're so keen about the place, why not insist upon going? Wives don't trouble overmuch about obedience nowadays; most of them seem to do whatever they please."

"Do they? Well, then, I suppose it pleases me to go where my husband likes best."

"Very dutiful, indeed!" A shadow of a sneer lurked beneath his bantering tone, and she reddened again.

"It's not dutiful at all. It's simply because——" She broke off short. "Oh, I think you're horrid this afternoon. I expect people to make themselves pleasant when I let them come out with me."

"Well, I'm sure I do my best. But one can never tell where to have you. Goodness knows I've shown you plainly that I'm ready to be your friend—to any extent; and you've seemed to accept it readily enough——"

"Well, of course. I like men to like me. I always did——"

"*Men?*"

"Yes, men," she nodded, smiling. "I don't trouble much about women—except Honor; and *she's* worth all the men in creation put together."

"Desmond included?" Again the covert sneer lurked in his tone, and she drew herself up with a pretty air of dignity.

"That's not any concern of yours."

"But I tell you it is!" He pressed closer. "More than you've chosen to realise so far. D'you suppose you can go on indefinitely blowing hot and cold with a man; snubbing him one minute and drawing him on the next?"

"Oh dear! Oh dear! I never bother to suppose things! Haven't I said that if you want me to be nice, you mustn't plague me with stupid questions? At any rate, you're seeing a lot of me now. And you're riding a lot with me now—isn't that enough?"

"No. It's not enough, Mrs Desmond—Evelyn——"

"Oh, hush—hush! You mustn't say that!" she murmured ineffectually; but he paid no heed.

"You find this sort of thing pleasant enough while Desmond's away; but *will* you keep it up when he comes back? Tell me that——" He leaned closer; but she turned her head away, avoiding his gaze.

"Oh, I don't know. How can I possibly tell?" she answered, half plaintively, half petulantly. "Why *are* men so tiresome? They never seem able to enjoy things peaceably without making tragedies and getting too much in earnest——"

"But how if I am in earnest—in desperate earnest?"

He spoke with sudden vehemence. Something in his tone startled her into a recollection of the incident at Lahore. And there was no Theo at hand to protect her now.

Forgetful of the loosened rein, and of her insecure hold on the stirrup, she struck the mare more sharply than she knew. The astonished animal bounded forward, stumbled on a round stone, and came down on her knees, pitching Evelyn over her head into the dust of the metalled road.

Kresney stifled an oath. "What the devil did the little fool do that for?" he muttered between his teeth.

Springing to the ground, he shouted to a passing native child to hold the two horses, and hurried to Evelyn's side, reflecting as he went that, if she were not seriously injured, the accident might have its advantages. She was on her knees when he reached her, and was pressing both hands to her temples.

"Are you badly hurt?" he asked, anger banished by real anxiety.

"I don't—know. Oh—my head—my head!"

The words ended in a sob; she swayed as if she would fall, and quick as thought his arm went round her, pressing her close. But at his touch she recovered herself as if by magic; and pushing him fiercely aside, staggered panting to her feet.

Kresney stood regarding her for a moment, an evil expression in his eyes.

"Well, I'm damned!" he broke out at length. "I'm not a disease that you should shake me off in that fashion."

"I'm sorry," she said with quick-coming breaths. "You meant to be kind, I know, but—don't touch me again, please."

"I only wanted to keep you from falling in the dust," he retorted huffily.

"I know. But—I would rather fall in the dust."

She spoke almost in a whisper, yet with such obvious sincerity that he set his teeth viciously and answered nothing.

She remained standing before him, helpless, tantalising, unapproachable, in her childlike dignity. Her head was dazed and throbbing. Her knees shook under her so persistently that she gave it up at last, and sank down in the road, covering her face with her hands.

"Oh, how *am* I going to get home?" she moaned, more to herself than to him.

He came and stood near her again. He was surprised to find how keenly her distress hurt him, and now that his anger was past, her flash of independence made her more alluring than ever.

"If you won't let me lay a finger on you," he said in an altered tone, "I don't see how I can be any use. But if you will condescend to use me as a prop, I'll put you up on the mare, and walk beside you; then you can hold on to me if you feel shaky. We are not far off now, and the boy can take my pony on. Will that suit you?"

She looked up gratefully through a mist of tears.

"Thank you. It is nice of you to be so kind to me after—what I said."

"No man in his senses could be anything but kind to *you*." And bending down he once more encircled her with his arm, raising her to her feet, and taking his time over the proceeding. For an instant, in mere weakness, she leaned her light weight upon him; and his sense of triumph was complete.

"No hurry," he assured her gently. "You're very shaky still, you know."

But she stiffened at the cautious tightening of his arm, and stumbled forward, so that he had some ado to repress his irritation.

He lifted her to the saddle; and, seemingly oblivious

that he had offered himself as a mere prop, took such full advantage of the permission to support her till they reached the bungalow, that she was vaguely troubled, though too dazed and shaken to attempt further remonstrance.

"May I come in?" he asked, as he set her on the ground.

"Yes, please come. Won't you stay to dinner?"

"I should like to, awfully."

"Very well then, do."

She managed to walk into the drawing-room; but as he laid her on the sofa, her head fell limply backward, and she fainted.

He stood watching her intently for a few seconds. Then he bent over her, low and lower, till his lips almost rested upon hers. But at this point something checked his despicable impulse—perhaps the purity of her face, or merely its unresisting stillness. Perhaps he chose to defer the pleasure till a more acceptable moment. He straightened himself with a jerk; and hastening into the hall, shouted for brandy and soda-water.

Very soon a faint colour crept back into her cheeks. She opened her eyes and smiled up at him.

"Drink some of this," he said. "It's very weak, and you need it."

She took a few sips and set down the glass.

"Better now?" he asked, and leaned over her again, his hand on the sofa back, his lips perilously close to her hair. At that critical moment, Wyndham's tall figure appeared in the doorway, closely followed by Honor Meredith.

Kresney's back was towards him; and the tableau presented by the pair was equivocal, to say the least of it. For an instant Paul stood still in sheer stupefaction; then he turned to the girl, his grey eyes ablaze with indignation, and she had never liked him better than at that moment.

As he stepped forward, Kresney started up with a stifled oath; and the two men confronted one another, in silent, undisguised hostility, while Honor hurried to Evelyn's side.

"What is wrong with Mrs Desmond?" Paul asked coldly, concealing his natural anxiety for Theo's wife.

"Oh, she has had a spill. The mare came down with her; and she fainted when I got her home."

Kresney's pronounced frigidity was more ludicrous than

impressive; and the shadow of a smile lurked beneath Paul's moustache as he addressed himself to Honor.

"Wouldn't it be well to send for Conolly?" he asked. But Evelyn interposed.

"No,—no,—I don't want Dr Conolly. I'm all right now."

She raised herself on her elbow in proof of her statement.

"Mr Kresney was very kind to me. I have asked him to dinner. Won't you stay too?"

"Thanks. I'll go and change, and come back later. You will do the same, I presume?" And he looked directly at Kresney, who had wit enough to perceive that the situation was untenable.

"It's very good of you to want me, Mrs Desmond," he said, elaborately ignoring Wyndham's remark, "but I'd better not stop to-night. You won't be fit for much talking after that nasty tumble."

"Perhaps not. You must come some other night instead. I won't forget."

She held out her hand with marked graciousness, flashing a defiant glance at Paul, who, in sublime unconsciousness, followed Kresney out into the verandah, and remained standing on the steps till he had ridden out of sight.

No words passed between them except a mutually formal "Good-night." But Paul succeeded in conveying the impression that he regarded himself as Desmond's representative; and in making Kresney feel more acutely uncomfortable than he had felt for many a long day. If he had done no actual harm, the fault did not lie with him; and his conscience sprang painfully to life under the lash of Wyndham's contemptuous silence.

In the drawing-room, conversation fared little better.

"Why on earth was Major Wyndham so dignified and disagreeable?" Evelyn queried in a tone of frank annoyance. "It isn't *his* affair."

"You seem to forget that he is Theo's oldest friend."

Restrained anger quivered in the girl's low voice.

"He has news for you—from the Samana," she added. "There has been sharp fighting. Theo's squadron has done a very dashing bit of work;—Major Wyndham will tell you about it, *if* you care to hear. Now you had better lie quiet till you dress for dinner." And without waiting for an answer she left the room.

Next morning, while she sat at work, wondering how she could broach the forbidden subject, Evelyn herself came and stood before her with a purposeful air of decision.

"Honor," she said, "I don't want anybody to say anything to—Theo about my accident. Do you see? It is my business to tell him, and not any one else's. Will you let Mrs Olliver know that, please? I don't care to speak to her about it myself."

Honor glanced up quickly.

"No, Evelyn; it would be just as well not. She happened to be crossing this hill yesterday when you and Mr Kresney were on the lower road; and—she saw you together."

"Just the sort of thing she *would* do! I hate Mrs Olliver! Always spying on me; and I dare say she won't believe the truth even now. But I won't have her talking to *Theo* about me, whatever she may imagine."

"You know her very little if you think she could do that," Honor answered quietly. "She only spoke to me because she fancies I have influence with you. But that seems to be over now. You have chosen to go your own way. It is a very dangerous way. However, I can say nothing more on the subject."

Evelyn choked back her rising tears.

"Honor, can't you *see* that—that I'm frightened and miserable about Theo, and I must have something to help me forget? It's no use trying to make *you* understand how it feels to have him away up there—always in danger——"

Honor started and flushed. "Indeed, dear, I do understand," she answered, not quite steadily.

Evelyn shook her head.

"You think you do, but you can't really. I know you are great friends with him, and you'd be very sorry if—if anything happened. But it's ever so much worse for me, because I am—his wife. Now I must go and write to him about all this."

And Honor, left alone, leaned back in her chair, hiding her face in her hands.

"God forgive me!" she murmured. "How dare *I* find fault with her, blessed child that she is!"

CHAPTER XXI.

I AM YOURS.

> "I knew thee strong and quiet—like the hills;
> I knew thee apt to pity, brave to endure."
> —R. L. S.

PAUL WYNDHAM's hopes were on the ascendant at last. After a full year of waiting, he saw himself drawing steadily nearer to his hour of reward.

He studied Honor Meredith as a man only studies that on which his life's happiness depends; and during the past few weeks he had become aware of a mysterious change in the girl's bearing. Her beauty—which had seemed to him so complete—was now unmistakably enhanced by some transformation within. Her whole nature seemed to have become more highly sensitised. Her colour came and went upon the least provocation; her frank friendliness was veiled by a shy reserve, that had in it no hint of coldness; and, more significant than all, her eyes no longer met his own with that disconcerting directness of gaze which had sealed his lips when they were upon the verge of speech.

For all his modesty, Wyndham could not fail to interpret these signs according to his heart's desire; and when, on the night of Evelyn's accident, Honor promised him an early ride, prefaced by *chota hazri*[1] in the verandah, he told himself that he need wait no longer—that the great moment of his life had come at last.

On the stroke of seven he mounted the verandah steps. A camp table, set with fruit, freshly made toast, and a tea-

[1] Early breakfast.

tray, awaited him in a shadowed corner. Two thick bamboo blinds, let down between the wide arches, converted that end of the verandah into a room, its low-toned coolness broken only by an arrow of sunlight, shooting through a gap in one of the blinds, like a streak of powdered gold. Wyndham's eyes lingered approvingly on every detail of the homely scene; and he caught himself wondering what his sensations would be half an hour hence; what words he should speak to her when the dreaded, longed-for moment arrived.

A light footstep reached his ears; and he turned sharply round to find her standing in the open doorway.

She did not come forward at once, nor did she speak. For the man's face was transfigured. She beheld, in that instant, his unveiled heart and spirit—foresaw the ordeal that awaited her.

Noting her hesitation, he came forward with unconcealed eagerness.

"Good morning," she murmured mechanically. There seemed nothing else that could be said.

Then a wave of colour surged into her face; for he kept the hand she gave him, and drew her towards the privacy of the tea-table. She would have sacrificed much at that moment for the power to speak to prevent the pain she was bound to inflict; but her heart seemed to be beating in her throat; and she endured, as best she might, the controlled intensity of his look and tone.

"You know—surely you know what I find it so hard to say—I love you,—Honor, with all there is of me. I want you—God knows how I want you! And—you——?"

He bent his head to receive the answer that need not be spoken in words. But all vestige of colour was gone from her face, and the unsteadiness of her beautiful mouth cut him to the heart.

"Oh, forgive me!" she pleaded. "I have been thoughtless, selfish,—blind. But you seemed so entirely my friend—I did not guess. I would have given the world to have spared you—*this*."

He straightened himself like a man under the lash; but he did not relinquish her hand.

"I can't let you reproach yourself," he said quietly, "because I misunderstood signs that seemed to tell me your heart was awake at last. But now—now you know how it is with me, at least you will let me hope——?"

"I wish I might," she answered, so low that he could scarcely hear. "But—it's impossible!"

"Am I so entirely unworthy—unlovable?"

"No, oh no. It is not that."

"D'you mean—I was not mistaken. Is there—any one else?"

"Yes."

It was impossible to lie to him, and the blood rushed back into her face at the confession.

"Is he *here?*" Paul demanded, with sudden energy.

"You mustn't ask any questions about—him—about it, please."

"Only this one. Shall you—marry him?"

"No. Never."

Sheer incredulity held him silent; and when he spoke there was rebellion in his tone.

"Your life and my own are to remain broken, unfulfilled, because of—this incomprehensible thing?"

"There is nothing else possible."

He relinquished her hand at that, giving it back to her, as it were, with a quiet finality of renunciation that shattered her self-control. She sank into a chair and hid her face in a vain attempt to conceal the tears that came in spite of herself.

He stood beside her for several seconds in a heartbroken silence; then gently touched her arm.

"Honor—Honor, is it really so impossible—as you think? I tell you plainly I can't understand——"

She uncovered her face and looked up at him.

"Can any one ever understand—this sort of thing? Isn't it a force outside the control of reason, of even the strongest will?"

"You are right," he answered gravely; and sitting down leaned towards her, his elbows on the table. "But there remains the fact that sooner than lose you outright, I am willing to marry you—on any terms. If you have no hope for yourself, could you not bring yourself to partially fulfil mine? Will you—in mercy to me—reconsider your decision?"

She looked up quickly with parted lips; but his raised hand enjoined silence.

"My suggestion deserves thinking over for a few minutes, if no longer. And in the meanwhile—" he smiled with a touch of his old humorous resignation to things in general—"we might do worse than have some *chota hazri*. What a brute I was to upset you before you had had a morsel to eat!"

She shook her head, with a faint reflection of his smile.

"I don't want anything to eat."

"Oh yes, you do! I suppose I must set you an example of common-sense behaviour."

He peeled two bananas with deliberate care, and set one on her plate. Then he lifted the cosy.

"That tea must be strong by this time; but the water's hot, and you can doctor it with that. Now—begin."

He himself began upon his banana, and she glanced at him in astonishment, not untinged with admiration, at his effortless transition from controlled passion to the commonplaces of everyday life. They got through the short meal after a fashion; and both were devoutly thankful when the demands of common-sense had been fulfilled.

Wyndham rose, and lit a cigarette.

"Now, I'll leave you to yourself for five minutes," he announced. "It is getting late. But before we go for our ride this matter must be settled once for all." He laid both hands on the table and looked steadily into her face. "You are the most just-minded woman I know. Look all round the question before you decide. Try to realise a little what it will mean for me to give up all hope. In losing you, I lose everything. There can be no question of any one else for me. Take me or—leave me, I am *yours* for the rest of my life."

He turned away to save her from the necessity of answering, and walked to the far end of the verandah, leaving her alone with the strongest temptation she had yet experienced—the temptation to trample on her own imperious love, and to accept this man's selfless devotion in the hope that it might one day conquer and monopolise her heart.

Had marriage with Wyndham entailed immediate removal from the atmosphere of Theo Desmond, hesitancy might have ended in capitulation. But life-long intimacy with him, as the wife of his closest friend, was unthinkable for a moment; and if by the wildest possibility Paul should ever suspect the truth——!

She shuddered and glanced in his direction.

"Major Wyndham," she said softly.

He hastened back to her at once. But one look at her face sufficed. The eagerness faded from his eyes, leaving them cold as a winter sky after sunset.

"It was wrong of me to keep you in suspense even for a few minutes," she said, her gaze riveted on the table. "Please forgive me that I am driven to hurt you so, and please believe that I do realise what I am losing——"

"The loss is—not yours," he said on a note of restrained quietness: and in the stillness that ensued, the impatient horses could be heard champing their bits.

He sank into his chair with a gesture of unfeigned weariness; and she glanced at his face. Its mingled pain and patience pierced her heart. But when at last he spoke, his voice was natural and controlled.

"I have only one word more to say. I confess I have not the courage to let you go altogether out of my life. Since nothing else is possible, will you at least accept me as your permanent and—devoted friend?"

She turned upon him in frank surprise.

"Do you mean that—really? *Can* you do it? Men always say——"

He smiled a trifle bitterly.

"Do they? No doubt they are right—for themselves. But I know I have the strength to accept what I ask, or I would not dare ask it. You won't refuse me that much, will you—Honor?"

"No, indeed, no," she answered, greatly moved. "I can deny you nothing that I am not forced to deny you—Paul."

"Ah, there is no woman in the world to compare with you! Let me say it this once, as I may never tell you so again."

He rose in speaking, braced his shoulders, and stood looking down upon her, a strangely glad light in his eyes.

"I have *not* lost you, after all," he said.

She rose also, and gave him both her hands. "No. You have gained me—for good. I—care now ever so much more than I did when I came out to you this morning."

"You *do?*"

"Yes—I do."

He drew her towards him. "Promise me this much," he said, "that if you should ever find it possible to—marry me on any conditions—even the hardest—you will tell me so at once, because after this morning I shall never open my lips on the subject again."

"I promise. Only—you must not let yourself hope."

He sighed. "Very well, I will shut out hope, since you command it. But I shall still have love and faith to live upon. You cannot deprive me of those—Honor. Now shall we go for our ride? Or would you rather go in and rest after all this?"

"No. We will have our ride. I can rest later if I need it."

"Let me put you up then. Come."

And she came without a word.

CHAPTER XXII.

THE CHEAPER MAN.

"No proposition Euclid wrote,
 No formulæ the text-books show,
Will turn the bullet from your coat,
 Or ward the tulwar's downward blow;
Strike hard, who cares—shoot straight, who can;
The odds are on the cheaper man!"
 —RUDYARD KIPLING: *Arithmetic on the Frontier.*

THE second week in March found the little force from Kohat still skirmishing energetically through a network of ravines, nullahs, and jagged red hills; still dealing out rough justice to unrepentant Afridis in accordance with instructions from headquarters; or as nearly in accordance with them as Colonel Buchanan's pronounced views on the ethics of warfare would permit. For Buchanan was a just man of independent character, a type not ostentatiously beloved by heads of departments. He had a reprehensible trick of thinking for himself and acting accordingly—a habit liable to create havoc among the card-houses of officialdom; and like all soldiers of the first grade, he was resolute against the cowardly method of striking at the guilty through the innocent; resolute in limiting the evils of war to its authors and active abettors.

He had taken full advantage of his temporary rank to run the expedition on his own lines; and although his instructions included the burning of crops, he had kept rigid control over this part of the programme; giving officers and men free scope for activity in the demolishing of armed forts and towers, and in skirmishes with the wild tribes who harried their transport trains, rushed their pickets, sent playful bullets whizzing through the mess-tent at night, and generally enjoyed themselves after the rough and ready fashion of the hillsman across the Border.

The Afridis in truth were merely tired of behaving like good children. The unstained knives at their belts cried shame on them for their prolonged abstinence from the legitimate joys of manhood;—the music of bullets whistling down a gorge, the yielding of an enemy's flesh under the knife.

Therefore, when Colonel Buchanan and his little force started punitive operations, they were met by a surprisingly concerted and spirited resistance. The cunning tribesmen, having got what they wanted in the shape of excitement, were determined to make the most of it. Thus, the expedition had flared up into one of those minor guerilla campaigns which have cost England more, in the lives of picked officers, than she is ever likely to calculate; being, for the most part, careful and troubled about weightier matters.

The sweeping movement, organised to include all villages implicated in the raid, took longer than had been anticipated. The demolishing of Afridi watch-towers, manned by the finest natural marksmen in the world, and built on bases proof against everything but gunpowder, is no child's play; and at almost every village on the line of route the troops had found their work cut out for them. That they carried it out gallantly and effectively need hardly be said, since we are dealing with the pick of India's soldiers, the Punjab Frontier Force.

Their daily march led them along broken tracks or boulder-strewn beds of torrents, winding through a land where "the face of God is a rock";—a land feigning death, yet alive with hidden foes who announced their presence from time to time by the snick of a breech-bolt, the whing of a bullet, or a concerted rush upon the rear-guard from some conveniently narrow ravine.

Little interruptions of this sort helped to keep all ranks on the alert, and to make things cheerful generally; but they also took up time. And although the middle of

March found them back within twenty-one miles of Kohat, there seemed little hope of quieting the country under another week or two at least.

On the evening of the 16th, after two days of skirmishing and a broken night under the stars, imperative need of water compelled them to encamp at the open end of a valley whose enclosing heights narrowed abruptly to the northward into an ugly-looking gorge.

Tents sprang up right and left; lines for horses and mules established themselves in less time than it would take the uninitiated to see where and how the thing could be done; and that eighth wonder of the world, the native cook, achieved a four-course dinner with a mud oven, army rations, a small supply of looted fowls, and a large supply of ingenuity. A party of cavalry, having reconnoitred the ravines branching off into higher hills, reported no signs of the enemy. A cordon of sentries was told off for duty; and the posting of strong pickets on the near hill-tops, and in the neighbourhood of the camp itself, completed the night's arrangements. Clanking of accoutrements, jangle of harness, and all the subdued hum of human life, died away into stillness; lights dropped out one by one; and the valley was given over to silence and a multitude of stars.

Touched into silver here and there by the ethereal radiance—for starshine is a reality in India—the scene presented a Dantesque mingling of beauty and terror,—the twin elements of life, which are "only one, not two."

At a little distance behind the clustering tents the ground sloped boldly upward to summits dark with patches of stunted forest; and beyond these again the snow-peaks of the Safed Koh mountains stood dreaming to the stars. Lower down, at rare intervals, dwarf oaks and the "low lean thorn" of the desert stood out, black and spectral, against the lesser darkness of rocks and stones. In the valley itself the stones had it all their own way;—a ghostly company, rounded and polished by the stream, which crept among them now a mere ribbon of silver, but in four months' time would come thundering through the gorge in a garment of foam, with the shout of a wild thing loosed from bondage. The triumph of desolation was reached in the savage peaks that almost fronted the camp and descended to the valley in a cataract of crags. Here even the persevering thorn-bush could take no hold upon a surface of bare rock, split up into clefts, and chiselled to such fantastic shapes that the whole might have inspired Dante's conception of the ravine by which he descended to the nether hell.

Absorbed in the requirements of earth, and untroubled by ghostly imaginings, officers and men slept soundly, with one eye open, as soldiers experienced in Frontier warfare learn to do; and when at last the earth, turning in its sleep, swung round towards the sun and the still air quivered with foreknowledge of morning, a sudden outcropping of life, where no life should be, amply justified the need for vigilance.

From the darkness of a ravine some distance above the camp, a shadowy mass of figures poured hurriedly, stealthily, into the valley—men of splendid physique, in loose dark draperies or sheepskin coats, carrying leathern shields and the formidable Afridi knife, bone-handled, with a two-foot blade that will halve a man's head as if it were a lemon.

By a preconcerted arrangement they divided into two parties, and keeping within the deepest patches of shadow, bore down upon the nearest pickets with a fierce, soundless rush,—the most disconcerting form of attack to sleepy sentries in the small hours, when life and courage are at their lowest ebb. But the picket sentries happened to be Sikhs; and they are ill men to tackle at close quarters or to spring on unawares.

Close upon the first determined rush came a scuffle, a smothered shout, the sharp crack of rifles in quick succession; and before the hills had flung back the volley of sound, the whole camp hummed with life from end to end, like a broken ant-heap.

A fusilade of shots rang out on all sides. Men hurried about among the tents, concentrating at the two points of attack. Here and there, amid the puffs of smoke that rose and vanished in the blue, a lifted sword or sabre gleamed like a flash of light.

A number of Afridis forced their way into the camp,

lunging at every tent-rope within reach of their long knives, and in the dim light it was not easy to distinguish friend from foe. But the first sharp shock of encounter past, it became evident that the troops were getting the best of the affair; and the Afridis, whose valour is not always tempered with discretion, saw fit to beat a rapid retreat up the valley, hoping to reach the ravine before the cavalry started in pursuit.

The men in camp, meanwhile, had leisure to breathe freely, after their rough awakening; to look about and recognise one another, and exchange cheerful congratulations on the resolute stand made by the Sikhs.

"That you, Desmond?"

The Colonel's voice greeted Desmond as he emerged from his tent where his servant had been pressing on him a half-cold cup of cocoa; and the two men faced each other, bareheaded, in shirt and breeches, unmistakable stains upon their naked blades.

"The Ressaldar's falling in your squadron," Buchanan said briskly. "Lose no time, and follow 'em up like hell. They'll break away into the hills, of course. But the chances are they'll concentrate again in the gorge and try to catch the main body as it passes through. So if they give you the slip now, ride straight on and secure the defile for us. I'll send out a detachment of infantry at the double to crown the heights; and I can safely leave all minor details to your discretion."

"Thank you, sir." And Desmond departed to carry out his orders with high elation at his heart.

There is no compliment a soldier appreciates more keenly than one which takes the practical form of leaving details to his own discretion; and, coming from Buchanan, it was doubly acceptable. For, in Desmond's opinion, there were few men in the world like the Colonel, hard and uncommunicative as he was; and it never occurred to him that his strong, unspoken admiration was returned with interest by the reserve-ridden Scot.

During the next fifteen minutes he fully justified his sobriquet of "*Bijli-wallah* Sahib." Before the Afridis were out of sight a hundred and sixty sabres, headed by himself and

Denvil, dashed along the rugged pathway in gallant style, the men leaning well forward, and urging their horses to break-neck speed. But the enemy were well ahead from the start, and in any case, they had the advantage on their own rough soil. The squadron overtook them—breathless and eager—just as the final stragglers plunged into a lateral cleft, which would hold the darkness for another half-hour at least.

Further pursuit was out of the question; and, by way of consolation, the foremost sowars were ordered to dismount and open rapid fire in the direction of the fugitives. Groans, curses, and the thud of falling bodies testified to its effect; and with laconic murmurs of satisfaction the men remounted, and rode on up the rapidly narrowing gorge.

By now, along the silver snows to eastward, the great change had begun. The sky was blue above them; and the last of the stars had melted in the onrushing tide of light, which had already awakened the sandstone peaks to the warm hue of life.

The party mounted the ascent at a foot's pace to ease their horses; and Desmond's eyes and mind, being as it were "off duty," turned thoughtfully upon the Boy who rode at his side, a very incarnation of good health and good spirits. It seemed that the outcome of his critical inspection was approval, for it ended in a nod that confirmed some pleasant inward assurance. During the past few weeks Denvil had proved himself thoroughly "up to the mark";—hot-headed but reliable; square and upright in mind as in body; a fine soldier in the making. He had not yet arrived at the older man's keen mental interest in his profession; but closer intimacy with Desmond had kindled in him an answering spark of that idealism, that unswerving subordination of self to duty which justifies and ennobles the great game of war. He coveted action, risk, responsibility—three things which the Staff Corps subaltern, especially on the Frontier, tastes earlier than most men; and which go far to make him one of the straightest specimens of manhood in the world. In Denvil's eyes the whole expedition was one tremendous spree, which he was enjoying to the top of his bent; and Desmond, remembering the good years of his own apprenticeship, could gauge the measure of that enjoyment to the full. He felt justified in expecting great things of the Boy, and decided to work him hard all through the hot weather;—in his eyes the highest compliment a man could pay to a promising junior.

"By the way, Harry," he said suddenly, as the defile, deep-sunken between towering rock, loomed darkly into view, "I've got a word of encouragement for you before we part company. You did an uncommonly gallant bit of work in that skirmish yesterday. The Colonel spoke of it; and congratulated me on having the smartest subaltern in the regiment. Of course I've known it myself this long while; and I don't think it will hurt you to know it too."

Denvil flushed hotly through his tan.

"I should be rather a poor sort of chap if I didn't manage to do pretty well—under you," he said, with awkward bluntness, looking straight between his charger's ears.

Desmond laughed. "Very neatly turned off, old chap. Now, I'm bound to call a halt till the Sikhs come up with us. Hope to goodness they'll be quick about it. Confounded nuisance having to wait."

Both men reined in their horses, and their consuming impatience. The squadron followed suit; and in an amazingly short time the Sikhs came into view, toiling lustily up the incline at their utmost speed.

Desmond turned in his saddle and raked the hillsides with his field-glasses.

"Looks empty enough, in all conscience," he remarked.

The words were hardly spoken when a single shot startled the echoes of the rocks, and instant alertness passed like an electric current through the squadron. The advance guard, which had already entered the defile, consisted of three promising young Pathans from Denvil's troop; and anxiety for the fate of his favourites pricked the Boy to keener impatience.

"I say, Desmond," he urged, "can't I take twenty men and push on to find out what's up. They'll be taking pot-shots at my men, unless I put a stop to it. For God's sake, let me go."

Desmond could not repress an approving smile at an

impetuosity that matched his own. He glanced down the valley at the advancing Sikhs, and saw that he would not be long delayed in following on. Moreover, he shared the Boy's anxiety for his three picked men; and a shot fired, being tantamount to a declaration of hostilities, justified immediate advance to the scene of action.

"Go ahead then," he said. "Advance warily; and good luck to you."

The Boy needed no second bidding. Eagerly, yet with all due precautions, he went forward with his handful of Pathans; and was soon lost to sight and sound in the darkness of the giant cleft.

Desmond, left alone, could hardly contain himself till the infantry came up. Dividing into two flanking parties, they scrambled up the steep slopes into the full radiance of dawn; while Desmond, with his squadron ready drawn up, awaited the signal, "All's clear," before entering the defile.

In due time it came; and they moved on between the frowning cliffs at a pace as rapid as the exigencies of the situation would permit.

Here night fronted them, dank and chill. It was as if the clock had been put back four hours. Only a jagged strip of sky, between projecting crags, announced the advent of day. No living thing seemed to inhabit this region of perpetual twilight. At intervals a gnarled and twisted bush grew out of a cleft, lifting spectral foliage toward where the sun should be, and was not. Silence pervaded the dusk like a living presence; unseen, but so poignantly felt that the whisper of the stream and the crunch of shingle under the horses' hoofs seemed an affront to the ghostly spirit of the place; and the sowars, when exchanging remarks among themselves, instinctively refrained from raising their voices.

Desmond, closely followed by his trumpeter, rode ahead of the troopers, chafing at their leaden-footed progress. A hand-gallop would have been too slow for the speed of his thoughts, tormented as he was by anxious wondering what had become of the Boy; while his ears were strained to catch the first sounds of contest from the heights, which were already widening out a little, and beginning to slope towards lower ground.

Sounds came at length—harsh and startling;—the unmistakable note of the jezail; answering shots from his own men;—proofs incontestable that a sharp engagement was in progress up above.

"Ambuscaded,—by Heaven!" was Desmond's instant thought. Mercifully the exit was already in sight; and flinging brisk instructions to the Ressaldar to follow him closely with a hundred sowars, leaving the remainder to take charge of the horses, and hold the opening till further orders, Desmond made for it full tilt, spurring Badshah Pasand as he had never been spurred in all his days. On dashing out into the sunlight he was greeted by a rattle of musketry from behind a tumbled mass of rock; and a dozen bullets buzzed about him like bees.

One riddled his helmet, stirring his hair as it passed. A second struck his left shoulder, inflicting a flesh wound of which he was not even conscious at the moment; for Badshah Pasand lunged ominously forward; swayed, staggered; and with a sound between a cough and a groan, fell headlong, flinging his rider clear on to the rough upward slope.

Luckily for him, Desmond pitched on to his sound shoulder; and though bruised and shaken, was none the worse for his fall. The foremost of his men dismounted and opened fire upon the treacherous rock, without eliciting response; and quick as lightning he sprang to his feet, mad with rage and pain. A single glance showed him that his charger's wounds were mortal. Two well-directed bullets had entered the chest; and the great soft eyes were glazing fast.

With a swift contraction of the heart, Desmond turned away, and issued hurried orders for a hundred men to dismount and take the hill at full speed. Half a dozen of Denvil's Pathans—left in charge of the discarded horses—gave information that the Sahib had taken his sowars up some time before, commanding them to await his return.

Distracted by anxiety, Desmond awaited the dismounting of his troopers, revolver in hand. The instant they were ready he bounded over the broken ground, his trumpeter dogging him like a shadow, and a self-imposed bodyguard of six sowars following close upon his heel. Behind these again the mountain-side was alive with clambering men; and the small party left below enviously watched their ascent.

Only by the impetus of his spirit did Desmond manage to keep ahead of his men; for in general the native outstrips the Englishman in this form of mountaineering. One thought hammering at his brain goaded him to superhuman exertion: "Those devils shall not murder Harry before I reach him."

Breathless and resolute, he hurried on, stumbling now and again from sheer excess of haste, clenching his teeth to keep the curses back. A dull stain spread slowly across his left shoulder, where the blood was soaking through his khaki coat.

The slope ended in a twenty-foot wall of rocks, massed so as to form huge irregular steps, that led to an abrupt bit of level, whereon the fighting appeared to be taking place. Sounds came to him now that lashed him to a frenzy; the clash of knives and sabres, the thud of many feet; the fierce shouts without which it is impossible for primitive man to slay or be slain.

Desmond never quite knew how he climbed those formidable steps; and as he vaulted up the last of them, the whole dread scene sprang abruptly into view.

Denvil and his fifteen Pathans had been ambuscaded and outnumbered; and in the cramped space a sharp hand-to-hand encounter was in progress. A small party of Sikhs had already come up with him; but even so the odds were heavily on the wrong side. It was simply a case of "dying game";—of adding one more to the list of "regrettable incidents" which figure too frequently in the record of Border warfare.

A new risen sun smiled serenely down upon it all; and the awakened earth was frankly indifferent to the issue.

But amid the stirring confusion of a struggle at close quarters Desmond saw one thing only; and the sight struck at his heart like a sword-thrust.

Harry Denvil, hard pressed by four Afridis brandishing long knives and leathern shields, stood with his back against a rock, fighting for dear life.

Five of his men and several of the enemy lay dead or

wounded around him. His left arm was disabled; his helmet gone; his hair gleaming red-gold in the sunlight; his young face, white and desperate, disfigured by an ugly cut across the forehead and cheekbone, from which the blood trickled unheeded in a sluggish stream.

He had flung away his empty revolver; and was warding off blows right and left, using his sword with a coolness and dexterity which would have surprised him had he been aware of it. But he was aware of nothing except a fierce desire not to die yet—not yet; and to get a straight cut at one of the dark faces that pressed in upon him with such pitiless persistence.

At sight of Desmond a great cry broke from him.

"Desmond!" he shouted; "Desmond—thank God!"

For answer Desmond ran blindly forward, sheer lust of slaughter in his heart; trumpeter, bodyguard, and the foremost troopers following as closely as their captain's ardour would permit.

But an unreasoning sense of safety put Harry momentarily off his guard. He took a hasty step away from the rock, making it possible for the first time to strike at him from behind: and, in the same instant, Desmond fired. Before his bullet could reach its destination, the long knife had descended, swift and certain. And even as the man who wielded it dropped like a log, Harry Denvil stumbled forward; and, with a thick sob, fell face downward at Desmond's feet.

There was no time to stoop and ascertain whether the knife had completed its work. Striding across his subaltern's body, Desmond turned upon his assailants, all the natural savage in him lashed to a white heat of fury, and fired twice in quick succession, with deadly effect. But the knife of a third man bit into his flesh like fire, inflicting deep gashes on the left arm and hand, while another slipped behind him, his uplifted blade glinting in the sunlight.

By this time Rajinder Singh was behind him also; and like a lightning-streak, his tulwar whizzed through the air, cleaving the man's head from his body at a blow.

Desmond swung sharply round to find his reinforcements swarming over the plateau's edge.

"Well struck, Sirdar Sahib!——"

But the sentence was never finished. A puff of smoke from behind a distant rock, the boom of a jezail, and Desmond fell beside the Boy, stunned by a well-aimed shot on the edge of the cheek-bone, the slug glancing off perilously close to the right eye.

A shout of rage went up from his men. "The Captain Sahib,—the Captain Sahib!" But Rajinder Singh promptly assuming command, bade them turn upon the Afridi devils and smite their souls to hell; and, forming a protective ring about their fallen officers, they obeyed with right goodwill.

The arrival of supports, however, made it clear to the enemy that they themselves were now heavily outnumbered; and after a desultory resistance they broke up and fled, the sowars zealously speeding their departure.

The whole incident had passed in an incredibly short space of time; and now, with a low cry, Rajinder Singh sank on his knees beside Desmond, cold fear at his heart, his lean fingers trembling as they pushed up the watch-strap and pressed the smooth tanned wrist.

"He lives!—*Parmeshwar*[1] be praised;—the Captain Sahib lives!" the old man murmured ecstatically, shaking his head at the same time over the wound in the cheek-bone, which had an ugly look.

In Denvil's wrist no flutter of life was left. The Boy's soul had passed unstained to its account; and the Ressaldar's stern eyes softened as they rested on the bright, blood-stained hair.

Very gently, as though Denvil were merely asleep, he turned him over and closed the unseeing eyes. No shadow of pain marred the repose of the lips. They looked as if they had just left off smiling and meant very soon to smile again.

The Ressaldar sighed, and shook his head thoughtfully once again.

"Doubtless it was written, . . . it was the will of God," he decided, with the pious stoicism of the East; and thereupon issued immediate orders to his signallers to open up communication with the main body of troops in the valley,

[1] God.

enumerating casualties, and adding an urgent request for an ambulance party to be pushed forward at the utmost speed.

A short stab of pain jerked Desmond back to consciousness with a curse upon his lips. He found himself lying in a hospital doolie set in the shade on a slab of rock. Both flaps had been flung up, and James Mackay stood beside him, investigating the wound in his face with conscientious thoroughness. It was not a pleasant proceeding. Hence Desmond's protest, which brought a twinkle of satisfaction to the doctor's eyes.

"Curse away, old man. It's a treat to hear you," he said heartily. "Just take a drop of this now, to keep you all there," and he held a glass of brandy and water to Desmond's lips. "They've given you a nasty wound here. Wants looking to at once. I'm going to hurt you like hell, I know; but you must put up with it. Swear at me as much as you please, if it eases you at all."

He probed a peculiarly tender spot as he spoke. Desmond clenched his teeth and "put up with it" in silence. Free permission to swear had quenched the desire—a common trick of human perversity; and just as he began to feel that one minute more of it would stretch endurance to breaking-point—the thing was done. A sloping bandage encircled his head, eclipsing his right eye; and he discovered that the Colonel was standing by the doolie, tugging at his grey moustache — sure sign of mental disturbance — and listening attentively to the wiry little doctor, who spoke in an urgent undertone.

He turned when Mackay left off speaking.

"Bad business this, Desmond," he said laconically. "Thank God it was no worse, though."

And Desmond had but two words for answer, sharp and anxious.

"The Boy?"

"We've lost Denvil," Buchanan growled between his teeth. "And we could very ill spare him."

Desmond closed his eyes and drew a deep breath. Speech was beyond him. His mind, dizzy with pain and loss of blood, refused to grasp the truth. Two hours ago the Boy had been radiantly, vigorously alive. It was rank foolishness to expect a man to believe that he would never hear him speak or laugh again.

He was roused by Buchanan's hand on his arm.

"Look here, Desmond," he said, "we must be moving again now. I merely came to see how things were going with you before pushing on."

"Thank you, Colonel. I'm in the rear for the present, I suppose?" And he tried to smile.

"Not exactly. As we are within two days' march of the station and there's little left to do but sweep up the rubbish, I have told off a strong escort to return to Kohat with the wounded men,—Denvil, and yourself. You've been badly knocked about, and you need careful seeing to at once."

"Won't you leave me out of the programme, sir? You know I'm hard as nails; I'm sure I could manage to hang on to the saddle, and be fit for light duty in a few days' time. Give me the chance, anyway. I'll do my level best."

"Never knew you do anything else," Buchanan answered gruffly.

Then there was a short silence. Hard as he was, the man rebelled against the thing he had to say; and Desmond's unconquerable spirit put him in no better humour for his task.

"My dear fellow," he began, "I'm no hand at beating about the bush; I can only tell you straight that for the present you must give up all hope of getting back to duty, light or otherwise. Mackay is not satisfied about that wound in your face. The slug went too close to the eye, and may possibly—have injured the nerve."

Desmond started and clenched his hand.

"Good God, Colonel!" he broke out hoarsely. "D'you mean—blindness?"

The ring of open fear in a brave man's voice is not a pleasant thing to hear. Buchanan felt he had been too blunt, and regretted not having allowed Mackay to speak.

"Don't jump to hasty conclusions, man," he said quickly. "We have to recognise the possibility in order to prevent it,—that's all. Mackay returns with you. He'll get a second opinion, if necessary; and we've signalled the news to Wyndham in full. All you've got to do now is to knock under like a man, and give your eyes every possible chance; even if it means lying in the dark for a week or two; you understand?"

"Yes—I understand."

There was bitterness in the studied resignation of his tone.

Colonel Buchanan put out his hand and kept firm hold of Desmond's arm while he spoke.

"You'll be reasonable then, and—obey orders? You ought to find the coast clear going back and have no trouble. Young Spence commands the party, and Rajinder Singh takes thirty of your men. The old chap begged for permission to accompany you. See you again in a fortnight, if not sooner. Keep up a good heart; and take every possible precaution, for your own sake and—for the sake of the Regiment."

The final injunctions, jerked out brusquely, were in the nature of an achievement for this man of few words; and Desmond knew it. He wrung the iron-hard hand that held his own with all the force still left in him; and Colonel Buchanan returned to his waiting charger.

That afternoon, under a brilliant sky, the little ambulance party set out for Kohat—thirty cavalry and twenty infantry, with six swaying doolies in their midst. And among all the occupants of those comfortless conveyances, Harry Denvil was the only one for whom that journey was not a prolonged torment of pain and unrest.

CHAPTER XXIII.

YOU GO ALONE.

"It is poor work beating butterflies with a cart-rope."
—LUCAS MALET.

ON the morning of that eventful 17th of March, Evelyn and Honor left the bungalow directly after breakfast, bent upon such shopping as Kohat could afford.

The nearest approach to shops, in the accepted sense of the word, were the open stalls in the native city. But there could be no question of exploring these; and the manifold needs of Western womanhood were inadequately met by the regimental go-downs attached to each corps in the cantonment. These consisted of spacious buildings, shelved from floor to ceiling, and stocked with a fine medley of human requirements, ranging from bone buttons to champagne, from quinine and chlorodyne to rolls of silk for evening gowns. A new consignment from "down-country" came up every month or so; and it was quite one of the events of life in Kohat to go the round of the go-downs as soon as possible after the arrival of these, so as to secure the pick of the market while the goods were fresh and the choice comparatively varied. Herein lay ample scope for those small spites and jealousies that are more than bread and meat to women of a certain type.

Evelyn had actually sent for gloves and shoes by this means, from a cheap Calcutta firm, instead of despatching an order to Simla regally regardless of cost. They by no means satisfied her fastidious taste; but she felt exalted to a superhuman pitch of virtue as she bore them home in her dandy.

"I don't believe Theo will like these shoes one bit!" she remarked with a satisfied laugh to Honor who rode beside her. "He will tell me to order the next ones from Simla straight away, and I shall be ever so dutiful and obey him without any fuss—shan't I, you grave, wise Honor?"

"I should be an inhuman monster if I could keep grave and wise in your company!" Honor answered, laughing back at her. "You will go on buying expensive shoes to the end of the chapter, if that's what you are driving at. Why have your spirits gone up with such a run this morning?"

"I don't know. It's nice enough that they *are* up. I got a lovely letter from Theo—that's partly why, perhaps." Her eyes softened at the remembrance of that letter. "He'll be home again in less than a fortnight."

"Yes; in less than a fortnight," Honor repeated, and wondered where she should go when that time arrived. She had not yet found courage to face the idea in detail.

Evelyn kept up an unbroken ripple of hilarity till the verandah was reached, laughing as Honor had not heard her laugh since Theo had left.

"You're 'fey,' child," she said, as she helped her out of the dandy. "I shall have you in floods of tears before night."

"No, you won't; I don't feel as if anything *could* happen to make me cry to-day. Hullo! there's Major Wyndham's horse out there."

Honor started.

"What can he want over here so early? Come in quick and find out."

They hurried through the hall into the dining-room, Evelyn leading, a swift premonition of evil killing the laughter on their lips.

Paul stood by the piano looking at Desmond's photograph; his arms folded; his "February face" more eloquent than he knew.

"Good-morning, Mrs Desmond," he said; and his sympathetic hand-clasp sent her mercurial spirits down to zero.

"What is it?" she asked, blanching visibly. "You have brought bad news?"

Paul assented in silence.

"If it is very horrible—don't tell me—I won't hear it!" She held up both hands, as if warding off a blow. But Honor, coming quickly forward, put both arms round her.

"Hush, dear, hush!" she said soothingly. "That is nonsense. We *must* know what has happened, at once."

"Let him tell *you*, then; it won't hurt you like it hurts me." And disengaging herself, she went over to the verandah doorway, and stood there, looking out into the sunshine; her back to the room; her small hands clasped; every nerve strained to miss no word of what was passing behind her.

Honor turned promptly on Paul, an anguish of suspense in her eyes.

"Is it—the worst?"

"No—no—not that," he reassured her hastily.

"Tell me everything, please."

"I only know bare facts; the news came by helio. It seems there was a sharp hand-to-hand engagement. The Boy and some of his men were taken by surprise. Just as Theo reached them Denvil was—killed!"

A stifled sound broke from Evelyn.

"And—Theo?" Honor's low voice seemed to come from very far away.

"Theo has been badly cut about. Four wounds. The most serious is a bullet wound in his face—close to the right eye. They seem afraid that he may possibly—lose his sight."

"It is not true—oh, it is *not* true!" Evelyn's hands went up to her head with a desperate cry. Then she swayed, tottered backward, and fell prone among the sofa cushions.

"Honor—come to me—I'm frightened!" she moaned, without lifting her head; and in an instant Honor was bending over her, murmuring brave words of encouragement, removing her hat, and mechanically smoothing her hair.

"Is—he still here?" Evelyn asked under her breath.

"Yes, dear. Do you want him?"

"No—no; send him away. I want you—only you!"

Wyndham was already nearing the door and Honor followed him out into the hall.

"You see she's a little off her balance, poor child."

"Yes, I see," he answered wearily. "And I thank God with all my heart that *you* are here. Will you tell Mrs Desmond that an escort is returning to-day with Theo and —the Boy. They will reach Kohat to-morrow evening."

Honor straightened herself suddenly.

"I will tell her. To-morrow evening. Does Frank know too?"

"Yes; she was in when I came. It upset her very much. Not a soul in the regiment—officers or men—will have a minute's peace of mind till the result of this wound is known for certain. In all the misery of it, one is proud to realise that."

Something of his own grief showed in his voice for the first time, and Honor's heart contracted with too keen a sympathy.

"Ah, Paul! you speak of it so calmly—as if you were just one with the rest. But I, at least, can guess what the pain and suspense must be for you."

His face softened at the tender inflection of her voice.

"No," he said, "even you cannot guess that. Now go back to his wife. If I can be of any use at all send for me. I shall not come round otherwise till I bring him here to-morrow evening. I mean to ride out with a small escort and meet them on the way."

Honor found Evelyn rigid and tearless among her cushions. The strange mingling of coldness and terror in her eyes startled the girl. She hurried to the sofa and knelt down at her side.

"Don't look like that, Evelyn," she said. "It's horrible! Only think, Theo will be here to-morrow evening. Paul told me so just now."

"To-morrow—to-morrow? He will be here, in this house—to-morrow?" She repeated the word with stunned iteration, and there was no feeling in her tone, only an uncanny fear, that chilled the blood in Honor's veins.

"I never thought—it would be so soon. How can we manage about getting away?"

"Getting away—where—in Heaven's name?" Honor rose abruptly. She began to feel as though she were moving in a nightmare.

"Oh, anywhere, away from here. I can't—I won't see him, when he is 'badly cut about' and—half blind. I thought—if you would take me to Murree—Mrs Olliver would be quite glad to look after him. And when he is better, he could come up too. But if—if he is really going to be—blind——"

She closed her eyes and shuddered. No flicker of pity stirred in Honor's heart. It needed all her force of will to control her temper, even for a few minutes longer. But a grim curiosity urged her to discover how far it was possible to travel along such incredible lines of thought and feeling.

"Well, what then?" she demanded coldly.

"Then—I know I could—never come back to him—never!" Theo's wife answered slowly, without raising her eyes, or the look in Honor's face would surely have frozen the words on her lips. "To feel that he was always in the dark would frighten me out of my life. And he would never be left alone, I know. There are so many—others."

But Honor could bear no more. Bending down, she caught hold of Evelyn's shoulders and fairly shook her, as though she would shake her back to life and human feeling. Her blue eyes blazed with indignation.

"How *dare* you talk like that!" she said in a low note of concentrated wrath. "How dare you think such despicable thoughts! Of course there are others who would give their lives to save him from a minute's pain; and you would let them take your place,—yours? And you can actually expect that *I*—of all people—will back you up in your desertion of him? No indeed! If you go, you go alone; and I shall never have a word to say to you again. I may be speaking hotly, because I am furiously angry. But I mean every word I say; and my actions will prove it. What's more, *I will not let you go.* You *shall* stand by him, however frightened you may be. You talk of—loving him, and you would treat him as I should be ashamed to treat a dog! Evelyn! Evelyn!"—her voice broke suddenly, and tears started to her eyes,—"tell me you did not mean what you said; or I don't know how I am to go on helping you at all!"

There was more of command than of entreaty in the last words, and Evelyn looked up at the transfigured beauty of her face with a slow shivering sigh.

"You are very wonderful, and very—terrible, Honor," she said. "I never imagined you could be as terrible as that." Then her lips quivered, and she caught at the girl's skirt, drawing her nearer. "You *must* go on helping me, or everything will go to pieces."

"So long as you remain a loyal wife to—Theo, I cannot choose but do so, with all my heart."

She knelt down again now; and Evelyn, flinging both arms round her neck, broke into a passion of weeping.

"I think I was half mad," she moaned through her tears, clinging to Honor as a drowning woman clings to a spar. "And I am dreadfully frightened still. But I will do whatever you tell me. I will try to be a loyal wife, even if——"

"We won't think of that at all," Honor interposed hastily. "It cannot—it shall not happen!"

But Evelyn's tears flowed on unchecked. The fire of Honor's just anger had melted the morsel of ice in her heart; and in a very short time she had cried herself to sleep.

Then Honor gently unlocked the clinging fingers, and went straight to Frank Olliver's room.

CHAPTER XXIV.

I WANT LADYBIRD.

"So free we seem; so fettered fast we are."
—BROWNING.

A LOW sun was gilding the hill-tops when two doolies, borne by sturdy *kahars* and escorted by Wyndham and Mackay, passed between the gate-posts of Desmond's bungalow. Honor stood with Evelyn at the head of the verandah steps; but as the *kahars* halted, and the officers prepared to dismount, she moved back a space, leaving her to welcome her husband alone.

The blood ebbed from Evelyn's face as she watched Theo mount the steps, slowly, uncertainly, supported on either side by Wyndham and the doctor—he who, in normal circumstances, would have cleared them at a bound and taken her in his arms. His appearance alone struck terror into her heart. Was this the splendid-looking husband who had ridden away full of life and energy,—this strange-seeming man, whose face was disfigured and more than half-hidden by an unsightly bandage and a broad green shade; whose empty coat-sleeve, slashed and blood-stained, suggested too vividly the condition of the arm strapped into place beneath?

It was all she could do not to shrink back instinctively when the men moved aside, as Honor had done, to afford husband and wife some small measure of privacy, and Theo held out his hand.

"They've sent me back rather the worse for wear, Ladybird," he said, with a smile; "but Mackay will put the pieces together in good time."

"Oh, Theo—I hope so!—It's dreadful to see you—like that."

The hand she surrendered to him was cold as ice; and the attempt at welcome in her voice was checked by a paralysing fear and constraint. Thirty-six hours of severe pain in body and mind had failed to break his spirit; but the thing was achieved by a dozen words from his wife. He knew now what to expect from her; and for the moment he was stricken speechless.

"I am so—sorry," she murmured, "about——"

"Yes—yes, I know," he took her up quickly; and there was an awkward silence.

"Who—what—is in that other doolie?" she asked, in a hurried whisper.

"The Boy."

"But, Theo—you're not going to——"

"For God's sake shut up!"

He swayed a little in speaking, and promptly Paul was at his side. No one had heard what passed; and when Mackay, returning to his post by the wounded arm, gently urged Desmond forward, Paul signalled to Evelyn to take his place, while he went back to the doolie.

"Just a minute, Mrs Desmond," he said in a low tone.

Evelyn, startled by the request, stood irresolute; and since there was no time for hesitancy, Honor came forward and put her hand under Theo's elbow. She felt a jar go all through him at her touch, and knew that he had heard Wyndham's request.

"Ah, Honor," he said, by way of greeting, "I'm afraid I've come back a mere log on your hands."

An undernote of bitterness in his tone gave her courage to speak the thought in her mind. "We are only too thankful to have got you back safe—in any condition," she murmured.

He did not answer at once; and she moved away to make place for Paul, whose face was set in very rigid lines.

"Take me to the *duftur*," Desmond commanded curtly. "I'll not be put to bed."

"No, no, man; we'll settle you up in your long chair," Mackay answered soothingly. He perceived that by some means Mrs Desmond had jarred his patient, and was in high ill-humour with her accordingly.

At the study door, Amar Singh almost laid his head at Desmond's feet. Within the room they found Frank Olliver arranging pillows and a rug on the deck-chair, and on a table beside it a light meal awaited him.

The meal ended, they all left him with one accord, instinctively making way for his wife—who was crying her heart out in the next room.

Paul was the last to leave. He remained standing by Desmond, resting a hand on his sound shoulder. But there are silences more illuminating than speech; and Theo Desmond knew all that was in his friend's heart at that moment—all that could never be spoken between them, because they were Englishmen, born into a heritage of incurable reserve.

"You're going to pull through this," Paul said quietly.

"Am I? Ask Mackay."

"No need for that—I'm sure of it; and—in the mean while——" A tightening of his grasp supplied the rest.

"Thanks, old man. I know what you mean."

Then Paul went reluctantly out, and on into the drawing-room, where he found Mackay and Honor Meredith in close conference. The little doctor was laying down the law in respect of his patient with characteristic bluntness.

"Now, Miss Meredith," he had said, as he met her in the hall, and drew her aside into the empty room, "I'm a plain man, and you must put up with plain speaking for the next few minutes. It's no light matter to be responsible for a chap like Desmond. Not a morsel of use talking to his wife! She seems to have upset him already. The Lord alone knows how women do these things. Fools men are to care! But Desmond is what you call finely organised; and you can't handle a violin as you would a big drum. Frankly, now, his eyesight's in danger; and that wound in his cheek is an ugly one in any case. He wants careful nursing, and I refuse to put him into Mrs Desmond's hands. I'd deserve hanging for murder if I did! Remains Mrs Olliver, or yourself. 'Twould be awkward for Mrs Olliver to take his wife's place when there is a capable woman on the spot. So now, will you take charge of Desmond for me, and put yourself under my orders?—that's the real *mutlub*[1] of the whole matter. You're welcome to say I don't think Mrs Desmond strong enough, if you feel bound to tell a polite lie on the subject."

[1] Gist

Ꮋonor had listened to the doctor's brusquely-delivered ech with a growing sense of helplessness, as of a mouse ght in a trap. His statement of the case was uncomfort- y plain. He left her no loophole of escape; and by the e he fired his final question at her, she had decided on sent capitulation.

"Yes, I will take charge of him," she said. "Only Mrs smond must have some share in the nursing—for his sake her own."

"Oh, well—well, I suppose she must. The less the better his sake; and you've got to consider Desmond before ry one else at present. I insist on that."

Honor smiled faintly at the superfluous injunction; and it was at this point that Paul entered the room.

Mackay turned on him a face of open jubilation.

"Congratulate me, Wyndham! I've secured Miss Meredith's services for Desmond."

"Thank God," Paul answered fervently; and he thanked Honor also with his eyes.

"I shall move into the bungalow myself after the funeral, and give you what help I can. He will need a good deal of companionship to keep him from chafing at his helplessness. He wished the Boy to be brought here and buried from his house. I am making all arrangements; and we shall be round quite early in the morning. Can I see Desmond again to-night?"

Mackay pursed his lips.

"He'll do best with just the women-folk this evening. Look in after Mess, if you like—last thing."

"Was Evelyn with him when you left?" Honor asked suddenly, a flash of apprehension in her tone.

"No."

"I must go and see what has come to her," she said, visibly disturbed. "I shall see you both after Mess."

She hurried out, and listened intently at the study door. No sound broke the stillness; and with an aching dread at her heart she passed on to the next door.

The brief dusk of India was already almost spent; and finding Evelyn's room in semi-darkness, she paused on the threshold.

"Are you there, dear?" she called softly; and was answered by a stifled sound from the region of the bed, where Evelyn lay prone, her face buried in the pillows. At that Honor came forward, and laid a firm though a not unkindly hand upon her.

"Evelyn, this is childish selfishness. Get up and go to him at once."

The sole answer vouchsafed to her was a vehement shaking of the fair head; a fresh paroxysm of distress.

"My dear — my dear," she urged, bending down and speaking more softly, "you *must* pull yourself together. This is no time to think of your own trouble. He is wounded, anxious, and terribly unhappy and—he wants you. Do you call this being a loyal wife? Remember, you promised——"

Thus appealed to, Evelyn lifted her head, supporting it on one elbow, and showed a grief-disfigured face.

"Yes, I know. But—couldn't you go to him, just for now, Honor? You're not upset, like I am; — and say I — I'll come when I'm better."

Honor went white to the lips,

"No, Evelyn," she said, her anger rising as she went on. "There are things that even *I* must refuse to do for you. I have done all that is in my power; but I *will* not take your place with—your husband."

Astonishment checked Evelyn's sobbing, and a spark of unreasoning jealousy shot through the mist of her tears.

"I don't *want* you to take my place with him. He's *mine!*"

"Then don't ask me to go to him now."

The counter-stroke was unanswerable. Evelyn made a genuine attempt to still the uncontrolled quivering of her body, and actually got upon her feet. But abandonment to misery had so shaken her that, even as Honor put out a steadying hand, she fell back among her pillows with a choking sob.

"It's no use," she moaned. "Go, Honor—go *now;* and say I—I'm coming."

The girl set her teeth hard. A strange light gleamed in the blue of her eyes. She moved across to the washing-stand and poured out a stiff dose of sal volatile.

"Here, Evelyn," she said, all the tenderness gone from

her voice, "drink this at once. Then get up as soon as you can, and make yourself presentable. I shall not be gone many minutes, and you *must* be ready to go to him the instant I come back."

Evelyn choked and spluttered over the burning mixture.

"Oh, thank you, Honor, thank you. Only — don't look so angry about it, please."

"I *am* angry—I am bitterly angry," Honor answered with sudden vehemence, and went quickly from the room.

Once outside, she paused; her whole soul uplifted in a wordless prayer for strength and self-control. It seemed to her that Evelyn's reception of Theo went far to make her own departure a matter of imperative necessity, cruelly hard though it was to risk being misjudged at such a crisis.

With heart and spirit braced for her ordeal, she entered the room.

But at sight of him, who was the incarnation of life, cheerfulness, and vigour, lying stricken in heart and body, her courage deserted her, and she could neither speak nor move. On the lower end of the long chair Rob nestled in an attitude of perplexed watchfulness; satisfaction and bewilderment contending for the mastery over his faithful soul; and Desmond's right arm supported his stunned and aching head.

As Honor paused on the threshold, he stirred uneasily. "That you, Ladybird?" he asked; and his tone, if listless, was unmistakably tender.

"No, Theo. It is I—Honor," the girl answered in a low voice without moving forward.

"Where's Evelyn, then?"

"She's coming soon—very soon."

"What's gone wrong with her? Has she fainted? You might come a little closer to a fellow, Honor. I feel cut off from everything and every one, with this damnable green wall in front of my eyes."

At that cry from the man's tormented heart all thought of her own pain, all doubt as to her own strength, was submerged by a flood-tide of pure human compassion; and she came to him straightway, kneeling close beside his chair, and laying one hand lightly on the rug that covered him.

"There, Theo—there. Can you see me a little now?" she asked tenderly. "You mustn't think hard things of—Ladybird—please. She let herself go so completely after seeing you in the verandah, and it was impossible for her to come to you while she was in such a state of collapse. I have given her a strong dose of sal volatile, and she begged me to explain things to you; so—I came. I can't tell you how sorry I was that it should be—only me."

He raised his head at that.

"You've the grit of all the Merediths in you, Honor," he said, and his changed tone assured her that she had, in some measure, fulfilled her purpose. "I can't have you talking about 'only me' in that deprecating fashion. Goodness knows what Ladybird would have done without you. No doubt she'll pull herself together when she has got more used to the hideousness of it all—myself included——"

"She will—I am sure she will," the girl declared with pardonable insincerity; "and I really believe that if—if *I* were not here, Evelyn might make more of an effort to stand on her own feet than she does now. Please don't misunderstand me, Theo,"—her brave voice faltered on the words—"please believe that I myself would far rather be here at a time like this. I would not dream of deserting my post if I were not quite sure that there are many others ready to look after you as carefully and willingly as I would do myself. Indeed, I am honestly suggesting what I think would be best for us all round—Evelyn especially. Won't you let me go, Theo, and at least try how it works?"

Desmond shook his head with cautious deliberation, since hasty movements had proved to be dangerous.

"My dear Honor," he objected, "you, who know Ladybird even better than I do, must surely know by now that nothing will force her to stand upon her own feet. To-day gives final proof of it. What's more, Paul will probably establish himself here. I can't have him criticising her, even in his own mind; and who but you can I rely on to prevent it, by keeping her up to the mark? You see, I am taking you at your word, and not misunderstanding you, and I ask you frankly to stand by us till this trouble is over, when you shall both go straight to the Hills."

"Very well, Theo; I will stay."

But her voice had an odd vibration in it. There was no refusing a request so worded; but she knew her decision was only deferred to a more seasonable moment.

"Thank you with all my heart," he said. "You'll not regret it, I feel certain."

During the pause that followed, the wounded man made a futile attempt to change his position. In an instant her hands were at his pillows, shifting them quickly and dexterously, supporting his shoulders with her arm the while.

"There, that's better, isn't it?" she asked; and the mother-note sounded in her voice.

"It's just beautiful, thank you. Now—I want Ladybird."

Honor's colour ebbed at the words, and she may be forgiven if a pang of rebellion stabbed her. All the hard tasks, it seemed, were to be hers; while for Evelyn was reserved the full measure of a love and tenderness which she seemed little able to rate to their true value. But there was no trace of emotion in her voice as she replied, "You shall have her at once; only she mustn't stay long. You have already talked more than is good for you."

"Talked?" he echoed, with a sudden outburst of impatience. "What else is there for me to do? I can neither read, nor write, nor move. Am I to lie here like a log, with my own black thoughts for company? I'm not ill, in spite of all."

"No, Theo, you are not ill now," the girl reasoned with him in all gentleness, "but with a wound like that so near your temple you soon will be ill, if you refuse to be moderately careful. Evelyn shall stay for a quarter of an hour. After that you *must please* obey me and lie quiet, so as to get a little sleep, if possible, after your cruel journey. Amar Singh shall sit here, and I will leave the drawing-room door open and play to you;—something invigorating—the Pastoral, to start with. Will that do?"

His prompt penitence caught at her heart.

"Forgive me, Honor," he said. "I was an ungrateful brute, and you're a long way too good to me. I'll obey orders in future, without kicking against the pricks. The music will be no end of a comfort. Just like you to think of it!"

CHAPTER XXV.

THE MOONLIGHT SONATA.

"The depth and dream of my desire,
The bitter paths wherein I stray,
Thou knowest, who hast made the Fire,
Thou knowest, who hast made the Clay."
—KIPLING.

WHEN the bedroom door opened, Desmond lifted his head, in a distracted attempt to see more of his wife than the shade would permit, and held out his hand.

"Come, Ladybird. I want you."

She came at his bidding, and put her hand in his. But, unwittingly, she stood no nearer than the action demanded; and in her bewildered misery she forgot that he would expect her to stoop and kiss him. It was a fatal omission—how fatal she did not realise till later.

He drew her closer with quiet decision; and she submitted, as she would have submitted to anything he might have chosen to do just then.

"Am I so very dreadful that you can't bear to come near me?" he asked, with a brave attempt at lightness.

"Oh, Theo, don't say that " she pleaded. It came too painfully near the truth. "Only—I can't seem able to believe that—it is really you."

"Well, I give you my word it *is* really me—the very same Theo who won the Punjab Cup, and danced with you at Lahore three months ago." Then he bit his lip sharply; for the thought smote him that he might never sit a pony or dance with her again.

The sob that had been clutching at her throat escaped, in

spite of herself. "Lahore!" she murmured. "It was all so beautiful at Lahore!"

"Don't cry about it, darling. It will be just as beautiful again, in time. Sit down on the floor—here, close to me. I can't get a sight of you any other way."

She sat down, but in such a position that he had only a scant view of her tear-disfigured face. He pushed the damp ringlets back from her forehead. In his eyes it was her misfortune, rather than her fault, that she should be so inexorably chained to her own trouble.

Her spirit and her love revived under the magic of his touch. She caught his hand and pressed it against her burning cheek. It was cool and steady and sustaining—the hand of a brave man.

"Poor child," he said gently. "I'm an uncomfortable sort of husband for you. But little accidents of this kind will happen to soldiers. Don't say you wish you hadn't married this one!" And he smiled.

"No—no. But, Theo, did you get all these wounds and things trying to save the Boy?"

"Yes; more or less."

"And it wasn't a scrap of use?"

"No. One had the satisfaction of killing the men who did for him. That was all!"

"And you might just as well have come back strong and splendid, like you went away?"

"No use thinking of what might have been, darling. We've got to set our teeth and face what *is*."

"Oh, Theo—you are very brave."

"Needs must, Ladybird. If a man fails in that, he had better not have been born. And you are going to be brave too,—my wife."

"Yes,—I hope so. But—it's much more horrible than I ever imagined; and if it's going on for weeks and weeks——"

The prospect so unnerved her that she leaned her head against him, sobbing bitterly.

"Oh, I can't—I can't——!"

The low cry came straight from her heart; and Desmond understood its broken protest to the full. The effort to uphold her was to be useless after all. He compressed his lips and gently released her hand.

"If it's as bad as that, my dear, and you really feel it will be too much for you," he said in a changed tone, "I might arrange for Honor to take you away in a day or two, till I am well enough to follow on. They all know here that you are not strong. One need not degrade you by telling—the whole truth."

"But, Theo, I couldn't leave you like that—just now, could I?"

His smile had a hint of scorn.

"Goodness knows! There is nothing to prevent you——"

"Yes—there is!" she spoke hurriedly, with downcast eyes. "Honor would never take me. She thinks it's dreadful that I should go. I never saw her so angry before. She—she said—terrible things——"

"Good God! What do—you—mean?"

Desmond spoke slowly. Anger and amazement sounded in his deep voice; and his wife saw what she had done.

"Theo!—Theo!" she cried, clasping her hands, and wringing them in distraction at her own foolishness, "I never meant to say that. I—I——"

"No—but you meant to do it," he said, breathing hard and speaking with an effort. "You actually thought of—going—before I came? You would have simply—bolted, and left me to come back to an empty house, if Honor had not prevented you? Great heavens! I can well believe she said terrible things."

His wife knelt upright now and caught at his hand. But he withdrew it hastily.

"Theo—will you listen to me and not be so angry? You are very unkind!"

"Am I? Don't you think it is the other way about? I confess I'm in no humour to listen to you just now. I've had about as much as I can stand to-night; and Mackay told me I must not upset myself about things." He laughed harshly—a sound that chilled her blood. "But no mere man could anticipate *this!*"

"Well, I never *meant* to say it, and I think you're horrid, you don't understand——"

"No; thank God, I don't understand—cowardice and desertion. Get up now and leave me alone, please. It's the greatest kindness you can do me; and yourself also, I imagine."

"Oh, don't say that. It's not true; and I'm not going to dream of leaving you. Won't you let me explain?"

"To-morrow, Evelyn, to-morrow," he answered wearily. "I shall be able to give you a fairer hearing by then; and I pray God I may have misjudged you. Now—go."

She bent down and kissed his hand; then rose and slipped silently back into her own room.

Theo Desmond lay motionless, like a man stunned. This third blow, dealt him in quick succession, left him broken in heart and spirit, as he had never been broken in all his days.

It is written that a man must be defeated in order to succeed; and in that moment Desmond bit the dust of the heart's most poignant tragedy and defeat—the shattering of faith in one who is very near to us. Nor was it the shattering of faith alone. The shock of his wife's unwitting revelation, coming when he stood supremely in need of her loyalty and tenderness, struck a mortal blow at his love for her; though in his present state he was not capable of recognising the truth. He only knew that, for the first time in his life, he felt unutterably alone—alone in a dimness which might deepen to permanent darkness; and that the wholesome vigorous realities of life seemed to have slipped for ever out of reach. He only knew that his wife would have turned her back upon him in his hour of extremity—openly disgracing herself and him—but for the intervention of Honor Meredith.

Her mere name called up a vivid vision of her beauty, a remembrance of the infinite compassion in her voice when she had knelt beside him, soothing and strengthening him by some miracle of womanly intuition, urging him to make allowance for his wife's distress.

A sudden glow thrilled through him from head to foot. He stirred slightly; and tried, without success, to turn in his chair. It was as if the compelling spirit of her had dragged him back from the brink of nothingness to renewed life, to the assurance that in his utmost loneliness he was not—nor ever would be—alone. And, in that moment of awakening, the voice of sympathy came to him—tender, uplifting, clear as speech.

Honor Meredith had begun to play.

By way of prelude she chose a piece of pure organ music—the exquisitely simple Largo of the Second Sonata. From that she passed on to the Pastoral itself, opening it, as of custom, with the fine Andante movement—the presage of coming storm.

None among all that wondrous thirty-two is so saturate with open-air cheerfulness and vigour as this Sonata, aptly christened the Pastoral. Here we are made accomplices of Nature's moods, and set in the midst of her voices. Here, in swift succession, are storm and sunshine; falling rain-drops; the plash and ripple of mountain streams; bird notes of rare verisimilitude, from the anxious twitterings before the thunder-shower, to the chorus of thanksgiving after it has swept vigorously past. And Theo Desmond, lying in semi-darkness, with pain for his sole comrade, knew that the hand of healing had been again outstretched to him,—not all in vain.

The Sonata ended in a brisk ripple of sound; and for a while Honor sat motionless, her shapely hands resting on the keyboard as if awaiting further inspiration.

Desmond moved again uneasily. He wondered what her unfailing intuition of his need would lead her to play next; and even as he wondered, expectancy was lulled into a great rest by the measured tranquillity of Beethoven's most stately and divine Adagio—the Moonlight Sonata.

There are some people who get deeper into a piano than others, who breathe a living soul into the trembling wires. The magic of Honor's music lay in this capacity; and she exerted it now to the limit of her power.

The Moonlight Sonata is cumulative from start to finish, passing from the exalted calm of the Adagio, through the graciousness of the Allegretto, to that inspired and inspiring torrent of harmony the Presto Agitato. Its incomparable effect of the rush and murmur of many waters, through which the still small voice of melody rings clear as a song dropped straight from heaven, leaves little room in a listener's soul for the jangling discords of earth. Into that movement the great deaf musician seems to have flung the essence of his impatient spirit;—that rare mingling of ruggedness and simplicity, of purity and passionate power, which went to make up the remarkable character of the man, and which sets Beethoven's music apart from the music of his compeers. Wagner, Chopin, Grieg,—these range the whole gamut of emotion for its own sake. But in the hands of the master it becomes what it should be—the great uplifting lever of the world.

The listener in the darkened room drew a long breath, and clenched his teeth so forcibly that a spasm of pain passed, like a fused wire, through the wound in his cheek. But the keener stress of mind and heart dulled his senses to the pin-prick of the flesh. For in the brief space of time since the music began, Theo Desmond — the soldier of proven courage and self-forgetfulness—had fought the most momentous battle of his life;—a battle in which was no flourish of trumpets, no clash of arms, no medal or honour for the winning.

But the price of conquest had still to be paid. There were still practical issues to be faced, and he faced them with the straightforward simplicity that was his. He saw as in a lightning-flash, the hidden meaning of this girl's power to stimulate and satisfy him; saw the unnameable danger ahead; and in the same breath decided that Honor must go. There must be no risk of disloyalty to Evelyn, were it only in thought.

He could not as yet see how he was to retract his request for her presence. His stunned brain refused to cope with such harassing details. The thing must be said; and no doubt he would find strength to say it aright. For him that was enough; and he deliberately turned his back on the subject.

The Presto was drawing to a close now in a cascade of single notes, as stirring to the ear as the downrush of a waterfall to the eye; and during the silence that followed upon the last crashing chords, the bitter thought came to him that Honor's departure would mean not only the loss of her comradeship, but of the music, which had again become one of the first necessities of his life.

With a sensation altogether strange to him, since it had in it an element of fear, he heard her shut the piano and come towards the door of his room. Closing his eyes, he lay very still, in the hope that she might believe him to be asleep. Ordinary speech with her seemed an impossibility just then.

He felt her come in, and pause beside his chair. His stillness clearly deceived her, for she said nothing; neither did she move away, as he had devoutly hoped she would do.

Remembering that his eyes were hidden, he opened them; and was rewarded by the sight of her cream-coloured skirt, and her hands hanging loosely clasped upon it. An intolerable longing came upon him to push off the shade; to satisfy himself with one glimpse of her face before banishing it out of his life. But strength was given him to resist, and to realise his own cowardice in deceiving her thus.

Then, because he was incapable of doing anything by halves, he made a slight movement and put out his hand.

"Thank you," he said simply. "You have heartened me more than I can say."

"I am so glad," she answered in a low tone, allowing her hand to rest for a mere instant in his. "Now I want you to shut all trouble out of your mind, and go to sleep for a long time. Will you?"

At that the corners of his mouth went down.

"Easier said than done, I'm afraid. But it's sound advice; and I'll do my best to act upon it."

"In that case—you are bound to succeed."

And, without waiting for his possible answer, she slipped quietly out of the room.

CHAPTER XXVI

STAND TO YOUR GUNS.

"It is so that a woman loves who is worthy of heroes."
—R. L. S.

WYNDHAM, returning to the bungalow soon after ten o'clock, found it readjusted to its new conditions. Frank Olliver had returned to her empty home; and Desmond, at his own request, had had his camp-bed made up in the study, that he might in no way disturb his wife. She herself had retired early, without going in to him again. Honor noted and wondered at the omission; but since Evelyn had said nothing about her short interview with Theo, she forbore to question her or press her unduly at the start.

When Paul arrived Desmond was sound asleep, wearied out with pain of body and mind; while Honor moved noiselessly to and fro, setting in readiness all that might be wanted before morning. Paul came armed with Mackay's permission to remain on duty for the night, taking what little rest he required on the drawing-room sofa; and Honor could not withhold a smile at his satisfaction.

"I believe you're jealous!" she said. "You want to oust me, and have him all to yourself!"

"You are right," he answered frankly; and going over to the bed, stood looking upon his friend in an unspeakable content, that even anxiety was powerless to annul.

For all that, it was late before Honor managed to leave her patient, and slip away into the bare room where Harry Denvil lay awaiting the dawn.

Save for the long scar across his face, no suggestion ot

that last desperate fight was visible; and in the presence of the Great Silence, her own turmoil of heart and brain was stilled as at the touch of a reassuring hand. She knelt a long while beside the Boy. It pleased her to believe that he was in some way aware of her companionship; that perhaps he was even glad of it—glad that she should feel no lightest shrinking from the temple that had enshrined the brave jewel of his soul.

Arrived in her own room, she found Parbutti huddled on the ground, in a state of damp and voluble distress. She could not bring herself to dismiss the old woman at once; though her heart cried out for solitude, and weariness seemed suddenly to dissolve her very bones. She saw now that her love had deepened and strengthened during Desmond's absence, as great love is apt to do; and the shock of his return, coupled with the scant possibility of her own escape, had tried her fortitude more severely than she knew.

She submitted in silence to the exchanging of her tea-gown for a white wrapper, and to the loosening of her hair, Parbutti crooning over her ceaselessly the while.

"Now I will soothe your Honour's head till weariness be forgotten, O my Miss Sahib, daughter of my heart! Sleep without dreams, my life; and have no fear for the Captain Sahib, who is surely favoured of the gods by reason of his great courage."

While her tongue ran on, the wrinkled hands moved skilfully over the girl's head and neck, fingering each separate nerve, and stilling the throbbing pulses by that mystery of touch, which we of the West are just beginning to acquire, but which is a common heritage in the East.

"Go now, Parbutti," Honor commanded at length. "Thy fingers be miracle-workers. It is enough."

And as Parbutti departed, praising the gods, Honor leaned her chin upon her hands, and frankly confronted the decision that must be arrived at before morning.

To her inner consciousness it seemed wrong and impossible to fulfil her promise and remain; while to all outward appearance it seemed equally wrong and impossible to go. She could not see clearly. She could only feel intensely; and her paramount feeling at the moment was that God asked of her more than human nature could achieve.

The man's weakness and dependence awakened in her the strongest, the divinest element of a woman's love, and with it the longing to uphold and help him to the utmost limit of her power. It was this intensity of longing which convinced her that, at all costs, she must go. Yet at the first thought of Evelyn her invincible arguments fell back like a defeated battalion.

If she had sought the Frontier in the hope of coming into touch with life's stern realities, her hope had been terribly fulfilled.

"Dear God, what *ought* I to do?" she murmured on a note of passionate appeal. But no answer came out of the stillness; and sheer human need was too strong upon her for prayer.

Rising impulsively, she went over to the wide-flung door that led into the back verandah, and rolled up the "chick," flooding the room with light; for a full moon rode high in the heavens, eclipsing the fire of the stars. She stepped out into the verandah, and passed to the far end, that looked across a strip of rocky desolation to the hills.

The whole world slept in silver, its radiance intensified by patches of blue-black shadow; and with sudden distinctness her night journey of a year ago came back to her mind. What an immeasurable way she had travelled since then! And how far removed was the buoyant-hearted girl of that March morning from the woman who rebelled with all her soul against the cup of bitterness, even while she drank it to the dregs!

Deliberately she tried to gather into herself something of the night's colossal calm, to wrest from the starved scrub of the desert a portion of its patience, its astounding perseverance; to stifle her craving for clear unprejudiced human counsel.

By a natural impulse her thought turned to Mrs Conolly, who alone possessed both will and power to satisfy her need. To speak of her own trouble was a thing outside the pale of possibility. Death itself were preferable. But to consult her friend as to what would really be best for Evelyn was quite another matter. She would go and see Mrs Conolly before breakfast and be ruled by her unfailing wisdom.

Having arrived at one practical decision, her mind grew calmer. She went back to her room, lowered the "chick" and knelt for a long while beside her bed—a white, gracious figure, half-veiled by a dusky curtain of hair.

Habit woke her before seven; and she dressed briskly, heartened by a sense of something definite to be done. A sound of many feet and hushed voices told her that Wyndham and the Pioneer officers had arrived. Chaplains were rare on the Border in those days; and Wyndham was to read the service, as he did on most occasions, Sundays included.

When Honor came out into the hall she found the chick rolled up and the verandah a blaze of full-dress uniforms. No man plays out his last act with more of pomp and circumstance than a soldier; and there is a singular fitness in this emphasis on the dignity rather than the tragedy of death.

The girl remained standing afar off, watching the scene, whose brilliance was heightened by an untempered April sun.

A group of officers, moving aside, revealed two scarlet rows of Pioneers; and beyond them Paul's squadron, striking a deeper note of blue and gold. The band was drawn up ready to start. Slanting rays flashed cheerfully from the brass of trumpets, cornets, bassoons; from the silver fittings of flutes; from the gold on scarlet tunics. And in the midst of this ordered brilliance stood the gun-carriage, grey and austere, its human burden hidden under the folds of the English flag. Behind the gun-carriage the Boy's charger waited, with an air of uncomplaining weariness, the boots hanging reversed over the empty saddle.

With an aching lump in her throat Honor turned away. At that moment the shuddering vibrations of muffled drums ushered in the "Dead March" and each note fell on her heart like a blow.

In passing the study door she paused irresolute, battling with that refractory heart of hers, which refused to sit quiet in its chains. It argued now that, after all, she was his nurse; she had every right to go in and see that all was well with him. But conscience and the hammering of her pulses warned her that the greater right was — to refrain; and straightening herself briskly, she went out through the back verandah to Mrs Conolly's bungalow.

She had not been gone twenty minutes when Evelyn crept into the study, so softly that her husband was not aware of her presence till her fingers rested upon his hand.

He started, and took hold of them.

"That you?" he said gently. "Good-morning."

There was no life in his tone; and its apathy—so incredible a quality in him—gave her courage.

"Theo," she whispered, kneeling down by him, "is it any good trying to speak to you now? Will you believe that—I am ever so sorry? I have been miserable all night; and I am not frightened any more,—see!" In token of sincerity she caressed his empty coat-sleeve. "Will you please—forgive me? Will you?"

"With all my heart, Ladybird," he answered quietly. "But it's no use speaking. A thing like that can't be explained away. It is simply wiped off the slate — you understand?" And almost before the words were out she had kissed him.

Then she slid down into a sitting position, one arm flung lightly across the rug that covered him.

In that instant the thunder of three successive volleys shook the house; and heart-stirring trumpet-notes sounded the Last Post. With a small shudder Evelyn shrank closer to her husband, resting her head against his chair; and Desmond lay watching her in silent wonderment at the tangle of moods and graces which, for lack of a truer word, must needs be called her character. He wondered also how much might have been averted if she had come to him thus yesterday instead of to-day. Impossible to guess. He could only wrench his thoughts away from the forbidden subject; and try to beat down the strong new yearning that possessed him, by occasionally stroking his wife's hair.

It is when we most crave for bread that life has this ironical trick of presenting us with a stone.

Honor, in the meanwhile, had reached Mrs Conolly's

bungalow. She found her in the drawing-room arranging flower-vases, and equipped for her morning ride.

"Honor? You? How delightful!" Then catching a clearer view of the girl's face: "My dear—what is it?"

Honor smiled.

"I am afraid you were going out," she said, evading the question.

"Certainly I was; but I am not going now. It is evident that you want me."

"Yes—I want you."

Mrs Jim called out an order to the waiting *sais;* and followed Honor, who had gone over to the mantelpiece, and buried her face in the cool fragrance of a cluster of Gloire de Dijons.

Mrs Conolly took her gently by the arm.

"I can't have you looking like that, my child," she said. "Your eyes are like saucers, with indigo shadows under them. Did you sleep a wink last night?"

"Not many winks; that's why I am here."

"I see. You must be cruelly anxious about Captain Desmond, as we all are; but I *will not* believe that the worst can happen."

"No—oh no!" Honor spoke as if she were beating off an enemy. "But the trouble that kept me awake was—Evelyn."

"Ah! Is the strain going to be too much for her? Come to the sofa, dear, and tell me the whole difficulty."

Honor hesitated. She had her own reasons for wishing to avoid Mrs Conolly's too sympathetic scrutiny.

"You sit down," she said. "I feel too restless. I would rather speak first." And with a hint of inward perplexity Mrs Conolly obeyed.

"It's like this," Honor began, resting an arm on the mantelpiece and not looking directly at her friend, "Dr Mackay has asked me to take entire charge of Theo for the present. He spoke rather strongly,—rather cruelly, about not leaving him in Evelyn's hands. I think he wanted to force my consent; and for the moment I could not refuse. But this is Evelyn's first big chance of rising above herself; and if I step in and do everything I take it right out of her hands. This seems to me so unfair that I have been seriously wondering whether I ought not to—go right away till the worst is over." And she reiterated the arguments she had already put before Theo, as much in the hope of convincing herself as her friend.

Mrs Conolly, watching her with an increasing thoughtfulness, divined some deeper complication beneath her unusual insistence on the wrong point of view; and awaited the sure revelation that would come when it would come.

"You see, don't you," Honor concluded, in a beseeching tone, "that it is not easy to make out what is really best, what is right to be done? And Evelyn's uncertainty makes things still more difficult. One moment I feel almost sure she would 'find herself' if I were not always at her elbow; and the next I feel as if it would be criminal to leave her unsupported for five minutes at a time like this."

"That last comes nearer the truth than anything you have said yet," was Mrs Jim's unhesitating verdict. "Frankly, Honor, I agree with Dr Mackay; and I must really plead with you to leave off splitting straws about your 'Evelyn,' and to think of Captain Desmond—and Captain Desmond only. Surely you care more for him, and for what comes to him, than your line of argument seems to imply?"

Honor drew herself up as if she had been struck. The appeal was so unlooked for, the implication so unendurable, that for an instant she lost her balance. A slow colour crept into her cheeks, a colour drawn from the deepest wells of feeling; and while she stood blankly wondering how she might best remedy her mistake, Mrs Conolly's voice again came to her ears.

"Indeed, my child, you spoke truth just now," she said slowly, a fresh significance in her tone. "It must be *very* hard for you to make out what is right."

Honor threw up her head with a gesture of defiance.

"Why should you suddenly say that?" she demanded, almost angrily. But the instant her eyes met those of her friend the unnameable truth flashed between them clear as speech and with a stifled sound Honor hid her face in her hands.

Followed a tense silence; then Mrs Conolly came to her and put an arm round her. But the girl stiffened under the touch of sympathy implying mutual knowledge of that which belonged only to herself and God.

"How could I dream that you would guess?" she murmured, without uncovering her face—"that you would even imagine such a thing to be possible?"

"My dearest," the other answered gently, "I am old enough to know that, where the human heart is concerned, all things are possible."

"But I can't endure that you should know; that you should—think ill of me."

"You know me very little, Honor, if you can dream of that for a moment. Come and sit down. No need to hold aloof from me now."

Honor submitted to be led to the sofa, and drawn down close beside her friend. The whole thing seemed to have become an incredible nightmare.

"Listen to me, my child," Mrs Conolly began, the inexpressible note of mother-love sounding in her voice. "I want you to realise, once for all, how I regard this matter. I think you know how much I have loved and admired you, and I do so now—more than ever. An overwhelming trouble has come upon you, by no will of your own; and you are evidently going to meet it with a high-minded courage altogether worthy of your father's daughter."

Honor shivered.

"Don't speak of father," she entreated. "Only—now that you understand, tell me—tell me—what *must* I do?"

The passionate appeal coming from this girl—apt rather to err in the direction of independence—stirred Mrs Jim's big heart to its depths.

"You will abide by my decision?" she asked.

"Yes; I am ready to do anything for—either of them."

"Bravely spoken, my dear. In that case I can only say, 'Stand to your guns.' You have promised to take over charge of Captain Desmond, and a soldier's daughter should not dream of deserting her post. Mind you, I would not give such advice to ninety-nine girls out of a hundred in your position. The risk would be too serious; and I only dare give it to you because I am *sure* of you, Honor. I quite realise why you feel you ought to go. But your own feelings must simply be ignored. Your one hope lies in starving them to death, if possible. Give Evelyn her chance by all means, but I can't allow you to desert Captain Desmond on her account. You must be at hand to protect him, and uphold her, in case of failure. In plain English, you must consent to be a mere prop—putting yourself in the background and leaving her to reap the reward. It is the eternal sacrifice of the strong for the weak. You are one of the strong; and in your case there is no shirking the penalty without an imputation that could never be coupled with the name of Meredith."

Honor looked up at that with a characteristic tilt of her chin, and Mrs Conolly's face softened to a smile.

"Am I counselling cruelly hard things, dear?" she asked tenderly.

"No, indeed. If you were soft and sympathetic, I should go away at once. You have shown me quite clearly what is required of me. It will not be—easy. But one can do no less than go through with it—in silence."

Mrs Conolly sat looking at the girl for a few seconds. Then:

"My dear, I am very proud of you," she said with quiet sincerity. "I can see that you have drawn freely on a Strength beyond your own. Just take victory for granted; and do your simple human duty to a sick man who is in great need of you, and whose fortune or misfortune is a matter of real concern to many others besides those near and dear to him. I know I am not exaggerating when I say that if any serious harm came to Captain Desmond it would be a calamity felt not only by his regiment, but by more than half the Frontier Force. He has the 'genius to be loved,' that is perhaps the highest form of genius——"

"I know—I know. Don't talk about him, please."

"Ah! but that is part of your hard programme, Honor. You must learn to talk of him, and to let others talk of him. Only you must banish him altogether *out of your own thoughts*. You see the difference?"

"Yes; I see the difference."

"The essence of danger lies there, and too few people recognise it. I believe that half the emotional catastrophes of life might be traced back to want of self-control in the region of thought. The world's real conquerors are those who 'hold in quietness their land of the spirit'; and you have the power to be one of them if you choose."

"I do choose," Honor answered in a low level voice, looking straight before her.

"Then the thing is as good as done." She rose on the words, and drew Honor to her feet. "There; I think I have said hard things enough for one day."

Honor looked very straightly into the elder woman's strong plain face.

"I know you don't expect me to thank you," she said; "we understand each other too well for that. And we will never speak of this again, please. It is dead and buried from to-day."

"Of course. That is why I have spoken rather fully this morning. But be sure you will be constantly in my thoughts, and—in my prayers."

Then she took possession of the girl, holding her closely for a long while; and when they moved apart tears stood in her eyes, though she was a woman little given to that luxury.

"This has been a great blow to me, dear," she said. "I had such high hopes for you. I had even thought of Major Wyndham."

Honor smiled wearily.

"It was perverse of me. I suppose it ought to have been —Paul."

"I wish it had been, with all my heart; and I confess I am puzzled about you two. How has he come to be 'Paul' within this last fortnight?"

"It is simply that we have made a compact. He knows now that he can never be anything more than—Paul—the truest friend a woman ever had."

"Poor fellow! So there are two of you wasted!"

"Is any real love ever wasted?" Honor asked so simply that Mrs Conolly kissed her again.

"My child, you put me to shame. It is clearly I who must learn from you. Now, go home; and God be with you as He very surely will."

Then with her head uplifted and her spirit braced to unflinching endurance, Honor Meredith went out into the blue and gold of the morning.

CHAPTER XXVII.

THE EXECRABLE UNKNOWN.

> "Doubting things go wrong,
> Often hurts more than to be sure they do."
> —SHAKESPEARE.

HONOR found Evelyn in a state of chastened happiness, buttering toast for Theo's breakfast, which stood ready on a tray at her side.

"Would you like to take this in yourself?" she said, as she completed her task. "I think he would be pleased. He was asking where you were."

The suggestion was so graciously proffered that Honor deposited a light kiss on the coiled floss silk of Evelyn's hair as she bent above the table. Then she took up the tray, and went on into the study.

She entered, and set it down without speaking; and Desmond, who was lying back with closed eyes, roused himself at the sound.

"Thank you, little woman," he said. Then, with a start, "Ah, Honor,—it's you. Very kind of you to trouble. Good-morning."

The contrast in his tone and manner was apparent, even in so few words; and Honor was puzzled.

"I hope you got some sleep last night," she said, "after that cruel thirty-six hours."

"More or less, thanks. But I had a good deal to say to Paul. You and he seem to have become very close friends while I have been away."

"We have; permanently, I am glad to say. I should have come in to you when I got up, but I was sure he would have done everything you could want before leaving."

"He did; and he'll be back the minute he's through with his work. He is an incomparable nurse; and with him at hand, I shall not need to—trespass on so much of your time, after all."

Honor bit her lip and tingled in every nerve, less at the actual words than at the manner of their utterance—a mingling of embarrassment and schooled politeness, which set her at arm's length, checked spontaneity, and brought her down from the heights with the speed of a dropped stone.

"It is not a question of trespassing on my time," she said, and in spite of herself a hint of constraint invaded her voice. "But I have no wish to deprive Paul of his privilege and right. You can settle it with Dr Mackay between you. Now, it's time you ate your breakfast. Can you manage by yourself? Shall I send Evelyn to help you?"

"No, thanks; I can manage all right."

He knew quite well he could do nothing of the sort; but his one need was to be alone.

"Very well. I shall be busy this morning with mail letters. Evelyn will sit with you till Paul comes; and Frank is sure to be round during the day. I pointed out to you yesterday that there were plenty of—others able and willing to see after you."

Before he could remonstrate she was gone. He drew in his breath sharply, between set teeth, and struck the arm of his chair with jarring force.

"I have hurt her—clumsy brute that I am. And I must do worse before the day's out. But the sooner it's over the better."

It was his invariable attitude towards a distasteful duty; and he decided not to let slip a second opportunity. Weak and unaided, he made what shift he could to deal with the intricacies of breakfast, choking back his irritability when he found himself grasping empty air in place of the teapot handle, sending the sugar-tongs clattering to the floor, and deluging his saucer by pouring the milk outside the cup. For the moment, to this man of independent spirit, these trivial indignities seemed more unendurable than the loss of his subaltern, the intrusive shadow threatening his self-respect, or the fear of blindness, that lay upon his heart cold and heavy as a corpse

And on the other side of the door, Honor stood alone in the drawing-room, trying to regain some measure of calmness before returning to the breakfast-table.

Red-hot resentment fired her from head to foot. Resentment against what, against whom? she asked herself blankly, and in the same breath turned her back upon the answer. Chiefly against herself, no doubt, for her inglorious descent from the pinnacle of stoicism, to which she had climbed barely an hour ago. It seemed that Love, coming late to these two, had come as a refiner's fire, to "torment their hearts, till it should have unfolded the capacities of their spirits." For Love, like Wisdom, is justified of all her children.

Breakfast, followed by details of housekeeping, reinstated common-sense. After all, since she had resolved to remain in the background, Theo had simplified affairs by consigning her to her destined position. She could quite well keep her promise to Dr Mackay, and superintend all matters of moment, without spending much time in the sick-room. Evelyn had agreed to accept her share of the nursing; and, as she had said, there were others, whose right was beyond her own.

Shortly after tiffin, Wyndham arrived with Rajinder Singh; and finding them together in the drawing-room—after the short interview permitted by Paul—Honor took the opportunity of fulfilling a request made by Theo on the previous evening.

"I have to write to Mrs Denvil," she said to Paul. "Would the Sirdar mind giving me a few details about the fighting on the 17th?"

Paul glanced approvingly at the old Sikh, who stood beside him, a princely figure of a man, in the magnificent mufti affected by the native cavalry officer—a long coat of peach-coloured brocade, and a turban of the same tint.

"Mind? He needs very little encouragement to enlarge on Theo's share in the proceedings."

"I would like to hear all he can tell me about that," she answered on a low note of fervour.

"You could follow him, I suppose?"

"Yes, perfectly."

"You hear, Ressaldar Sahib." Paul turned to his companion. "The Miss Sahib desires full news of the attack and engagement on Tuesday morning, that she may write of it to England."

The man's eyes gleamed under his shaggy brows, and he launched into the story, nothing loth; his eloquence rising as he warmed to the congenial theme.

Paul Wyndham stepped back a few paces into a patch of shadow, the better to watch Honor Meredith at his ease. She had balanced herself lightly on the arm of a chair; and now leaned a little forward, her lips just parted in the eagerness of anticipation. A turquoise medallion on a fine gold chain made a single incident of colour on the habitual ivory tint of her gown; threads of burnished copper glinted among the coils of her hair; and the loyal loving soul of her shone like a light through the seriousness of her eyes.

And as he watched, hope—that dies harder than any quality of the heart—rose up in him and prevailed. A day must come when this execrable unknown would no longer stand between them; when she would come to him of her own accord, as she had promised;—and he could wait for years, without impatience, on the bare chance of such a consummation.

But at this point a growing change in her riveted his attention—a change such as only the eyes of a lover could detect and interpret aright. She sat almost facing him; and at the first had looked towards him, from time to time, certain of his sympathy with the interest that held her. But before five minutes were out he had been forgotten as though he were not; and by now all else about her was forgotten also. Not her spirit only, but her whole heart glowed in her eyes; and Paul Wyndham, standing watchful and silent in the shadow, became abruptly aware that the execrable unknown—whom he had been hating for the past fortnight with all the strength of a strong nature—was the man he loved better than anything else on earth.

The Ressaldar was nearing the crowning-point of his story now. Honor listened spellbound as he told her of the breathless rush up that rugged incline, and of the sight that greeted them after scaling the mighty staircase of rock.

"None save the fleetest among us could keep pace with the Captain Sahib, wounded as he was," the Sikh was saying, when Wyndham, with a hideous jar, came back to reality. "But God gave me strength, though I have fifty years well told, so that I came not far behind; and even as Denvil Sahib fell, with his face to the earth, at the Captain Sahib's feet, he turned upon the Afridi devils like a lion among wolves, and smote three of them to hell before a man could say, 'It lightens.' Yet came there one pig of a coward behind him, Miss Sahib. Only, by God's mercy, I also was there, to give him such greeting as he deserved with my Persian sword, that hath passed from father to son these hundred and fifty years, and hath never done better work than in averting the hand of death from my Captain Sahib Bahadur, whom God will make Jungi-Lat-Sahib[1] before the end of his days! For myself I am an old man, and of a truth I covet no higher honour than this that hath befallen me, in rendering twice, without merit, such good service to the Border. Nay, but who am I that I should speak thus? Hath not the Miss Sahib herself rendered a like service? May your honour live long, and be the mother of heroes!"

Rajinder Singh bowed low on the words, which brought the girl to her feet and crimsoned her clear skin from chin to brow. By a deft question she turned the tide of talk into a less embarrassing channel; and Paul Wyndham, pulling himself together with an effort, went noiselessly out of the room.

Passing through the hall, he sought the comparative privacy of the back verandah, which was apt to be deserted at this tine of day. Here he confronted the discovery that tortured him—denied it; wrestled with it; and finally owned himself beaten by it. There was no evading the witness of his own eyes; and in that moment it seemed to him that he had reached the limit of endurance. Then a sudden question stabbed him. How far was Theo responsible for that which had come about? Was he, even remotely, to blame?

Had any living soul dared to breathe such questions in his hearing Wyndham would have knocked the words down his throat, and several teeth along with them, man of peace

[1] Commander-in-Chief.

though he was. But the very depth of his feeling for Desmond made him the more clear-eyed and stern in judgment; and the intolerable doubt, uprising like a mist before his inner vision, held him motionless, forgetful of place and time; till footsteps roused him, and he turned to find Honor coming towards him.

"Why, Paul," she said, "what brings you here? I have been looking for you everywhere. I thought you had gone to him. Evelyn says he is alone, and he wants you."

The unconscious use of the pronoun did not escape Paul's notice, and he winced at it, as also at the undernote of reproof in her tone.

"Sorry to have kept him waiting," he said quietly, and for the first time his eyes avoided her face. "I will go to him at once."

But on opening the study door he hesitated, dreading the necessity for speech; glad—actually glad—that his face was hidden from his friend. For all the depth of their reserve, the shadow of restraint was a thing unknown between them. But the world had been turned upside down for Wyndham since he left the familiar room half an hour ago. A spark that came very near to anger burned in his heart.

Desmond turned in his chair. Two hours of undiluted Evelyn had left him craving for mental companionship.

"Paul, old man," he said on a questioning note, "can't you speak to a fellow? Jove! what wouldn't I give for a good square look at you! It's poor work consorting with folk who only exist from the waist downward. You've not got to be running off anywhere else, have you?"

"No; I am quite free."

"Come on then, for Heaven's sake, dear chap! I have been wanting you all the morning."

The direct appeal, the pathos of his shattered vigour, and the irresistible friendliness of words and tone dispelled all possibility of doubt, or of sitting in judgment. Whatever appearances might suggest, Paul stood ready to swear, through thick and thin, to the integrity of his friend.

He came forward at once; and Desmond, cavalierly ousting Rob, made room for him on the lower end of his chair.

CHAPTER XXVIII.

YOU SHALL NOT—!

very sore shame if like a coward I shrink away from battle. Moreover, my own soul forbiddeth me."—HOMER.

QUITE a little party of a quiet kind assembled in the drawing-room for tea—Frank Olliver, Mrs Conolly, Wyndham, and his subaltern George Rivers, a promising probationer of a year's standing. The funeral of the morning, and anxiety as to the fate of Desmond's eyes, gave a subdued tone to the attempt at cheerfulness that prevailed, But Evelyn was grateful even for so mild a reversion to a more normal condition of things.

Each in turn had paid a short visit to the wounded hero in the study; but now they were grouped round the tea-table, leaving him temporarily alone. Evelyn had just filled his cup; and being in no mood to interrupt her exchange of light-hearted nothings with George Rivers, she glanced across at Wyndham, who promptly understood the situation and the mute request.

Honor, standing apart from the rest, noted the characteristic bit of by-play, and with a pang of envy watched Paul receive the cup and plate destined for Theo's room. It seemed a century since she had left him in the morning, with words wrung from her bitterness of heart and regretted as soon as they were uttered; and because of the longing, that would not be stifled, she refrained from the offer that came instinctively to her lips.

But, as if drawn by the magnetism of her thoughts, Paul came straight up to her.

"Won't you take these yourself?" he said in a low tone. "He has seen plenty of me this afternoon; and when I spoke of you just now he said you had not been near him since breakfast. Is that your notion of taking charge of a patient? It isn't mine, I can tell you!"

He spoke lightly, easily; for if life were to be tolerable, the discovery he had made must be ignored, without and within.

"It is not mine either," she answered, flushing at the unmerited reproof. "But I am by way of handing over my charge to you. Doesn't the arrangement suit you?"

"By all means. But Mackay rightly chose you. Besides, I am not so selfish that I should want to deprive Theo of the pleasure of your ministrations."

"Deprive him? You are judging him by yourself! It is hardly a question of deprivation, surely."

Wyndham glanced at her keenly.

"Hullo!" he said, "one doesn't expect that sort of tone from you where Theo is concerned. What do you mean me to understand by it?"

"Nothing—nothing at all! Only—he happens to prefer *your* ministrations. He almost told me so. You or he can settle it with Dr Mackay to-night. But I will take these in to him—if you wish."

"Purely as a favour to me?"

Her face lit up with a gleam of irrepressible humour.

"Purely as a favour to you!"

She took the cup and plate from him, still smiling, and passed on into the study.

As she bent above the table, Desmond lifted his head in a vain effort to get a glimpse of her face.

"Thank you—thank you—how good of you!" he said, his constraint softened by a repressed eagerness, which gave her courage to speak her thought.

"Why am I suddenly to be discomfited by such elaborate thanks, such scathing politeness?" she asked in a tone of valiant good-humour.

"I didn't mean it to be scathing."

"Well, it is. Overmuch thanks for small services is a poor compliment to friendship. I thought you and I agreed on that point."

He answered nothing. He was nerving himself to the effort of decisive speech, which should set danger at arm's length and end their distracting situation once for all.

She set the small table closer to his side.

"I will look in again, in case you should want some more," she said softly, "if you will promise me not to say 'thank you!'"

"I promise," he answered with a half smile; and she turned to go. But before she had reached the door his voice arrested her.

"Honor,—one minute, please. I have something particular to say."

The note of constraint was so marked that the girl stood speechless, scarcely breathing, wondering what would come next—whether his words would break down the barrier that held them apart.

"Well?" she said at length, as he remained silent.

"I have been thinking," he began awkwardly, "over what you said yesterday—about Evelyn. You remember?"

"Yes."

"And I have been wanting to tell you that I believe you were right. You generally are. I believe we ought to give her the chance you spoke of. Besides—I asked too much of you. This may be a slow business; and really we have no right to trade on your unselfishness to the extent I proposed. You understand me?"

For the life of him he could not ask her to go outright; his excuse appeared to him lame enough to be an insult itself. A fierce temptation assailed him to push up the detested shade and discover whether he had hurt this girl, who had done so infinitely much for him. But he grasped the side of his chair, keeping his arm rigid as steel; and awaited her answer, which seemed an eternity in coming.

Indeed, if he had struck her, Honor could scarcely have been more stunned, more indignant, than she was at that moment. But when she found her voice it was at least steady, if not devoid of emotion.

"No, Theo," she said. "For the first time in my life I *don't* understand you. But I see clearly—what you wish; and if you feel absolutely certain that you are making the right decision for Evelyn, I have no more to say. For myself, you are asking a far harder thing to-day than you did yesterday. But that is no matter, if it is really best for you both—I don't quite know what Dr Mackay will say. I will see him about it this evening; and you will please tell Evelyn—yourself."

He knew now that he had hurt her cruelly; and with knowledge came the revelation that he was playing a coward's part in rewarding her thus for all she had done; in depriving Evelyn of her one support and shield, merely because he distrusted his own self-mastery at a time of severe mental stress and bodily weakness.

His imperative need for a sight of her face conquered him at last. Quick as thought his hand went up to the rim of the shade. But Honor was quicker still. The instinct to shield him from harm swept everything else aside. In a second she had reached him and secured his hand.

"You *shall not* do that!" she said—anger, fear, determination vibrating in her low tone.

Then, to her astonishment, she found her own hand crushed in his, with a force that brought tears into her eyes. But he remained silent; and she neither spoke nor stirred. Emotion dominated her; and her whole mind was concentrated on the effort to hold it in leash.

For one brief instant they stood thus upon the brink of a precipice—the precipice of mutual knowledge. But both were safeguarded by the strength that belongs to an upright spirit; and before three words could have been uttered Desmond had dropped her hand, almost throwing it from him, with a decisiveness that might have puzzled her, but that she had passed beyond the region of surprise.

Still neither spoke. Desmond was breathing with the short gasps of a man who has ran a great way, or fought a hard fight; and Honor remained beside him, her eyes blinded, her throat aching with tears that must not be allowed to fall.

At last she mastered them sufficiently to risk speech.

"What *have* I done that you should treat me—like this?"

There was more of bewilderment than of reproach in the words, and Desmond, turning his head, saw the white marks made by his own fingers upon the hand that hung at her side.

"Done?" he echoed, all constraint and coldness gone from his voice. "You have simply proved yourself, for the hundredth time—the staunchest, most long-suffering woman on God's earth. Will you forgive me, Honor? Will you wipe out what I said—and did just now? I am not quite—myself to-day; if one dare proffer an excuse. Mackay is right, we can't do without you—Evelyn least of any. Will you believe that, and stay with us, in spite of all?"

He proffered his hand now, and she gave him the one that still tingled from his pressure. He held it quietly, closely, as the hand of a friend, and was rewarded by her frank return of his grasp.

"Of course I will stay," she said simply. "But don't let there be any talk of forgiveness between you and me, Theo. To understand is to forgive. I confess I *have* been puzzled since—yesterday evening, but now I think we do understand one another again. Isn't that so?"

"Yes; we understand one another, Honor," he answered without a shadow of hesitation; but in his heart he thanked God that she did not understand—nor ever would, to her life's end.

Relief reawakened the practical element, which had been submerged in the emotional. She was watching him now with the eyes of a nurse rather than the eyes of a woman.

When he had spoken, his arm fell limply; and he leaned back upon the pillows with a sigh of such utter weariness that her anxiety was aroused. She remembered that his hand had seemed unnaturally hot, and deliberately taking possession of it again, laid her fingers on his wrist. The rapidity of his pulse startled her; since she could have no suspicion of all that he had fought against and held in check.

"How *is* one to keep such a piece of quicksilver as you in a state of placid stodge!" she murmured. "I suppose I ought to have forbidden you to talk. But how could I dream that—all this would come of it? You must lie absolutely quiet and see no one for the rest of the evening. I will send at once for Dr Mackay; and, look, your tea is all cold. You shall have some fresh—very weak—it will do you good. But not another word, please, to me or any one till I give you leave."

"Very well; I'll do my best to remain in a state of placid stodge, if that will ease your mind," he answered so humbly that the tears started to her eyes afresh. "Won't you let me smoke, though? Just one cigarette. It would calm me down finely before Mackay comes."

Without answering she took one from his case and gave it to him. Then, striking a match, held it for him, till the wisp of paper and tobacco was well alight; while he lay back, drawing in the fragrant smoke, with a sigh in which contentment and despair were strangely mingled.

It is to be hoped that, to the end of time, woman's higher development will never eradicate her delight in ministering to the minor comforts of the man she loves.

"As soon as I have seen Paul, and sent for Dr Mackay," Honor said, "I will come back and stay with you altogether for the present."

"Thank you." He smiled directly the word was out. "I forgot! That's against regulations! But I swear it came straight from my heart."

"In that case you are forgiven!" she answered, with a low laugh.

It was such pure pleasure to have recaptured the old spontaneous Theo, with whom one could say or do anything, in the certainty of being understood, that even anxiety could not quell the new joy at her heart.

Re-entering the drawing-room, she beckoned Wyndham with her eyes and passed on into the hall. So surprisingly swift are a woman's changes of mood, that by the time he joined her anxiety had taken hold of her again, to the exclusion of all else.

"What is it?" he asked quickly.

"Oh, Paul, you did well to reprove me! We must send the orderly for Dr Mackay at once. He has fever now—rather high, I am afraid. Did you notice nothing earlier?"

"No; he seemed quiet enough when I was with him."

"I think he has been worrying over something, apart from his eyes and the Boy; but I can't get at the bottom of it. No need to make the others anxious yet; only—I won't leave him again. I intend to stick to my charge after all," she added, with a sudden smile. "There was some sort of—misunderstanding, it seems. I don't quite know what, but there's an end of it now."

"Thank God!" The words were no mere formula on Paul Wyndham's lips. "Misunderstandings are more poisonous than snakes! Go straight back to him, and I'll send the orderly flying in two minutes."

There was little sleep for either Wyndham or Honor that night.

The girl persuaded Evelyn to go early to bed, merely telling her that as Theo was restless she would have to sit up with him for a while; and Evelyn, secretly relieved at not being asked to do the sitting up herself, deposited a light kiss on her husband's hair and departed with a pretty air of meekness that brought a smile to Honor's lips.

She had felt mildly happy and oppressively good all day. The tea-party had helped to lighten the hushed atmosphere of the house; and her last waking thought was of George Rivers' deep-toned voice and frankly admiring eyes. She decided that he might "do" in place of Harry Denvil, who must naturally be forgotten as soon as possible; because it was so uncomfortable to think of people who were dead.

Desmond's temperature rose rapidly; and the two, who could not bear to leave his side, divided the night watches between them. Amar Singh, his chin between his knees, crouched dog-like on the mat outside the door, presenting himself, from time to time, with such dumb yearning in his eyes that Honor devised small services for him in pure tenderness of heart.

Paul took a couple of hours' rest at midnight, on the condition that Honor should do the same towards morning; and since she was obviously reluctant when the unwelcome hour arrived, he smilingly conducted her in person to the threshold of her room.

"Good-night to you,—Miss Meredith! Or should it be good-morning?" he said lightly, in the hope of chasing the strained look from her face.

"Good-morning, for preference," she retorted, with an

attempt at a laugh. "You can take a horse to the water, but you can't make him drink! I shan't sleep even for five minutes."

"You think so; but Nature will probably have her way with you all the same."

He moved as if to go, but she came suddenly nearer; and the hidden fear leaped to her lips.

"Paul—is there any real danger because of this fever? One is so afraid of erysipelas with a wound of that kind; and it would be—fatal. Has Dr Mackay said anything definite? Tell me—please. I must know the truth."

In the urgency of the moment she laid a light hand upon him; and Wyndham, bracing the muscles of his arm, tried not to be aware of her finger-tips through his coat-sleeve.

"You evidently know too much for your own peace of mind," he said. "But Mackay is as inscrutable as the Sphinx. One could see he was anxious, because he was ready to snap one's head off on the least provocation; but beyond that I know no more than you do. We can only do our poor utmost for him every hour, you and I, and leave the outcome—to God."

"Yes, yes,—you are right. Oh, Paul, what a rock you are at a bad time like this!"

Unconsciously her fingers tightened upon his arm, and a thrill like a current of electricity passed through him. Lifting her hand from its resting-place, he put it aside, gently but decisively.

"I may be a rock," he remarked with his slow smile, "but I also happen to be—a man. Don't make our compact harder for me than you can help. Good-night again; and sleep soundly—for Theo's sake!"

Before she could find words in which to plead forgiveness, he had almost reached the study door; and she stood motionless, watching him go, her face aflame with anger at her own unwitting thoughtlessness, and humiliation at the exquisite gentleness of his rebuke.

Surely there were few men on earth comparable to this man, whose heart and soul were hers for the taking. A cold fear came upon her lest in the end she should be driven to retract her decision; to forego all, and endure all, rather than withhold from him a happiness he so abundantly deserved.

"*Why* is it such a heart-breaking tangle?" she murmured, locking her hands together till the points of her sapphire ring cut into the flesh. But she only pressed the harder. She understood now how it was that monks and fanatics strove to ease the soul through torments of the flesh. A pang of physical pain would have been a positive relief just then. But there was none for her to bear. She was young, vigorous, radiantly alive. She had not so much as a headache after her anxious vigil. The high gods had willed that she should feel and suffer to the full. There is no other pathway to the ultimate heights.

The soft closing of the study door sounded loud in the stillness; and she went reluctantly into her own room.

CHAPTER XXIX.

THE UTTERMOST FARTHING.

"We then that are strong . . ."

—St Paul.

To say that Owen Kresney was annoyed would be to do him an injustice. He was furious at the unlooked-for interruption, which bade fair to cancel all that he had been at such pains to achieve. Pure spite so mastered him, that even the news of Desmond's critical condition—which stirred the whole station the morning after the funeral—awakened no spark of pity in that region of concentrated egotism which must needs be called his heart.

The "counter-check quarrelsome" would have been welcome enough. But this impersonal method of knocking the ground from under his feet goaded him to exasperation. He had not even the satisfaction of knowing that he had wrought jealousy or friction between husband and wife. Desmond had practically ignored his existence. There lay the sting that roused all the devil in Kresney; and the devil is a light sleeper in some men's souls. But the Oriental strain in the man made him an adept at a waiting game; and finding himself cavalierly thrust aside, he could do no otherwise than remain in the background for the present, alert, vigilant, cursing his luck.

In the blue bungalow a strained calmness prevailed. The work that must be done could only be carried through by living from hour to hour, as Paul had said; and Evelyn could now no longer be shielded from the pain of knowledge.

On the morning after her first night of vigil, Honor came to her; and, keeping firm hold of both her hands, told her, simply and straightly, that the coming week would make the utmost demands upon her strength and courage.

Evelyn listened with wide eyes and blanching cheeks.

"Did—did *I* make him bad?" she asked in an awe-struck whisper, for she had not been able to keep her own counsel in regard to her fatal interview with Theo.

"I think not—I hope not," Honor answered gravely. "But you did wound him cruelly; and whatever happens, you *must* not fail him now."

Evelyn looked up with a distressed puckering of her forehead.

"I don't want to—fail him, Honor. But you know I'm not a bit of use with sick people; and I can't all of a sudden turn brave and strong, like you."

Honor's smile expressed an infinite deal, but she did not answer at once. She wanted to be very sure of saying the right word; and it is only when we try to grapple with another's intimate need that we find ourselves baffled by the elusive, intangible spirits of those with whom we share sunlight and food and the bewildering gift of speech. Honor was wondering now whether, by a supreme concentration of will, she could possibly infuse some measure of the soldier spirit into Theo Desmond's wife; and the extravagant idea impelled her to a sudden decision.

She drew Evelyn nearer.

"Listen to me, darling," she said. "We have *got* to pull Theo through this between us, you and I; and you always say I can help you to do difficult things. Very well. I am quite determined that you *shall* be a brave wife to him, for the next two weeks at least. And when I make up my mind about a thing, it is as good as done, isn't it?"

She spoke very low, and her eyes had a misty softness. But behind the softness lay an invincible assurance, which Evelyn felt without being able to analyse or understand.

"I don't know how you are going to manage it, Honor," she murmured. "But I believe you could make *any*body do *any*thing—especially me!"

Honor's eyes twinkled at the incoherent compliment.

The visionary moment had passed, and she was her practical self again, the richer by a fixed resolve.

"At that rate we shall work wonders," she said cheerfully; "and I promise not to make you do anything alarming. You shall begin by taking Theo's breakfast to him at once."

The ill news brought Frank Olliver round later in the morning. She did not stay long; and the look in her eyes as she parted from Paul in the verandah touched him to the heart.

"You'll send me word how he goes on, won't you?" she said. "I'll not be coming round much meself. There's plenty of you to look after him, and you'll not be needing any help from me. 'Tis the first time I could say so with truth," she added, smiling through moist lashes. "An', no doubt, 'tis a wholesome set-down for me self-conceit!"

"I don't believe you can say it with truth yet," Paul answered promptly. "I shall get a chance to talk things over with Honor this morning, and you shall hear the result. May I invite myself to tea, please?"

"Ah, God bless you, Major Wyndham!" she exclaimed, with something of her natural heartiness. "It's a pity there's not more o' your sort in the world."

A compliment, even from Mrs Olliver, invariably struck Paul dumb; and before any answer occurred to him she had cantered away.

The first time he could secure a few minutes alone with Honor he put in an urgent plea for Mrs Olliver's services, and had the satisfaction of going round to her bungalow at tea-time, armed with a special request from the girl herself.

Evelyn accepted, with a slight lift of her brows, Honor's announcement that Mrs Olliver would be only too glad to help in nursing Theo. These odd people, who seemed to enjoy long nights of watching, the uncanny mutterings of delirium, and the incessant doling out of food and medicine, puzzled her beyond measure. She had a hazy idea that she ought to enjoy it in the same way, and a very clear knowledge that she did no such thing. She regarded it as a sort of penance, imposed by Honor, not altogether unfairly. She had just conscience enough to recognise that. And as the hushed monotone of nights and days dragged by, with little relief from the dead weight of anxiety, it did indeed seem as if Honor had succeeded in willing a portion of her brave spirit into her friend. What had passed in secret between God and her own soul resulted in a breaking down of the bounds of self—an unconscious spiritual bestowal of the best that was in her, with that splendid lack of economy in giving which is the hall-mark of a great nature. And Evelyn took colour from the new atmosphere enveloping her with the curious readiness of her type.

Desmond himself, in moments of wakefulness, or passing freedom from delirium, was surprised and profoundly moved to find his wife constantly in attendance on him. At the time he was too ill to express his appreciation. But a vision of her dwelt continually in his mind; and the frequency of her name on his lips brought tears of real self-reproach to her eyes as she sat alone with him through the dread small hours, not daring to glance into the darkest corners or to stir unless necessity compelled her; overpowered by those vague terrors that evaporate like mist in the cold light of definition.

In this fashion an interminable week slipped past, bringing the patient to that critical "corner" with which too many of us are familiar. Neither Paul nor Mackay left the study for twenty-four hours; while the women sat with folded hands and waited—a more arduous task than it sounds.

With the coming of morning, and of the first hopeful word from the sick-room, an audible sigh of relief seemed to pass through the house and compound. It was as if they had all been holding their breath till the worst was over. It became possible at last to achieve smiles that were not mere dutiful distortions of the lips. James Mackay grew one degree less irritable; Wyndham one degree less monosyllabic; Amar Singh condescended to arise and resume his neglected duties; while Rob—becoming aware, in his own fashion, of a stir in the air—emerged from his basket, and shook himself with such energy and thoroughness that Mackay whisked him unceremoniously into the hall, where he sat nursing his injured dignity, quietly determined to slip back, on the first chance, into the room that was his by right, though temporarily in the hands of the enemy.

It was some five days later that Desmond, waking towards morning, found his wife standing beside him in expectant watchfulness.

The low camp-bed lent her a fictitious air of height, as did also the unbroken line of her blue dressing-gown, with its cloud of misty whiteness at the throat. A shaded lamp in a far corner clashed with the first glimmer of dawn; and in the dimness Evelyn's face showed pale and indistinct, save for two dusky semicircles where her lashes rested on her cheek. Desmond saw all this, because at night the shade was discarded, though the rakish bandage still eclipsed his right eye. He lay lapped in a pleasant sense of the unreality of outward things, and his wife—dimly seen and motionless—had the air of a dream-figure in a dream.

Suddenly she leaned down, and caressed his damp hair with a familiar lightness of touch.

"I heard you move, darling," she whispered. "I've been sitting such a long, long while alone; and I badly wanted you to wake up."

"Such a brave Ladybird!" he said, imprisoning her fingers. "You seem to be on duty all the time. They haven't been letting you do too much, have they?"

"Oh no; I'm not clever enough to do much," she answered, a little wistfully. "It is Honor who really does everything."

Desmond frowned. Mention of Honor effectually dispelled the dream. "I choose to believe that everything *isn't* her doing," he said with unnecessary emphasis.

But for once Evelyn was disposed to extol Honor at her own expense. She had been lifted, for the time being, higher than she knew.

"It *is*, Theo—truly," she persisted, perching lightly on the edge of the bed, though she had been reminded half a dozen times that the "patient's" bed must not be treated as a chair. "I don't know anything about nursing people. Honor just told me that I was going to do it beautifully, that I wasn't really frightened or stupid at all; and somehow, she has made it all come true. She's been ever so kind and patient; and I'm not half so nervous now when I'm left alone all night. She writes out every little thing I have to do, and sits up herself in her own room. She's sitting there now, reading or writing, so I can go to her any minute if I really want help. She knows it comforts me to feel there's some one else awake; and she does her own nights of nursing just the same. I often wonder how she stands it all."

Desmond drew in his breath with a sharp sound. The infinitely much that he owed to this girl, at every turn, threatened to become a torment beyond endurance.

Evelyn caught the sound and misunderstood it.

"There now, I'm tiring you, talking too much. I'm sure you ought to be having something or another, even though you are better."

She consulted her paper; and returning with the medicine-glass half filled, held it to his lips, raising his head with one hand. But at the first sip he jerked it back abruptly.

"Tastes queer. Are you sure it's the right stuff?"

"Yes. Of course."

"Better look and see."

She took up the bottle, and examined it close to the light. There was an ominous silence.

"Well?" he asked in pure amusement.

"It—it was the—lotion for your eyes!"

The last words came out in a desperate rush, and there was tragedy in her tone. But Desmond laughed as he had not laughed since his parting with the Boy.

"Come on, then, and square the account by doctoring my eyes with the medicine."

"Oh, Theo, don't! It isn't a joke!"

"It is, if I choose to take it so, you dear, foolish little woman!"

She handed him the refilled glass; then, to his surprise, collapsed beside the bed and burst into tears.

"Ladybird, what nonsense!" he rebuked her gently, laying a hand on her head.

"It's not nonsense. It's horrible to be useless and—idiotic, however hard you try. It might easily have been—poison, and I might have—killed you!"

"*Only* it wasn't—*and* you didn't!" he retorted, smiling. "You're upset, and worn out from want of sleep; that's all."

She made a determined effort to swallow down her sobs, and knelt upright with clasped hands.

"No, Theo, I'm not worn out; I'm simply stupid. And you're the kindest man that ever lived. But I mustn't cry any more, or you'll get ill again, and then Honor will be really angry!"

"Oh, shut up about Honor!" he broke out irritably; and set his teeth directly the words were spoken.

Evelyn started. "I won't shut up about Honor! I love her, and you're very ungrateful not to love her too, when she's been so good to you."

She spoke almost angrily, and he made haste to rectify his slip.

"No. I'm not ungrateful. I—love her right enough."

He thought the statement would have choked him. But Evelyn noticed nothing, and for a while neither spoke.

"Look here, Ladybird," he said suddenly, "I can't have you calling yourself names as you did just now. You only get these notions into your small head because I have condemned you to a life that makes demands on you beyond your strength. I ought to have seen from the start that it was a case of choosing between the Frontier and you. At all events, I see it clearly now; and—it's not too late. One can always exchange into a down-country regiment, you know. Or I have interest enough to get a Staff appointment somewhere—Simla, perhaps. How would that suit you?"

The suggestion took away her breath.

"You don't *mean* that, Theo—seriously?" she gasped; and the repressed eagerness in her tone sounded the death-knell of his dearest ambitions.

"I was never more serious in my life," he answered steadily.

"You would leave the Frontier—the regiment—and never come back?"

"You have only to say the word, and as soon as I am on my feet again I'll see what can be done."

But the word was not forthcoming; and in her changed position he could see nothing of her face but its oval outline of cheek and chin. He waited; holding his breath. Then, at last, she spoke.

"No, Theo. It wouldn't be fair. You belong to the Frontier. Every one says so. And—I shall get used to it in time."

She spoke mechanically, without turning her head; and Desmond's arm went round her on the instant.

"But you haven't got to think of me," he urged. "I want to do what will make you happy. That's all."

"It—it wouldn't make me happy. And, please, don't talk about it any more."

At that he drew her down to him.

"God bless you, my darling!" he whispered. But even in speaking he knew that he could not accept her sacrifice; that her courage—barely equal to the verbal renunciation—would be crushed to powder in the crucible of days and years. For the moment, however, it seemed best to drop the subject, since nothing definite could be done without Honor's consent.

"Now I ought to be attending to my business!" she said, freeing herself with a little nervous laugh. "It's getting too light. I must put out the lamp and dress you up in your shade again, you poor, patient Theo. Then we'll have *chota hazri* together."

She moved away from him quickly, and not quite steadily. She had let slip her one chance of escape, and she did not know why she had done it. The impulse to refuse had been unreasoning, overpowering; and now it was all over she only knew that she had done what Honor would approve, and what she herself would regret to the end of her life. How far the girl whose soul had been concentrated on Evelyn's uplifting was responsible for her flash of self-sacrifice, is a problem that must be left for psychologists to solve.

Desmond had only one thought in his brain that morning —"How in the world am I going to tackle Honor?" He foresaw a pitched battle, ending in possible defeat; and decided to defer it till he felt more physically fit for the strain. For he possessed the rapid recuperative power of his type; and, the fever once conquered, each day added a cubit to his returning vigour.

One night, towards the close of the second week of his

illness, he awoke suddenly from dreamless sleep to alert wakefulness, a sense of renewed health and power thrilling through his veins. He passed a hand across his forehead and eyes, for the pure pleasure of realising their freedom from the disfiguring bandage, and glanced toward the writing-table, whence the too familiar screened lamp flung ghostly lights and shadows up among the bare rafters twenty feet above.

It was Honor who sat beside it now, in a loose white wrapper, her head resting on her hand, an open book before her. The light fell full upon her profile, emphasising its nobility of outline—the short straight nose, the exquisite moulding of mouth and chin; while all about her shoulders fell the burnished mantle of her hair.

For many moments Desmond lay very still. This amazing girl, in the fulness of her beauty, and in her superb unconsciousness of its effect upon himself, had him at a disadvantage; and he knew it. The disadvantage was only increased by waiting and watching; and at last he spoke, scarcely above his breath.

"Honor—I am awake."

She started, and instinctively her hand went to her hair, gathering it deftly together. But he made haste to interpose.

"Please leave it alone!"

His tone had in it more of fervour than he knew, and she dropped the heavy mass hastily, thankful to screen her face from view. Then, because silence had in it an element of danger, she forced herself to break it.

"You were sleeping so soundly that I thought you were safe not to wake till morning; and it was a relief to let it down."

"Why apologise?" he asked, smiling. "What is it you are reading? Won't you share it with me? I feel hopelessly wide-awake."

"It would be delightful to read to you again," she said simply. "But you might prefer something lighter. I was reading—a sermon."

"I have no prejudice against sermons. We get few enough up here. What's your subject?"

"The Responsibility of Strength."

"Ah!—" There was pain in the low sound. "*You* must know a good deal about that form of responsibility,—you who are so superbly strong." And again she was grateful for her sheltering veil of hair. "The text is from Romans, I suppose?"

"Yes. 'We then that are strong ought to bear the infirmities of the weak.'"

"It's a heavy penalty," he mused. "But one is bound to pay it to the uttermost farthing. Isn't that so?"

"Yes,—to the uttermost farthing."

She was thinking of herself, and his answer amazed her.

"Then, let me off that promise I gave you last April. It was a fatal mistake, and it's not fair on Ladybird."

She stifled an exclamation of dismay. It had been one thing to plead with him a year ago; but now it seemed impossible to speak a dozen words on the subject without risk of self-betrayal.

Her silence pricked Desmond to impatience.

"Well," he said, "what's the difficulty? You'll do what I ask, of course?"

"No, I can't. It is out of the question."

A suppressed sound of vexation reached her.

"I thought you cared more for Evelyn than that amounts to," he said reproachfully.

"I *do* care for her. You know I do."

"Yet you intend to hold out against me?"

"Yes."

"In spite of all it may involve—for Ladybird?"

"Yes."

The brief finality of her answers was curiously discouraging, and for the moment Desmond could think of nothing more to say.

He closed his eyes to concentrate thought and shut out the distracting vision of her bowed head. When he opened them again she was standing close to him—a white commanding figure, in a dusky cloak of hair reaching almost to her knees.

"Theo," she said softly, with an eloquent gesture of appeal, "you don't know how it hurts me to seem hard and unfeeling about Ladybird, when I understand so much too well the spirit that is prompting you to do this thing. I frankly confess you are right from your point of view. But there remains my point of view; and so long as I have the right to prevent it, you shall not spoil your life and hers."

Desmond would have been more, or less, than man if he could have heard her unmoved; and as he lay looking up at her he was tempted beyond measure to take possession of those appealing hands, to draw her down to him, and thank her from his heart for her brave words. But he merely shifted uneasily.

"I don't quite understand you, Honor," he said slowly. "It is strange that you should—care so much about what I do with my life."

The words startled her, yet she met them without flinching.

"Is it? I think it would be far more strange if I had lived with you for a year without learning—to care. That is why I can never say 'Yes' to your request."

"And I am determined that you shall say 'Yes' to it in the end."

The note of immobility in his low voice made her feel powerless to resist him; but she steeled herself against the sensation by main force of will.

"At least I can forbid any further mention of it till you are fitter to cope with such a disturbing subject. Are you aware that it's only two o'clock? And you need sleep more than anything else just now. I'll give you some beef-jelly, and sit in my own room for an hour, or I believe you will never go off again at all."

But when she returned at the end of an hour she found him still awake.

"Honor,"—he began; but she checked him with smiling decision. "Not another word to-night, Theo, or I must go altogether."

The threat was more compelling than she knew; and sitting down by the table, she took up her vigil as before

CHAPTER XXX.

SHE SHALL UNDERSTAND.

"The light of every soul burns upward; but we are all candles in a wind; and due allowance must be made for atmospheric disturbances."
—GEO. MEREDITH.

CERTAIN souls, like certain bodies, cannot breathe for long at a stretch the rarefied atmosphere of the heights; and towards the end of the second week Evelyn's zeal began to wear thin. Dr Mackay had at last spoken hopefully as to the fate of Desmond's eyes. Night-nursing was no longer a necessity; and with the relief from anxiety, from the effort to meet the demands upon her small stock of strength, came the inevitable drop to the comfortable commonplaces of everyday life.

Nor was she alone in her sensations. In varying degrees they affected every inmate of the blue bungalow during that last week of Desmond's imprisonment; and it is probable that Honor unconsciously relaxed her mental concentration upon Evelyn which had been responsible for more than either knew. Her midnight talk with Desmond, and the knowledge that a second contest lay before her, gave her food for much troubled reflection; while the comparative lightness of sick-room duties left her free to grapple with arrears of letters, work, and household accounts. Thus, being only human, and very much absorbed in matters practical, she made the fatal mistake of relaxing her vigilance at the very moment when Evelyn needed it most. But it is written that "no man may redeem his brother"; and, soon or late the relapse must have come. Honor could not hope to lay permanent hold upon the volatile spirit of her friend.

Desmond himself, whose patience under the burden of illness and of a nerve-shattering fear had amazed even those who knew him best, was approaching the irritable stage of convalescence,—the strong man's rebellion against Nature's unhurried methods; against enforced restriction and imprisonment, when renewed life is pulsing through every artery, renewed vigour stirring the reawakened brain.

Nor were matters enlivened by Mackay's decree that, if risk were to be avoided, the detested shade must be worn for three full weeks or a month. Thus to imprisonment was added the gall and wormwood of total dependence upon others; the unthinkable prospect of parting with Paul, with the Border itself—with everything that had hitherto made life worth living; and, worse than all, the undercurrent of striving to ignore that veiled danger, which he refused to name, even in his thoughts, and which lay like a millstone upon his heart.

Thus there were inevitable moments when his spirit kicked against the pricks; when his return to life and health seemed a parody of a blessing, a husk emptied of the life-giving grain. In these moods Evelyn found herself powerless to cope with him; and was not a little aggrieved when she discovered that his unvarying need, on black days, was the companionship of Paul Wyndham, whose insight detected some hidden trouble, and who, as a matter of course, devoted every spare moment to his friend.

One thing Desmond missed beyond all else—the sound of music in the house. Since the terrible evening of his home-coming, the piano had not been opened; and his recent experience of the effect Honor's music could produce on him made him chary of asking her to play.

He saw very little of her in these days. Now and then she would come and read to him; but their former open-hearted intercourse seemed irrevocably a thing of the past. With the return of the troops, however, interests multiplied. Desmond's hold on the hearts of all who knew him had seldom been so practically proven; and the man was moved beyond measure at that which he could not fail to perceive. His small study was rarely empty, and often overcrowded with men—Sikhs, Gunners, Sappers, and, above all, his own brother officers, who filled the place with tobacco-smoke, the cheerful clink of ice against long tumblers, and frequent explosions of deep-chested laughter; while Desmond threw himself whole-heartedly into the good minute and enjoyed it to the full.

To Evelyn this new state of things was a little disconcerting. During Theo's illness she, as his wife, had enjoyed special attention and consideration; and since her incomprehensible refusal of his offer to throw up the Frontier, had even regarded herself as something of a heroine, if an unwilling one. Now, all of a sudden, she felt deserted, unimportant, and more or less "out of it all." The past fortnight seemed an uplifted dream, from which she had awakened to find herself sitting among the dust and stones of prose and hard facts. Yet she could not complain definitely of anything or any one. Honor and Theo were kind and tender, as always; but the one was temporarily busy, and the other very naturally enjoying a reversion to masculine society. Nobody seemed to want her. There seemed no particular use for her any more.

To make matters worse, the whole station wore a subdued air. The Club compound was practically deserted; and Evelyn's first outing in that direction left her with no desire to repeat the experiment for the present. The Sikhs had lost a popular captain; while a Gunner subaltern, who had returned seriously wounded, was being nursed by Mrs Conolly and the only woman in the battery.

This sort of thing was, as Theo had said, "part and parcel" of life on the Frontier; it was to this that she had condemned herself for the next twenty years at least; by which time she supposed she would be far too old to care for the frivolities of life at all! If only Theo would be generous and give her a second chance, she would not let it slip this time—she would not indeed!

Altogether the aspect of things in general was sufficiently depressing. Then one afternoon she met Owen Kresney; and all at once life seemed to take on a new complexion. Here, at least, was some one who wanted her, when every one else seemed only to want Theo; some one who was really glad to see her—rather too emphatically glad, perhaps; but the eagerness of his greeting flattered her, and she had overlooked the rest. She had been returning in her jhampan from her melancholy outing to the Club, when he had caught sight of her in the distance, and cantering up to her side, had dismounted, and shaken hands as though they had not met for a year.

"How awfully white and pulled down you look!" he had said with low-toned sympathy. "They must have been working you too hard. They forget that you are not a strapping woman like Miss Meredith."

"No one has worked me too hard," she answered, flushing at the veiled implication against her husband. "I wanted to do as much as the others."

"Of course you did. But you are too delicate to work like that, and it isn't fair to take advantage of your unselfishness. I hope you're going off to the Hills very soon, now that Desmond is better?"

"Yes, I hope so too."

Her voice had an unconscious weariness, and he bent a little closer, scanning her face with a concern that bordered on tenderness. "We have thought of you a great deal these two weeks, Mrs Desmond," he said. "We hardly cared to go out to tennis, or anything, while you were in such trouble. But now it has all come out right, you must be dreadfully in want of cheering up. Won't you come home with me and have a talk, like old times? Linda would be awfully pleased to see you again."

The temptation was irresistible. It emphasised her vague sense of loneliness, of being left out in the cold. The longing to be comforted and made much of was strong upon her.

"It is very nice of you to want me," she had said, as simply as a child. To which he had replied with prompt, if somewhat cheap, gallantry that no one could possibly help wanting her; and his reward had been a flush, as delicate in tint as the inner surface of a shell. This man had one strong point in his favour—he invariably talked to her about herself; a trick Desmond had never learnt, nor ever would.

She had spent more than an hour in Miss Kresney's stuffy, dusty drawing-room, and had left it with a pleasantly revived sense of her own importance; had left Kresney himself in a state of carefully repressed triumph; for she had promised him an early morning ride in two days' time.

It was all harmless enough so far as she was concerned—merely a case of flattered vanity and idle hands. But the strong nature, the large purpose, lies eternally at the mercy of life's little things.

She said nothing to Honor or Theo of her meeting with Kresney, or of the coming ride. A fortnight of submission to the former had evoked a passing gleam of independence. They would probably make a fuss; and since they neither of them needed her, she was surely at liberty to amuse herself as she pleased.

On her return a buzz of deep voices greeted her from the study, and it transpired that Honor had gone over to Mrs Conolly's. Thus she had leisure before dinner to argue the matter out in her mind to her own complete justification. If Mr Kresney chose to be polite to her, why should she rebuff him and hurt his feelings, just because Theo had some stupid prejudice against him? On the other hand, where was the use of vexing Theo, when every one was doing their best to shield him from needless irritation? As soon as his eyes were right they would go to the Hills together. She would have him all to herself; and Kresney sank into immediate insignificance at the thought.

Meanwhile the man's assiduity and thinly veiled admiration formed a welcome relief in a desert of dulness. Besides, one was bound to be pleasant to a man when one practically owed him two hundred rupees.

Unwittingly she shelved the fact that Kresney was beginning to exercise a disturbing fascination over her; that the insistence underlying his humility alternately pleased and frightened her; the lurking fear of what he might say next gave a distinct flavour of excitement to their every meeting.

The slippery path that lies between truth and direct falsehood had always been fatally easy for her to follow; and she followed it now more from natural instinct, and from the child's dread of making people "cross," than from any deliberate intent to deceive. It was so much easier to say nothing. Therefore she said nothing; and left the future to look after itself.

On returning from her first ride with Kresney, she found Honor in the verandah giving orders to a sais. The girl lifted her out of the saddle, and kissed her on both cheeks.

"Such a very early Ladybird!" she said, laughing. "You might have let me come too."

Accordingly they went out together the next morning, but on future occasions Evelyn returned more cautiously, and changed her habit before appearing at the breakfast-table. She went out once or twice in the afternoons also, and Honor's thoughts flew to the Kresneys as a matter of course; but remembering a certain incident at Murree, she held her peace. She was disheartened, and very far from satisfied, nevertheless.

In this fashion ten days slipped uneventfully past. Then, on a certain afternoon, Kresney again met Evelyn by chance,—and begged her to come back with him to tea before going home. Her consent was a foregone conclusion; and as they neared Kresney's whitewashed gate-posts, Captain Olliver trotted past. He had already met Miss Kresney jogging out to tea on a long-tailed pony of uncertain age; and glancing casually back over his shoulder, he saw Mrs Desmond's jhampan entering the gateway. Whereat he swore vigorously under his breath, and urged his pony to a brisker pace.

But of these facts Evelyn was blissfully unaware. Her uppermost thought was a happy consciousness of looking her best. From the forget-me-nots in her hat to the last frill of her India muslin gown all was blue—the fragile blue of the far horizon at dawn. And Kresney had an eye for such things.

She started slightly on discovering that the drawing-room was empty.

"Where's Miss Kresney?" she asked, stopping dead upon the threshold.

"Why, what a fool I am!" the man exclaimed with a creditable air of frankness. "I clean forgot she had gone out to tea. But you're not going to desert me on that account! You wouldn't be so unkind!"

Evelyn felt herself trapped. It would seem foolish and pointed to go; yet she had sense enough to know that it would be very unwise to stay. She compromised matters by saying sweetly that she would come in just for ten minutes, to have a cup of tea before going back in the sun.

Kresney looked his gratification—looked it so eloquently that she lowered her eyes, and went forwards hurriedly, as if fearing that something more definite might follow the look.

But the man, though inwardly exultant, was well on his guard. If he startled her this first time, he could not hope to repeat the experiment. He chose the most comfortable chair for her; insisted on an elaborate arrangement of cushions at her back; poured out her tea; and plied her assiduously with stale sponge-cake and mixed biscuits. Then drawing up his own chair very close, he settled himself to the congenial task of amusing and flattering her, with such success that her ten minutes had stretched to an hour before she even thought of rising to go.

Captain Olliver, meanwhile, had ridden on to the blue bungalow, which chanced to be his destination; and had spent half an hour in desultory talk with Desmond, Wyndham, and the Colonel, who had fallen into a habit of dropping in almost daily.

As he rose to take his leave, a glance at Wyndham brought the latter out into the hall with him.

"What is it?" he asked. "Want to speak to me about something?"

"Yes. Can we have a few words alone anywhere? It concerns Desmond, and I can't speak to him myself."

Paul frowned.

"Nothing serious, I hope. Come in here a minute." And he led the way into his own Spartan-looking room.

"Now let me hear it," he said quietly.

But Olliver balanced himself on the edge of the table, tapped his pipe against it, and loosened the contents scientifically with his penknife before complying with the request.

"The truth is," he began at length, "that it's about Mrs Desmond and that confounded cad Kresney."

"Ah!" The note of pain in Wyndham's voice made the other look at him questioningly.

"You've noticed it, then?"

"Well,—it was rather marked while Desmond was away. Nothing to trouble about, though, if it had been any other man than Kresney."

Olliver brought his fist down on the table.

"That's precisely what my wife says. You know what a lot she thinks of Desmond; and I believe she's capable of tackling the little woman herself, which I couldn't stand at any price. That's why I promised to speak to you to-day. Hope it doesn't seem infernal cheek on my part."

"Not at all. Go on."

Each instinctively avoided the other's eyes; while Olliver, in a few curt sentences, spoke his mind on the subject in hand.

The bond that links the inhabitants of small isolated Indian stations is a thing that only the Anglo-Indian can quite understand. Desmond's illness, and the possible tragedy overhanging him, had roused such strong feeling in Kohat, that his wife's conduct—which at another time would merely have supplied material for a little mild gossip—had awakened the general sense of indignation, more especially among the men. But men are not free of speech on these matters, and it was certain pungent remarks made by little Mrs Riley of the Sikhs which had set Frank Olliver's Irish temper in a blaze. The recollection of what she had seen during Desmond's absence still rankled in her mind; and her husband, with a masculine dread of an open quarrel between the only two ladies in the Regiment, had accepted the lesser evil of speaking to Wyndham himself.

"Mind, I give Mrs Desmond credit for being more passive than active in the whole affair," he concluded, since Paul seemed disinclined to volunteer a remark. "But the deuce of it is, that I feel sure Desmond knows less about the thing than any one else. Can you see him putting up with it under any circumstances?"

Wyndham shook his head; and for a while they smoked in silence thinking their own thoughts.

"You want me," Paul asked at length, "to pass all this on to Desmond? Is that it?"

"Yes; that's it. Unless you think he knows it already."

"No,—frankly, I don't. But is it our business to enlighten him?"

"That's a ticklish question. But I'm inclined to think it is. We can't be expected to stand a bounder like Kresney hanging round one of our ladies. Why, I met him as I came here, taking her into his bungalow; and I had only just passed the sister on that old patriarch she rides. I call that going a bit too far; and I fancy Desmond would agree with me."

Wyndham looked up decisively.

"I wouldn't repeat *that* to him, if my life depended on it."

"No, no. Of course not. You can make things clear without saying too much. Beastly unpleasant job, and I'm sorry to be forcing it on you. But you must know that you're the only chap in the Regiment who could dream of speaking two words to Desmond on such a delicate subject."

Paul acknowledged the statement with a wry smile under his moustache.

"I doubt if he will stand it, even from me; and I'd a deal sooner wring Kresney's neck. But I'll do the best I can, and take my chance of the consequences to myself."

Thus reassured, Olliver departed, and Wyndham, watching him go, wondered what he intended to say.

There are few things more distasteful to a well-bred man than the necessity of speaking to a friend, however intimate, on the subject of his wife's conduct or character; because there are few things a man respects more intimately than his fellow-man's reserve. Wyndham knew, moreover, that the real sting of his communication would lie less in the facts themselves than in Mrs Desmond's probable concealment of them; and his natural kindliness prompted him to a passing pity for Evelyn, who, in all likelihood, had not yet penetrated beyond the outer shell of her husband's strongly marked character.

The only means of tempering the wind to the shorn lamb lay in speaking first to Honor; and on that idea Wyndham unconditionally turned his back. Mrs Desmond had brought this thing upon herself. She must face the consequences as best she might.

But on entering the study, the words he had come to say were checked upon his lips.

Desmond stood beside the writing-table, where the green shade lay discarded; and a noticeable scar on his right cheek was all that now remained of the wound which had threatened such serious results. His whole attention was centred upon Rob, who pranced at his feet with ungainly caperings, flinging dignity to the winds, and testifying, with heart and voice and eloquent tail, to the joy that was in him.

Paul's sensitive soul revolted from the necessity of imparting ill news at such a moment; and it was Desmond who spoke first.

"Mackay's been here this minute making a final examination of my eyes. Gave me leave, thank God, to discard *that* abomination; and Rob hasn't left off congratulating me since I flung it on the table. The little beggar seems to understand what's happened just as well as I do." He turned on Wyndham with a short satisfied laugh. "By Jove, Paul, it's thundering good to look *you* squarely in the face again! But why,—what's the trouble, old man? Have you heard bad news?"

"Not very bad, but certainly—unpleasant."

"And you came to tell me?"

"Yes, I came to tell you."

Desmond motioned him to a chair; and, as he seated himself with unhurried deliberation, laid a sympathetic hand on his shoulder.

"What is it?" he asked. "The Regiment or yourself?"

"Neither."

"Well, then——?"

"It concerns *you*, my dear Theo," Paul answered slowly. "And it is about—your wife."

Desmond frowned sharply, and Wyndham saw the defensive look spring into his eyes.

"Do you mean——? Has there been an accident?"

"No—no; nothing of that sort. I'm sorry to have been so clumsy."

"She is quite safe? Nothing wrong with her?"

"Nothing whatever."

Desmond's mouth took an expression Wyndham knew well. An enemy might have called it pig-headed.

"At that rate, there can be no more to say about her."

And he went leisurely over to the mantelpiece, where he remained, leaning on one elbow, his back towards his companion. Paul saw plainly that he was ill at ease, and cursed the contingency which compelled him to further speech.

"Forgive me if I seem intrusive, Theo," he began, "but I am afraid there is more to be said. This afternoon Olliver spoke to me——"

Desmond swung round again, with blazing eyes.

"What the hell has Olliver got to do with *my wife?* I have never interfered with his."

Paul Wyndham looked very steadily into the disturbed face of his friend. Then he brought his hand down on the green baize of the table before him.

"Theo—my dear fellow," he said, "it is hard enough for me, in any case, to say what I must. Is it quite generous of you to make it harder?"

The fire died slowly out of Desmond's eyes, giving place to a look of stubborn resignation.

"Forgive me, Paul. Sorry I lost my temper. Let me have the bare facts, please. Though I probably know them already."

And he returned to his former attitude, the fingers of his left hand caressing mechanically the stem of a tall vase.

His last remark made Paul watch him anxiously. He was wondering whether Theo's determination to shield his wife would possibly goad him into a direct lie; and he devoutly hoped not.

"Well," he began at length, "Olliver spoke to me because there seems to be rather a strong feeling in the Regiment about Mrs Desmond and—Kresney being so constantly together again just now——"

The vase Desmond was handling fell with a crash on the concrete hearth, and the blood spurted from a surface cut on his finger. But beyond thrusting the scarred hand into his coat pocket, he made no movement.

"Go on," he said doggedly; and Paul obediently went on, addressing his unresponsive back and shoulders.

"You see, it was rather—noticeable while you were away.

Perhaps the fact that we all dislike Kresney made it more so; and it naturally strikes one as very bad taste on his part to be forcing himself on your wife at a time like this. It seems there was some slight talk at the Club too—not worth noticing, of course. But you know Mrs Olliver takes fire easily, where any of us are concerned; and Olliver seemed afraid she might speak to Mrs Desmond, unless I came to you. He met them again this afternoon; and he felt you ought at least to know exactly how matters stand——"

"He might have taken it for granted that I should do that without *his* interference."

Desmond's temper was flaring up again; and his words brought the anxious look back to Paul's eyes. Theo was sailing very near the wind.

"We all know you too well to believe that you would—tolerate such a state of things—*if* you were aware of them," he answered slowly, choosing his words with care. "Please understand, Theo, that it is Kresney who is criticised; and that Olliver put the whole thing before me as nicely as possible. I feel I have been clumsy enough myself. But it goes against the grain to say anything at all, you understand?"

Desmond's sole answer was a decisive nod of the head. Then silence fell—a strained silence, difficult to break. Yet it was he himself who broke it.

"I can do no less than thank you," he said stiffly. "It was a hateful thing to have thrust upon you; but Frank's intrusion would have been unendurable. The truth is—" he paused, for the words were hard to bring out—"I have known—all along that my wife was more friendly with—these Kresneys than I quite cared about. One could make no valid objections without seeming uncharitable, and she is still too new here to understand our point of view. But I must see to it now that she *shall* understand, once and for all. It is intolerable to have one's brother officers—making remarks, even with the best intentions. Will you ask Honor to tell my wife, when she comes in, that I want to see her?"

Silence again; and Paul rose to his feet. It hurt him

to leave his friend without a word. But the attitude Desmond had adopted precluded the lightest touch of sympathy, and Wyndham could not choose but admire him the more.

"By the way"—Desmond turned upon him as he went with startling abruptness—"*Honor* isn't in any way mixed up with all this, is she?"

Something in his look and tone made Wyndham glance at him intently before replying. "Of course she saw how things were while you were away. But she has been out very little lately; and as far as I can judge, she knows nothing about the talk that is going on now."

"Thank Heaven!" Desmond muttered into his moustache; but Paul's ear failed to catch the words.

"Won't you have a 'peg' or a cup of tea, Theo?" he asked gently.

"No, thanks."

"I think you ought to have one or the other."

"Very well, whichever you please. Only, bring it yourself, there's a good chap."

Paul's eyes rested thoughtfully upon his friend, who, absorbed in his own reflections, seemed to have forgotten his presence. Then he went slowly away, revolving the matter in his mind.

While avoiding the least shadow of false statement, Desmond had succeeded in shielding his wife from the one serious implication suggested by her conduct, or at least would have so succeeded, but for the tell-tale crash of glass upon the hearthstone. Yet the most vivid impression left on Paul by their short interview was the look in Theo's eyes when he had asked that one abrupt question about Honor Meredith.

Was it possible——? Was it even remotely possible——?

Wyndham reined in the involuntary thought, as a man reins in his horse on the brink of a precipice. Common loyalty to the friend he loved, with the unspoken love of half a lifetime, forbade him to look that shrouded possibility frankly in the face.

CHAPTER XXXI.

THE LOSS OF ALL.

"The loss of all love has to give,
Save pardon for love wronged."
—G. MEREDITH.

"HERE I am, Theo. Honor says you want to see me."

Evelyn Desmond closed the door behind her; and at sight of her husband transformed into his very self—freed at last from all disfigurements—she ran to him with outstretched arms.

"Theo, are you really all right again? I can hardly believe it."

But Desmond had no answer to give her. He simply squared his right arm, warding off her hands.

Then she saw the hard lines of his mouth, the inexpressible pain in his eyes; and, clutching at his rigid forearm, tried to force it down. She might as well have tried to shift a bar of iron.

"What's the matter with you now?" she asked, half petulant, half fearful. "Has anything else gone wrong? Haven't we had enough misery and depression——?"

"There's no more call for acting, Evelyn," Desmond interposed with an ominous quietness more disconcerting than anger—"Doesn't your own conscience tell you what may have gone wrong?"

At that the colour left her face. "You mean—is it about —me?" she asked with shaking lips.

"Yes. About you." Her pitiful aspect softened him; he took her arm and set her gently down upon a chair;—

the selfsame chair that Paul had occupied half an hour ago. "Don't be frightened," he said gently; "I won't hurt you more than I must. Ever since we married I have done my utmost to help you, spare you, shield you; but now—we've got to arrive at a clear understanding, once for all. First I want you to answer a question or two, straightly, without prevarication. You went out early, it seems. Where?"

"To Mrs Riley's——"

"And after?"

"I met Mr Kresney—quite by chance. He wanted me to come in to tea. He said Miss Kresney would soon be home—and I—I——"

"No need for polite fabrications;" he took her up quickly. "You went in. Miss Kresney did *not* come home. Is this the first time he has trapped you with a convenient lie? Tell me that."

Words and tone roused her to a passing flash of retaliation.

"If you're going to get so angry, Theo, I won't tell you *any*thing, and I *won't* be questioned like a creature in a witness-box! Some one's been saying horrid things of me. Major Wyndham, I suppose. You wouldn't listen to any one else. It's very mean of him——"

Desmond took a hasty step forward. "How dare you speak so of the straightest man living!" he cried with imperious heat. "You, who have taken advantage of my blindness to deceive me deliberately a second time, on account of a cad who isn't fit to tie your shoe-strings. I've been blind in more than one way lately. But that is over now. I am not likely to repeat the mistake of trusting you implicitly—after this."

She cowered under the lash of his just wrath, hiding her face and crying heart-broken tears—the bitterest she had yet shed. In snatching at the shadow it seemed she had lost the substance past recall.

"Oh! You are cruel—horrible!" she wailed, with her disarming, pathetic air of a scolded child that made a rough word to her seem cowardly as a blow.

"No need to break your heart over it," he said more

gently; "and as to cruelty, Evelyn, haven't you abused my faith in your loyalty and dragged my pride in the dust by letting your name be coupled with that man's, though I told you plainly I had good reasons for distrusting and disliking him. I suppose he made a dead set at you while I was away—cowardly brute! But what hits me hardest of all is not your indiscretion; it's your persistent crookedness that poisons everything. It was the same over your bills last year—as I told you then. It's the same now. It's a poor look-out if a man can't trust his own wife; but I suppose you must have lied to me—and to Honor, a dozen times this last week."

It had cost him an effort to speak so plainly and at such length; but his wife's uneven breathing was the only answer he received.

He came closer and laid an arm round her shoulder.

"Evelyn—Ladybird—have you nothing to say to me?"

"N—no," she answered in a choked voice, without uncovering her face; "it wouldn't be any use."

"Why not? Am I so utterly devoid of understanding?"

"No—no. But you brave, strong sort of people can't ever know how hard little things are for—for people like me. It has been so—dull lately. You had—all those men, and—I was lonely. It was nice to have some one—wanting me—some one not miles above my head. But I knew you would be cross if I told you—and—and—" tears choked her utterance—"oh, it's no good talking. You'd never understand."

"I understand this much, my dear," he said. "You are done up with the strain of nursing, and badly in need of a change. But we shall soon get away on leave now; and I will see to it that you shall never feel dull or out of it again. Only one thing I insist upon—your intimacy with—that man is at an end. No more riding with him; no more going to his bungalow. From to-day you treat him and his sister as mere acquaintances."

She faced him now with terror-stricken eyes. For while he spoke, she had perceived the full extent of her dilemma.

"But, Theo—there isn't any need for that," she urged, with a thrill of fear at her own boldness. "They would think it so odd. What excuses could I possibly make?"

"That's your affair," Desmond answered unmoved. "You are a better hand at it than I am. My only concern is that you shall put an end to this equivocal state of things for good."

At that she hid her face again, with a sob of despair. "I can't do it—I *can't*. It's impossible!" she murmured vehemently more to herself than to him.

Her unexpected opposition fanned his smouldering wrath to a blaze. He took her by the shoulder—not roughly, but very decisively.

"*Impossible!* What am I to understand by that?"

It was the first time he had touched her untenderly; and she quivered in every nerve.

"I—I don't know. I can't explain. But—it's true."

For one instant he stood speechless;—then:

"Great Heavens, Evelyn!" he broke out, "don't you see that you are forcing upon me a suspicion that is an insult to us both?"

She looked up at him in blank bewilderment, then jerked herself free from his hand.

"I—I don't understand what you mean. But if you *will* think horrid things of me you may. I can't explain and—I won't!"

"You—*won't*," Desmond repeated slowly, frozen incredulity in his eyes; and she, fearing she had gone too far, caught at the hand she had shaken off.

"Oh, Theo, what *does* it matter after all?" she urged between irritation and despair, "when you know quite well it's you—that I love?"

The appeal was too ill-timed to be convincing; and Desmond's smile had a tinge of bitterness in it.

"You have an uncommonly original way of showing it," he said coldly; "and the statement doesn't square with your refusal to explain yourself. You have broken up the foundations of—things to-day, Evelyn! You have killed my trust in you altogether. You may remember, perhaps,—what that involves." And withdrawing his hand he turned and left her.

But he had roused her at last by the infliction of a pain too intense for tears. She sprang up, knocking over the chair that fell with a thud on the carpet, and hurried after him, clinging to his unresponsive arm.

"Theo, Theo, take care what you say! Do you mean—truthfully that you don't—love me any more?"

"God knows," he answered wearily. "Let me alone now, for Heaven's sake, till I can see things clearer. But I'll not alter my decision about Kresney, whatever your mysterious impossibilities may be."

Freeing himself gently but deliberately, he went over to the verandah door and stood there, erect, motionless, his back towards her, looking out upon the featureless huts of the servants' quarters with eyes that saw nothing save a vision of his wife's face, as it had shone upon him, more than two years ago, in the Garden of Tombs.

And it was shining upon him now—had he but guessed it,—not with the simple tenderness of girlhood; but with the despairing half-worshipping love of a woman.

When he heard the door close softly behind her, he came back into the room, mechanically righted the chair, and sitting down upon it buried his face in his hands.

CHAPTER XXXII.

EVEN TO THE UTMOST.

"How can Love lose, doing of its kind,
Even to the utmost?"
—EDWIN ARNOLD.

WHEN Evelyn Desmond stumbled out of her husband's presence, stunned, bewildered, blinded with tears, the one coherent thought left in her mind was—Honor. Amid all that was terrifying and heart-breaking, Honor's love stood sure; a rock in mid-ocean—the one certainty that would never fail her, though the world went to pieces under her feet.

But Honor was not in the drawing-room; and Evelyn knocked timidly at her door.

"Come in," the low voice sounded from the other side. The girl was standing before the looking-glass, pinning on her hat.

"I was going across to ask after Mr Bradley," she explained, completing the operation before looking round. But at sight of Evelyn's face she hurried forward, holding out her arms.

"Dearest, what *has* happened to make you look like that?"

"Everything's happened! It's all finished between Theo and me. Broken up. He said so—and—I'm going away. There are—other people who care. I won't stay with a man who doesn't love me—or trust me——"

But Honor, holding her closer, looked searchingly into her face. "Evelyn, that is *not true!*"

"Well, he said so. And *he* doesn't tell lies!"

"Oh, you poor, poor child!" Honor murmured, kissing her with a strange fervour of sympathy. "But tell me—what's the reason of all this? If Theo did say such terrible things, he must have been cruelly hurt or very angry——"

"He was—very angry. I'm sure he won't forgive me this time; and I do believe it would be better all round if I went right away and left him in peace with his polo and his squadron and his precious Frontier Force——"

Honor's hand closed her lips. "My dear! Are you *quite* mad?"

"No. But I think I will be—very soon."

She spoke with such tragic certainty that the girl smiled in spite of herself. "Why? What have you done? Tell me—quick!"

"Oh! It's not *me* that's done," Evelyn declared with her engaging air of injured innocence. "It's other people—Major Wyndham, I believe—making remarks to him about me and—Mr Kresney."

"You've been *there* again. I was half afraid——"

"Why on earth shouldn't I? But now Theo's simply ordered me to drop them. It's quite impossible. I—I told him so."

"And you did not tell him why?"

"No. That would have been worse than all."

"But you will tell *me*. You must—if I am to help you."

Evelyn regarded her with a misty smile. "You're very wonderful, Honor. But even *you* can't help now. You see—it's money——"

"Money? How? What?"

"Promise you won't stop loving me and be angry—like Theo was," Evelyn pleaded, the incurable child flashing out in the midst of her distress. "I've had enough for to-day."

"I promise, dear. Go on."

Then the small sordid tragedy came out in broken snatches, to the last particle. For once in her life Evelyn Desmond spoke the unvarnished truth, adorning nothing, extenuating nothing; and Honour listened in an enigmatical silence—a silence which held even after the last word had been spoken. Evelyn looked up at her nervously.

"Honour, you *are* angry inside. I can see you are."

"No,—I am not angry," Honor answered slowly. "Where would be the use? I am simply—astounded that you could *dare* to run such risks with the love of a man who is one among a thousand."

She spoke the last words with unguarded enthusiasm; not perceiving, till they were out, the intent look on Evelyn's face.

"I knew you were friends with Theo, Honor," she said, "but I never thought you admired him as much—as all *that*."

The girl caught the note of jealousy, and coloured to the roots of her hair.

"I am not alone in my opinion," she said with an uneasy laugh. "There are dozens of others who would say no less. It is only that I want you to realise your good fortune before it is too late."

"But it *is* too late. If he's angry now he'll be furious when he knows. And unless I go away he will *have* to know."

"You shall not go away. And he must never know. He has suffered enough as it is——"

"Haven't *I* suffered just as much? You always think of him——"

"I am thinking of you both. How much is it that you still owe these Kresneys?"

"A hundred and fifty—no, two hundred. And I can't possibly pay it for months and months."

By this time Honor had crossed to the chest of drawers near her bed and had taken out a small japanned cash-box. Evelyn watched her movements with ecstatic enlightenment.

"Honor—what *are* you going to do?" she asked breathlessly.

But the girl neither answered nor turned her head. She took out a small sheaf of notes, locked the cash-box, and put it away. Then taking an envelope from her rack, she sealed and addressed it, while Evelyn leaned against the dressing-table, white and speechless from the shock of relief.

"The whole amount is in there," Honor said, handing her the envelope, and speaking in a repressed voice. "Luckily I had hardly touched my month's money. This makes you free to do as Theo wishes. I don't want a penny of it back

—ever. And Theo is never to know anything about the whole transaction. Promise me that; and don't *dare* to break your word."

"I promise faithfully. Oh, Honor, you are my good angel! Shall I take it now—at once?"

"No. Not you. I must go myself. It ought to be delivered to him in person, and I must have a stamped receipt."

"Honor, how horrid! Just as if he were a shop! Besides—nobody but *me* can give it—or explain——"

"How can you explain? What will you say?"

"Just whatever comes into my head. Married women understand these sort of things. I shall know what to say—at the time."

"So will he. And then——"

"There you go!" Tears threatened again and her voice shook. "You talk about loving me and you don't trust me any more than Theo does. If I mayn't do this my own way I won't take the money at all."

"Don't talk nonsense, child," Honor cried desperately, her own self-control almost at an end. "You *must* take it. And if you insist on running risks with your eyes open, there's no more to be said except make haste and get the wretched thing done with. Go at once, in your jhampan—and *don't* leave it. Ask for Miss Kresney; and—shop or no shop—mind you get a proper receipt. Then come straight home and tell Theo you will do what he wishes. He will have had time to think things over and it will be all right. I know it will. Perhaps you would like me to speak of it to him, if I get the chance?"

"Yes—yes. Do, please! You dear, wonderful Honor! I don't know how to say thank you enough——"

But Honor disengaged herself something hurriedly. The ache of rebellion at her heart made Evelyn's effusiveness unendurable.

"Don't thank me at all," she said. "I don't want your thanks. I don't—deserve them. Take care of that envelope; it is worth more than two hundred rupees to you—and to me. Now go!"

And taking her by the shoulders, she put her gently outside the door. Then, drawing a deep breath of relief, stood alone with the realisation of all that had passed.

It seemed that she was not to be spared one drop of the cup of bitterness; that to her had been assigned the task of Sisyphus, the ceaseless rolling upward of a stone that as ceaselessly rolled down; the continual re-establishment of Evelyn in the shrine of her husband's heart. And there would be no end to it, even after John's return. So long as these two had need of her, heart and brain and hands would be at their service. She did not definitely think this, because true heroism is unaware of itself. "It feels, and never reasons; and therefore is always right."

Honor was aware of nothing just then, but the keen pang of self-reproach. "God forgive me!" she murmured, forming the words with her lips. "I did it for *him*."

Then she started, and the blood flew to her face. For Desmond's voice, imperious, entreating, rang clear through the quiet of the house.

"Ladybird, where *are* you? Come back!"

And without a thought of what she intended to say, Honor went out to the completion of her day's work. That was her practical way of looking at the matter.

"It will be easy enough," she reflected as she went. The entreaty in Desmond's voice assured her of that.

But in the drawing-room doorway she stood still, extraordinarily still. For Desmond himself confronted her; and she had not anticipated the ordeal of a face-to-face encounter.

Involuntarily, inevitably, their eyes met, and lingered in each other's depths. It was their first real greeting since his return; and they felt it as such. It was the first time also that Desmond had seen her completely since his lightning-flash of self-knowledge; and in the same instant the same thought sprang to both their minds—that, in the past three weeks, the detested shade had served them better than they knew.

For a full minute it seemed as if these two, whose courage was above proof, did not dare risk movement or speech. But it was no more than a minute. Each was incapable of suspecting the other's hidden fear; and now, as always, Evelyn was the foremost thought in the minds of both.

Desmond broke the spell by one step forward.

"I want Ladybird," he said abruptly. "Where is she?"

"I'm sorry. She has just gone out; but she won't be long."

Honor knew what must come next; knew also that she could neither lie to him nor tell him the truth.

"What possessed her to go out again? Do you know where she went?"

"Yes, Theo, I do know," she answered, coming into the room, and speaking with a noble directness that was like a light thrown across tortuous ways. "It was unavoidable. I would rather not say any more. You can trust me, can't you?"

"As I trust God and my own soul," he replied with profound conviction. "Did she seem—much upset?"

"Yes,—terribly upset. Not without reason. She told me everything. May I speak of it, Theo? You won't think me—intrusive?"

He gave her a quick, reproachful glance.

"*You?* Say what you please. I was a brute to her; and I know it. But I swear I wasn't hard on her till she refused to break with Kresney. Did she give you any sort of reason for that?"

"Yes; and I have quite cleared up the difficulty; though I'm afraid you mustn't ask me how."

"You seem hedged about with mysteries this evening," he remarked, a trifle curtly. "I confess I like daylight, and straight roads."

"Not more than I do, Theo. But you have said you can trust me; and at least I can assure you that there was no question of personal reluctance. Whatever Evelyn's failings may be, I know that *you* are the one big thing in her life."

Desmond compressed his lips, and looked down thoughtfully at the bearskin under his feet; while Honor allowed her eyes to dwell on the goodly lines of his face. Then he squared his shoulders and looked up at her.

"Honor—if that is true—and I think it is—you are bound to let me help her by the only means in my power. Give me back that promise of mine. I am strong enough now to tackle the subject; and I warn you fairly that I mean to have my own way. So don't waste time by beating about the bush."

The unexpected attack unbalanced her, and the blood left her face; but there was no hint of yielding in her eyes. They were equally matched these two—strength for strength; will for will. The ultimate victory might rest with either.

"Theo!" she protested, "you can ask that of me—to-day?"

"Yes, precisely—to-day. My mistake—my selfishness, has been very painfully brought home to me in the last hour; and I don't ask it of you—I demand it."

Honor drew herself up to her full height.

"You cannot command it, though," she said quietly. "And—I refuse."

The hot blood mounted to his temples, but he shut his teeth to keep back hasty speech. Then, as the silence grew and deepened between them, anger gave place to an unbounded admiration.

They were standing now face to face, beside the mantelpiece, exactly as they had stood on that eventful April afternoon a year ago. The memory came to them simultaneously; and each saw the light of it spring into the other's eyes. Honor's face softened.

"You remember," she urged. "I see that you remember; and the arguments you admitted then hold even more strongly now. Besides—you said I had earned the right——"

"So you have—ten times over since then. But to-day I see my duty to Ladybird so clearly, that no one—not even you—must stand in the way of it. You would realise better how I feel, if you had heard her pitiful excuses. She was 'dull.' She was 'lonely.' I had 'all those men,'—so I had. She was right, poor child! Truth is, my life is so richly filled with 'all those men,' that I sometimes wonder if I was justified in bringing a woman into it at all. But having done so, I'm bound to take her where she won't be tempted to entangle herself with cads like Kresney, just because she feels dull and lonely. That's the source of half the catastrophes one hears of in this country; and in nine cases out of ten I blame the husband more than the wife. You see, I happen to believe that when a man takes a woman's life into his hands, he makes himself responsible not only for her honour, but for her happiness and well-being. I'm not setting up a standard for other fellows, remember. I am simply stating my own by way of explanation."

Honor's eyes shone with a very tender light.

"I can only say that Evelyn is—a singularly fortunate woman. If most men held such views there would be ninety per cent fewer marriages in the world."

"Possibly. But that doesn't put me in the wrong. Now, I have set the picture before you as I see it——"

"Yes, with the core of it left out,—the loss to you and to the Regiment."

"Oh, hang it all!" Desmond protested with an embarrassed laugh. "One's bound to leave out something. That's the whole art of making a decent picture! But it strikes me we've had enough of argument. Whether I have convinced you or not, Honor, you *must* let me off that promise."

The girl held her breath, nerving herself for a last desperate stand.

"Forgive me, if you know how, Theo," she said; "but I cannot—I will not give up my right to save you from yourself."

Desmond simply raised his head and looked at her, as though he could not believe that he had heard aright; and when at last he spoke, his voice had the level note of authority which she had been dreading to hear.

"At the risk of seeming brutal, Honor, I warn you that I'll not give you one minute's peace till you unsay those words—for Ladybird's sake."

Then, to his unspeakable consternation, she took a step backward and sank into the chair behind her, pressing both hands over her eyes.

"Do whatever you think right," she murmured brokenly. "You are too strong for me altogether."

There are victories more bitter than defeat; and Desmond had no words in which to answer this girl, who cared so strangely, so intensely, much what became of him.

When a woman breaks down utterly in the presence of the man who loves her—whether he dare acknowledge it or no

—words are not apt to meet the exigencies of the case; and Desmond had no other panacea at his command. He could only stand looking down upon her, his hands thrust deep into his pockets, as if he feared that they might go out to her of their own accord; his eyes darkened with such intensity of pain that it was well for both that hers were shielded from sight of them.

He longed, beyond all things on earth, to kneel down and comfort her. He knew that three words from him would put an end to her distress, and cancel his own quixotic plan of action. But the words were not uttered; and he remained standing on the hearth-rug with his hands in his pockets. There was no sign in the quiet room that anything noteworthy had taken place. Yet on those two prosaic details the future of three lives depended—a man silent when he might have spoken; planted squarely on his feet when he might have been on his knees.

Rob got up and stretched himself elaborately, vented his boredom in a long musical yawn, then settled down to sleep again in a more expansive attitude; and Evelyn's French clock struck six with cheerful unconcern.

The silence, which seemed interminable, might possibly have lasted three minutes, when Honor let fall her hands, and looked up at the man who had mastered her. He looked what he was—unconquerable; and if she had not loved him already, she must infallibly have loved him then.

"Please understand," she said, and her voice was not quite steady, "that I have not *given* my consent to this. You have simply wrenched it from me by the sheer force of—your personality. You have not altered my conviction by a hair's-breadth. What you have set your heart on is a piece of unjustifiable quixotism; and I have only one thing to beg of you now. Do nothing decisive till you have spoken to Paul."

Desmond sighed.

"Very well. I will tackle him to-morrow."

"What a hurry you are in!" And she smiled faintly.

"I believe in striking while the iron's hot."

"And I believe in giving it time to cool. May I—first, say one word to Paul?"

"No, certainly not." The refusal came out short and sharp. "If you two combined forces against me I should be done for! Leave me to manage Paul alone."

With a sigh she rose to her feet.

Then, quite suddenly, her calmness fell away from her.

"Theo—Theo," she protested, "if you really persist in this, and carry it through, I don't think I shall ever forgive you."

The pain in her voice was more than he could bear.

"For God's sake spare me that!" he pleaded. "I am losing enough as it is."

And now his hands went out to her irresistibly, in the old impulsive fashion, that seemed an echo from a former life.

With superlative courage she turned and surrendered both her own. She wanted to prove herself, at all points, simply his friend; and he gave her no cause to repent of her courage, or to suspect the strong restraint he put upon himself during that brief contact, which, at a moment so charged with emotion, might well have proved fatal to them both.

"Thank you, Honor," he said quietly.

But for her, speech was impossible. She bowed her head, and left him standing alone, with the dregs of victory.

On reaching the blessed shelter of her own room she bolted the door; and for once in her life grief had its way with her unhindered.

She could not guess, while railing against Desmond's tenacity of purpose, that the same passionate self-reproach which had urged her to go all lengths for Evelyn, was urging him now to a supreme act of self-devotion to his wife's happiness.

CHAPTER XXXIII.

THE ONE BIG THING.

"The sky that noticed all makes no disclosure;
And earth keeps up her terrible composure."
—BROWNING.

HIS wife herself was, in the meanwhile, journeying hopefully back to the Kresneys' bungalow, on the shoulders of four long-suffering jhampanis, who murmured a little among themselves, without rancour or vexation, concerning the perplexing ways of Memsahibs in general. For the native of India the supreme riddle of creation is the English "Mem."

They had but just cast aside their liveries and, squatting on their heels in a patch of shadow, had embarked on leisurely preparations for the evening hookah and the evening meal. The scent of curry was in their nostrils; the regular "flip-flap" of the deftly turned chupattie was in their ears; when a flying order had come from the house—"The Memsahib goes forth in haste!" With resigned mutterings and head-shakings they had responded to the call of duty, and the *mate*,[1] who was a philosopher, had a word of comfort for them as they went. "Worse might have befallen, brothers, seeing that it hath pleased God to make our Memsahib light as a bird. Had it been the Miss Sahib, now——" A unanimous murmur testified that the Miss Sahib would have been a far weightier affair!

And on this occasion they must have found their mistress even lighter than a bird; for instead of lying back among

[1] Headman.

her cushions, she sat upright, in strained anticipation, pressing between her hands the miraculous envelope which was to buy back for her all that she had so lightly flung away.

Honor had spoken truth when she said that Desmond was the one big thing in Evelyn's life. Everything else about her was small as her person, and little more effectual. But this impetuous, large-hearted husband of hers—whose love she had been so proud to win, and had taken such small pains to keep—could by no means be chiselled into proportions with the rest of the picture. He took his stand, simply and naturally, on the heights; and if it was an effort to keep up with him, it was a real calamity to be left behind. Understand him she could not, and never would; but it sufficed that she saw him fearless, chivalrous, admired on all sides, and singularly good to look at. This last should perhaps have been set down first; for there is no denying that her remorse, her suffering, had been less overwhelming without that unexpected vision of his face.

But things were going to be all right soon. She would never hide anything from him again—never. And the resolve may be counted unto her for righteousness, even if there could be small hope of its fulfilment.

Such absorbing considerations crowded out all thought of Honor's generosity. It was just Honor. No one else would ever give you two hundred rupees, at a moment's notice, as if it were sixpence. But you might expect anything from Honor—that was how she was made. And the one important point was—Theo. Nothing else really mattered at all.

As Kresney's bungalow came in sight she found herself fervently hoping that he might have gone out; that she might have to encounter nothing more formidable than Miss Kresney, or, better still, the bearer.

But before the gate was reached, she caught sight of him in the verandah, taking his ease very completely in one of those ungainly chairs, with arms extending to long wooden leg-rests, which seem to belong to India and no other country in the world. He had exchanged his coat for a Japanese smoking jacket, whose collar and cuffs could ill afford to brave daylight; and his boots for slippers of Linda's making, whose conflicting colours might have set an oyster's teeth on edge! His own teeth were clenched upon a rank cigar; and he was reading a paper-bound novel that she would not have touched with a pair of tongs.

He had never appeared to worse advantage; and Evelyn, fresh from her husband's air of unobtrusive neatness and distinction, was conscious of a sudden recoil—a purely physical revulsion; to which was added the galling thought that she owed her recent suffering and humiliation to her intimacy with a man who could look like that!

As she turned in at the gate, he sprang up and ran down the steps. Her return astounded him. He was prepared for anything at that moment, except the thing that happened—a common human experience.

"Back again, Mrs Desmond!" he cried cheerfully. "This is a most unexpected pleasure. *Rukho jhampan.*"[1]

But Evelyn countermanded the order so promptly that Kresney's eyebrows went up. She handed him her note, clutching the wooden pole nervously with the other hand.

"I had to come out again—on business," she said, with that ready mingling of the false and true which had been her undoing. "And I thought I could leave this for Miss Kresney as I passed. Will you please give it to her. I am sorry she is not in."

He took the envelope, and watched her while she spoke with narrowed eyes.

"You are in trouble?" The intimate note in his voice jarred for the first time. "Something has upset you since you left? You are quite knocked up with all this. You ought to have been in Murree two weeks ago."

And, presumably by accident, his hand came down upon her own. She drew it away with an involuntary shudder; and Kresney's sallow face darkened.

"You have no business to say that," she rebuked him with desperate courage; "I prefer to be with my husband till he is well enough to go too. You won't forget my note, will you? Good-night."

"Good-night, Mrs Desmond," he answered formally, without proffering his hand.

[1] Set down the jhampan.

As he stood watching her depart, all that was worst in him rose to the surface and centred in his close-set eyes. "By God, you shall be sorry for that!" he muttered.

But in mounting the steps his curiosity was awakened by the bulkiness of Linda's letter. He turned it over once or twice; pressed it between his fingers and detected the crackle of new bank-notes.

"So that's it, is it? Well, I can forgive her. No doubt she had a jolly hot quarter of an hour; and I hope that fellow is enjoying himself now—*like hell!*" Then, without a glimmer of hesitation, he opened his sister's letter.

And, out in the road, Evelyn's jhampanis were experiencing fresh proof of the indubitable madness of Memsahibs.

No sooner were their faces set cheerfully homeward, than they were brought up short by an order to turn and carry her in the opposite direction. No destination was specified; and the road indicated led out towards the hills. Hookahs and chupatties tugging at their heart-strings, roused them to mild rebellion. The mate, as established spokesman, murmured of *khana*[1] and the lateness of the hour; adding that the road behind them led away from the Sahibs' bungalows to the boundary of the station.

But Evelyn, whose Hindustani was still a negligible quantity, made no attempt to follow the man's remarks. She reiterated her wish, adding irritably, "Make no foolish talk. It is an order!"

Those magic words, *Hukm hai*, are the insignia of authority through the length and breadth of India; and consoling one another with the reflection that if the Memsahib had small understanding, the Sahib was great, they jogged obediently along the lonely road toward the hills.

Evelyn's order had been given on the impulse of a moment. The idea of confronting her husband again in less than ten minutes had overpowered her suddenly and completely. She had only one thought—to gain time; to screw up her courage for the ordeal; and to realise a little what she intended to say. It is only the strong who dare to trust that the right words will be given them.

[1] Food.

Her interview with Kresney had unnerved her; and a lurking doubt quenched the spark of hope at her heart. Would Theo accept her tardy obedience without asking unanswerable questions. Or would he simply put her aside, with his inexorable quietness, that was far more terrible than any spoken word?

In all the pain and bewilderment of their short interview, nothing had so smitten her as his recoil—first and last—from the touch of her hands. The bare possibility that he might treat her so again made return seem out of the question. And her unhappiness struck deeper than the fear of the moment. For the first time she realised her own instability of feeling and purpose; and with the realisation came a new paralysing fear of the future—of herself.

For the first time it dawned upon her that she was unworthy of the love and faith that had been given her in such generous measure;—which was proof conclusive, though she did not guess it, that Honor Meredith had not laboured in vain. To know oneself unworthy is to have achieved the first step upward. A year ago she would have been incapable of such knowledge; and now that it had come to her she was afraid.

Sudden cessation of movement roused her; and the mate, turning his head, spoke with respectful urgency.

"Protector of the Poor, it is not well to go farther. Behold the swift going of the sun. Before your servants can reach the bungalow there will be no more light, and it is against orders—— The Sahib will make angry talk."

Evelyn did not follow the whole of this appeal; but the man's anxiety was evident. She caught the words "Sahib" and "angry" with an inward shudder; she had endured enough of the Sahib's anger for one day, and her own common-sense told her that she had behaved foolishly.

Even outlying bungalows were no longer in sight. A boundary pillar gleamed ghostlike a few hundred yards ahead. The last rim of the sun had already slipped behind the hills. Their harsh peaks black against a sky of faint amber, had a threatening look; and darkness was racing up out of the east. The mate was right. It would be upon them almost before they could reach the bungalow; and to be out after sunset was strictly against the rules of the station.

Sudden terror clutched her; a nameless dread of the country—of the natives—which she had never been able to shake off; a paralysing sense that she was alone in their midst—alone on the verge of night.

Fear unsteadied her voice as she answered the man. "Turn, turn at once, and go quickly,—run; the Sahib will give *backsheesh*—run!"

But before they could obey, a white figure sprang up from behind a cluster of rocks. Quick as thought followed a flash, a report, a heart-piercing scream; and the men, with a cry of "Ghazi! Ghazi!" unceremoniously set down their mistress and fled.

The fanatic fled also, certain of a passport into Paradise; and as Evelyn Desmond fell back among her cushions, a shadow, that had not been there before, crept slowly across the shoulder of her muslin dress. The oncoming darkness mattered nothing to her now; and she herself, a mere atom of life, blown out like a candle, mattered less than nothing to the desert and the imperturbable hills.

But justice does not invariably tarry. The arm of the Lord is not shortened, though in these days of omniscience man has a larger faith in his own; and the Ghazi, heading post-haste through the dusk plunged unwittingly into a group of villagers and cattle returning home.

A short scuffle ensued, shouts and the tramping of feet—sounds which brought the flying jhampanis back in a twinkling, surcharged with voluble valour and explanations. Resistance was useless. Moreover, to the fanatic, death is the one great gift. With stoical indifference the man found himself overpowered and disarmed. Zealous villagers, unrolling turbans and kummerbunds, made fast his arms, bound him securely about the waist and neck, and in this ignominious fashion led him back to where Evelyn Desmond lay untroubled and alone.

The jhampanis shouldered their burden once more; and fell to discussing, in lively detail, the hanging and subsequent burning that awaited the Taker of Life, who walked unconcernedly in their midst.

CHAPTER XXXIV.

C'ÉTAIT MA VIE.

"C'était toute petite, ma vie:
Mais c'était ma vie."
—ANATOLE FRANCE.

"HONOR, come out! I want you."

Desmond's voice, followed by a peremptory rap on the door, startled the girl back to a realisation of the flight of time. The sun had set, and a grey light filled the room. Without a passing thought of the tears upon her face, she lowered the bolt and confronted Evelyn's husband.

"Ladybird isn't back yet," he said quickly. "It'll be dark in ten minutes. I *must* know where she went to, and go after her myself."

Honor bit her lip. To tell him at such a moment would be madness; yet he was in an ill mood to oppose.

"Can't you send the orderly?" she asked, with something less than her wonted assurance.

"No. I am going myself. This is no time to fuss over trifles. Something may have gone wrong——"

"Hush,—listen! What's that?"

The shuffling and grunting of jhampanis, and the thud of the lowered dandy, were distinctly audible in the stillness.

"There she is!" Desmond said eagerly; and a moment later the blood in his veins was chilled by a long-drawn wail from the verandah. "Hai—hai—*mere Memsahib murgya!*"[1]

Before the cry had spent itself he was through the "chick," down the verandah steps at a bound, and bending over his unconscious wife. Her head had dropped down to one shoulder, and on the other ominous stains showed darkly in the half light.

[1] My mistress is dead.

"Great God—*murder!*" Desmond muttered between his teeth. "What devil's work is this?" he added, turning upon the cowering jhampanis.

"Ghazi, Sahib; Ghazi," they told him in eager chorus, with a childish mingling of excitement and terror; and would fain have enlarged upon their own valour in pursuing the Taker of Life, but that Desmond's curt "*chupraho*"[1] checked them in mid-career.

"Stay where you are, Honor," he added to the girl, who had followed him, and now stood at the head of the steps. "I am bringing her in."

"Is she—alive?"

"God knows. Look sharp and get some brandy."

He took up one limp hand and laid his fingers on her wrist. A faint flutter of life rewarded him.

"Thank Heaven!" he murmured; and lifted her tenderly in his arms. But at the foot of the steps he paused.

"Nassur Ali—the Doctor Sahib. Ride like the wind!" Then turning again to the jhampanis, big with harrowing detail, added: "The devil who did this thing, hath he escaped?"

"*Nahin, nahin,*[2] Sahib. Would your Honour's servants permit? The jackal spawn is even now in the hands of the police. May his soul burn in hell——"

"It is enough—go!" Desmond commanded in the peremptory vernacular; and mounted the steps with his burden.

Honor stood awaiting him in the drawing-room, white as her dress, tears glistening on her cheeks and lashes, yet very composed withal.

At sight of his face she started; it was grey-white and set like a rock. Only the eyes were alive—and ruthless, as she had never yet seen them, and prayed that she never might see them again.

"They've got the man," he said between his teeth. "I wish to God I could shoot him with my own hand."

Then he went forward to the sofa, and laid his wife upon it. His quick eye detected at once the nature of the wound. "Lung," he muttered mechanically. "No hope."

With the same unnatural calmness, he drew the long pins out of her hat—the poor, pretty hat which had so delighted

[1] Be quiet. [2] No, no.

her six hours ago; and as she moved, with a small sound of pain, he applied the spirit to her lips.

"What is it?" she murmured. "Don't touch me."

The faint note of distaste struck on her husband's heart; for he did not understand its meaning.

"Ladybird—look!" he entreated gently. "It is Theo." She opened her eyes, and gazed blankly up at him, where he leaned above her.

Then, as recognition dawned, he saw the shadow of fear darken them, and instantly dropped on one knee enclosing her with his arm.

"Ladybird, forgive me! You must never be frightened of me—never!"

The intensity of his low tone roused her half-awakened brain.

"But you were so angry, I was—afraid to come home."

"My God!" the man groaned under his breath. But before he could grasp the full horror of it all, she shrank closer to him, clutching at his arm, her eyes wide with terror.

"There's blood on me—look! It was—that man. Is it bad? Am I going—to die?"

"Not if human power can save you, my dear little woman. Mackay will soon be here."

But pain and fear clouded her senses, and she scarcely heard his words.

"Theo—I can't see you properly. Are you there?"

"Yes, yes. I am here."

The necessity for speech tortured him. But her one coherent longing was for the sound of his voice

"*Don't* let me die, please—not yet. I won't make you angry any more, I promise. And—it frightens me so. Keep tight hold of me; don't let me slip—away."

Desmond had a sensation as if a hand had gripped his throat, choking him, so that he could neither speak nor breathe. But with a supreme effort he mastered it; and leaning closer to her, spoke slowly, steadily, that she might lose no word of the small comfort he had power to give.

"I am holding you, my darling; and I will hold you to the very end. Only try—try to be brave, and remember that—whatever happens, you are safe—in God's hands."

A pitiful sob broke from her.

"But I don't understand about God! I only want—you. I want *your* hands—always. Where is the other one? Put it—underneath me—and hold me—ever so close."

He obeyed her, in silence, to the letter. She winced a little at the movement; then her head nestled into its resting-place on the wounded shoulder, with a sigh that had in it no shadow of pain; and bending down he kissed her, long and fervently.

"Theo—darling," she breathed ecstatically, when her lips were free for speech, "now I *know* it isn't true—what you said about not—caring any more. And I am—ever so happy. God can t let me—die—now."

And on the word, a rush of blood from the damaged lung brought on the inevitable choking cough, that shattered the last remnant of her strength. Her fingers closed convulsively upon his; and at the utmost height of happiness—as it were, on the crest of a wave—her spirit slipped from its moorings; —and he was alone.

Still he knelt on, without movement, without thought, almost it seemed without breathing, like a man turned to stone; holding her, as he had promised, to the very end, and—beyond.

Honor, standing afar off, dazed and heart-broken, one hand clasping the back of a chair for support, heard at last the rattle of approaching hoofs, and nerved herself for the ordeal of speech. But when Mackay entered with Paul Wyndham, Desmond made no sign. The little doctor's keen eye took in the situation at a glance; and at the unlooked-for relief of Paul's presence, Honor's strained composure deserted her. She swayed a little, stretched out a hand blindly towards him, and would have fallen, but that he quietly put his arm round her, and with a strange mixture of feelings saw her head drop on to his shoulder. But it was only for a moment. Contact with the roughness of his coat roused her on the verge of unconsciousness. She drew herself up, a faint colour mantling in her cheeks, and tried to smile.

"Come away," Paul whispered, leading her to the door. "We can give him no help—or comfort—yet."

AFTERMATH.

"Had he not turned them in his hand, and thrust
Their high things low and laid them in the dust,
They had not been this splendour."

I.

Some two weeks after that day of tragedy—a tragedy that had stirred and enraged the whole station—Theo Desmond and Paul Wyndham left Kohat on furlough, long over-due to both. Such a wander-year, spent together, had, from early days, been one of their cherished dreams; but, as too often happens, there proved little family likeness between the dream and the reality. In the dream, Desmond was naturally to be the leading spirit of their grand tour. In the reality, all practical plans and considerations had devolved on Paul, and Theo it was who assented, unquestioning, uncaring, so long as he could put half the world between himself and Kohat.

His long illness, the fear of losing his sight, the double shock of self-revelation and loss had affected him mentally as blow on blow affects a man physically. Since the night of his wife's death none had seen him strongly moved, either by sorrow, pleasure, or anger. He had said and done all that was required of him with a strained unnatural precision. Even to the few who had drawn nearest to him in former times of trouble, he seemed now like a house whose every door is locked and every shutter drawn.

Outwardly unmoved, he had endured the ordeal of Evelyn's funeral, the storm of public surprise and indignation aroused by her murder. Though British officers, not a few, have been victims to fanaticism in India, no Englishwoman had ever been shot at before, and the strong feeling aroused by so dastardly a crime had been long in subsiding. The news had been wired to Peshawur. The Commissioner had galloped across thirty miles of desert next morning; and before Evelyn's funeral, at sundown, her death had been openly avenged by the hanging of her murderer and the burning of his body.

On that day Honor had gone over to Mrs Conolly's bungalow, there to remain till Meredith's arrival; and in the two weeks that followed, Desmond had seen little of her—or of any one save Paul. She had helped him in disposing of Evelyn's personal belongings; and at his earnest request, had accepted one or two of her trinkets, the remainder being sent home to her mother. At his request also, Honor had taken over charge of his piano while he was away; and if a touch of constraint marked their parting, neither was aware of it in the other.

By one sole distinction he had set her apart from the rest. To her, and her only, he could and did speak of his wife; for the simple reason that in her he recognised a love and a sorrow that matched his own—a sorrow untainted by the lurking after thought, "Better so"; and that tacit recognition had been for Honor the single ray of light in her dark hour. Once, before parting, she had spoken of it to Paul, who thenceforward knew his friend's aloofness for what it was—not the mere reserve of the strong man in pain, but the old incurable loyalty to his wife that had kept them all at arm's length in respect of her while she lived.

So they two went forth together on their sorrowful pilgrimage; and, once gone, there fell a curtain of silence between Desmond and those he had left behind. Week after week, month after month, that silence remained unbroken, though Olliver and his wife wrote and John Meredith wrote also on his return; though they plied him with questions, with news of the Regiment and Border politics, never a sight of his handwriting came to cheer them. But for Paul's unfailing, if discouraging bulletins, no word of him would have reached them at all.

Honor herself wrote twice, without avail; and thereafter accepted the fiat of silence, gleaning what comfort she might from a steady correspondence with Paul. It was not in her to guess how those fortnightly letters, so frank in expression, so reserved in essence, had upheld him through the darkest and most difficult months of his life; months in which he could only stand aside and wait till the man he loved, as Jonathan loved David, should come forth out of the house of sorrow and take up the broken threads of life once more.

Meantime, with inexhaustible patience, he continued to try one place after another, one distraction after another, with small result. It was a costly prescription, and though Desmond imagined he contributed his share, the chief of it was paid by his friend. During those first months he read little, talked little, and rarely expressed a definite wish. He would go anywhere, do anything in reason, so long as no mental effort was required of him; but music—to Paul's utter mystification—he decisively refused to hear. For the time being the man's whole nature seemed awry, and there were moments when Paul's heart contracted with dread of the worst.

Christmas found them at Le Trayas, on the Esterelles coast, an isolated paradise unprofaned by sight or sound of the noisy, restless life of the French Riviera. Here Theo Desmond had spent whole hours at a stretch, basking in the temperate December sunshine, under feathery mimosa bushes, that glorify the foothills,—silent as ever, yet seemingly content.

Still he wrote no line to the Regiment, that for thirteen years had stood second only to his God, and very rarely asked for news of it or his friends. By now their letters betrayed hints and more than hints of increasing anxiety. The men wrote tentatively; but Frank Olliver, nothing if not direct, poured forth her loving, unreasoning Irish heart on closely-written sheets of foreign paper, to Wyndham's alternate distraction and delight.

"Is there no manner of wild tale you could invent now to rouse the blessed man?" she wrote about this time. "Sure it's past believing that his pretty doll of a wife—who went near to ruin him living—should stand between him and us that love him, worse than ever now she's dead. The fear of it haunts me like a bogey and makes me go red hot inside."

The selfsame fear made Paul Wyndham go cold in the

small hours; but he could not bring himself to write of it, even to Frank.

At last, in the second week of the New Year, there came news that wrought a change in Desmond; news from John Meredith of his father's broken health and his sister's immediate departure for England. She would sail in a week, he wrote, and would travel overland.

Paul, reading the letter to his friend, had a sudden inspiration.

"Theo, let's go and meet her at Marseilles!" he said eagerly, "and see her safe into the express. It would please Meredith—and her too."

For the fraction of a second, an answering eagerness glowed in Desmond's eyes; then vanished, leaving his face a politely interested mask. But Paul had seen the flash and pressed his point accordingly.

"Of *course* you'll come, Theo. A sight of her will do us both good. I'm glad I thought of it."

"So am I," Desmond agreed, without a particle of gladness in his level tone. "But—you can leave me out of the programme. One of us is enough—for all that is needed; and it's only right it should be you."

"I don't quite follow the logic of that."

Desmond's set face softened to a smile. "Don't you, old man? Then you must take my word for it."

In spite of that smile Paul heard the note of finality in his friend's voice and said no more.

On the appointed morning he set out alone to meet the ship, pain and elation contending in his heart. But when, at last, he set eyes on Honor Meredith, and saw her whole face lighten at sight of him, complexities were submerged in a flood-tide of simple, human joy.

But the exalted moment was short-lived. He could not fail to see how, instinctively, her glance travelled beyond him; how her lower lip was indrawn for the space of a heart-beat; and when their hands met, he, as instinctively, answered her thought.

"I couldn't persuade Theo to come. He is still difficult to rouse or move. The news of your father did seem to stir him and I am hoping he will write."

She let out her breath unsteadily. "Oh, if he only would! This interminable silence seems—so inhuman. In a way, I understand it; but the others, out there, are getting terribly unhappy over it; John and Frank more than all. *You* don't think—do you—that there is really any fear——?"

The look in her eyes recalled that terrible night of March when they two had watched over Theo in turn; and Paul knew that now—as then—she craved no cheap consolation, but the truth.

"There have been bad moments," he admitted, "when one was afraid—— But now I honestly believe that he *will* fight again and live again with his old zest; and I want you to believe it too, with all your heart."

"I will believe it—with all my heart," she answered very low and steadily. "Have you any plans—beyond Le Trayas?"

"Nothing definite. I just keep my eye on him and act accordingly. In April, I think Bellagio would be a sound move. There, if anywhere, the call of the spring should prove irresistible. At least it's a prescription worth trying."

She smiled; and, even in smiling, he noted the pathetic droop of her eyelids and the corners of her lips.

"How wise you are for him, Paul! And you *will* come home for a little before going back?"

"I hope so, devoutly, if Bellagio proves a success."

The crowd about them, surging chaotically to and fro, recalled them to prosaic considerations of luggage and a corner seat in the express, which Paul—unhurried yet singularly efficient—did not fail to secure. That done, Honor was confided to the care of an assiduous guard, and was supplied with fruit, chocolate, and more newspapers than she could possibly digest;—trifling services which the girl, in her great loneliness, rated at their true value.

By that time the platform had emptied its contents into the high, dingy-looking carriages of the Paris-Lyons Express. A gong clanged. Honor put out an ungloved hand and had some ado not to wince before it was released.

"Thank you—for everything," she murmured, sudden tears starting to her eyes. "I only wish Theo could have come too!"

"I'll tell him that. It may do him good!"

In spite of herself the blood flew to her cheeks. But before she could answer, the train jolted forward—and she was gone.

Paul Wyndham stood a long while motionless, looking into empty space; then, with a sensible jar, he came very completely back to earth.

It was near sunset when he reached their haven of refuge, a small hotel set in a rocky garden overlooking the sea. No sign of Theo within doors,—and Paul strolled down the narrow pathway that led to his friend's favourite seat. There, at the far end, leaning upon the balustrade, he sighted an unmistakable figure black against a blazing heaven rippled with light clouds that gave promise of greater glory to come.

Footsteps behind him roused Desmond. He started and turned about with a new eagerness that was balm to the heart of his friend.

"Ah—*there* you are! It's been a long day." His eyes scanned Wyndham's face. "You've seen her?" he asked abruptly.

"Yes—I have seen her."

"How did she look? Well?"

"She looked very beautiful," Paul answered simply, an odd thrill in his voice. "But not—not like her old self. One can see—she has suffered."

Desmond bit his lip and turned away again. A sudden mist blurred the sunset splendour, the bronze and purple iridescence of the sea. Paul went on speaking.

"She sent you a message, Theo—she wished you had come too."

"Did she? That was kind of her.—Sir John no worse?"

"Apparently not. She will write from Mavins."

"Good."

He leaned on the balustrade as before and tacitly dismissed the subject; but Wyndham, regarding him thoughtfully, and remembering Honor's tell-tale blush, fell to dreaming of a golden future for these two who were dearer to him than his own soul.

Suddenly Desmond spoke again in an altered tone.

"Paul—I've been thinking——"

"Have you, indeed! You do very little else these days. What's the outcome?"

"Nothing brilliant. Quite the reverse. I'm a coward at heart. That's all about it."

Paul smiled as a mother might smile at the vagaries of a beloved child.

"Can't say I've seen any symptoms of the disease myself."

"Well—you're going to, old man, plain as daylight. It's like this——" he squared his shoulders with a jerk and thrust both hands into his pockets. "I can't face—going back to Kohat. I've suspected it for some time. Now I know it. There's too much—that is to say—there *are* reasons. Pretty big ones. But they don't bear talking of. Think me a broken-backed cornstalk if you must. It'll hurt. But it can't be helped."

For an instant Paul's heart stood still. Then: "Don't talk that brand of nonsense to me, old man," he said gently. "But if you really can't go back—what then?"

"I said—to Kohat. The reliefs will take us to Dera in the autumn. Well—I want to work another six months on urgent private affairs——" he tried to smile. "Do you think the Colonel will come within a hundred miles of understanding and be persuaded to back me up?"

"I think, just at present, he would be loth to refuse you anything, Theo. But still——"

"Well—*what?*"

His tone had a touch of defiance, almost of temper, purely refreshing to hear.

"Well, naturally—I was thinking of the Regiment——"

"Damn the Regiment!" Desmond flashed out, and turning on his heel strode off toward a wooded headland, whose red rocks took an almost unearthly glow from the setting sun.

For several seconds Paul looked after him, scarcely able to believe his ears. If Theo had arrived at damning the Regiment, Frank's fear might not prove to be chimerical after all; and yet the flash of temper, the renewed energy of speech and movement were symptoms of the best.

Paul sat down on the bench, folded his arms, and proceeded to consider, in practical fashion, how they could secure the desired extension of leave. Theo might dub himself coward if he would. Paul knew better. He had long ago guessed that stronger forces were at work in his friend than mere sorrow for the loss of a wife, however dear—and he had guessed right. It was Desmond's sensitive conscience that had been his arch tormentor throughout those months of silence and strangeness that had brought him near to madness and Paul near to despair.

Tragedy on tragedy—loss of the Boy, dread of blindness, the shock of his own discovery of Evelyn's defection, and the awful fashion of her death—had so unsteadied and overwrought his strong brain that, even now, he could neither see nor think clearly in respect of those most terrible weeks of his life. Obsessed by an exaggerated sense of his own disloyalty to the wife who should never have been transplanted to such stony soil, he saw himself virtually her murderer, in the eyes of that God who was, for him, no vague abstraction but the most commanding reality of his consciousness.

Day after day, week after week, he had lived over and over again the events of that fateful month, from the moment of his return, to the last bewildering, unforgettable scene with his wife. Always he discovered fresh excuses for her. Always he lashed himself unsparingly for his own failings;—the initial folly of bringing her to the Frontier, his promise to Honor that had delayed his determination to exchange, and more than all, that final straight speaking—wrung from him by pain and shame—that had made fear of him outweigh even her childish terror of the dark. In the hidden depth of his heart he had been untrue to her, and his passionate attempt at reparation had come too late. There had even been fevered moments when he told himself that he, Theo Desmond, not the crazy fanatic in quest of sainthood—should by rights have been hanged and burned on the day of her death.

The whole tragical tangle, blurred and distorted by incessant repetition, had come at last to seem almost a separate entity; a horror, outside his own control, that now shrank to a pin-point and now loomed gigantic, oppressive, till all true sense of proportion was lost. The silence that he could not force himself to break, infallibly made matters worse. And now came Honor, re-awakening the great love he had wrestled with and trampled on to very small purpose; a love beside which his chivalrous tenderness for Evelyn showed like the flame of a candle in the blaze of noon.

Her sudden return, the perturbing sense of her nearness, had for the first time wrenched him away from the obsession of the past. But even now he dared not frankly face the future; dared not let his mind dwell on the colourless emptiness of life without her. Neither could he, as yet, face the only alternative—to tell her, of all women, that he had loved her before his wife's death. Besides, there was Paul, who obviously cared, in his own repressed fashion, and who must not be baulked of his chance.

Yet to-night, as he tramped the whole round of that rocky headland—in the glow of a sky rippled by now with feathers of flame—his blood was in a fever for sheer desire of her, and he cursed the folly that had impelled him to refuse the morning's golden opportunity.

Returning later, in a more chastened mood, he found Wyndham sitting still as a statue, seemingly forgetful of his existence; and of a sudden his heart contracted at thought of his friend's inexhaustible patience, his unquestioning acceptance of moods to which he did not hold the key. Stepping lightly, Desmond came up behind him and laid both hands on his shoulders..

"Forgive me, old man. I didn't precisely mean all that——"

Wyndham scarcely started.

"I thought as much! Don't apologise!" he said, looking up with his slow smile. "It was a pure pleasure to hear you swear again!"

Desmond laughed abruptly. "You'll get more than enough of that kind of pleasure if they refuse me my six months!—But look here, I'm thinking I can't keep *you* away from them any longer——"

"My dear Theo," Paul interposed with gentle decision. "So long as you stay—I stay. That goes without saying.

Meredith will fix it up for us—no fear. Come on now. It's time we went indoors."

They sauntered back up the gravel path together without further speech, yet with thoughts more closely linked than either guessed; thoughts that flew instinctively as homing doves to the one beloved woman—Honor Meredith.

II.

A late April evening on Lake Como:—for the initiated there is magic in the very words; magic of light and warmth and colour; glory of roses and wistaria, that everywhere renew the youth of ancient ruins and walls and weave a spring garment even for the sombre cypress who has none of his own. Love-song of birds, laughter of men and women, the passionate blue above, the sun-warmed cobblestones underfoot—in these also there is magic, unseizable, irresistible as the happiness of a child. There is nothing great about Como, nothing in the measured beauty of her encircling hills to uplift or strike awe into the soul of a man. She is exquisite, finished; a garden enclosed, a garden of enchantment that speaks straight to the heart; and the banner over her is peace.

Here Paul Wyndham—with the instinctive understanding that belongs to a great love—had chosen to round off the the wander-year devoted to his friend. Throughout that year he had done all that one man may do for another in his dark hour; and each week his conviction grew stronger that Honor—and none but Honor—could do the rest. Let them only meet again, in fresh surroundings, and Theo—already so very much her friend—could not fail to come under her spell. His present seeming disposition to avoid her Paul set down to her intimate association with his wife. Six months' extension of leave had been granted to both, and Paul looked to a summer in England to establish what Italy had already begun.

Since that night at Le Trayas, when Theo had damned

the Regiment and confessed his dread of returning to Kohat, Paul had begun to be aware of a change in his friend. Apathy had given place to restlessness, to a craving for distraction that neither Nature nor Art could satisfy. From place to place he had shifted like a man pursued. He fled as an animal flies from a gadfly securely fastened into his flesh. Go where he would, the passionate voice of his own heart spoke louder than books and pictures, mountains and the sea, urging him always in the one direction that his will was set to avoid.

Wyndham—aware of some inner struggle, while far from suspecting its nature—reckoned it all to the good, since it implied that the real man was astir at last. His suggestion of the Hotel Serbelloni at Bellagio—diplomatically broached—had been hailed almost with enthusiasm; and a month of Italy's April at its radiant best had proven, past question, the wisdom of the move.

In those four weeks they had explored the length and breadth of the lake with the restless energy of their race; had tramped the stony roads of North Italy and climbed every height within reach.

Better than all, it was now Theo who planned their expeditions, studied guide books and discussed local legends with his very good friend the Head Waiter. Flashes of temper had become more frequent. He could even be lured into argument again and grow hot over a game of chess. Trivial details—but for Wyndham each was a jewel beyond price. And Desmond was writing again now; fitfully but spontaneously, as of old. He had written to Sir John, and to the Colonel; and there had been two thick envelopes addressed to Frank; but never a one to Honor Meredith.

It had needed only this to fill Paul's cup of content; but Desmond—though he talked more openly of other matters—seldom mentioned the girl.

As on his return from the Samana, so now, he had fought his hidden fight and come off conqueror. All things conspired to convince him that Paul was the man—the infinitely worthier man—of her choice; and their steady correspondence seemed proof conclusive. At that rate there was nothing for it but to stand aside, leaving Paul to go in and win; only—he could not bring himself to be present at the process.

So these two friends, united by one of the closest ties on earth, lived and thought at cross purposes, for the simple reason that even of so fine a quality as reserve it is possible to have too much of a good thing.

And now an end of peaceful isolation. To-morrow they would cross to Menaggio homeward bound; and on this their last evening they climbed the cobblestoned, corkscrew of a path that winds to the ruins of Torre di Vezio above Varenna. The fine outlook from the summit was Desmond's favourite view of the lake. He himself had planned the outing, and now strode briskly ahead of his friend, with more of the old vigour and elasticity in his bearing than Paul had yet seen. To-day, too, for the first time, he had discarded the crepe band from the sleeve of his grey flannel suit; a silent admission that the spirit of resurrection had not called to him in vain.

Paul, noting these significant trifles, decided that he could have chosen no time more propitious for the thing he had to say. That morning's post had brought a letter from Sir John Meredith begging them both to come straight to his country house in Surrey for a week. Paul saw that invitation as Theo's God-given chance to discover the treasure that was his for the asking; and all day he had patiently awaited the given moment for speech. Now he recognised it, and did not intend to let it slip through his fingers.

The grey stone walls and towers of the Torre di Vezio stood four-square and rugged in the last of the sun; their battlements jewelled with fine mosaic work of lichens, their feet in the young grass of April starred with cowslips and late primroses. Near the old wooden door two cypresses stood sentinel, and the gnarled olives in the foreground loomed ancient and unresponsive as the walls themselves. The light wind of the morning had dropped with the sun; and the lake, far below them, showed delicately blurred mirages of townlets, hills, and sky. Southward, toward Como and Lecco, all was saturated in the magical blue atmosphere, the aura of Italy. Northward, toward Gravedona, the lesser Alps gloomed grey-violet under a mass of indigo cloud that blotted out the snows.

Theo Desmond, standing very erect, with the sun in his eyes, felt the peace and beauty of it all flow through his veins like wine.

"It's good to be up here. Very good. Sit down, old man."

Paul obeyed. They settled themselves on a green ledge near a bold outcrop of rock. Desmond, leaning forward, sunk his chin on his hand and fell into one of his brooding silences that had grown rarer of late.

So long it lasted that Paul began to fear he might lose the given moment after all. Yet every line of his friend's face and figure spelled peace; and he was loth to break the silence. Taking the letter from his pocket he opened it with ostentatious cracklings. He read it through twice, very leisurely; and still Desmond sat motionless, absorbed in the changing lights on the water and the hills. Then Paul gave it up and spoke.

"Theo—I've had a letter from Sir John. They're delighted to hear we're coming home."

Desmond started and frowned without changing his position. Only his stillness took on a more rigid quality. It had been natural; now it was forced.

"The old man going on well?" he asked, feeling that some remark was expected of him.

"Yes. He's almost himself again. He and Lady Meredith want us to go straight to Mavins for a week. What do you think?"

This time an answer was imperative; but it stuck in Desmond's throat.

"Very good of them. All the same—I think not," he said slowly; then made a clumsy attempt to modify the blank refusal. "You see, though I've taken this extra leave, I don't mean to spend it in loafing. We've had our fill of that. As soon as I get to town, I shall start reading in earnest for my promotion."

Paul, puzzled and dismayed as he was, could not lightly relinquish his castle in the air.

"I'm glad you feel up to work again, Theo," he said

"But a week in the country wouldn't seriously delay matters; and, in the circumstances, it seems ungracious to refuse. It would cheer the old man up. And it goes without saying that Honor would be glad to see us again."

The last appeal roused Desmond effectually. He jerked himself upright and faced his friend; faced also the ordeal of open speech after months of evasion.

"Yes—yes. You're always right, old man," he said, eyes and voice superbly under control. "I'm a selfish brute to monopolise you and—er—stand in your light. A sight of you will do them all good; and *you'll* be glad to see—Honor again. I used to wonder—long ago—what hindered you from fixing things up—you two."

It was Paul's turn now to start and change colour.

"You wondered?" he echoed blankly; then his voice dropped a tone. "Well, Theo, since you've touched on the subject, I'd as soon you knew the truth. I—spoke to Honor last March, while you were away; and—she refused."

"Refused—*you?*"

In that flash of amazement and sympathy with his friend's pain, Desmond escaped, if only for a moment, from the tyranny of his own tormented soul. His gaze travelled back to the hills.

"I'd have given her credit for more perception," he said quietly; and Paul, regarding him with a whimsical tenderness: "Has love anything to do with that sort of thing?"

"No—no. I'm a blatant fool. But still—a man like you——!" He broke off short, and there was a moment of strained silence. But the real Desmond was awake at last, and he forced himself to add: "Women change sometimes—once they know. Have you never been tempted to try again?"

"No; and never shall be, for a very good reason. There's some one in the way—some other man——"

Desmond drew in his breath sharply.

"Good Lord!" he muttered in a low dazed voice, as if thinking aloud. "But where the deuce *is* he? Why hasn't he come forward? He must be a rotten sort of chap——"

Paul caressed his moustache to hide a smile. "Not

necessarily Theo. I gather, from what she said that—there were difficulties——"

"Difficulties—?" Again he broke off, stunned by the coincidence, yet incapable of suspecting the truth. Then, pulling himself together, he spoke in his natural voice: "Well, anyway, Paul, *you'd* better accept Sir John's invitation, since you can still manage to be friends with her in spite of that infernal chap in the background."

This time Paul smiled outright; but Desmond saw nothing. His chin sunk in his hand, he sat still as a rock, raging inwardly—as he had not raged for a full year—at thought of that same "infernal chap" whose difficulties might not be permanent; who might even now——

Suddenly he became aware that Paul was answering his last remark.

"Yes, Theo, I can just manage it," he was saying in a voice of grave tenderness. "It has not been easy; but the truth is that—when it came to the wrench—I hadn't the courage to let her go quite out of my life."

"You had not the *courage!*" Desmond flashed round on him, a gleam of the old fire in his eyes. "It's like you to put it that way, Paul. The real truth is that you had the courage to put mere passion under your feet. *I* should feel rather, in such a case, that she *must* go quite out of my life. There's the root difference between us. I should not have the courage to accept friendship when I wanted—the other thing. But we're not discussing my affairs—" He dismissed himself with a gesture. "The point is, you'll go to Mavins and make my excuses to Sir John."

"Yes, if you really wish it, I'll go alone, a little later on. Only—you must furnish me with something valid in the way of excuse. You know, as well as I do, that *you* are first favourite with the old man. But I take it for granted you have some good reason at the back of your mind——"

"You're right there. I have—the strongest reason on earth." He paused and set his teeth, bracing himself to the final effort of confession. "What's more—I unintentionally stated it a minute ago, in plain terms." He faced Wyndham squarely now and a dull flush mounted to his temples. "Since the ice is broken at last, there can be nothing less than absolute truth between us," he said simply; and there was no more need for the clumsy machinery of speech.

Paul's eyes, that neither judged nor questioned, rested on his friend like a benediction. In that moment he had his reward for months of silent service, of patience strained almost to breaking point, of anxiety that bordered on despair.

Minute after minute they sat silent, while the splendour in the west blazed and spread till it challenged the oncoming shadow in the north; and the near hills grown magically ethereal, stood in a shimmer of gold, like hills of dream.

Then Desmond spoke again very quietly, without looking round.

"Now perhaps you better understand—this last year?"

"Yes, Theo, I do understand," Paul answered in the same tone, and Desmond let out a great breath.

"God! The relief it is to feel square with you again!"

III.

In a third-floor sitting-room, facing east, breakfast was laid for two. Every item of the meal bespoke furnished apartments; and even the May sunshine, flooding the place, failed to beautify the shabby carpet and furniture, the inevitable oleographs and the family groups that shared the mantelpiece with pipes, pouches, and a tin of tobacco. A hanging bookcase held some military books, a couple of novels, and a volume of Browning—the property of Paul. After Bellagio—Piccadilly; and their year abroad constrained them to economy at home.

Theo Desmond sauntering in, scanned every detail with fastidious distaste. To-day, for the first time, a great longing possessed him for the airy ramshackle bungalows of the Frontier he loved, for the trumpet-call to "stables," for a sight of his squadron and the feel of a saddle between his knees.

His wandering gaze lighted on a letter near Paul's place. The address was in Honor's handwriting. He stood a moment regarding it, then turned sharply away and went over to the window. There he remained, seemingly absorbed in the varied traffic of Piccadilly, actually consumed by such jealousy as he had never suffered while he imagined that her heart was given to his friend.

For Paul's sake he could and would endure all things; but this detestable unknown who had won her and could not claim her was quite another affair. There could be no thought of standing aside on his account. It was simply a question of Honor herself. She was not the woman lightly to withdraw her love, once given. And yet—in a year—who could tell? Love, like the spirit, bloweth where it listeth; and Paul's failure did not of necessity predicate his own. For all her sudden bewildering reserves, she had drawn very near to him in those last terrible weeks at Kohat; and now—now—if he could believe there was the veriest ghost of a chance—!

The mere possibility set heart and blood in a tumult; a tumult checked ruthlessly by the thought that if Honor Meredith was not the woman to change lightly, still less was she the woman to approach with that confession which, at all hazards, he was bound to make. Speaking of it to Paul had cost him such an effort as he ached to remember. Speaking of it to her seemed a thing inconceivable. And yet—in that case—what hope of escape from this unholy tangle, from this fury of jealousy that had stabbed his manhood broad awake at last?

In Italy he fondly believed that he had fought his fight and conquered. Yet now, behold, it was all to do over again!

"Theo, my dear chap, there *is* such a thing as breakfast!" Paul's voice brought him back to earth with a thud. "Will you have a congealed rasher or a tepid egg—or both?"

"Neither, confound you!" Desmond answered, swinging round with an abrupt laugh and strolling back to the table.

Inevitably he glanced at the perturbing envelope, open now and propped against the milk-jug, and as inevitably Paul answered his look.

"Honor is in town for a few days," he said, putting the letter near Theo's plate, "staying with Lady Meredith's sister. She hopes I can go in and see her this morning.

She seems under the impression that you are too busy, just now, to be included in any invitation."

Desmond buttered a leathery triangle of toast with elaborate precision. "You may as well encourage that notion, old chap. It simplifies things. You're going yourself, I suppose?"

"Yes."

"Lucky devil!"

He scowled at the envelope by his plate and tacitly dismissed the subject by an excursion into the *Morning Post.*

They talked politics and theatres till the unappetising meal was ended and Paul pocketed his treasure with a sigh. It was the first time Theo had ignored one of her letters; and the simple-hearted fellow—quite unaware that his mention of the other man had been a master-stroke of policy—felt almost at his wits' end. Standing by the mantelpiece mechanically filling his pipe, he watched Desmond set out his books and papers on the table near the window, intent on a morning of abnormal industry; and the pathos of it all caught at his heart. For the first time in his controlled and ordered life he felt impelled to carry a situation by storm—the result possibly of playing Providence to Theo for the space of a year.

But Theo plus a woman, loving and beloved, whom he obstinately refused to meet, was a problem demanding far more of diplomacy, of intimate human experience than Paul Wyndham had been blest withal. The one obvious service required of him was easier to recognise than to achieve. By some means these two must be brought together in spite of themselves; but for all his forty years he was pathetically at a loss to know how the deuce one contrived that sort of thing. It was a woman's job. Mrs Olliver, now, could have fixed it all up in a twinkling; while he—poor clumsy fool!—could only sit there smoking and racking his brain, while his eyes perfunctorily scanned the columns of the *Morning Post.*

The doings of the world and the misdoings of those in power, earthquakes, shipwrecks, and rumours of wars—all these were as nothing to him compared with the insignificant tangle of one man and one woman among the whole seething, suffering throng. But concern brought him no nearer to the unravelling of their tangle; and when the time came to go he could think of nothing better than a direct appeal to his friend.

Desmond still sat at the table, head in hand, absorbed in the intricacies of military tactics.

Paul rose and went over to him. "I'm going now, old chap." The matter of fact statement was made with indescribable gentleness. "I'll be back in an hour or so. Wish to goodness you were coming too."

"Damned if you can wish it more than I do," Desmond answered without looking up.

"Well then—come. Is it really—so impossible as you think?"

Desmond nodded decisively. "Can't you see it for yourself, man? Even if she *was* quit of that other confounded fellow, how could I face telling her—the truth?"

For a moment Paul was silenced; not because he found the question unanswerable, but because of that hidden knowledge which he might not disclose, even to save his friend.

"My dear Theo," he said at last, "I know—and you know—that, sooner than lose her, you could go through any kind of fire. Besides, I have an idea she would understand——"

"So have I," Desmond answered gruffly, "that's the deuce of it all. But it doesn't make a man less unworthy——"

"If it comes to that," urged the diplomatist, "are any of us worthy?"

Desmond flung up his head with an odd laugh.

"Possibly not! But there happen to be degrees of unfitness—yours and mine for instance, you blind old bat! Go along now, and enjoy the good you deserve. As for me—I have sinned and must take the consequences without whining."

"There is a radical difference, Theo," Paul remarked quietly, "between temptation and sin."

"Casuist!" was all the answer vouchsafed to him; and

baffled—but not yet defeated—he went out into the May sunlight, quite determined, for once in his life, to take by storm the citadel that seemed proof against capitulation.

Before reaching his destination he had devised a plan so simple and obvious that it might have occurred to a child; and like a child he gloried in his unaided achievement. The fact that it involved leading them both blindfold to the verge of mutual discovery troubled him not a whit. Heart and conscience alike asserted that in this case the end justified the means; and it needed but the veiled light in Honor's eyes at mention of Theo's name to set the seal on his decision.

For near an hour they talked, with that effortless ease and intimacy which is the hall-mark of a genuine friendship; and at the end of it Honor realised that, without any conscious intention on her part, Theo—and little else but Theo—had been their topic as a matter of course. Never dreaming of design on the part of Paul, she merely blessed him for a devotion that almost equalled her own, and accepted, with unfeigned alacrity, his suggestion that they should meet next morning at the Diploma Gallery.

"I've not been there for a hundred years!" she declared with more of her old lightness than he had yet seen in her: "It will take me back to bread-and-butter days! And I believe they have added some really good pictures since then."

Paul exulted as an angler exults when he feels his first salmon tug at the line; but his tone was casual and composed. "Come early," he said. "Then we shall pretty well have the place to ourselves. Eleven? Half-past?"

"Somewhere between the two."

"Good."

And Paul Wyndham—the devout lover, who had trampled passion underfoot to some purpose—walked back to Piccadilly like a man reprieved. Honor was secure. Remained the capture of Theo—a more difficult feat; but, in his present mood, he refused to contemplate the possibility of failure.

A morning of unclouded brilliance found Desmond

frankly bored with tactics and topography; the more so, perhaps, because Paul with simple craft took his industry for granted.

Soon after eleven, he put aside the inevitable pipe and newspaper and took up his hat. "Well, Theo," said he, "you won't be needing me till after lunch I suppose?—I'm off."

"Where to, old man?" Desmond yawned extensively as he spoke, and pushed aside his little pile of red books with a promising gesture of distaste. "What's your dissipated programme?"

"An hour in the Diploma Gallery, and a stroll in the Park," Paul replied with admirable unconcern. "D'you feel like coming?"

"I feel like chucking all these into the waste-paper basket! When England takes it into her capricious head to do this sort of thing in May, how the devil can a human man keep his nose to the grindstone? Come on!"

Paul's heart beat fast as they stepped into the street; faster still as he glanced at Theo striding briskly beside him, head in air all unconscious that he was faring toward a tryst far more in tune with the season and the new life astir in his blood than his late abnormal zeal in pursuit of promotion.

To Paul it seemed that the heavens themselves were in league with him. Overhead, scattered ranks of chimney-pots were bitten out of a sky scarcely less blue and ardent than Italy's own. In every open space young leaves flashed, golden-green, on soot-blackened branches of chestnut, plane, and lime. And there were flowers everywhere—in squares and window-boxes and parks; in florists' and milliners' windows; in the baskets of flower-sellers and in women's hats. The paper-boy—blackbird of the London streets—whistled a livelier stave. Girls hurried past smiling at nothing in particular. They were glad to be alive—that was all.

And Theo?

He too was glad to be alive, to be free, at last, from the conquering shadow of memory and self-reproach. If penance were required of him, surely that black year must suffice. Now the living claimed him; and that claim could no longer be ignored With a heart too full for speech he walked beside his friend; and halting at last, on the steps of Burlington House, he bared his head to the sunlight and drew a deep breath of content.

"I vote we don't waste much of this divine morning on pictures, Paul," he said suddenly. "Why bother about them at all?"

Wyndham started visibly; but in less than a minute he was master of himself and the situation.

"Well, as we're here, we may as well look in," he answered casually; and without waiting further objection, turned to enter the building.

Desmond, following, laid a hand on his shoulder.

"Anything to please you, old man," said he smiling.

"God knows you've danced attendance on *my* whims long enough!"

No sign of Honor in the cloistered coolness of the first room; only a small group of people in earnest talk before one of the pictures, and an artist, with stool and easel, making a conscientious copy of another.

Desmond made a cursory tour of the walls and passed on into the second room. Paul, increasingly anxious every moment, lagged behind and consulted his watch. It was twenty-five minutes past eleven. Would she never come?

The second room was empty, and there Desmond's aimless wandering had been checked by a battle picture; a vigorous and tragic presentment of Sir John Moore's retreat from Corunna.

"Here you are, Paul. Here's something worth looking at," said he as Wyndham joined him; and, soldier-like, they soon fell to discussing the event rather than the picture. Desmond—his head full of tactics and military history—held forth fluently quite in his old vein; while Paul—who heard scarce one word in six—nodded sagely at appropriate intervals.

Hope died hard in him. A clock outside, chiming the half-hour, rang its knell with derisive strokes that seemed to beat upon his heart. It was just his luck. She would never turn up. A hundred contingencies might arise to prevent her—a street accident, a headache, bad news of her father——

Sudden silence from Theo cut short the dismal list; and one glance at him told Paul that his hour was come indeed. For Desmond stood rigid, a dull flush burning through his tan; and his eyes looked over Paul's shoulder towards the entrance into Room Number One.

"My God!" he muttered hoarsely, "Here's Honor!"

Without a word Paul turned on his heel and saw how she, too, stood spellbound, there by the doorway, her cheeks aflame, her eyes more eloquent than she knew. Taken completely unawares, each had surprised the other's secret, even as Paul had foreseen. In that lightning flash of mutual recognition, the end he had wrought for, and agonised for, was achieved. Obviously they had no further need of his services—and, unnoticed by either, he passed quietly out of the room.

For one measureless minute they remained confronting each other; scarcely daring to breathe lest they break the spell of that passionate unspoken avowal. Then Honor came forward slowly, like one walking in her sleep—and the spell was gone. In two strides Desmond had reached her and grasped her outstretched hand.

No attempt at conventional futilities marred their supreme moment. Words seemed an impertinence in view of the overwhelming fact that he stood before her thus—his face transfigured and illumined by love unutterable, by a discovery scarcely realised even now.

There was so much to tell, and again, so little after all, that there seemed no need to tell it. Yet Honor could not choose but long for the sound of his voice; and to that end she tried very gently to withdraw her hand.

Desmond—suddenly aware that they were alone—tightened his grasp. "No—no," he protested under his breath, "unless—you wish it. *Do* you—Honor?"

"I don't wish it," she answered very low, and her eyes, resting on his, had a subdued radiance as of sunlight seen through mist.

Haloed in that radiance Desmond beheld the "infernal chap" he had been cursing for weeks; realised instantaneously all that the recognition implied; and, capturing both her hands, crushed them between his own.

"Honor—my splendid Honor!"

He still spoke under his breath; and still his eyes held hers in a gaze so compelling that it seemed as though he were drawing her very soul into his own with a force that she had neither will nor power to resist.

In that long look she knew that, for all her passionate intensity of heart and spirit, this man, whom she had won, surpassed her in both; that in all things he rose above her—and would always rise. And because she was very woman at the core, such knowledge gladdened her beyond telling; crowned her devotion as wedded love is rarely crowned in a world honeycombed with half-heartedness in purpose and faith and love.

THE END.

Printed in Great Britain by
WILLIAM BLACKWOOD AND SONS.

1892797R0020

Printed in Great Britain
by Amazon.co.uk, Ltd.,
Marston Gate.